DUDLEY PUBLIC LIBRARIES

The loan of this book may be renewed if not required by other
readers, by contacting the library from which it was borrowed

K
is
sc
sl
S/
is

PENGUIN BOOKS
RED CARD

Kautuk Srivastava is a Mumbai-based writer and comedian. He a member of the popular comedy collective SnG Comedy. As a screenwriter, he has written many successful TV and Web-based shows, including MTV Reality Stars, Snog, Sumbhal Taja and Shaitaan Haveli. His previous stand-up special, Anatomy of Aukaard, is featured on Amazon Prime Video. This is his debut novel.

RED CARD

KAUTUK SRIVASTAVA

PENGUIN BOOKS

An imprint of Penguin Random House

PENGUIN BOOKS

USA | Canada | UK | Ireland | Australia
New Zealand | India | South Africa | China

Penguin Books is part of the Penguin Random House group of companies
whose addresses can be found at global.penguinrandomhouse.com

Published by Penguin Random House India Pvt. Ltd
7th Floor, Infinity Tower C, DLF Cyber City,
Gurgaon 122 002, Haryana, India

First published in Penguin Books by Penguin Random House India 2018

ISBN 9780143441953

Typeset in Bembo Std by Manipal Digital Systems, Manipal
Printed at Replika Press Pvt. Ltd, India

www.penguin.co.in

MIX
Paper from
responsible sources
FSC® C016779

To my parents.
Looking back, I realize that the tenth standard was harder
on you than it was on me.

FIRST
HALF

July 2006

ON A HOT evening in Berlin, France are playing Italy in the World Cup final. The scores are level. France 1–Italy 1. The match is in the second half of extra time. At the 110th minute precisely.

France's captain, Zinedine Zidane, is jogging away from a miserable free kick. Tailing him is Italy's Marco Materazzi, his arm wrapped around the Frenchman's torso like a boa constrictor as he proceeds to administer what in common Indian parlance is known as a *pungi* on Zidane's left nipple. And, as any pungi victim will testify, this annoys Zizou. He shrugs Materazzi off. Words are exchanged. Though Zidane jogs a few steps ahead, more words fly in his direction. Suddenly, he spins around with that classic, career-defining grace and rams his big bald head squarely into Materazzi's chest.

The stadium erupts—one half in indignation and the other in disbelief. The whistle is blown sharp and clear. The ball comes to an abandoned stop. The players freeze. The only pair of feet streaking down the pitch belong to the referee. He's hurtling towards them. The Italian defender is writhing in pain, clutching his chest. Zidane towers over him, snorting like a rhinoceros, fumes rising from his cannonball head. Finally, the referee reaches the spot and, in a fatal flourish, raises a red card in the air.

Zidane darts his eyes towards the card flashing in front of his face. He begins explaining to the referee why a man at the peak of his powers, in the last match of his footballing career, playing the biggest match a footballer can play in, would choose to headbutt an opponent. A pretty solid tale it must have been too. Referees, however, are an obstinate bunch, and after patiently hearing Zidane out, he points to the exit.

Zidane hands over the captain's armband to Willy Sagnol and makes the long walk to the dressing room. He's taking off the tape around his hand as he goes. He steps off the field. The World Cup, glinting golden, sits seductively on a pedestal beside the touchline. Zidane walks right past it with neither a wistful glance nor rueful resignation. All he sees in the last moments of his career is a flaming red card.

Many, many miles away, in suburban Thane, four jaws dropped so low that a dentist could have worked on them without complaint.

'What the hell—' began Abhay Purohit.

'Impossible!' said Rahul Rawat, peeking at the screen through his fingers.

'This sucks . . .' breathed Sumit Awasthi. He slumped further in the sofa.

'Yes!' said Rishabh Bala and fist-pumped the air. A fifteen-year-old of medium height, he had an oval face that was redeemed by the presence of cheekbones and the faint trace of a jawline. On his chin and the prime real estate of his cheeks grew a beard. It wasn't fuzzy like his classmates'. It was well defined and bristly from a full year of shaving—an early gift from puberty, which had also left him with six pimples that almost exactly formed the Big Dipper constellation on his forehead. Rishabh wore his wavy dark hair brushed back. He thought it made him look like David Beckham. On his nose rested rectangular glasses that definitely made him look like David Beckham's accountant.

For that night, Rishabh was an Italy supporter. Not like he particularly liked them, though. The only reason he had been cheering for them was because the other three had their hearts set on France winning. 'No fun if we all support the same team, no?' he'd said. And he had warmed to his adopted team rather quickly. He'd howled in anguish when they conceded and whooped with delight when they'd scored, and now he gloated at the ignominy of Zidane's exit.

'If only he had headed the ball that well,' he said.

'Shut up. If you want to live to see tomorrow, just shut up,' growled Sumit. This was no empty threat. Sumit could have waded into a pond full of hippos and they would have welcomed him as one of their own.

Rishabh turned his head to the screen, but not before sticking up his middle fingers at the French supporters. The match went on, bathing the dark hall in blue.

When Italy scored the winning penalty, Rishabh took off his shirt and ran up and down the length of the house, screaming soundlessly. His parents were sleeping, and, though he was happy for Italy, he wasn't happy enough to incur their wrath. He did, however, do a victory dance right in the faces of his dejected friends. Puro hurled a cushion at him in disgust.

'Fuuucck!' he bellowed. It echoed in the dim hall.

'Hey!' said Rishabh, putting a finger to his lips. 'Parents.'

Puro continued cursing under his breath.

'Oh well, happens,' said Sumit, crossing his arms and closing his eyes. As far as he was concerned, the match was over—a team had won, another had lost—and now it was time to sleep.

'How could Zidane do this?' spat Puro with venom in his voice. 'Who gets a card like that?'

'Zidane would normally *never* act like that. Materazzi must have said something really bad,' said Rahul, as if he were Zidane's long-time girlfriend.

'Please! It was plain stupid. The guy is clearly nuts,' said Rishabh.

'I'm telling you, it's Materazzi's fault. That was Zizou's last match. There's no way he would *choose* to end his career that way.'

'I want to kill that Italian bastard!' said Puro, punching a wall. Abhay Purohit felt a special kinship with Zinedine Zidane. They were both number 10s, captains of their respective teams, the one the rest of the team looked to for inspiration, and both were blessed with talent and temper in equal measure. That's where the similarities ended. Unlike Zidane, Puro was a short, scrawny boy with a headful of messy hair. He was the smallest member of the school football team but made up for the missing inches with his leonine ferocity—which was on display even now, as he prowled about the hall, gnashing his teeth and swinging blows at an imaginary Materazzi.

'Well, you lost. That's all that matters. You losers owe me three vada pavs,' said Rishabh, deciding to take care of business before everyone forgot.

Just then, they heard three shrill toots of a horn, and Puro's demeanour went from a pacing lion's to a leaping kitten's. He sprang to the window and peeled back the curtain an inch.

'I'll see you tomorrow,' he muttered and dashed out the door.

Rahul and Rishabh looked out the window and saw Puro's father atop his bike. Vijay Purohit had a scowl on his face. His burly arms rested on the fuel tank. The bike, its ignition left on, puttered steadily, in sync with Purohit Senior's furiously moving moustache. Puro emerged soon, apologizing. The father glared at his son and jerked a thumb towards the back seat. Puro got on and they sped off.

Puro lived just down the road from Rishabh's house, but his father never let him stay over. He knew his son would run amok through the streets if left alone even for a single night. With a son like Puro, the dread wasn't exactly misplaced. But it did leave Puro feeling like he had grown up in a high-security prison.

The boys turned in for the night. Rahul and Rishabh had to hoist a slumbering Sumit up from the sofa and all the way to the bedroom—an act of kindness that was also a year's worth of weight training. They deposited him on a mattress on the floor and got into bed. Rahul shut his eyes, but his mind was filled with scenes from the match.

'I'm telling you he had a good reason for doing what he did,' he whispered.

'I'm sure,' said Rishabh, 'but what could possibly be worth losing for?'

7

Rishabh opened his eyes to a dull grey room. Surly clouds hung in the sky. Electricity crackled in the air. He glanced at the alarm clock—7.30 a.m. Springing out of bed, he smacked Rahul on the back of his head and kicked Sumit awake. As they grumbled to consciousness, the door opened and his mother entered.

'Finally, thank God! I've been trying to wake you up for an hour,' said Chitra Bala. 'Hurry up, have a bath and run!'

So the three of them took express showers, slipped into their school uniforms—white shirt and brown pants—hoisted their bags and trooped out the door. Mrs Bala handed them a banana each as they went.

That morning, the corridor and classrooms of the tenth standard of Shri Sunderlal Sanghvi School were divided. The boys staggered around in a sleep-deprived stupor, with yawning dark circles around their eyes, as they fervidly discussed the game and 'that incident'. Meanwhile, the majority of the girls, fresh and rested, wondered how the boys could be so affected by something they had so little to do with. The bell rang. The chatter reached a crescendo as the students raced to get their final words in, before the plodding footsteps of approaching teachers sent them scampering to their classes.

Rishabh and Puro were one of the last to vacate the corridor. Eventually they ambled into 10 F. Their class teacher, Kaul Miss, frowned at them. 'And which garden are you two strolling in? Go on, go to your desks!' she said, glaring at them over her large bifocals.

'Yes, miss . . . sorry, miss,' piped Puro, giving her a cheeky grin.

'The same specimens *every* year,' she muttered to herself.

Rishabh liked Asha Kaul. Behind her prickly comments was a kindly warmth, and behind her gold-rimmed spectacles were the twinkly eyes of the easily amused. Her laid-back attitude could lull one into a false sense of security, but with one swift throw of the duster, Asha Kaul would establish the boundaries once again. She launched them with unnerving ease and unerring accuracy, and had she not been a Hindi teacher, she would most definitely have been an international darts champion. 'This is a duster, and Kaul Miss doesn't use it to wipe the board,' were her first words to the batch.

That had been a mere week ago, but to Rishabh's mind it seemed a lot longer. The tenth standard was turning out to be just as hectic as advertised. Nearly everyone in the batch was going to two dozen after-school tutorials. Rishabh and Puro went to Basu's for English, Prasad's for Hindi and Oswal's for maths and science. Thankfully history and geography weren't deemed complicated enough for their own tuition. Between school, coaching classes and the extra hours of study their parents insisted on at home, every brain in the tenth standard had begun to feel like an empty tube of toothpaste after only the first week of school—flattened, rolled up and with nothing left to give.

In class, Kaul Miss had departed, and the first period had begun. Rishabh gazed out the window. A chilly wind rippled through the room. Raindrops spluttered in. The gloom was barely dispelled by the dim tube lights. Chatter had erupted in class, which Barkha, the scrupulous class monitor, was finding hard to quell. Another gust of wind blew in and Rishabh felt it wiggle into his shirt. He shivered. He turned to Puro, who sat behind them. 'You feeling cold too?'

Puro nodded. 'I'm a Puro-flavoured popsicle.'

Rishabh laughed as he got up to shut the window. He was still tugging at one of the jammed frames when a high-pitched shriek rang out. 'STOP THIS NOISE AT ONCE!'

He whirled around to see Poulomi Bobde standing at the door, her eyes popping like the purple of her sari. 'SHUT UP! ALL OF YOU!' she yelled. Her wild eyes roved the classroom and then fell on Rishabh. Just when he thought he would get blasted with another high-intensity sound wave, Rishabh saw Bobde's face break into a smile. Her eyes softened. 'And what are you up to, young man?' she said.

'I was shutting the window, miss,' said Rishabh.

'How about you SHUT YOUR MOUTH!' roared Bobde.

Rishabh was taken aback by how quickly she shifted gears from sweet to savage. He mumbled an apology and slunk back to his seat. He had hated the new English teacher from the first minute she sashayed into the classroom with a smug expression on her face. His hatred was justified when she began her class with 'Shakespeare was written by Julius Caesar.' What's more, he had made the mistake of correcting her. She had studied him with a cold-blooded stare. 'Next time you say a word without raising your hand, rest assured that I will raise mine.' Then she'd smiled at him with the innocence of Heidi, leaving him and the rest of the class wondering whether it was the same woman who had just threatened a student with violence. Years later, Poulomi Bobde would be diagnosed with bipolar disorder, and if the students of 10 F were to hear about it they would say, 'Aha! We knew it!'

That morning, Poulomi Bobde asked them to open their poetry textbooks to page 103. Everyone rummaged in their bags and then ruffled through the pages until they arrived at 'The Listeners' by Walter de la Mare. Bobde read the poem aloud with the cadence of a preschool teacher—another thing Rishabh couldn't stand. From behind him, he heard a murmur. 'You have a pencil or what?' asked Puro.

Rishabh turned around. Puro, hanging low, was asking Mansi Shenoy, the girl he had been crushing on since the minute he'd seen her at the start of term.

'Rishabh,' boomed Bobde, 'this is a final warning. Don't talk when I'm reading. Understood?'

Rishabh was indignant. 'Miss, I didn't say anything. I was just—'

'QUIEEEET!'

Bobde flicked her head and went back to reading. Rishabh was seething. He didn't care much for getting yelled at, especially when he was blameless. He gulped large breaths of air to calm himself and tried to return to Mr De la Mare's verse.

A minute later came another urgent whisper. 'Mansi, pass rubber also, no.' This time he didn't look behind himself. The whisper, however, floated to Bobde's ears, and she traced it to the same source.

'RISHABH! WHAT DID I TELL YOU? YOU CAN'T UNDERSTAND ENGLISH?'

'Miss, I really didn't—'

'SHUT UP! I don't want to hear another word from you. UNDERSTOOD?'

So Rishabh didn't say a word. His teeth were gnashing.

'Answer me!'

He nodded.

'Good,' Bobde said and blithely returned to the poem.

Puro patted him on the back. 'Sorry,' he whispered.

Rishabh shrugged him off. Colours were flashing in front of his eyes. He yanked out his notepad and scribbled a message. He tore it out, folded it neatly until it was a little chit and then slipped it to Amay Khatri, who sat to his right. 'Pass it on,' he said, the arch of his eyebrows indicating the direction.

Khatri slipped it to Parth Popat, who gave it to Priyal Pandey, who palmed it to Bhargav Chigulur. Chigu fumbled it.

Bobde saw the awkward exchange and was at Chigu's desk faster than you could say, 'Manic-depressive disorder.' She smiled and held out her palm. Chigu dropped the chit in it.

Poulomi Bobde began smoothing out the creases. 'Let's see what you kids have written. I'm sure it's better than Walter de—'

In it were the words:

Still not talking.

She looked up at Rishabh, who smiled back sweetly.

Poulomi Bobde rocked in her place. She had never experienced insolence. Then, slowly, she regained her composure . . . and erupted. She screamed so loud that Devi Miss, who was teaching 10 E, peeped in to see if all was well.

Bobde demanded Rishabh's calendar and inaugurated the 'Remarks' page with a venomous account of his behaviour. 'It's not over. You, Rishabh Bala, will bring me nimbu pani— on a tray—from the canteen to the staffroom . . . every recess, for the whole week. This is not punishment. The way you're going, this is just practice for your future.'

The bell rang. Poulomi Bobde swayed out of the classroom with her nose in the air. A cold gust of wind swept in from the open window.

Rishabh exited the staffroom, having delivered Bobde's nimbu pani. She had smiled at him so pleasantly that Rishabh wondered if he had handed over the glass to Bobde's nicer twin sister. He glanced at his watch. Seven minutes still remained for class to begin, and he trotted towards the tenth standard corridor, determined to make the most of them. He bounded up the steps three at a time and at the top of the flight, ran into Rakshit Dave. He waved at Dave and was continuing on his way, when Dave called out to him.

'Rishabh! Rishabh! Have you seen Tamanna today?'

'No . . .' said Rishabh.

'You should,' said Rakshit with a cackle. 'Go find her . . . *quickly.*' He patted Rishabh on the shoulder and descended the stairs, still chuckling to himself.

Rishabh knitted his eyebrows for a second and then straightened them immediately. Rakshit Dave, the twiggy, curly-haired goalkeeper of the school team, was notorious for his sly sense of humour. *He's just teasing me*, thought Rishabh.

But before long, four completely unrelated people asked him the same question: 'Have you seen Tamanna?' The last to ask this was Anshul Ghosh, a boy who only spoke to answer a question in the maths period. Now Rishabh was intrigued. He wanted to know what it was that Tamanna had done that was as important as trigonometry. He ran into Puro near the toilets and asked him if he knew what was up with her.

'You don't know?' snorted Puro.

'No!' said Rishabh, exasperated. 'What the hell is going on?'

He had to wait a good minute for Puro to stop laughing before he heard the news. Tamanna had apparently shown up to school sporting a hairstyle so terrible that it made Hitler's comb-over look fashionable. The reviews were in:

'A stunning disaster'—Rahul Rawat

'Like a rat ate her hair while she slept'—Aurobindo Ghatak

'Is that a scrambled egg on her head? Oh, it's her hair'—Dhriti Karekar

Puro's voice suddenly dipped. 'In fact, if you turn around right now, you can see the horror at first hand,' he whispered.

Rishabh whipped around and saw Tamanna Vedi and, like always, the air exited his body in a dreamy sigh. To his mind, she was like the *Mona Lisa*. Not in the way that she had a high forehead but that she was mysterious, and he wanted to look at her all the time. She had slender legs, thin arms and an angular face on which sat a nose so sharp it deserved a sheath. Her eyes always twinkled, and he used them to navigate the corridors every lunch break, like a Phoenician sailor pursuing the North Star. And, unlike the majority of the batch, puberty had only done her favours. While the rest of them had turned into pimply ogres, Tamanna had returned after the eighth-standard summer vacation with a suspiciously tight-fitting pinafore.

But something was different about her that day. Rishabh knew this because he had mapped the topography of her face through countless hours of sneaky glances. His eyes immediately went to her hair. Usually her locks were long and free-flowing. When left open, they made little waves that lapped against her face. Most of the time, they were shackled by a scrunchy into a jaunty ponytail. That day, however, there were neither waves nor a ponytail. The reports had been accurate; half her hair was indeed missing. However, they had been wrong in calling it ugly. To Rishabh's eyes, even the bowl-shaped crop of her curly, stringy, Maggi-like hair looked nothing short of wondrous. *She's so fashionable*, he thought, *she's . . . gorgeous*.

Rishabh was a little biased. Heavily biased, actually, because the truth was that he pined for Tamanna with that intense, hormonal, butterflies-in-the-stomach adolescent love that leaves gawky boys slack-jawed and speechless. He had contracted young love all at once in the seventh standard, when he had seen the prefect Tamanna as she manned the bridge on the second floor. And he'd developed a crush proper when she had told him to walk silently as he passed. *Why can't I feel my stomach?* he'd wondered. *And why is the world suddenly all pink?*

For weeks he had dreamed about her, and his knees wobbled each time he passed her in the corridors, but he hadn't had the courage to tell her how he felt. She'd found out anyway, though, because he had made the mistake of telling Puro about it.

'Don't tell anyone, but I love Tamanna,' he had said.

That's when Rishabh found out that the fastest way to tell everybody was to tell somebody not to tell anybody. Sure enough, the next day when he'd come to school, the corridors erupted in wolf whistles and a chant of 'Tamanna, haan-haan-haan?' She had made fleeting, embarrassed eye contact with him before pivoting and walking off with a soft goose-step. He wondered what it meant. He never asked, and she never said.

Three years passed, and even now, in the tenth standard, theirs was a great, unfinished love story—a hot topic of gossip, speculation and even betting (the odds were in favour of Tamanna slapping Rishabh if he eventually did ask her out). Which is why Rishabh had been the first person everyone had flocked to after seeing Tamanna's fresh mop.

'I like it,' said Rishabh, a touch dreamily. 'It frames her face perfectly.'

Puro scanned Rishabh's for irony and, spotting none, sputtered with laughter. 'You know what? You should tell her that!'

'No, I can't. What will I say to—' But before he could finish that sentence, Puro yelled out to Tamanna.

Rishabh watched in horror as she and her posse of three girls came to a halt. Tamanna was always surrounded by these girls, whose only job, it seemed to Rishabh, was to leer at him and spit to Tamanna, 'He's looking at you again.'

'Yeah?' said Tamanna to Puro in a voice that sounded like an angel's harpsichord.

'He wants to tell you something,' blurted Puro, pointing at a rapidly shrinking Rishabh before pushing him forward.

The posse sniggered as Tamanna looked on awkwardly. Too much time had passed for Rishabh to remain silent any longer. Something had to be said, but his brain seemed to have shut down the machinery. Puro nudged him, and some words came unstuck.

'Your hairstyle. It's nice,' spoke Rishabh as if it were the first time he had ever spoken.

Tamanna smiled, and he felt his stomach unknotting. 'Thank you,' she said in Lata Mangeshkar's singing voice.

Now, it would have been a perfectly sweet compliment if he had just left it at that. But her smile changed everything. Rishabh reacted to that smile like a slam poet reacting to snapping fingers. *I must go on, my words are clearly magic*, he thought.

'It's not at all like what people are saying about it,' he insisted.

'What are people saying about it?' asked Tamanna, concern dancing on her eyebrows.

'Oh, you know, like a rat bit through your hair. Anything they are saying, haan! How is this an omelette? *Maybe* scrambled egg, but it's not even that—all rubbish they are saying.'

Behind Tamanna, Preetha Mahadevan rolled her eyes, Krupa Iyer sucked her teeth and Suman Bagh smacked her forehead with her palm. That's when Rishabh realized he had made a mistake. Tamanna breathed deeply and stalked off, her shapely chin bobbing in anger.

'But I really like it!' Rishabh yelled after her. 'God promise!'

Fortunately, the bell shrieked through the corridor, stemming the flow of any more stupid words from his mouth.

Many years later, Rishabh Bala would remember how the windy, flaky rain was pattering down from the skies when Sadashiv Ghadge, the physical education teacher, sent word for the football team to assemble in the gymnasium. They left their tiffin half-finished and tore through the corridors, joyously running to answer the call. It was always good news when Ghadge Sir summoned them for an 'impor-tent announcement'.

It was about time, too, that they got an 'impor-tent announcement', felt the fifteen boys who made up the school football team. Two weeks into the new term, and they were still without a coach. Their last coach had left for a more lucrative salary at another school. They had been badgering Ghadge Sir for a replacement almost every day, but all they'd get out of him was 'Yes, yes, I wheel get you coach.' And every day, the football team had been jealously watching the cricket and basketball teams train while wondering when they would get on the pitch. So when Ghadge Sir called them to the gymnasium that afternoon, fifteen boys shared a single thought: coach. They were excited to meet the new man and wondered if the one to lead them to glory had finally arrived.

Puro, the captain, went in first. The others crowded around him. Ghadge Sir looked up from his desk and gave them a weary nod. They tumbled into his office.

'You are all here?' said Ghadge Sir.

'No, sir,' said Puro.

Just then Aurobindo came huffing down the corridor and skidded to a halt.

'Yes, sir, now we are,' added Puro.

Ghadge Sir gave Aurobindo a withering look. 'Alvase late.'

'Sir, where's the new coach?' asked Rahul, keenly scanning the room for a football coach–shaped person but failing to find one.

Ghadge Sir's big bearlike face soured, and he swatted the comment aside with disgust. Then he gently put on his bifocals and riffled through some papers on his desk, found the ones he was looking for, inspected them and got up, grumbling. Chatter had broken out among the boys. Speculation about the nature of this 'impor-tent announcement' was on in full swing.

'Boys, keep quiet,' began Ghadge Sir, hitching up the waistband of his track pants till they bordered his enormous paunch. 'I haeo call you here to tell you about Subroto Cup. It is happen in phipteen days. You boys want to play?'

A chorus of yeses and a choreography of nods went around the group. The Subroto Cup was a national-level tournament—one of the oldest and most prestigious—that was hosted on a waterlogged ground in Ambarnath each year. The winners of the tournament became the proud holders of an ornate silver trophy that was so big and heavy that it had brought down many a trophy cabinet in its forty-six-year run.

'Good. Then I am giuing you phorms. I want philled back latesht by Whedneshday. Undershtand?' said Ghadge Sir.

'Yes, sir!' came the unanimous cry.

'And giu with three pashport photographs. Okay?'

'Yes, sir!'

The only person who didn't seem enthused was Puro. Rishabh spotted his jaw working. It was a sign that Puro was indeed concerned. As the din subsided, he spoke up, 'But, sir, how will we play without a coach?'

Ghadge frowned. These boys just didn't let up about the coach. 'How many times I haeo sed, I wheel get you coach, I wheel get you coach. Coach is growing on trees or what? Giu me some time. This Subroto Cup, you want to play or not?'

'We want to, sir, but—'

'Then phill the phorms and submit phasht. Purohit, you only collect and bring. Okay?'

'Yes, sir.'

'And don't worry. I wheel get you coach bephore the match.'

Ghadge Sir distributed the forms and dismissed them. The boys buzzed with anticipation as they filed out of the gymnasium. They were going to play again! Another chance to *finally* win a trophy had presented itself.

'What if we win the Subroto Cup?' said Pinal Oza.

'Puro won't be able to lift it,' said Abel Floyd Thottapalli.

'But he'll easily fit in it,' offered Rahul.

They laughed and jabbered on as they made their way back to class. The bell rang; tiffin boxes were clanged shut, desks thumped and chairs scraped into place. Rishabh looked out a window and studied the ground. The restlessness he had been feeling in the past month seemed to have cooled. They were set to play at last; the year had finally begun.

The next Monday, the boys submitted their forms with three photographs each. Ghadge Sir filed them away but when asked about procuring a coach, he winced with annoyance once again. 'I wheel get bephore tournament. Now don't ashk one more time,' he chafed.

Three days crawled by, each heavy with the anticipation of a coach's arrival, but a coach never came and those days of practice were lost. The last bell rang on Thursday and as a sea of students filled the corridors, Purohit told Rishabh to meet him at Upvan Lake at seven o'clock that evening. They could meet at leisure because it was one of those rare days when they didn't have tutorials.

At 6.45 p.m., Puro rang Rishabh and told him to get ready. The latter sprayed on deodorant and dashed out. He sprang up the hump of road that separated their houses. He jogged past the medical store, the dry-cleaners, the *kirana* store, the municipal corporator's bungalow and the ice-cream parlour before coming to a stop at the gate to Nataraj Heights. Rishabh stood there in a blue French jersey with 'Zidane' and the number '10' written on the back.

The two boys continued up the curving road, rounded the bend and ascended until they felt the cool breeze of Upvan Lake in their hair. Rishabh always thought that Upvan was a lake only in the most generous use of the word 'lake'. At less than a kilometre in radius, it was less a lake and more a pond that had let itself go. What the boys found even more amusing was that at the entry to the lake was a board that read 'Beware of crocodile'. Rishabh thought this was fitting— if Upvan could be a lake, then any garden lizard in it could be a crocodile.

Puro leaned over the railing and cast an ominous look across the water. 'What are we going to do, my boy?' he said. 'Only ten days left, and we haven't trained even a single day.'

'Isn't Ghadge Sir finding us a coach?'

'Who knows, yaaaar,' said Puro. He bent down, picked up a stone and hurled it into the water with all his strength. It landed with a distant plop. 'All I know is that we can't win the cup like this,' he continued. 'Our last training session was in April. It's July. Look at the team. We haven't played together in so long. Stamina is zero. Fitness is finished. Look at Aurobindo—the only running he does is to McDonald's. We're going to lose again. Fuckin' hell!'

Rishabh shared Puro's frustration. Every decade, with some luck, a school was blessed with a full complement of players. A batch arrived that seemed predestined for greatness. And after many decades of sporting drought, theirs was the batch that was unanimously dubbed the Golden Generation. Ever since they had broken into the under-14 team in the sixth standard, Ghadge Sir, their former coach, Amar, and every passing spectator had reported goosebumps on seeing them play. It had been predicted that when the boys came of age, they would sweep every trophy. The years had passed, and though they'd improved and matured each year, the only sweeping they had done was of the dust that gathered in the empty trophy cabinet.

'Let's start coaching them,' said Rishabh. He was angry in the way that made foolish ideas seem appealing.

Puro looked at him and saw his stern eyebrows. 'Meaning?'

'Meaning you and I coach the bloody team. Remember the exercises Amar taught us?'

'The two exercises? "Shot on goal, shot on goal" and "Pay the fees, pay the fees"?'

'We'll come up with new ones. At the very least, let's get everyone running. Do rounds, get match fit. We can set up five-a-side games.'

'You think it'll make a difference?'

'Look, I don't know if we'll win, but I know we have to try.'

Puro fell silent. The dark water shimmered in front of them. Finally he spoke. 'And why should anyone listen to us?'

'Everyone *will* listen to you. Captain's orders.'

Puro laughed. 'You're mad or what? No one will train because I said so. I'm Abhay Purohit, not Zinedine Zidane.'

Rishabh Bala's eyes lit up. 'What did you say?'

'They won't listen to me.'

'No, after that!'

'I'm not Zidane?'

'*They* don't know that!'

Puro looked at his friend, concerned. He was pretty sure everyone knew he wasn't a retired bald French footballer. 'I'm sorry?' he asked cautiously. He had read that one mustn't provoke lunatics.

'I'll tell you!' said Rishabh, dragging Puro away.

In the middle of the lake, there was a shallow ripple.

'Guys, do you know what this is?' said Puro, holding up a lime-green file. Fourteen pairs of eyes blinked back at him.

'This file has Zidane's training techniques. Every drill, every set and every repetition he ever did is in *this* file.'

The fourteen pairs of eyes widened simultaneously.

'How did you get it?' whispered Floyd.

Puro looked at Rishabh, who nodded supportively. 'Rishabh and I, we found it on the Net.' Floyd nodded. It seemed a plausible explanation. Puro, seeing that the ruse was working, went on. 'We have ten days left. We need to follow this for these next ten days. If we do exactly as is written, down to the last crossing–heading exercise, for ten straight days, there is no way we will not win!'

Puro threw his hands up in the air, and as he did so, the pages slipped out of the file—first a few and then the whole bundle—and wafted to the ground. Floyd picked up a sheet.

'It's blank,' he said sourly.

'This isn't Zidane's training technique, it's Puro's brain!' said Rahul, holding up a spotless sheet.

'Not this one,' said Khodu Madon, the burly stopper, while scowling at a page. 'On this is written, "Run three rounds. Defence drill. Passing drill. Shooting practice." . . . Rishabh, this is your handwriting, no?'

But Rishabh didn't hear Khodu because he was busy arguing with Puro about the filing of the papers.

'I bought the file. You had to file them.'

'I thought you already did it.'

'I told you I hadn't.'

'Bullshit.'

'Why didn't you check?'

'I wouldn't need to check if you'd done your job!'

'Fellows,' began Khodu. They turned to look at him. He shoved the single page of instructions into Rishabh's hands. 'You dropped this. Call us when we have a real coach.'

Khodu pushed through the team to leave, and others began following his lead. They shook their bowed heads and their shoulders sagged as they shuffled away. Then, suddenly, from behind them came a fierce growl. 'GET BACK IN HERE!'

It was Puro, his eyes aflame under his hooded eyebrows.

'All of you, here, *right now*. We will coach you, and that's final! I am captain of this team. I am submitting a team sheet next week, and if you're not here for training then you sure as hell won't be on that sheet. Got it?'

Khodu thought of saying something but, on seeing Puro's blazing eyes, remained silent.

'So can we start this bloody session?'

All fourteen boys stood rooted in place. Then a booming voice went up from the back. 'Let's do it,' said Sumit, stamping the ground with his studs.

'Yes, coach,' said Rahul, winking as he stepped forward.

The heads now nodded, the shoulders straightened and the majority mumbled in agreement.

'So plan B, then,' whispered Rishabh.

On the second day of training, the new coaches faced their first test. The team was on the field, in the middle of stretching, when Govind Sir, the coach of the cricket team, strode up to them and told them to clear off.

'Cricket has the ground right now.'

'Yes, sir. But we just need a small area of the ground. Just the patch near the goalposts,' said Puro, still bent midway from touching his toes.

'Who has given you permission to train here?' asked Govind Sir.

'Sir, we have a tournament in a few days,' explained Rishabh.

'And we've come here to eat papdi chaat, no?' sneered Govind Sir. 'Get off the pitch. Come on, fast, fast!'

The team followed Puro as he led them to the minuscule ground in front of the canteen. It was a bald, muddy patch, but at least they had it all to themselves. Once they had finally finished stretching, Puro ordered them to run ten rounds.

By the third round, most of the boys began to pant. Gone were the jokes and banter of the first lap. The smiles of the second round had disappeared too. By the fourth, the group splintered, and the fifth and sixth saw Aurobindo and Bhupinder Chatwal slow to a walk. Puro, Rishabh, Rahul and Khodu still jogged steadily and by the eighth circuit, had overtaken Aurobindo and Bhupinder, who were as close to crawling as two boys can be while still walking upright.

At the end of the final round, Puro turned and said, 'Okay! Now, shooting practice?' He got no reply, because people close to fainting aren't usually a vocal lot.

For the next few days, the boys were sore and achy in places they didn't know were capable of being sore and achy. They hobbled into training, bent and wincing, but Puro showed no mercy. They circled the ground with ragged motion and laid themselves flat on the muddy earth when it was over. They practised through rain and dirt. To make the best of their collective knowledge, different leaders were assigned to each drill, depending on their talents. Puro took the passing drills, Rishabh dictated crossing, Rahul taught them to move the ball quickly despite the sinking mud, Floyd led the heading exercises. The defenders were getting better, as they were finally managing to keep their eyes open when making contact. Vipul Dutta, the tall ninth-standard central defender had been struggling until Puro told him that heading the ball didn't lead to hair loss. The only one to not join in was Khodu. On the third day, he sulked through training and then stopped coming altogether. He was the best defender in the team and knew the only way his name would be omitted from the team sheet would be if Puro decided they wanted to concede half a dozen goals or so.

Soon their legs found strength and the stitches in their sides disappeared. They passed quicker and ran faster. They remembered the rhythms and patterns of their teammates and anticipated each other's movements. But the most marked change in them wasn't their physical fitness, it was the laughs. Puro and Rishabh observed happily as the ground buzzed with chatter. The jokes increased more steadily than the stamina. Floyd's *hyuk-hyuk* guffaw became the soundtrack of their training sessions.

As the days ticked by, they grew more obsessed. No amount of play was ever enough. Puro and Rishabh trained in the evenings, then ran for tutorials—restlessly sitting through the class with mud-caked ears—after which they played some more in the small court in Rishabh's apartment complex. Mrs Bala watched anxiously as Rishabh started packing his football kit with more care than his school bag.

Each day they would pick up the balls from the gymnasium and ask Ghadge Sir when the coach would arrive, and each day Ghadge Sir supplied the same reply: 'I wheel get you coach bephore tournament.' It was a question that had lost meaning fairly quickly, but they continued asking out of habit.

On the second last day of practice, they had split into teams and were playing a match when Tamanna came to the canteen.

Rahul spotted her first and yelled across the pitch, 'Rishabh, time to score!' Soon everyone had eyes on the girl in the brown pinafore asking for a vada pav at the counter. Wolf whistles rang out, and Tamanna's face turned scarlet. Rishabh tried to silence them with as menacing a look as he could muster, but his embarrassment only fuelled the rabble.

After that, it was less a game of football and more a game of who could kick the ball towards the canteen so Rishabh could get it back. Tejas Thackeray, a left-winger, seemed to be comfortably winning at this new game with a total of five kicks, all of them landing the ball just inches away from Tamanna. By the end of lunch break, Rishabh had run from the ground to the canteen at least a dozen times. He would hoof the ball back, run on to the pitch and then watch the ball sail over his head towards Tamanna again. He would run up the three steps again, half-smiling, half-shrugging at Tamanna, before kicking the ball back. Once she even returned his smile. It made him inhale sharply and when he kicked the ball, it rocketed to the far end of the pitch.

When they met at Prasad's Hindi tutorial that evening, Rishabh asked Puro, 'Why'd you guys have to do that?'

Puro's eyes shone as he said, 'The question, my boy, is, why did she stay?'

The night before the tournament, Rishabh's breath quickened as he packed his bag. His hands and feet trembled, and he had a fleeting vision of victory. He had already slipped his studs into their olive-green nylon shoe-bag and, along with it, had tossed in a face towel, a roll of crêpe bandage, a can of Relispray (you never knew when you would need it during a match) and a can of deodorant (you always knew when you would need it after a match).

Their first draw was tomorrow. Rishabh had been wondering whom they would be up against. Suddenly he swung his foot in mid-air, and commentary crackled to life in his head: 'He's smashed it . . . and it's a goooooooooal!' Rishabh wheeled away in celebration but stopped short when he saw his father at the door.

'All okay?' asked Mr Bala.

'Yes, Papa,' said Rishabh, sheepishly getting back to his bag.

Mr Bala *hmm*-ed—as he always did when he was unconvinced—nodded and left. Had he probed further, he would have found that things were a little more than okay for his son. Shri Sunderlal Sanghvi School's football team had successfully managed to confuse excitement for confidence. They were so eager to play that they believed they were ready to play.

Rishabh carefully zipped up his bag, switched off the lights and neatly pulled the blanket over himself. From beyond his darkened window came the soothing patter of raindrops hitting the concrete. When he opened his eyes again, he found the blanket twisted around him. The bed sheet had undergone a thorough kneading. It was like he had played an entire match in his sleep. Outside his window, the sky was a light grey and a drizzle persisted. He shook his head and turned off his alarm before it went off.

At school, everyone turned to look when the football team walked through the corridor wearing jeans and bright T-shirts.

'Why are you dressed like that?' was the standard question.

'We're going for a tournament,' each said with pride.

When the bell rang, Krupa Iyer—a stringy girl with wild, wiry hair, whose thick black frames were trumped only by her huge crush on Floyd—cornered the object of her affection outside class. She ran across the corridor, screaming, 'Abel! Abel!' Unfortunately for her, Floyd didn't reciprocate her sentiments, and when he saw her bounding towards him, he bolted for the safety of the classroom. But he was too slow. She put an arm around his shoulder and held him in place as if he were a Barbie doll.

'Abby—do you mind if I call you that?'

'I do.'

'Great! Abby, I made something for your big day. Here . . .' She thrust a small card made of chart paper into his hand. It was covered in glitter and gleamed so bright that even the people who hadn't noticed Krupa and Abel now stopped and stared.

'Can I tell you something?' said Krupa, her dish antenna–sized eyes blinking dreamily behind her spectacles.

'No,' said Abel, cringing.

'Great, come here, no. I'll whisper it in your ear.'

She pulled a reluctant Floyd close to her. But instead of whispering a secret, she passed the border of his ear, entered the land of his cheek and, in an act of romantic terrorism, planted a thunderous kiss upon it. The smack reverberated down the corridor. Doors rattled, windows shook. Then the corridor erupted in cheers.

Krupa bit her lower lip and, giddy with excitement, dashed off to her classroom. Abel stood still. His face turned an angry red, as if a wasp had stung him, as he stalked into class.

The second the morning assembly ended, Puro and Rishabh hoisted their bags, sauntered down the aisle and stopped at Kaul Miss's table. She glanced up at them from the attendance sheet and raised an eyebrow.

'On duty, ma'am,' they said in unison and watched as Kaul Miss's face dissolved into grudging acceptance. They exited the classroom, leaving a murmur of jealousy behind them. Turning into the corridor, they joined the stream of players as they trickled out of each class. The boys walked to the parking area, where bus no. 11 waited for them. Ghadge Sir stood beside it, scowling.

'Come on, phasht, phasht! We are getting late,' he barked.

Puro, Rishabh, Rahul, Floyd and Paras Apte, the diminutive striker, took up residence at the back of the bus.

'Look at Floyd, all glowing and all,' said Rahul.

'Fuck off, yaar,' groaned Floyd.

'What did she give you?' asked Puro.

'A kiss . . . Didn't you see?' said Rishabh.

'No, no, she gave him some paper also, no,' said Puro.

'I'll give all of you anything to shut up,' pleaded Floyd.

'Where is it?' asked Paras. 'Where's that paper? Let's see it.'

'I threw it out the window,' declared Floyd.

Rahul sneaked up behind Floyd and yanked his bag from beside him. Floyd swore in Malayalam and lunged to retrieve it. But the boys were too quick and passed it among each other until it landed in the lap of the tiny left back Arnav Vade, who managed to extricate the letter and fling it to Rishabh before Floyd pounced on him. In the scuffle, Vade's hand hit Khodu with a soft thud. He slowly turned around and pointed a stern finger at Vade, who shrank back in his seat.

Dave, now swaying down the aisle, patted Khodu on the head and said, 'Calm down, Khodu. You know we love you.' He swung towards the back. He didn't like being left out when mischief was being made.

'Okay, okay! Just finish this,' said Floyd, defeated.

Rishabh carefully opened the card so as to not contaminate himself with glitter, cleared his throat and boomed, '"Abby! You are my star! You are the most talented footballer I ever saw. You run like a horse." A horse! Is it just the running, Abby?'

'Shut up, na, fucker.'

'"You kick with lotsa power. You play with lotsa passion." This is getting very personal, guys!'

'Give it back,' demanded Floyd.

'Okay, okay. Wait, it's almost over. "You are so happy with the football that I know I will always be second best in your eye. But I am OK with that. Best of luck and keep shining, my star."'

Rahul pretended to throw up.

'I think you should ask her out,' said Rishabh.

'If you liked the note so much, you ask her out,' said Floyd.

'I already have Tamanna.'

'You have Tamanna as much as Puro has height.'

'What the fuck! Floyd, you son of a bitch, I would have punched you, but I can't make that face any uglier,' retorted Puro.

31

'Calm down, everyone,' said Tejas. 'Let's not forget we have a tournament to win. Especially you, Floyd.' He continued. 'Do you want to be Krupa's shining star or not?'

So the clamour rose again, and only when the bus rounded the final bend, and the sprawling ground could be seen through the grilles on the windows, did they finally fall silent.

Stepping off the bus, they were met with a chilly wind that made them shiver. It wasn't raining just then, but the road was wet and pocked with puddles. They could hear intermittent shouts from the ongoing match.

'Boys, I wheel be back. Jusht you shtay here,' said Ghadge Sir.

'Yes, sir,' said Puro. Then he turned to Rishabh, nodded and said, 'Okay, everyone, shut up. Rishabh, take them through the Final Strategy.'

The Final Strategy was a plan of action that Rishabh and Puro had devised across many periods, tutorials and phone calls. It combined Rishabh's academic knowledge of football tactics and Purohit's deep-seated belief that their team wouldn't be able to execute any of them, till they finally arrived at a system they felt would be clever yet simple enough to pull off.

'Here's the plan,' began Rishabh. 'Be quick with your passing. Treat the ball like a virus; and always pass forward. It's simple: get the ball to Rahul. If you have to kick it, throw it, head it, shoulder it, liver it, kidney it—doesn't matter. Just get the ball to Rahul. Got it?'

'And then what?' quizzed Rahul.

'And then you figure out a way to not fuck it up,' said Rishabh.

Everyone agreed this was a great plan. Rishabh now went on to the finer details of the Final Strategy. 'Defence, I need you to be in formation. A straight line at all times, got it?'

'Are you sure? Shouldn't the defence line be a curve?' asked Sumit from behind him.

Rishabh furrowed his brow. 'Good joke, Sumo. Keep to a straight line, okay? Now, this is for everybody. Make sure you stay in your positions. And mark your players.'

'What if the mark goes out of position? Do we stay in position or do we mark him?' asked Sumit over Rishabh's shoulder again.

'Shut the fuck up, Sumo! You're on the fucking bench anyway. That's your position, stay there and—'

It was then that Rishabh saw Sumit's hulking frame in *front* of him, a wide grin on his face. Rishabh, though not a genius, was smart enough to grasp that if a boy was standing in front of him, grinning, then he couldn't also be behind him.

He whipped around to see a tall, lanky man with a bright orange, mehendi-stained moustache and floppy black hair. He wore a blue tracksuit, a black T-shirt and a blue windcheater, and stood with his legs wide apart and his arms casually crossed across his chest. An amused smile shaped his lips.

'Aye, Ghadge, why you got me here? You already have such a good coach,' he said.

'Boys, this is Mehphouz Noorani, new phootball coach. What you are waiting for, say good morning!'

The team sang good morning, but Mehfouz Noorani dismissed them with a wave.

'What I had sed?' said Ghadge Sir emphatically, waggling his eyebrows. 'I wheel get you coach bephore tournament. And look, tournament is not shtart and coach is here.'

Now, for most people, it's always a little awkward coaching a bunch of boys fifteen minutes after you've met them, but Mehfouz Noorani was not most people. The boys didn't know it, but they were in the presence of a legend.

Mehfouz Noorani had played five seasons with the legendary Kolkata football club Mohun Bagan AC. As a spry, mousy-faced, floppy-haired striker, he had been so effective that Bagan fans had nicknamed him The Mongoose. He had made his international debut at the mere age of twenty-one. Spectators who had watched the Mongoose in his prime recalled not his goals as much as his constant screaming at teammates to stop strolling on the field like they were in a garden. He had been on course to become India's youngest captain when Shabbibur Rahman, East Bengal FC's bullish centre back, took out his knee and the rest of his career. Every time he thought of that incident, the only thing the Mongoose really lamented was that Shabbibur didn't even get carded.

Once he had been forced off the pitch, he was bumped around a string of sports quota jobs, but his feet always twitched under his desk and his colleagues didn't appreciate him constantly yelling at them for sitting around like they were in a garden. So one night, he assessed his savings and found they'd be enough for the education of his three children as well as one family vacation to Manali. The next morning, he set down his ID card on his superior's desk and said he was resigning. That day, Mehfouz took his wife out to lunch. They ordered rice and fish, and Nazneen asked him why he kept staring at her. Mehfouz said she looked just as beautiful as the day they were wed, and Nazneen asked him what he had done this time. He told her he had resigned, and she laughed and said he was still as mature as the day they were wed.

His first few weeks at home had been happy—Mehfouz took over the television and inspected his children's homework. But soon he'd begun drifting like a ghoul from the living room to the bedroom, from the kitchen to the bathroom, looking for something to do. Every time he'd try helping around the house, Nazneen intercepted him and told him to relax. He was tired of relaxing and had no one to yell at.

That's when Ghadge had called about a coaching position at Shri Sunderlal Sanghvi School and would Mehfouz know anyone who could do the job. It had been hard for Mehfouz to keep the eagerness out of his voice when he'd said he was interested himself. Ghadge had been stunned. He couldn't believe the Mongoose would coach his boys. How incredible! It would be an honour, Ghadge had said.

When Mehfouz had asked when he could begin, Ghadge told him the team was going for a tournament the next day and, if he wanted, he would be more than welcome to join them in Ambarnath. And the Mongoose had said a tournament was as good a time to start as any.

The boys had changed into their kit: black shorts and a black jersey with an orange 'S4' emblazoned on the chest. They were forced to wear this kit from two years ago because, in their excitement, they had all forgotten that a new jersey needed to be made. Now they stood around awkwardly, their studs squelching in the muck, wearing jerseys so tight they constricted most of their blood vessels. In fact, Sumit had grown so rapidly that his jersey was now a crop top. Mehfouz winced just looking at them. Then he herded them together, introduced himself and asked them to do the same. The boys blinked at each other, wondering who would go first.

'You start. Name and position,' said Mehfouz, pointing at Rahul.

'Rahul, sir.'

'You don't have a last name?'

'Rahul Rawat, striker, sir,' said Rahul.

He focused on each boy with his flinty stare until he reached the last one. Then he clapped his hands and said, 'Okay, boys, very good. Now, as soon as that match ends, we have to get on the pitch. We have—' he consulted his watch, 'ten minutes to do that. I need you to warm up by then, got it?'

The boys nodded.

'Purohit, take charge.'

'Sir, who are we playing?' inquired Rishabh.

'Arre, how it matters? You have to beat whichever team it is,' said Mehfouz. 'Come on, start the warm-up.'

The boys formed a circle. Puro stood in the middle, leading the stretching. Leaning forward, they whispered their shared opinion—that the coach seemed like he had a prickly object wedged up his posterior.

'You don't have a last name or what?' mocked Rahul mid-stretch.

'And why won't he tell us who we are playing?' said Floyd, perplexed.

'He's going to be such a pain,' muttered Dave. 'Khodu, are you happy now?'

Khodu grimaced and continued stretching. Soon they began lightly jogging up and down the touchline.

'We're playing those guys,' said Sumit, jerking a thumb across the ground. A team in blue-and-white were bouncing up and down, out of sync, trying to pull through a chaotic warm-up routine.

'Which school is that?' asked Rishabh. 'Why won't Maksud tell us anything?'

'Mehfouz.'

'Yeah, yeah, whatever his name is.'

'Whatever *my* name is,' said Mehfouz.

Rishabh shut his eyes as he exhaled. It seemed he couldn't go five minutes without insulting the new coach. At this rate, it'd be a miracle if he even made it to the substitutes' bench. But Mehfouz had other things to worry about.

'Okay, everybody, come here,' called Mehfouz. He waited for the team to gather around. 'You're playing Balaji Anandrao School, Dombivli. Now, for this match, I want you to keep the line-up you had chosen.' He looked at Rishabh and asked, 'Rishabh, you were coaching, no?'

'Well, sir, I was just—'

'Did you have a team in mind?'

Rishabh murmured assent.

'Well, tell me, then.'

Rishabh called out the names: Dave, Rana, Khodu, Vade, Bhupi, Puro, Floyd, Tejas, Rahul and Paras. 'And myself.'

'You know your positions?' asked Mehfouz.

The team nodded solemnly.

Then the coach ran over some basic tactics that the boys hadn't known. They huddled around him and strained their eyes and ears. He kept it short as the referee had already walked on to the pitch, carrying a mud-stained ball in the crook of his arm.

Finally, Mehfouz crouched closer. 'Ghadge Sir said that you boys have trained yourselves. You've worked hard,' he said. 'For me, the most important thing is that you took responsibility. You made a plan, you took a decision. And I will say it: you did well. This is why I am confident about this match. If you can be so strong without a coach, with a coach you will be even stronger. Yes or no?'

Fifteen boys bobbed their heads.

'Say . . . yes or no?' said Mehfouz.

'Yes, sir,' came the mumbly reply.

'What is this meow–meow you're doing? Roar like bloody lions!'

'YES, SIR!' they roared.

Across the ground, the knees of many a Balaji Anandrao player shook in their blue stockings as they heard that bellow. The referee tooted his whistle and signalled for the teams to step on to the field.

In the moments right before a match, players always look like they have an ant running up and down the length of their clothes. They wiggle and shake, they jump and twist, they waggle their arms and jiggle their thighs. It is, in fact, a powerful cocktail of fear and excitement that makes them so jittery. If you cut a footballer open just before kick-off, adrenaline would pour out of them in spurts.

The boys of Sanghvi shook so badly that they looked like the top halves of really old mixers. Rishabh jogged over to the right wing. He surveyed the ground with a grim eye. The ground was so muddy that it looked like they were playing on a surface of rich chocolate ice cream. Down the wing was a pool of water so large that it demanded its own lifeguard. The Balaji boys bobbled just as nervously.

The referee called the captains to the centre circle for the toss. Rishabh watched as the coin remained suspended in mid-air for a second, as if the referee had tossed it through a viscous fluid. Puro called heads and fist-pumped when he saw the outcome. He elected to kick off. Thankfully, the Balaji boys decided to stay put in their half and the match could begin.

Rishabh trotted to the centre, where Rahul was standing with his hands on his hips and one foot resting on the ball.

'Rishabh,' said Rahul, 'make sure you find me.'

'I will. You just stick to the plan and don't fuck it up.'

The whistle is blown and Rishabh rolls the ball forward. Rahul swoops down on it as three Balaji players rush him. He neatly scoops the ball to Floyd, who is charging from behind him like a freight train. Floyd dinks the ball to Puro. The whole Sanghvi midfield pushes forward like a pack of wolves on the hunt. Puro tries an audacious pass to Tejas. The ball soars across the air and Tejas steadies himself in anticipation, but before it can land, a Balaji head blunders into it. The ball bobbles ahead and the Balaji player runs towards it with a satisfied grin, which leaves his face as soon as he sees the stork-like legs of Rana pinch the ball away.

Rana looks up and spots Puro waving his hands at him like a man marooned on a desert island waves at a passing ship.

He pokes the ball to Puro, who resumes the attack with a determined run. He skips past one defender and nears the edge of the D. He finds himself facing a thicket of Balaji players and coolly passes the ball out to Rahul. Every defender turns to the left, leaving the right exposed. Rishabh, not one to let an opportunity pass him by, flies down the wing and infiltrates the box. He screams, 'RAHUL! LOOK!'

Rahul spots him on the far right and side-foots a pass, just as the goalkeeper comes at him like a maddened rooster, with both arms flapping. Time slows down. Rishabh sees the goalkeeper rattling into Rahul. He sees the lolling pink tongue of a Balaji defender who is desperately running in to prevent this pass from meeting its target. The ball glides over the surface, dips viciously on to the mud and skips off it like a pebble on the surface of a pond. Rishabh watches in amazement as he unconsciously sticks a foot out and stops the ball.

I stopped it! he thinks. *Is my breathing always this loud? Wow. I sound like a harmonium. Wait, there's a ball at my feet . . . I'm in the middle of a game! That's right! Oh, look—the goal is in front of me. What luck! You'd better do something quick, Rishabh. That defender and his tongue are almost here.*

His eyes droop, his body slackens and he stabs at the ball in a relaxed manner. The ball, which was perfectly happy going one away, gets rudely diverted to another. It rockets into the net! Rishabh sees the mesh ripple and hears that delightful ripping sound, and he erupts in a howl.

'YAAAAAAASSSSSSSSS!' he screams as he wheels away. Puro slams into him, Rahul hugs him from behind and Floyd grips his cheeks with aggressive affection. The whole team, save Dave, land up at the right corner flag to celebrate. Bhupi is the last to reach as he waddles forward, hitching up his shorts as he comes.

'Bastard, you did it!' he pants.

The Balaji boys wait patiently as Bhupi waddles back to his position before they resume the match. Mehfouz is heard viciously yelling something from the touchline.

'Stay focused! Stay focused!' the words waft to the wing.

Why's he still shouting? thinks Rishabh. *Give us a break. This team is finished!*

The Balaji players do look defeated. They're slouching around the field, crestfallen at having conceded so early. They don't even make eye contact. The Sanghvi boys relax. The fatal bite has been administered, and now they can take their time with their prey. They prowl in their positions, baring their teeth and smiling in the gently falling rain.

But as the game restarts, they quickly realize why the coach has been frothing at the mouth. The Balaji boys don't roll over and die as scheduled. Instead, they begin putting passes together. Rishabh finds himself pulled further and further into his own half. He's marking a number 13, who has an annoying habit of wriggling past him. Their defence is under siege. Each time they clear the ball, it lands right back with a Balaji player, who politely decides to return to sender.

The Balaji boys prod and prod; unable to penetrate the flanks, they play the ball infield. Their centre midfielder receives it and drives forward. He comes up against Khodu, who seems alert but out of breath. Khodu starts and lunges at him with a tackle. The boy cuts the ball away from Khodu's sliding body and tears into the open space ahead of him. He aligns his body and kicks the ball inches away from Dave's fingertips.

It's Balaji's turn to celebrate, and Rishabh feels humiliated by their happiness. Khodu is still wallowing in the muck, heaving asthmatically. From the touchline comes a volley of abuse. The coach is positively bouncing with rage. Rishabh is alarmed by how far out the coach's eyeballs have ventured from their sockets. A few minutes later, the pressure is relieved by the whistles for half-time.

The boys trundled off the field. The Balaji team left in better spirits than Sanghvi's. The rain fell harder. Rishabh took off his glasses and wiped them with the hem of his shirt. At the school level, each match consisted of two ten-minute halves with a five-minute half-time break, and it properly knackered the young men.

'Sit down,' growled Mehfouz, 'drink water, shake your legs, take deep breaths.' He paused.

'You fuckers can't understand or what?' A gasp rose from the team. No adult had called them 'fuckers' before. It was both exciting and insulting. 'That goal was a bloody shame. And you,' he said to Khodu, 'you can't stay on your feet or what? Bloody fucker, stand your ground, no. You like rolling in mud or what? Are you a pig?' Khodu remained silent, gulping mouthfuls of air. 'Answer!' roared Mehfouz.

'No, sir.'

'Then don't slide in next time.'

The coach continued to savage them individually and collectively. Then, towards the end of the mauling, he said, 'But you boys are playing well.' Which led to the whole team tilting their heads quizzically. He praised their discipline in formation and their passing before dropping his voice to a low rumble. 'Just do one thing: attack them from the right side. They are slower there. And don't worry, it's only a matter of time—you boys will win.'

The boys cheered at this, loudly. Mehfouz's conviction was contagious. They got up and stretched. As they were about to head to the field, the coach called, 'Bhupinder?'

'Yes, sir,' said Bhupi, wincing in anticipation.

'Tie your shorts properly. When you are running ahead, they shouldn't run down.'

The second half gets under way and Sanghvi pounces on Balaji. The whole team seems unafraid. The Balaji boys start the half more tentatively and find themselves pushed back by wave upon wave of Sanghvi attacks. Puro begins asserting himself in the midfield, orchestrating the game with his array of passes. Rishabh sees Puro's features shaped by concentration. In this half, he's on the flank, where the coach is standing, and he hears constant commentary, like he's listening to a radio channel he can't turn off.

'Pass right,' the coach yells. 'Do what I told you! Aye, bloody Purohit! Pass right!'

Puro hears the coach but every time he looks to the right, he sees Rishabh closely marked, so he swivels and passes elsewhere. 'Get rid of your marker,' he whispers to Rishabh as they come together for a free kick.

Rishabh tries to shake off the left back, but the boy clings to him like his shadow. Rishabh is despondent. He looks around and spots Bhupi ambling down his line. An idea occurs to him. He jogs up to Bhupi and says, 'Next time Puro gets the ball, I need you to run down the flank, okay?'

'All right,' says Bhupi, expiring breath.

'Overlap me, okay?'

Bhupi gives him a thumbs up, unable to drum up any more air for words.

Moments later, Puro gets the ball. Rishabh turns to Bhupi. 'NOW!' he yells. Bhupi lets out one last almighty heave and charges up the field like a beach volleyball that's been given a good thump. He patters past Rishabh and his marker, who yelps. An intruder has bundled past him, right under his nose, as it were. The boy, enraged that someone could overtake him with such ease, tears after Bhupi, leaving Rishabh alone.

'Puro, here, here!' calls Rishabh.

Puro looks up, sees Rishabh unmarked and gladly lays the ball off to him. Rishabh darts into the box. Defenders, now alerted, begin swarming around him. He reaches the goal line and then spots Rahul unattended at the penalty spot. He cuts the ball back with a grunt. Rahul controls it, steadies himself and then pokes it with the toe end of his boot . . . and the ball zips into the net! Relief explodes in the centre of Rishabh's chest. The Sanghvites race forward, hollering, fully intending to mob Rahul. Rishabh is the first to get to him. He grabs Rahul's head in a lock and says, 'I told you I'd find you!'

'I'm dying. Need. Air,' rasps Rahul, choking in the vice-like grip. Rishabh lets go so the striker can receive thumps on his back as well as the many joyous *gaalis* from his teammates. At the touchline, the coach holds up both his thumbs and there's a hint of a smile beneath his moustache.

The score 2–1 is one that doesn't inspire much confidence. It's an unstable score, which constantly looks to tip over to a more even 2–2. It's a score that makes the rest of the match incredibly nervy for the boys of Sanghvi as they quell even more desperate attacks from the Balaji boys. They hold off the opposition most admirably . . . until the dying minutes, when the Balaji number 9 slinks past a hapless Khodu. The boy is about to pull the trigger when Dave flies off his goal line and smothers the ball without regard for life or safety. He does receive a good wallop in the thigh, which he would later dismiss by saying, 'Look, I'm just happy it wasn't two inches to the left.'

When the final whistle sounds, they break into such an orgy of shrieking and dancing that the Balaji boys wonder whether they were playing a final in the first round itself.

Their next match was in an hour's time. At school tournaments, teams would play two, sometimes three, matches in a day because it seemed tournaments were designed by the same people who had come up with Chinese sweatshops. Ghadge Sir dispensed food coupons, which they promptly exchanged for plates of idli sambar. Only when they got their hands on the plates did they realize how hungry they were. They scarfed the grub down in seconds and it warmed their shivering bodies.

The boys found a vacant section in the stands and flopped down. Their studs lay in disarray around them, their shin guards protruded out of their rolled-down stockings, hanging on with a single strap. Paras, who had spent most of the game running furiously with little reward, sighed deeply and shut his eyes. Dutta had made friends with a white stray dog and was petting it silently. The dog thumped his tail at the lavish attention. Tejas sat with a rag in his hand, fastidiously scrubbing his new Nike studs. He knew they were going to get dirty again but was compelled by some mania to keep them sparkling.

'Look at Tejas rubbing his magic lamps,' quipped Dave.

'Regular lamps. There's no magic in them,' said Floyd.

Tejas ignored them in favour of extracting a particularly resilient speck of mud.

'Aye, Tejas, play better passes, no,' said Puro, suddenly remembering what he had been meaning to tell him all through the game. 'Tejas!' he called louder and the left-winger looked up. He repeated his criticism and Tejas turned red.

'It's not my fault, yaar. What can I do if the ground is like this? The flanks are the worst. Ask Rishabh!'

'So we ask the second-worst player why the worst player played so badly?' sneered Rahul.

'Your mom scored or what?' said Rishabh.

'I did all the hard work. You just poked it in!'

'I still scored, no!'

'Aye, you let it be. Who scored the winning goal?'

Rishabh was about to tell him where he could shove his winning goal when they heard a cry for help. On the ground, a livid Rana was chasing a wailing Vade. 'Son of a bitch!' screamed Rana. They raced around before Puro yelled for them to stop.

'What's the matter?' he asked.

'He threw mud at me,' Rana said, then turned to Vade. 'Such a coward. Throwing from afar! I'll give you one . . . your teeth will come out of your ass!'

Puro admired the creativity of that insult but, as captain, told them to cut it out. He instructed them to get something to eat, sit down and conserve energy. 'You idiots will be crawling on the field later. Stay put, understood?'

Soon the coach came to the stands and asked Puro to have the team ready. Then he looked at Rishabh. 'You come here.' Rishabh hopped down the stands and joined the coach on the ground.

'Remove your specs,' said Mehfouz.

Rishabh took them off. All detail dropped from the world.

'I want you to wave at your friend Sumit,' said the coach.

'But why, sir?'

'Just do as I am saying.'

Rishabh squinted, trying to bring things into some focus. He stared at the many blurry blobs that milled about the stands. No, he was pretty sure Sumit was not in the stands. He turned towards the ground. In the distance, he saw a large frame hulking towards him. It was still a silhouette to his narrowed eyes but the proportions matched his memory of Sumit, so he stuck a hand out and waved.

'Put your specs back on,' instructed the coach.

'But, sir, what was this for?'

'I was checking if you can play without your specs. You can't,' concluded the coach.

Rishabh put on his spectacles and recoiled on seeing a cheery Ghadge Sir waving back at him. *He could have just* asked *me*, thought Rishabh as he joined the rest of the team at the base of the stands.

'Okay, boys, the draw has been announced,' said Mehfouz. 'You're playing Gyan Vikas High School. They are from Vasai, no, Ghadge?'

Ghadge Sir nodded.

'This is a knockout format. You lose one game, you're out. Each game is like a final, and you must win each game. So be alert. Now, some special things to keep in mind: I want both strikers to take more shots, okay? The team that takes more shots scores more goals. Defenders, never pass into the middle, always out. What is your name again?'

47

'Sir, Khodu.'

'Yes, Khodu. I saw you pass inside. Don't repeat that mistake. Always outside. And one tip for the entire team: The ground is sticky and muddy. To move the ball, scoop it. See what Rahul is doing. He is doing perfectly. Scoop and move, okay?'

'Siiiiirrrr,' came a trembling voice.

'Yes?' asked the coach.

'Sir,' said Vade, the owner of the trembling voice, 'th-there is a d-d-dog here.'

Vade's face was ashen and he had frozen in his place. Beside him stood the white dog that Dutta had been petting. The dog was sniffing Vade's shorts and merrily wagging his tail.

Mehfouz Noorani sighed. *The boys of today are girls*, he thought. 'Someone move that dog out,' he ordered.

'Yes, sir,' said Rana as he grabbed Vade by the collar and began dragging him away, saying, 'Shoo, shoo!'

The boys cackled, but the coach failed to find Rana's excellent joke funny. His eyes bulged. His moustache grew angry. This was possible because the coach's mehendi-dyed orange moustache had a personality of its own and, in time, the boys would be able to recognize its many moods. They saw it spray its bristles like the quills of a porcupine.

'Aye!' he yelled with a violence that didn't seem compatible with his lanky frame. 'AYE! How dare you! What do you think is going on? Fucking circus or what? If you don't have discipline, then get out from here right now!'

He waited, expecting all of them to leave, but they stood rooted with downcast eyes.

'Any idiot can kick a ball. I don't want footballers. I want champions. That means one thing and one thing only: discipline.' This apoplectic diatribe went on for a while, with the coach touching on many crucial themes, such as:

1. Discipline
2. Discipline
3. Dealing with dogs like a man, without disrupting crucial team conversations

After his passionate monologue ended, the coach realized there wasn't much time left for strategy and tactics. He chose instead to bolster the team's confidence, which he had, just seconds before, demolished. His tone softened and his voice dropped. His moustache became more genial. He spoke about the sparks of talent that had shone through their ill-disciplined exterior. He said their game was commendable for a team as feral and un-coached as they were. It just meant that they had natural talent, a resource so rare that only God dished it out. And they had talent by the bagful. If only they applied themselves correctly, they would be practically unbeatable.

Slowly, word by word, the boys' faces brightened. Like all good dictators, the coach had that rare ability to inspire confidence even after threatening genocide. He made football seem simple and victory a given. It was potent stuff, and they went into their warm-up with a disposition almost bordering on sunny.

As soon as Rishabh took to the field, he noticed three things about Gyan Vikas High School. First, every member of the opposition was positively microscopic. Their average height must have been just below five feet. They were as scrawny as they were short, and most of them looked like they hadn't had a whole meal in many months. Second, they didn't have a uniform. Instead, they had each donned a T-shirt sporting a different design but were unified by the colour red. With the shorts, they weren't even colour-coordinated, each wearing whatever took his fancy. One boy had showed up in bright blue Bermuda shorts, complete with a palm-tree print and the word 'aloha' emblazoned down his right hip. And lastly, they spoke—a lot. Even before kick-off, they were constantly yapping. But it was a shrill, rapid-fire barking that the Sanghvites—strain their ears as they did—couldn't understand, and it annoyed them.

At the toss, Puro towered over the Gyan Vikas High School captain. This was a first for him, and he felt awkward about the advantage. Yet again, though, he won the toss. The Vikas players seemed disheartened. Their screechy chattering reached a crescendo. Puro chose to kick off. The Vikas captain chose to switch sides. So the teams traded places.

'Rishabh, Rahul! Kick off!' shouted Puro.

The two boys jogged to the circle. The referee put the ball down.

'On my whistle,' announced the referee.

'I'll pass the ball, you play it back to Puro, I'll make a run and—' said Rahul.

Rishabh cut him off, 'No, no, no!'

'Why, what happened?'

'I'll play the ball. Last time I started it, and we won. It's lucky.'

Rahul didn't argue. There was no arguing with the 'L' word. Of all the supporters a team could have, fate was the best one.

As the match begins, something odd occurs. The rain, which has been falling at a polite patter, suddenly turns to an angry lashing. It shimmers across the ground in silvery sheets. It streams down Rishabh's glasses as he wishes that they came with wipers. But he can see clearly that he was wrong about their opponents. They're less shrinking marmots and more rabid, red-eyed rats.

Gyan Vikas High School comes at them harder and faster than the rain. They zip past the Sanghvi boys, squeaking and shrieking as they go. They even have the pluck to pick on Sanghvi's larger lads. Their forward goes head first into a tackle with the powerful Khodu and squeezes past him with the ball at his feet. Their captain is the epicentre of their game. He's a pinched-faced, spiky-haired roadrunner called Chotte. The Sanghvites know this because the Vikas players can't stop shouting his name. 'Chotte! Chotte!' they holler, even when Chotte is nowhere near the ball.

Meanwhile, on the wing, Rishabh is up against one of the most infuriating defenders he's ever played. The boy is so thin that a wristwatch could be his belt. He has a neat close-cropped haircut and wears his T-shirt tucked into his oversized pants. While he's being marked, Rishabh can hear an endless sniffling from behind him. From time to time, he sees the boy running the back of his hand across his leaking nose. The boy brushes against Rishabh.

'Don't touch me with your snotty hands!' shouts Rishabh, disgusted.

The boy doesn't even acknowledge him. His eyes robotically follow the passage of play ahead.

'. . . and eat something. I can hear your bones rattling.'

The boy sniffles but doesn't look at Rishabh.

'You're deaf or what?'

The boy still doesn't respond. A few moments later, the ball breaks into the right wing. Rishabh thunders towards it, waiting to shove his bamboo-shoot marker to the ground. The boy doesn't come. Rishabh sees a blur pass him by from the corner of his eye. He looks up to find that his marker has already intercepted the ball and is coolly passing it to a teammate. Rishabh stops in his tracks. The boy jogs back to him.

'All that fat is slowing you down,' he says.

Gyan Vikas High School keeps the pressure on Sanghvi for the rest of the first half. Their passing is precise and their movement is too quick to contain. When Sanghvi does get the ball, they're hesitant about what to do with it. They are a team that thrives on dominance and rhythm and are unable to find either. Puro yells, 'Chin up, chin up!' trying to raise their plummeting morale. At the touchline, Mehfouz is gesticulating more and more wildly.

That's when Khodu tackles Chotte and retrieves the ball at the edge of his own D. He looks up and sees Floyd making a run, and passes the ball to him. Floyd, however, has no intention of making any such run. He's panting from tracking back. He watches serenely as Khodu's pass lands at many feet in front of him. Before he can even react, a Vikas player latches on to the ball and dodges into the D.

He gambols lamblike past Khodu. But Puro comes charging from his blind side and kicks the ball off him. The ball bobbles towards Dave. All he has to do is calmly scoop it up like a dutiful goalkeeper. Instead, he hacks the ball with his boot. The ball smashes squarely into Puro's chest and ricochets towards a corner. A gasp escapes the Sanghvi players. The ball could have gone anywhere—and that includes the empty, open, ultra-wide Sanghvi goal.

Mercifully, the first half ended scoreless. The boys dreaded getting off the field because they could see Mehfouz prowling the touchline like an unfed panther. Their fears weren't unfounded for he exploded the minute they sat down.

'Where's that keeper?' he growled.

Dave raised a shaky hand. A broth of bubbling rage was ready to spill out of the coach's mouth. He was livid about Dave's last-minute clumsiness, which could have cost them a goal.

'You are the only player who can use his hands in a game called football!' he said incredulously. 'THEN WHY, MY FRIEND, ARE YOU NOT TAKING ADVANTAGE OF IT? Pick up the ball! Don't be like a rain cloud that only rains. If you have lightning, use it!'

It was the first of many statements that made the boys crick their necks as they pondered it. They would soon realize that the new coach had a knack for making analogies that bungee-jumped from the cliff of meaning: they almost didn't make sense but managed to survive through a single strand of interpretation.

Mehfouz then turned on Rishabh. 'Aye! How are you playing? Not one time you have kept the ball. And if you lose the ball that's fine, but at least try to get it back. Just standing there like a dadaji while another player runs off with it.'

But the core of the coach's anger was reserved for Khodu. He bombarded Khodu with a volley of abuse. Over two games, Khodu had been the player who was most at fault. He huffed and puffed towards the end of the games. His sloppy passes compromised the team.

'Right now, in the end, what you did? I told all the defenders to clear outside, then why you passed to the middle?'

'Sir, Floyd was making a run,' said Khodu.

'Aye! Don't give me bloody excuses. First of all, that boy was not even running. You don't know your teammates or what? First time you're playing together or what? Bloody hell!' The coach glared at him. 'Take your studs off. Who are the other centre backs?'

Dutta and Sumit raised their hands. The coach pointed at Sumit. 'You get ready.'

Sumit hesitated. He had been present for two dozen games and played in only two. His experience suggested he was a much better substitute than he was a player. He had seen the havoc the Vikas players were causing and heard the fiery invective delivered to Khodu. Truth be told, he didn't fancy doing a better job than the burly Khodu. If anything, he would be slower and even more misguided. Interpreting his fear as honesty, he cleared his throat and said, 'Sir, I think you should pick Dutta. He's better than me.'

The coach remained quiet for a long moment and then began chuckling. He was wondering if he had done the right thing by taking this job. In a twenty-five-year—and by all accounts—stellar career, Mehfouz Noorani had never once told a coach what to do. Maybe times weren't what they used to be, he thought. If the boy didn't want to play, there was little he could do about it.

'Superb. One defender is overconfident and one is under-confident.' He turned to Dutta. 'You please be just right. Start stretching and warming up.' The coach waited for Dutta to leave before continuing. 'Does anyone know the difference between confidence and arrogance?'

Nobody said a word because everyone rightly recognized this to be a rhetorical question.

'My coach Ramdin Sir used to tell us confidence means showing up and believing you'll win. Arrogance is believing you'll win because you showed up,' answered the coach. 'I can see it on your faces. You think this team is easy. That they are not tall, so they are weak. But they are *not* weak. They are efficient. And fast. Just like a mouse can scare an elephant, like that only, if you are not careful, they will beat you. What I had said in the start? Every game is a final. Every team needs respect. Don't underestimate anybody. It will be a very costly mistake. Chalo, now, get ready!'

The boys returned to the field curiously and played the second half cautiously. Once they stopped taking their opponents for granted, they played with greater control. They tracked back diligently and attacked aggressively. Gyan Vikas High School was worthy of their respect as they continued to press for a win while preventing Rahul and Paras from even sniffing at a goal.

The rain eased as the half progressed, but the two teams grew more frantic. The game shaped into a midfield tussle, with chains of passes forming and breaking, probing and searching, thirsting for that definite thrust that would decide the match. None was to be found. The referee called time on the contest and pointed to the penalty spot.

Victory now lay beyond the gates of nerves and chance.

Penalties are an odd way to clinch a football match. It's the process of dismantling a team sport into individual value. A player is never more in charge of his destiny and less in control of his nerves as during a penalty shoot-out. In the end, it is not a test of skill but of nerves.

The Vikas keeper knew this, for he bounced about the goal line, trying to faze Rahul. Puro had won the toss and elected to kick first. Rahul had stepped up to claim the first kick. In the stands, the other players, three unemployed locals, an alcoholic uncle and the dog were on their feet, craning and straining to see the shoot-out.

Rahul strode forward with the ball under his arm, his eyes trained on the ground beneath him, ignoring the antics of the Vikas keeper—who waved his arms about so wildly that it looked as if he were being attacked by an invisible swarm of bees. Rahul staggered three long steps back and waited with his hands on his hips. The referee blew the whistle. Rahul steadied himself and dispatched the ball with ease to the left of the keeper.

'Yes!' he howled, his voice ragged with relief.

Dave slouched between the sticks. His eyes bore into the Vikas player who stepped up with a laser stare, almost trying to scan the boy for signs of which way he would place the ball. Rishabh tried to deduce it too. The boy wore the number 9. He stood with his weight shifting from foot to foot.

His left foot was angled to the left. *Left*, thought Rishabh, *he's going left*.

The whistle was blown. The boy didn't go left. He went with clobbering the ball. He pushed his shoe through it with such venom that it flew within an inch of Dave's face. His hair was ruffled as the ball zoomed by. He gulped, realizing how close he had been to having his nose smashed. 1–1.

Next up was Puro, who sprang to the spot. He gathered some mud and made a little tee, on which he placed the ball. The Vikas keeper yo-yoed on the spot. The referee expelled air into the whistle. Puro nodded in acknowledgement and charged at the ball. He struck it neatly, and it whizzed into the lower-right corner of the goal, out of the keeper's reach.

Now the team stood with arms interlocked across their shoulders and felt a collective nervousness course through the line as Dave took up his position.

Mehfouz yelled, 'Hands wide!'

'Come on, Dave!' said Tejas.

Chotte stepped forward. He held a steady gaze and, when the time came to strike, coolly placed the ball into the top-right corner. Dave seemed paralysed. He hadn't even hopped to prevent it. Instead, he'd gazed at it like an astronomer on seeing a shooting star go by—with curiosity and wonder.

Then a nervous Floyd stepped forward. He chewed on the cuticles of his right hand as he made his way to the spot. He stared at the ball as the Vikas keeper danced on the goal line. When the whistle was sounded, Floyd took a large gulp of air and hammered the ball into the top-right corner of the goal. 3–2.

Vikas's number 8 stepped up to the spot. Dave crouched low, arms spread, eyes narrowed. The Vikas player licked his lips. This time Dave guessed correctly and dived left. The ball swung in his direction, but it was perfectly struck. It crashed into the left post and ricocheted into the net. The Vikas players clamoured from their huddle.

It was Rishabh's turn. He had volunteered to take the fourth kick. Now he felt a trepidation he hadn't felt when he had raised his hand. As he walked to the spot, he felt time had slowed down. He could see the drops of rain, individual and prism-like. In the goal, he saw the Vikas player bouncing the ball with both his hands. When he reached the spot, the keeper flung the ball at him. Rishabh caught it. There was a tremor in his hands that he couldn't control.

Be calm, he told himself. *It's all right*.

'Come on, Rishabh!' shouted Puro from behind him. His voice rang out like gunfire. He could see the shuffling wall of his teammates from the corner of his eye. The referee put the whistle to his lips. He could feel the blood, hot and dizzyingly fluid, swilling through him. His ears were burning up. The keeper was now jumping, hollering and flapping his arms all at the same time. *Pfffeeeet*, came the sound.

Right! To the right, said Rishabh's mind.

Done! said his feet.

Hold on a sec— went his heart.

His body moved forward and his foot connected at the right angle, but the kick had no power behind it. His foot caressed the ball like a gentle breeze. The ball bobbled ahead, skidded a bit and came to a halt three feet from the keeper, who giggled at the attempt. Cheers went up from the Vikas side, gasps escaped Sanghvi lips.

'WHAT THE FUCK WAS THAT!' bellowed Puro from behind him.

Rishabh couldn't believe it was over. There was a part of him that wanted to run up to the ball and knock it in. He could still score!

'Leave,' said a voice. He saw the referee glaring at him. He saw the stunned stands as he walked back to the team. He passed the coach in silence. No one said a word as he stood apart from the group. Not a hand on his shoulder, not a pat on his back, not a word. There was nothing anyone could say about a penalty that had hardly left the spot.

Vikas scored in their effort to pull ahead. 3–4. Now Tejas broke from the huddle to take the final kick. The pressure was on him to keep Sanghvi's slim hopes alive. Breathing heavily, he placed the ball on the ground, and retreating with tiny steps, waited for the whistle. When it sounded, Tejas charged at the ball and struck it well. It made a long, beautiful arc above the goal and disappeared into a tree. Tejas had missed and how.

Rishabh didn't see the Vikas keeper wheel away, screaming wildly, and get mobbed by his mates as if he had a part to play in the miskick. He didn't see Tejas crumble to the ground. He didn't hear the wail that went up from his teammates. All he heard was silence and all he saw was the brown earth and their tournament buried under it.

August 2006

RISHABH BALA STOOD in front of the mirror. He tilted his face down, arched his eyebrows, checked his right profile and then his left. *Cool*, he thought to himself. He brushed back his hair for the 117th time and yanked and tugged at a strand until it twirled gracefully over his forehead. Next, he picked up a can of deodorant and pressed down on the nozzle for a few minutes as he waved it all over himself. Grabbing his bag and umbrella, he dashed out of the house, yelling, 'Mummy, I'm going!'

Mrs Bala waved goodbye to the cloud of deodorant that blew out the house.

The reason Rishabh looked so spiffy was because he was going to Oswal's. It was only at this coaching class that he got an opportunity to be in the same room as Tamanna. He hadn't spoken to her yet but was certain that he was making her fall in love with him owing to his dashing sense of style. It was a day after the defeat, but he was confident about going a step further in impressing her today.

He entered the long, narrow classroom of batch A, trooped to the last bench on the left side and set his bag down. Tamanna and her gaggle usually occupied the last two rows on the right. Soon they entered the room, preceded, as usual, by laughter. They were always laughing and, for some inexplicable reason, Rishabh always thought they were laughing at him.

When they had settled down, Rishabh glanced at his watch; there were five minutes to the lecture. Enough time. He ran a clammy palm over his forehead, cleared his throat and, in a bold voice, said, 'Hey, Kunal! How are you, man?'

That was the sign.

Kunal Bedi, who sat only two benches away, replied with an equally loud 'Arre, Rishabh! I'm good, re. How are you?'

'I'm fine, yaar,' yelled Rishabh. 'Just recently played a football tournament. Nothing much.'

'Oh, right! The school football tournament, where you represented the school in football. How did it go?'

Rishabh darted his eyes to see if Tamanna was listening. She was in the middle of a chirpy conversation with Krupa, so he increased his volume some more.

'It was good, yaar! I scored the first goal—and we won!'

'We won because you scored the goal, no?'

'You could say that!'

'How did you score the goal?'

'Oh, it's a long story . . .'

'Okay, so tell me after class,' said Kunal.

Rishabh's eyes widened and his nostrils flared. He had carefully written the script himself and had spent the entire evening going over it with Kunal. Now the ass was forgetting his cues! 'Now! Now! Ask me the story NOW!' he mouthed.

Kunal blinked. He squinted his eyes. 'Wha-at?' he mumbled.

Rishabh went on. 'I can tell you now also if you want . . .' He vigorously nodded his head until Kunal hesitantly said, 'Yes, yes, I want to know now only.'

Rishabh glanced to the right. Tamanna was now thoroughly immersed in taking out a notebook from her bag. Krupa, on the other hand, was staring straight at him. It frightened him to see her goggle eyes boring into him. She smiled and nodded her head expectantly.

'Yeah, so I'll tell you, no, Kunal. See, I was surrounded by defenders. All around me. Fully covered. And Rahul passes the ball to me. I get hold of the ball, then I block it from one defender, then I run ahead. The second defender comes forward. I do a step-over and go inside the D. Then their captain tries to tackle me, but I chip the ball and leap over him. Now it's just me and the keeper, okay? It's a battle of nerves. He's got both the left and right post covered. He thinks I can't score. But I just kick the ball up and head it over him . . . and I scoooored!'

'Wooo!' cheered Krupa, clapping. 'Now tell us how you missed the penalty.'

'What?' said Rishabh, gagging. 'What penalty?'

'I heard you missed the final penalty.'

'Who told you that?'

'They did,' said Krupa, pointing at Rahul and Dave, who sat two benches ahead. They had been shaking with concealed giggles but were now howling with laughter.

'Act it out and show, no,' insisted Krupa.

'We'll show you how he missed it,' Rahul offered.

The bevy leapt out of their seats with unholy joy.

'I'm Rishabh,' began Rahul, 'and Dave is their keeper, okay?' Rishabh glanced at Tamanna, who suddenly seemed to be giving her full attention to this mockery.

'So he stands over the ball like Beckham for a long time, just like this.' Rahul kept an imaginary ball down, pouted theatrically and heaved with exaggerated nervousness. 'We all think he's going to score. Then he runs up to the ball and kicks it.'

Dave walked over and picked up the imaginary ball just an inch away from Rahul.

'That's also too far!' said Rahul over Krupa's loud cackles.

'Even the ball was saying, "You haven't had breakfast or what?"' jeered Dave.

'The referee was happy. He didn't even have to place the ball back on the spot. It had not moved only!' Rahul added.

Rishabh was livid. His face had turned so red you could use it to send people off the field. Then he looked at Tamanna. She was laughing, with her head thrown back and her body convulsing with hysteria.

It's because of me! he thought. *Eh, I'll take it.*

Seeing her laugh made him giggle, and soon he was laughing just as hard as the others until Hariharan, the maths tutor, came in and put an end to all happiness for the next two hours.

The bell trilled through the school and sent feet scurrying to class for morning prayers. Just as the chanting began on the PA system, two pairs of feet dragged across the white-and-brown tiles of the tenth standard corridor. The feet belonged to Rishabh and Puro. They shuffled to class like zombies. Their wet hair was uncombed, their shirts untucked; they struggled to carry their school bags and their legs felt like they were made of marble—marble that could feel pain.

'May we come in, miss?' they groaned once the prayer was over.

Kaul Miss was repulsed by their appearance. 'Come in. Why are you looking like this? Animals—both of you. Tuck your shirt in. Abhay . . . your fly is open,' she said and looked away with the embarrassment of a fifty-five-year-old schoolteacher.

Puro dazedly zipped up. 'Sorry, miss,' he mumbled.

'Go sit down,' said Kaul Miss with nothing short of disgust.

They hobbled past her and she sucked in her breath. 'What is this unearthly smell? You boys didn't have a bath or what?' Soon two whole rows of students were gagging as Rishabh and Puro made their way to their desks, emanating a smell so putrid that decomposing corpses would have asked them to do something about it.

'I think I'm going to retire,' said Rishabh. 'I've had enough football.'

'I can't feel my feet,' squeaked Puro.

This was the miserable condition of every footballer of Shri Sunderlal Sanghvi School after the first day of practice under the new coach. The Mongoose had conducted his first session on the Monday after the tournament loss. He had told them to take it easy over the weekend because they would begin intense training right from day one. He hadn't been joking. All the anticipation of training under the assured Mehfouz Noorani had been crushed out of them after a single day.

They had arrived on time (save for Aurobindo, who was consequently made to sit the session out) and found the coach reading the newspaper in the little shed that overlooked the ground. He peered at them over the rim of his reading glasses and asked them to kit up quickly.

A sack of balls lay on the ground, besides equipment they had never seen before: cones, markers, bibs and mini posts. The boys imagined these to be the paraphernalia that professionals played with. This must have been what they used in the training grounds in Manchester and Madrid. They raced to put their studs on and galloped to get to the ground. They couldn't wait to get started that cold Monday morning under an ice-grey sky.

The coach patted his pockets, then slapped his forehead. 'My whistle is in the office. I'll go bring it. You boys stay here.'

The minute the coach left, they ran over to the equipment. Rishabh, Puro and Sumit each picked up a cone or a bib and inspected it.

'So many balls!' exclaimed Rahul, shaking the sack.

'Having balls must be new to you, no, Rahul?' said Floyd.

Rahul took one out and flung it at him.

Rana had begun chasing after Vade again after the latter had jammed a cone on to his head. Tejas had slipped on a bib to see how it looked on him. Khodu was kicking a ball high in the air and trying to trap it.

'AYE!' bellowed the coach, sending a flock of mynahs into flight. 'WHAT ARE YOU DOING?'

Cones, balls and bibs dropped to the ground faster than you could say 'penalty'. The coach's moustache flared again. His eyeballs threatened to fly out of his sockets and hit them in the face.

'Sorry, sir,' said Puro. 'We got a little excited seeing all this. We were just looking. Really.'

'Did I tell you to touch that?' asked the coach.

'No, sir.'

'What did I tell you?'

'To wait for you.'

'Then why did you touch the stuff?'

There was no answer.

'You got excited seeing this? You want to train so badly? You are so happy to run around? Okay, I will make you use all the balls and all the cones. Come, line up.'

No one moved.

'I SAID, LINE UP.'

Once they were in two files, the coach ordered, 'Ten rounds of the ground. You like to run, I will make you run. Go!'

They jogged ten tiring circles and came to a stop, panting and huffing, but before they could catch their breath, the coach blew his whistle. He had set up the cones and now made them dribble around them. Whistle. They dropped to do push-ups. Whistle. Relay sprinting. Whistle. Knee-ups. Whistle. By the time they had to play a five-a-side match, they were finding it difficult to even don their bibs.

'You wanted to wear them, no?' queried the coach. 'Put them on now.' *Whistle.*

Just then, Bhupi staggered to the touchline and threw up a concoction of banana and milk out of sheer exhaustion.

'One team will have one player less,' said the coach coolly.

By the end of the session, they were as close to being dead as was possible while still having a pulse. Most of them lay collapsed on the ground with their arms splayed, waiting for the cold embrace of death. They got, instead, the grim spectre of the coach standing over their motionless bodies as he said in a low voice, 'What I told you? I want champions. Champions have discipline. If you can't be disciplined, I don't need you.

If I cannot trust you to stand in one place for five minutes, I can't trust you to win a game. It's that simple. Now, get up and go study.' *Whistle.*

In class, Meesha Pinto, the geography teacher, could see Rishabh's eyes shutting. On any other day, Pinto would have unleashed carnage upon a student who dared to sleep in her class, but seeing Rishabh's grimy face and dishevelled appearance, she felt pity instead of anger.

'Rishabh! RISHABH!' she called, firm yet concerned.

The boy opened his eyes and was startled to see the class staring at him.

'Stop dreaming in class,' said Pinto.

Meesha Pinto couldn't say for sure, but she thought she heard him say, 'But this is a nightmare.'

'Football is war, and I only go to war with those I trust,' the Mongoose had said. And by the tenth day of training, he had his squad. He hadn't picked them as much as let them do the picking for him. It had started with a gruelling five days, during which he had put them through a relentless program of drills and games. In the hour-long session each morning, he allowed them to rest a measly ten minutes. They spent the rest of the time on their feet, in constant motion and alert because of the coach's whistle or rebuke.

The reporting time was 6.30 a.m. sharp. Aurobindo, whose love for pav bhaji was only eclipsed by his love for sleep, found it impossible to wrench himself away from his pillow on time. He always bounced in around 6.45 a.m., smiling—he was one of those ever-smiling boys who grew up to be a cynical research assistant in a chemical factory—and was always bounced out by the coach with equal severity.

'This isn't a brothel, where you can come any time you want,' snarled the coach. 'Shut up!' he added in response to the giggling that followed the word 'brothel'.

On the third day, Aurobindo beat a personal record and was only five minutes late. Unfortunately, in the coach's book, late was late, no matter the minutes. He didn't even look in Aurobindo's direction. He simply held up a steady arm towards the gate. 'Out.'

'Please, sir. Sorry, sir,' said Aurobindo, the smile dimmed to a helpless grin.

'Don't come from tomorrow.'

'But sir—'

'People who are late are lazy. Do I want lazy people in my team? No.'

'No, sir! It's not like that . . . my rickshaw—'

'Lazy people always have excuse. Do I want people with excuse? No.'

'Sir . . . it's the truth—'

'It's the truth on one day, not three. You don't value my time, but I value yours. Don't waste any more. Get out.'

'Sir—'

'OUT!' yelled Mehfouz Noorani, once again scattering the mynahs.

Aurobindo never came back, and the rest of the team never came late.

On the fifth day, the coach had split them into two sides and assigned them positions for the five-a-side match.

'Khodu, right back,' said the coach.

'Sir, that's Bhupinder. I'm centre back.'

'Aye! You will play right back.'

'I'm not good in that position, sir. My best place is centre back, I'm telling you.'

'You will tell me now? You think I'm stupid here or what? Haan? Why am I putting you at right-back: because you have speed, stamina. You can run down the flank, box to box. In the centre-back position, what you do? Play dangerously. Play the ball inside. Try to attack from middle. You want to attack, go to the right-back position.'

'I don't want to play there.'

'Then I don't want you to play anywhere,' stated the coach. Khodu glowered at Mehfouz Noorani. It looked like he would punch the older man. Khodu's fuse was a short one. It took very little to make him feel insulted, but the coach didn't care much for Khodu's wrath. 'Leave the ground, and take your stare with you,' he said, putting his whistle to his lips.

Khodu clomped off the ground, muttering abuses under his breath. Although no one considered Khodu a bosom buddy, the boys were sad to see him go. It wasn't disputed that Khodu was the best defender in the team. His imperious build and savage aggression, though menacing off the field, were both comforting qualities when he was defending your goal. Besides, his replacements were Vipul Dutta and Sumit Awasthi, both of whom inspired little confidence. Puro asked the coach to forgive Khodu's petulance, but the coach refused.

'This team doesn't need players like him. You only think he is a good player because you haven't seen what I will make of you.' Saying so, the coach had welcomed new recruits in an effort to deepen the squad. None of them lasted beyond the week. Priyesh Manjarekar (laughing at a joke while the coach was speaking), Ojas Rahane (playing without warming up properly) and Vishwas Pannu (plain lack of talent) were all told to leave almost as soon as they had come.

On the tenth day, after practice, the coach blew his whistle in one long note. This was the signal for the boys to assemble. They staggered into a cluster around him. 'You are my team. Each of you I have chosen. Each of you is standing here because you have discipline and determination. Each of you knows how to play with your legs. Now you will learn to play from here,' he said and thumped his chest. 'Each of you I have picked for a reason. I know deep inside me that you will be champions. You will lift many, many trophies. Do you want to win?'

'Yes, sir!' roared the boys.

'Do you want to be champions?'

'Yes, sir!' went up an even louder shout.

'Good. In September, we are playing. We are playing a district-level tournament. But there is good news. This time you will be playing for the school in the school.'

Surprise washed over the faces that looked at the coach.

'The tournament is being held over here only, in this school, on this ground. The war has come home, and each of you will fight and all of us will win!'

'YES, SIR!'

Rishabh clenched his fists and shut his eyes. He would play in school, play in front of Tamanna. He would score, and it would make her leap up from her seat and clasp her hands. He would like that. He would really, really like that.

Ever since the tournament was announced, they could sense it. If you'd asked them what 'it' was, they couldn't have told you, but 'it' felt like a trophy was around the corner.

The boys were no longer tired of training. Their teeth didn't chatter in the rain. They made sacrifices without complaint. Most of it was because of the Mongoose. He was competent and confident, and both these qualities rubbed off on the team. The better they got on the pitch, the more they believed they were winners off it. Though he barked his orders and greeted mistakes with a fusillade of foul language, they had grown accustomed to the coach's tough love. What they admired most about him was his fairness. All his anger was filtered through the objective of improving them. To that end, it didn't matter who you were, how talented you were or how much he liked you; if you didn't display the discipline and dedication that was demanded of a top-class player, then Mehfouz Noorani would immediately let you know what he thought of you and your entire family.

The pressure had transformed Rishabh too, who now arose before his alarm rang. He had even started having a glass of milk with a raw egg in it. Each time he saw the gooey yolk rising in his glass like a malodorous sun, he reminded himself it was good for his stamina and then gulped it down before gagging.

They offered so much of themselves on the ground that there was little left to give beyond it. At school, Rishabh could feel the post-lunch drowsiness set in at 10 a.m. He tried his hardest to battle the blurring of vision and the shuttering of eyelids, but to no avail. One morning, Pillai Miss, the chemistry teacher, caught Puro and Rishabh nodding off and ordered them to go wash their faces. When the boys trooped into the loo, they found Dave, Rahul and Tejas already splashing water on their mugs. They were soon joined by Floyd and Pinal Oza, and they all agreed that training for a tournament was wearisome but worth it.

The bone-deep tiredness doubled at home. Rishabh would set his bag down and then discover that he had no more energy left in him, not even to get out of his uniform. He would then toddle over to the sofa, lie down and watch television for the remainder of the day. His mother grew alarmed at how much TV he was watching and how little he was studying. When she brought it up with him, he waved a hand in her general direction and said, 'I'm too tiiiiireeeed. I need some rest. Just a little while.'

'You've been watching TV for three hours, Rishabh.'

'It's getting over in two minutes.'

'When did you even start watching tennis?'

He had started watching tennis ever since it meant not thinking about his studies. It bothered him that every time his parents saw him, that's all *they* thought of. They didn't see their young son, they didn't see their tired boy; they saw a lazy student. He was itching to tell them he just wanted to be left alone, but could never muster the courage. The panic got under his skin. Each moment of every day, no matter what he did, he was trailed by the looming ghost of the 'boards', like a black beast inching closer and closer to devour him, destroy him.

The only time he didn't think of textbooks and results was when he had a ball at his feet. The tenth standard did not intrude on the football field. The fear and worry that had dogged him ever since the school year had begun couldn't keep up with him when he flew down the flanks. The coach was the only grown-up who didn't ask them what they wanted to be in life; the coach never hounded them to a desk; the coach was the only adult who didn't believe they would disappoint him.

Rishabh lay on the sofa and toggled through TV channels. Cricket dominated the sports channels and Animal Planet was airing a documentary about sea anemones, which was interesting only to other sea anemones. He was still wearing his school uniform—the sweaty, dusty shirt had congealed on his body—and sported the oiliness on his forehead like a headdress. Yet he stayed moored to the sofa, held back by paralysing lethargy.

The doorbell rang. His mother fluttered out of the kitchen to answer it. His father tromped in. Rishabh knew he should show some semblance of regard but couldn't get himself to summon the feeling. Mr Bala took one look at his son fertilizing the sofa while watching an English movie and grew red in the face. Had Dr Desai, their family physician, checked his blood pressure at the moment, he would have surely shaken his head and said, 'Mr Bala, you must learn to relax.'

And Mr Bala would have lashed out. 'But how can I relax if my only son is watching TV all day instead of studying for his boards! The boy is going to fail, disgrace the family. The only thing he is good at is changing the channels, and which job pays you to use a goddamn remote control!'

Enough was enough, Mr Bala thought; today he would confront his lazy boy. 'Rishabh! Shut that thing now!' he thundered.

Rishabh sighed and switched off the TV. Then he peeled himself off the sofa and assumed an upright position.

'Do you even realize the importance of this year?' said Mr Bala.

'Yes, Papa.'

'Don't answer back. I have never seen you study, not even once. Never seen an open textbook in your hands. Your goddamn desk is gathering dust. All I ever see you do is watch TV!' He goggled his eyes at his son, who seethed silently. He could see the boy's chest rising and falling.

'Maybe you shouldn't see me for only one hour at night,' came the reply, and Rishabh slunk off to his room.

Mr Bala wasn't one to stand motionless in a fight. When his temper flared, he could be a formidable opponent. But something about his son's chiding left him wounded in a visceral way. The unhappiness stung him. He wondered whether he should console his son. But he quickly brushed that impulse aside. Console him for what? For being told not to be a spoilt, lazy, sulking sack of potatoes? No. He had seen the trajectory of such a life. He knew he was right to be worried about his child's future. He knew he had been justified in reprimanding his son. He knew the boards were important. The only thing he didn't know was the mysterious mind of his moody son.

The next morning, there was a disconcerting commotion in the tenth standard corridor. A crowd swarmed around the noticeboard, writing pads and pens in hand, jostling and swaying as they scribbled something down. Rishabh sensed the anxiety from afar. He asked Pooja Matroo what the fuss was about.

'Exam timetable,' she said.

'Which exams?'

'Um, the first-term exams.'

'Oh, shit! Really? When is it?'

'Why don't you just read the noticeboard?'

Rishabh grimaced. He wondered why he even bothered asking Pooja. She was always too snarky for her own good. Walking up, he craned his neck to get a glimpse of the timetable but could barely read the print on the A4 page. *I'll copy it later,* he thought. *When there isn't a stampede.*

But, of course, he would forget to do it in the short break and it would completely slip his mind in the lunch break. In fact, it wouldn't be until two days later that he would finally get around to returning to the noticeboard, only to find the timetable had been yanked off by some miscreant. A scrap of paper still tacked on with a pin was the only sign of it ever having been there. *I'll just copy it from Puro*, Rishabh thought. *There's plenty of time.*

Still, the news of the impending exams finally settled in his stomach. It swirled and it churned and it made the school day insufferable. Rudely awakened to academics, he was surprised by just how adrift he was with his studies. He didn't know which chapter Kaul Miss was reading from, and his head hurt just trying to keep up with maths. During physics, he looked around and saw the rest of his class nodding attentively while he couldn't even grasp the gibberish Anita Miss had scrawled on the board. And it wasn't just because her handwriting was bad.

Fittingly finishing off a depressing day, the last period was English. Rishabh felt a gob of saliva collecting at the back of his throat as soon as Bobde sashayed into class in a revolting moss-green sari. She had a tired yet imperial look on her face, as if she were doing them a favour by showing up. It hadn't rained all day, and the air was sticky and oppressive. Rishabh could feel the rim of his collar sticking to the back of his neck. He just hoped this terrible day would end soon.

As it happened, it ended on a good note. Within five minutes, Bobde pulled up Rishabh and Puro for talking. They apologized half-heartedly. She autographed their 'Remarks' section and stationed them outside the classroom. They accepted the sentence a little too eagerly, Poulomi Bobde should have figured. Because when she went to check on them mid-lecture, she found the corridor empty. She would have had better luck finding them if she had only peered out the window that overlooked the ground.

At Oswal's the following day, Rishabh gave an award-winning performance as 'attentive pupil', a feat made more impressive by the fact that he kept it up for over four hours. At the end of the second lecture, he trickled out of class with his group and they puddled outside. It was Kunal who proposed the great idea. 'Let's watch a movie,' he said.

'Yeah, good idea,' said Sumit.

'We can go to Eternity Mall. It's close by,' said Parth Popat.

'I don't think I'm coming,' muttered Rishabh.

'Why?' asked Kunal.

'Look, I just got a bad remark yesterday. My parents are already super angry. If I tell them I went for a film today, they'll kill me.'

'Don't be a baby, yaar. Just come. It's only two hours,' said Kunal.

'I'm really sorry, guys. Some other time, pakka.'

'Accha, I just spoke to the girls,' said Amay Khatri, joining in. 'They're coming too.'

Rishabh turned around and saw Krupa, Suman, Preetha, Divya and Tamanna walking towards them. Krupa waved at Rishabh, and winked.

He turned to face the boys. 'So which movie are we going for?'

Like most teenagers, they didn't visit the mall, they stormed it. They travelled en masse, moving like one organism, a giant amoeba, pushing and pulling in different directions. They whirled through Planet M, picking up every CD and cassette in the store and putting them back in the wrong shelves. They blitzed through Pizza Hut, wolfed many pizzas and quaffed gallons of Pepsi. Finally, fed and spent, they came down to the main order of business: which movie to watch.

The one they settled on after much high-pitched squabbling was *The Da Vinci Code*, an A-rated movie. Not a pansy U, not a non-committal U/A; it was the full-fledged bold red capital letter 'A'. Plus the film had caused controversy for graphic violence as well as hurting religious sentiments. It had all the elements that piqued the interest of humans aged fifteen.

'Will they give us the tickets?' asked Preetha. Her pragmatism punctured the building excitement.

'I'll get them,' said Rishabh. He hadn't said much throughout the afternoon. *If I remain silent, I won't say anything stupid*, he had decided.

Now he stepped forward because he was confident that if anyone could get those tickets, it was him. This was not misplaced confidence. You see, Rishabh Bala was the victim of a strange affliction called premature bearding. At some point during the seventh standard, puberty had smacked him in the face. Unfortunately for him, it had struck him before everyone else in his standard. By the end of term, he'd had a moustache thick enough to put army colonels to shame. When he'd walk through the corridors, chants of 'Uncle! Uncle!' went up. When he'd enter classrooms, a chorus of 'Good morning, sir!' greeted him. It had been a nightmarish situation that had only been resolved a year ago when his older cousin finally ushered him into the loo and handed him a razor and foam.

To his dismay, people had then started teasing him for being clean-shaven. Shave Puri, they called him. There was no winning with people who played for both sides, so he'd stopped bothering with the jibes and soon they stopped bothering him. That day at the mall, Rishabh had suddenly realized that he could use his two-week-old goatee for the greater good. He collected the money and confidently stepped up to the counter.

'Ten tickets for *The Da Vinci Code*,' he said authoritatively.

The ticket seller saw a fifteen-year-old boy asking for tickets to an adult movie in a voice that had barely cracked and happily handed them to him. *Let the doorman deal with them*, he thought, counting the cash.

'Got them!' said Rishabh, waving the tickets in front of his bearded face. He had solved the problem. He was their hero. He thought he saw a glimmer of admiration in Tamanna's eyes.

Everyone was ecstatic. 'Hold on,' said Preetha, right on cue, 'we still have to get past the doorman.'

'What should we do?' asked Tamanna, forcing Rishabh to wonder how anyone could look that good even when they were worried.

'Arre, now they can't stop us,' said Kunal. 'We've paid for our tickets.'

'That's not true, haan,' Suman added her two cents. 'My brother and his friends weren't allowed to go in even after they bought tickets.'

'I knew this would happen!' Preetha sighed. She still wore her Oswal's ID card and flapped it around anxiously. Rishabh watched it hypnotically fluttering around her wrist.

'Wait a minute!' he said. 'Everyone has their Oswal's IDs?' Yes, they did.

'We show them to him as college IDs. Do it fast and he won't notice. If he says anything, just insist that Oswal's is a college in Thane East. Okay?'

'I'm not entirely sure . . .' mumbled Khatri.

'The film starts in ten minutes. You got any other plans?' said Rishabh.

'Okay, let's try it your way,' said Khatri.

Rishabh led the line. He walked slowly, maintaining steady, relaxed eye contact with the usher. He was assured in his robust hairiness. In fact, he half-expected the usher to say, 'Sir, you can pass but your kids will have to stay behind.'

The doorman nodded and let him pass. Rishabh walked into the cool environs of the air-conditioned theatre and bit his lip. He watched as the doorman stopped the rest of the gang. The trap was sprung. Each shoved their Oswal's ID under his nose. The swarm overwhelmed the doorman. He did his best to inspect the IDs on display, but the clamour was deafening and the swell of the bunch pushed against him.

'Go,' he croaked. The teenagers rushed past him, giddy with excitement and chuffed that they had passed off as adults.

'Rishabh, my man, you did it again!' Kunal slapped his back.

'My hero!' said Krupa.

This time he definitely caught a glint in Tamanna's eye, but it was gone in a flash.

'Screen 1!' she called, walking off a bit too quickly.

They ran into the theatre and filed into row F, seats 11 to 20. Rishabh noticed with a mix of horror and delight that the only seat left was the one next to Tamanna. *The clever bastards*, he thought. Kunal knocked him on the shin as he passed, Khatri winked and Parth told him that if he spilled his popcorn he would murder him.

'I guess, uh, I'll have to sit here,' said Rishabh to Tamanna without looking at any one in particular.

She hummed sympathetically.

Rishabh sat back in his chair, feeling hot under the collar. He was stock-still while the trailers played. He didn't even sing along to the national anthem, rightly surmising that she would find it creepy. At last, the movie began. Pictures flickered on the screen. Tom Hanks ran helter-skelter, trying to save the world.

But none of that mattered to Rishabh Bala. All he thought was: *I'M SITTING NEXT TO TAMANNA!* The voice in his head was so loud that he was sure she could hear him. In four years, this was the closest he had got to her. He was determined to remember it, all of it: the dark of the theatre, the white-blue-green light dancing on her face, bouncing off her hair, the way she was serenely staring at the screen and the grace with which she blinked. He tried sneaking a look at her as often as he could without it becoming obvious that he hadn't paid to watch the movie.

His biggest dilemmas were his hands. He suddenly realized that hands were the most awkward parts of the human anatomy and that they tended to get awkward-er when you were sitting next to the girl you liked. He didn't know what to do with his stiff, tense arms. He folded them across his chest but felt he appeared frigid. He put them on the armrest but they slid off. He propped them on his knees but that made his back ache. He knitted his fingers and supported them on his stomach but felt like he was approaching retirement. Finally, he let them dangle by his side like fishing rods. He felt the uncoolness wafting out of him. *What will she think if she sees me sitting slumped in my seat like a squid?* he thought. *I am a vertebrate; I must spine up.* So he continued wriggling and squirming in his seat, trying to play it cool, while Tamanna calmly followed the film flitting across the screen in front of her.

He didn't have money to buy popcorn in the interval. Tamanna didn't want anything to eat. So they both sat steadfastly, staring at the screen with the same intensity as when the movie was playing on it. When the second half started, Tamanna did something strange. She turned around and surveyed the theatre, and then mysteriously got up and left. This crushed Rishabh. *She can't stand sitting next to me. It must have been the hands that drove her away!*

'Rishabh!' came a hiss from his left. It was Parth, spitting at him from a distance. 'Go after her!'

'What . . . *why?*'

'She's gone behind to sit alone. Look.'

Rishabh looked, making sure he was as coy as could be. Tamanna had gone and perched herself on one of the empty seats higher up in the hall.

'So?' quizzed Rishabh.

'So go and give her company!' said Preetha, who couldn't tolerate more of the movie getting ruined by this dithering conversation.

'Are you sure?'

'Yes!'

'She won't mind, no?'

'There's only one way to find out,' stated Preetha, shoving Rishabh out of the seat.

Rishabh stood up as coolly as possible and tried to saunter up to Tamanna in row M. He asked as breezily as he could, 'Can I sit here?' This was a feat because his heart was fluttering in his chest, his stomach had come unmoored and his mouth had dried up. He wondered if he was having a seizure. *Please, God, not now. Dying would look so uncool to her.*

'Yeah,' she said, 'sure.'

'Cool, thanks,' Rishabh said and proceeded to squeeze past her awkwardly, trying not to crush her toes in his passage.

'You could have just sat here,' said Tamanna once he had settled down. She was pointing at the empty seat to her left, one that could have been reached with greater convenience.

'Ahhh . . . I didn't see that.'

'I couldn't see anything from those cheap seats. Plus the place is empty. Who's stopping us from sitting here, man?'

'Yeah. Nobody can stop us. Not even God!'

Tamanna's eyes narrowed.

Stupid, stupid, stupid. Why can't my mouth just shut up?

The theatre reverberated with Dolby surround sound but for Rishabh Bala there was only silence. He tried, bravely, many times to utter something smart or thoughtful, but his brain seemed to be jammed. To Tamanna it just sounded like the boy beside her couldn't stop clearing his throat. He felt time escaping like air from a balloon. Oh, how many days and nights he had dreamed to be alone with her! He had imagined saying a million beautiful and poignant things, but now when the chance had come, when she sat an armrest away, all he could do was sound like a car with engine trouble.

'I should have got popcorn in the interval,' said Tamanna after a long while.

'Sorry?'

'Nothing. I was just saying that I'm feeling a bit hungry.'

'Would you like a biscuit?' offered Rishabh, his heart picking up pace again.

'Yeah, okay. Which one do you have?'

'Threptin—they're high-protein supplementary biscuits,' he said, fishing out the tin from his bag.

She burst out laughing. 'Why do you carry these around?'

Rishabh always thought the biscuits were insipid but had to carry them on the insistence of his mother.

'You need the energy,' she would say. 'Constantly running around. It's good to always carry something to eat.'

'Can't it at least be tasty?' Rishabh would whine.

'Not everything is about taste,' his mother would answer. This was as true for her aloo methi as it was for the biscuits. Rishabh had been sullenly lugging them around for weeks without once touching them, but now he couldn't thank his mother's foresight enough.

'It's a long story. But they're good for hunger pangs. Try one. Pineapple flavoured, I think.'

She took one and liked it. So she took another. Rishabh suddenly found himself viewing the crumbly, powdery snack in a favourable light. They nibbled on their biscuits and sat in a more relaxed silence. Years later, Rishabh would think back to the time when he sat in a dark theatre with a tin of Threptin biscuits lying open in his lap and his heart beating like the wings of a hummingbird. He would wonder where romance went wrong and when it became just about dinners and dates.

Towards the end of the movie, Audrey Tautou and Tom Hanks shared a kiss. When it happened, Rishabh looked at

Tamanna and found her looking back at him. There was something in her eyes. They flickered brightly, her eyebrows quivered and she drew back. Words bubbled to his lips but fear froze them away once again. Finally, with great effort, he whispered, 'Did you like the biscuits?'

'I liked the biscuits more than the film.'

Rishabh liked her more than the film or the biscuits, but he agreed with her assessment anyway.

It's a real pity that life doesn't come with a soundtrack, thought Rishabh as Puro and he sauntered to class after training. Rishabh's bag felt light on his back. His shoulders were relaxed, his arms swung freely. Puro bounced on his instep. Their deodorant wafted into the classrooms, where the teachers had begun. Their droning stopped abruptly as El Paso entered their nostrils.

The boys reached 10 F and asked if they could enter. Before Pinto even said yes, they stepped in. Rishabh could feel her dark eyes dart towards them like two shoals of fish. He set his bag down and was astonished to see veins prominently snaking around his forearms like vines around a tree. Barkha's eyes sparkled with curiosity at the rivulets of blood but she looked away, embarrassed, when she saw Rishabh observing her.

Rishabh smirked. He had distracted Barkha from a textbook. He felt his shirt stick to his back. Under the slowly turning fan, his wet hair felt cool. A bead of sweat slid down a stray strand of hair from his otherwise brushed-back look (think early-era Beckham) and plopped on to his trousers. He flicked it off. Pinto had resumed her high-pitched description of the Brahmaputra River.

Less than a month ago, Rishabh used to feel broken in class. His legs—his shin bone in particular—would throb with a dull, insistent pain. His mind used to be fatigued, surprisingly worn out by an hour of football. *Why does my head hurt more than my legs?* he would wonder.

'You clearly never used to think in a game before,' the coach had said when he had voiced his predicament. The coach always justified his torturous drills and also demanded explanation for their actions.

'Why did you pass to Oza when Abel was open?' the coach would ask.

'Sir, I thought he was in a better position.'

'Who was closer?'

'Floyd?'

'You'll use your brain tomorrow or what?'

And the throbbing in Rishabh's upper machinery would begin. These drills, coupled with the inevitable quizzing afterwards, slowly taught the boys the meaning of tactics. Until recently, they'd mistake formation-making for strategic genius. Now they'd begun to understand positional awareness, zonal marking, link-up play, making intelligent runs and just plain old picking the right pass. Slowly, they had come to realize that the most tiring aspect of football wasn't the running—it was the thinking. And slowly, they had overcome the fuzziness that would cloud their minds towards the end of sessions.

Now, sitting in class, Rishabh's mind was clear. It felt like a white expanse in his head, clean and calm. It was this mental stillness and physical sturdiness that was transforming the football team. A quiet energy swirled around them.

Where they walked, the whispers began. Girls blushed at the sight of them. The reverence once reserved for the basketball team had now passed to them. No longer did they look scruffy and aimless. They looked like they were finally headed somewhere, and they knew it was towards victory. It was a doubtless belief that stemmed from the coach. He'd worked his magic in mysterious ways.

When Puro had been packing up his studs after training one morning, the coach had walked up to him and said, 'You'll play for India one day.' Saying so, he'd continued on his way.

Puro had sat confused till the words sank in, and then bloomed with happiness. He'd told everyone what had happened. The difference was enormous. Before that day, Puro had been a boy captaining a school team and after it, he was a man bent on representing his country.

'Confidence,' Mehfouz Noorani had once famously said, 'is like an erection. When you have it, it shows.'

When there were less than two weeks left for the first-term exams, Rishabh finally decided to start studying. He commenced his academic campaign by copying down the exam timetable from Puro.

'You sure it's correct, no?' he asked as he noted down the dates.

'Haan, bey,' said Puro, twanging a plastic ruler on his desk.

'But you've crossed stuff out and rewritten things all over this. See, here you wrote "physics", then you struck it out. Now it's "computers". Then again it's become "physics". What is this *icchadhaari* subject!'

'Arre, it's physics only. I couldn't see it because . . .'

'Because you're a dwarf?'

'You want the timetable or not?' growled Puro.

Rishabh conceded that he did want the timetable and finished copying it without any more mean comments. It took him two more days to will himself to sit at his desk and open a textbook. It physically pained him to do so. He felt like an invisible force was stopping him from even separating the pages.

However, he felt oddly confident. *There's enough time*, he thought. *I'll begin right after I watch this episode of* Friends. Three episodes and one tennis match later, he felt too sleepy. *No point studying in this state*, he ruled. *Might as well make a fresh start tomorrow.*

But the promises we make to ourselves are the hardest to keep. The next day disappeared in reading a book, watching Animal Planet and running to tutorials. *At least I studied at coaching*, he consoled himself. *That counts.*

'It doesn't,' said a voice inside him.

Shut up. I'll definitely be up to it tomorrow, he assured the voice.

Remarkably, he did plant himself at his desk the following day and opened the textbook briskly, before somnolence overpowered him. He began reading, but his eyes moved faster than his brain. He was reading the words but couldn't make much sense of them. So he had to reread them. This was frightfully dull work, and soon his mind made plans to shut up shop and take a nap.

'Rishabh! Study!' came a sharp bark from his mother, and Rishabh sprang to attention and shook his head as if to shake the sleep off.

He gave the textbook another shot, but soon an itch developed in his scalp. He dispatched a finger to take care of the emergency and, before long, found himself fascinated with the flakes of dandruff that fell from his hair. He couldn't believe his head housed so much of it! He was equally enthralled and appalled by the larger chunks. *They're as big as icebergs*, he marvelled. *No wonder I don't feel the breeze on my head!* So for the next hour, he occupied himself with personally scratching out each dandruff flake before deciding to shampoo his hair and confront this dermatological demon at the root. And another day passed.

The real problem was that Rishabh couldn't care less even if he tried. Studying just didn't have that dizzying excitement he felt when he was on the pitch. On the pitch he was confident, attentive, diligent, eager to learn and hard-working; at his study table he was lazy, reluctant, bored and asleep. He really did a lot of sleeping at his desk while preparing for the first-term exams.

It alarmed Mrs Bala. 'It's all this football that's tiring you out and putting you to sleep!'

'It's the bloody syllabus that's doing it, Ma,' he explained, only to be dismissed as a smart alec and have his TV rights revoked.

But he wasn't trying to be cheeky. He had given it an honest think. He felt alive when he was on the pitch. He felt every breath that entered his lungs, remembered every run and pass and goal. The sacrifices he made—getting up before most roosters, gulping down a raw egg in milk, tolerating abuse from the coach—seemed necessary to him. These things were worthwhile. He did them gladly because, unlike studies, football was something he actually liked doing.

As the exams drew nearer, even the teachers at Oswal's started feeling the pressure. They had to justify the criminal amount they charged in fees. The lectures became more focused, the breaks became shorter and the doubts were treated with greater scorn. Needless to say, the change in style didn't sit well with Rishabh. He hadn't exactly had a wild time there earlier, but now he despised Oswal's even more.

The only consolation, as ever, was the presence of Tamanna. He spent many a lecture staring at her attentive side profile, like a man holding on to a lifebuoy while drowning at sea. He had tried making contact with her many times since their movie outing, but none of their conversations had lasted longer than thirty-eight seconds. A strange gagging reflex kicked in every time he was near her, preventing him from speaking. But what he lacked in confidence he made up in perseverance. Now he always made it a point to say something, even if it was something inane, like 'Nice handwriting!'— in the hope that one day Tamanna would go, 'I love how Rishabh talks about things that don't matter whatsoever.'

It was about a week till the term exams when Rishabh had his longest conversation with Tamanna, at the end of which, he had a distinct impression that he had finally broken the proverbial ice. He walked into Oswal's that day and saw Tamanna sitting at the back with earphones plugged in. Spotting an opportunity for some light banter, he walked up to her and said, 'Hi, what are you listening to?'

Rishabh didn't have a booming voice to begin with, and his nervousness decreased his volume further. This ensured that he had the worst possible vocal equipment to get the attention of a girl who was sitting with her eyes closed and silently headbanging to really loud rock music. Hence proved: Tamanna completely missed his pithy conversation starter.

Now, Rishabh could have walked away and kicked himself for trying to talk to the love of his life, but he was the persevering kind. So he cleared his throat and said, only slightly more loudly, 'What are you listening to?'

He managed to get the attention of every person within a three-row radius, but Tamanna herself remained oblivious. He noticed that all eyes were on him. He was in too deep. Earlier he could have slid into his seat with no one the wiser about his sad attempt, but now he had an audience. He had to commit himself to the cause; the show had to go on.

Now Rishabh almost shouted his question at the object of his adoration and touched her on the shoulder for good measure. It was the first time he had touched her, and he felt the temperature of his blood rising. Tamanna's eyes flew open, and, gasping, she recoiled in horror.

'Sorry . . .' mumbled Rishabh.

There was a long, empty silence.

'I . . . I just wanted to know which song you were listening to . . .' said Rishabh.

Tamanna brought out her iPod, paused the music, yanked out her earphones and said, 'Oh.' This was followed by another stretch of radio static. '"Numb" by Linkin Park.'

Rishabh's eyes lit up. He knew Linkin Park. He had heard their song 'In the End' a couple of times. It was on that CD that Sumit had burned for him, which had music and a folder called 'New Folder' in which was a folder called 'School Project' and within which was 'Notes', within which were a whole bunch of films that were of a decidedly unacademic nature. But that was not the point. The point was that Tamanna had spoken of a band that Rishabh had heard of, and he sniffed an opportunity for conversation.

'Linkin Park! I love that band,' he said.

'You do?' said Tamanna, shifting in her seat to face him.

'Yup. "In the End" is my favourite song in the world,' lied Rishabh.

'I love that song!' squealed Tamanna.

'It's genius.'

'*Hybrid Theory* was awesome but *Meteora* is waaaay better.'

'I think so too!' said Rishabh, not knowing what any of those words were.

'Their lyrics are so perfect. I feel like "Numb" is about me only.'

'I feel the same way about "In the End",' said Rishabh, making it a point to not stray too far from known territory.

'I didn't know you liked them too.'

'How can you not like a band that made—'

'"In the End"?'

'Yes . . .'

Tamanna giggled. It was a sound so pure that it made Rishabh totter in his place.

'I like how much you like that song,' said Tamanna. 'It's damn cool.'

Rishabh blushed. He felt his breath quicken. A small voice inside him told him this moment was perfect—it was best that he left while she still thought he was cool.

So he winked at her.

In his head, it was what a cool guy did, except that when he executed it, his eye remained shut for too long and then his lips began twitching. Tamanna soon grew concerned by his contorted face.

'Are you okay?' she asked.

'Yeah, yeah,' said Rishabh, sweating to get his face under control. 'Okay, see you later . . .'

Rishabh turned away from her and sat down at his desk, his face in his hands. Kunal patted his back.

'It was going so well,' whispered Rishabh, prying open his left eye with his fingers.

'But in the end, it doesn't even matter,' said Kunal.

A week before the exams, football training was halted.

'There are complaints from parents about training during exam time,' said the coach. Dave and Floyd shifted uneasily, staring at their shoes. 'I don't want to give you a break and all before a big tournament but . . .' He held up his hands with his wrists criss-crossing each other, signifying that his hands were tied. 'Listen, all of you—I know you're not going to exercise but at least eat right for the next few days. No oil and vada pav and all. Home food only. I don't want fatties coming back, okay?'

'Yes, sir,' they chorused.

'Go now. All the best.'

Puro and Rishabh resolved that they would keep up a light fitness regime, exams be damned. In reality, it proved harder to do. As the countdown ticked closer to the papers, they felt genuine nervousness. No number of football trophies would spare them the wrath of their parents if they flunked their first-term exams, and that seemed like a real possibility.

Rishabh's fingertips would freeze as he flipped through the many pages he had to study. He would bunch them up and stare at the thickness of unstudied material in disbelief. It amazed him how little knowledge had penetrated his skull even though he had been physically present in each and every lecture. Many chapters were entirely new to him. The term seemed to have gone by like a drunken night out—he remembered how much fun he had at the beginning, then there were bits he remembered hazily and some he didn't recall at all, but now he had come to his senses and piecing it together made his head hurt.

Along with the anxiety came a slithering sense of regret. *Why hadn't I just paid attention?* he wondered as the clock stuck 2 a.m. and he was nowhere close to finishing the endless chapter on the freedom movement in India. 'I'm never doing this again. Next term, I'll be more careful. Just got to get through this. COME ON!'

He was up the whole night before the first paper: English. It was the only paper he felt confident about and even that had kept him up all night, frantically making notes, scanning wildly through the words, reading with wide-eyed intensity—almost like blinking was a luxury he couldn't afford. On the morning of the exam, he remembered God. He got ready and stood in front of the mandir for a good ten minutes, mumbling and grovelling, explaining to God that he had done his best and now he was leaving the rest in His hands.

His seat was at the head of the class, near the blackboard. He neatly arranged his notepad, pencil box and ID card on the desk, and waited. He felt the thump of his heart when Anita Miss, the invigilator, handed him the paper. At first glance, the paper didn't seem hard. However, as he began writing the answers, he suddenly realized how much he'd have to imagine and invent. By the time the bell rang, Rishabh was reasonably pleased with his effort. His English paper was 20 per cent fact and 80 per cent fiction, and, though he was tired and sleepy, he could see how fitting that was.

The next two papers were a blur. He managed to get four hours of sleep over two days, collapsing at his desk and then violently springing awake at the piercing scream of the alarm. Mrs Bala wondered how the coffee was getting over so quickly. She solved the mystery when she saw Rishabh bouncing off the walls of his room.

'Did you sleep at all?' she asked.

'Yes, Mumma,' lied Rishabh, his pupils pinball–ing in their sockets.

Each exam was equally exhausting. Though he wore a watch, he never managed to pace himself properly, always scribbling in long, incoherent scrawls until the paper was snatched from him. During the chemistry exam, he held on to the paper, writing desperately, even as Pillai Miss tugged and pulled at it with all her might. He only let go when the answer sheet threatened to get ripped apart.

The fourth exam was physics. Studying a subject he despised while being critically low on sleep tested his resolve. Yet he ploughed on, rubbing his eyes, splashing icy water on his face, pumping his system with dark brown coffee. The next day, even a bath couldn't wash the tiredness off his face. *I'm going to be happier on the other side of this paper*, he consoled himself.

He sat at his desk and stared vacantly at the blackboard. His mind raced through the phrasing of definitions as he double-checked if he remembered them. The bell rang, the nervous chattering ceased. Bobde handed out the question papers, and Rishabh received his with trepidation. He slapped it on the desk and rapidly scanned it for questions that seemed familiar, but there were none. It was the oddest physics paper he had ever received. He didn't know a single thing on it; in fact, not a single thing he had studied was on it.

He searched frantically for questions on light (refraction, reflection, lenses), energy, force, electricity, magnetism, at least Ohm's law . . . but instead he found that he was being asked to write code and explain functions and define constructors. Finally, his eyes slid to the top of the paper. 'Subject: Computers,' it said.

To say the world swam in front of Rishabh Bala would be an understatement. The world did the freestyle, butterfly and even the backstroke before coming to a stop. Rishabh, in his heightened sense of panic, heard every sound around him: the squeaking of the rotating fans, the agitated scrawling of pens, the swishing of Bobde's dangling foot. They drove him mad. *This can't be*, he thought.

He glanced at Puro across the room, who felt Rishabh's eyes on him and looked up. Helplessness was written all over his face. 'Sorry,' he mouthed. Rishabh flared up. He shouldn't have trusted Puro with the timetable! He should have taken it down himself. How could he have made such a mistake? Puro was prone to clumsiness, ditziness and irresponsibility—everyone knew that. It had always been hilarious. But not any more. These moments flashed in front of Rishabh's eyes and he saw them for what they were: immature stupidity, a kind of fatal foolishness that bred failure and despair. They were both going to flunk this paper, and all for what? Puro's silly mistake of wrongly copying the timetable and Rishabh's even sillier mistake of copying it from Puro.

There was no time for anger now, Rishabh reasoned. He still had to attempt answering the questions. Buckling down, he strained his memory, trying to recall any useful scrap of information. In his mind, the computer classes were a disjointed mass of reminiscences, mainly about the illegally downloaded football clips that were distributed across the network. He tried summoning what Vishala Miss had said about functions, but all he remembered was how annoying her voice had sounded. He also vividly recalled the hum of the ACs, the antiseptic smell of the room and the chill in his forearms, but about the subject itself he remembered nothing.

So he faffed his way through the questions, fusing half-remembered garble with invented wisdom, even shoehorning in his physics knowledge for good measure. When Vishala Nath would eventually go through his paper, she'd be appalled by how little he knew but also secretly impressed by his brave effort at bullshitting. The way he had weaved Ohm's law into iterations was truly admirable.

When the exam ended, Rishabh was the first one out of the room.

'Rishabh!' called Puro. 'I'm sorry, re!'

Rishabh didn't turn around. He was fuming. Puro ran up behind him, struggling to hold on to his writing pad, pencil box, the question paper and bag. He touched Rishabh on the shoulder, who shrugged him off.

'Fuck you,' said Rishabh. The menace in his voice stopped Puro in his tracks. He stood still and watched Rishabh stalk down the corridor.

There was no time to feel despondent. Three more excruciating papers awaited their attention. The only consolation was that Rishabh was prepared for the actual physics paper. Puro tried apologizing again. He called Rishabh's home and was told he was studying. Before each paper, Rishabh brushed him off and after the bell rang, shot off before Puro even got out of his seat.

The final paper was Hindi. Rishabh was so sleep-deprived by this point that he wrote his roll number for his name and his phone number for his roll number. Pinto was not happy about giving him a fresh supplement. As with every paper, it came down to the very last second. His fingers were numb with scribbling; he had to shake his wrist to get the blood flowing again. Finally, the exams were done. He could sleep. He sat back in his seat and dreamed of his bed.

When he looked up again, Puro was standing over his desk. Rishabh got up to leave.

'Here, take this,' Puro said solemnly and placed a rolled-up tube of paper on the desk.

Rishabh unrolled the paper. It was the poster of Ronaldinho that used to be stuck on Puro's wall. Rishabh could see it was freshly taken down. The poster had peeled where the tape had held it up. It was one of Puro's prized possessions, a poster of his favourite star. Rishabh frowned. He wanted to be angry with Puro, but he couldn't muster it any more. It pissed him off that he couldn't be more pissed off.

'Don't,' he said. 'It's fine.'

'I'm sorry, bro.'

'I know. Forget it, it was a mistake. What's done is done.'

'So we're still friends?'

'Of course.'

Puro darted his eyes to the poster and lingered on it.

'You can have this back.'

'You sure you don't want it?' said Puro a little too eagerly.

'Definitely.'

'Definitely want it or definitely don't want it?'

'Definitely don't want it. If it were Beckham, I would have kept it . . .'

'Ah,' said Puro, relieved. He rolled up the poster and carefully slid it back in his bag in record time. 'But I have something you'd definitely want.' He thrust a hand inside his pocket, rummaged about and then pulled out a small chit.

'It's a little late for copying.'

'Copy this!'

Puro held up the chit. Scribbled on it was a number. Rishabh looked at it quizzically and then waggled his eyebrows.

'Guess whose?'

Rishabh squinted. Then his eyes widened. 'It's her number?' he yelled. People turned to look. He dropped his voice. 'It's Tamanna's?'

'Her landline it is, my boy.'

'How'd you get this?'

'I have my sources.'

'Krupa?'

Puro nodded sheepishly.

'This is amazing!' said Rishabh. The exhilaration had left him feeling fresh and wide-eyed.

'I knew you'd like it.'

'How many exams do I have to fail to get her address?'

'Fuck you.'

September 2006

'I'VE NEVER BEEN to school on a Saturday,' said Puro.

'Me neither,' said Rishabh.

The first weekend of September was here. The exams were a distant and mostly suppressed memory. The textbooks had been cast aside and the studs had been brought back into circulation. The tournament they had been preparing for all term was finally about to begin. It was going to be an intense weekend of football, and the boys hoped that when they returned to school on Monday, they would be doing so as champions.

The two turned the corner and saw the expansive ground in front of them. In the grey light of the cloudy September sky, it looked lush, inviting and, most importantly, familiar. Dattatreya, the portly groundsman, was bent over as he put the finishing touches to the white lines on the pitch. He huffed with every step and adjusted his interrupting paunch to extend his reach. On the sidelines and all along the giant steps swarmed boys from the participating teams. They seemed enamoured by the ground and intimidated by the infrastructure. Rishabh had never felt prouder of the imposing three-storey facade of the school—of its towering beams and columns, of the high standards of cleanliness it boasted—as he was when he saw these outsiders ogling at it. He realized what a difference it made to play a tournament at home—where you knew the surface of the ground, were acquainted with its bumps and patches, had spent years shooting at and missing its white posts. It inspired a kind of love that Rishabh didn't think he could feel for a patch of land.

'Aye, you two! Where were you?' snarled the coach when he spotted them loitering near the cash counters—windows where the accountants of the school sat and collected the fees. The area was better known as the '*vasooli* zone'.

'Sir, we couldn't get a rickshaw,' said Puro.

'And we're only five minutes late,' added Rishabh.

'Late is late, remember? If you hadn't done all this fashion, maybe you would have come on time.'

The coach was referring to the windcheater-jeans-and-skullcap look that Rishabh was sporting and the wrist-chain-beanie-flip-flops-and-baggy-jeans ensemble that Puro was carrying off. The coach had an odd quirk: while he was avant-garde and brave on the pitch, off it he was a conservative middle-aged man with no regard for the sartorial needs of the modern footballer.

'Yes, sir . . .' said Rishabh.

'What "yes, sir"? Idiot. Go and change.'

They turned on their heels to head back to where they had come from.

'Not there. Go to 5 A. That is the changing room for you boys for the whole tournament,' said Mehfouz Noorani with his back to the two and his eyes trained on the ground.

'Sir . . . we have . . . a changing room?' Rishabh gaped at the coach.

'I said something different or what? Go to 5 A. Full team is already there.'

'Sorry, sir. Going, sir,' said Rishabh.

They darted into the nearest entrance and found that 5 A was the first classroom on the left. Puro shoved open the door and was greeted with a mighty uproar as the team were in various stages of undress. It turned into a boisterous welcome when they saw it was just Puro and Rishabh.

'Dressing room!' said Rahul with a happy glint in his eye as they made their way in. 'Like Chelsea.'

'Yeah, because Chelsea players change in fifth standard classrooms, no?' Dave rolled his eyes.

'Arre, at least it's better than the toilets,' reasoned Floyd.

'I swear,' said Bhupi, who had once fallen into a urinal while struggling to put on his shin pads. 'I hate changing there.'

'Good to change without holding my breath,' added Oza.

'That phenyl smell. Ugh.' Rakshit retched.

'And the urine,' said Bhupi.

'You would know,' said Rishabh.

'Change, change!' thundered Puro, knowing that a re-enactment of Bhupi's tumble was in the offing.

They sat kitted up—the coach had commissioned a new kit that matched their measurements—nervously tapping their feet. Rishabh's stomach was flipping around like a paratha on a tawa. *Let's go, let's get out there*, he thought. He couldn't it take any longer, sitting around with fourteen other jittery souls.

The room had grown stuffy with the tense energy escaping their bodies.

Finally, the door creaked open and Ghadge Sir stuck his large head in. 'Phootball team! Coach is calling you. Come phasht.'

Puro sprang up from the table on which he had been perched. He clapped his hands rapturously. 'Okay, boys! Time to go! Up, up!'

The boys began barking and hollering as they filed out, their cries echoing through the empty school.

The coach met them at the edge of the ground. He waited with crossed arms for them to rally around him. Then he said in a low rumble, 'Rehearsal time is over. Now it is time for the show. Are you ready?'

They woofed back.

'Good. I also think you're ready. I wanted you to train last week even, but the bloody exams . . . Anyway, we have the best chance to win. You have trained like champions.'

Rishabh's lips involuntarily parted in a smile. Every chin was pointed skyward.

'Now, the first draw has been announced, and it's good for us. You are playing Bodhi. I will tell you only one thing: don't be arrogant. You might think they are weak or stupid, but give them respect . . . and give your full best on the pitch.' Then the coach proceeded to name his team and dismissed them to start warming up.

When they set eyes on the boys from Bodhi Deenanath High School, they finally understood the coach's disclaimer. The Bodhi players didn't have a kit. In fact, by the looks of it, they didn't even have clothes. They were huddled together at the other end of the ground, wearing white banyans and uncoordinated shorts. A bunch of them didn't even have shoes.

They had shown up in bathroom slippers. The sight of them repulsed Rishabh. They looked pathetic—more to be pitied than to be pitted against.

But a draw was a draw, and when the referee called for the captains, Rishabh grew grim. This was their best chance to win a cup, and they had to make the best possible start. Looking at the Banyan boys, Rishabh felt like fate was on their side.

The Banyan boys are abysmal. They play worse than they look. They clearly don't have or know any tactics, getting hypnotized by the ball as they follow it in a flock.

A portly boy is inexpertly marking Rishabh. The name Ajinkya is written on his back in orange chalk. He is a keen conversationalist. 'You have a very nice school,' he says, stomping around in the mud in his slippers.

'Thanks,' replies Rishabh. The ball is with Tejas, who's doing step-overs while two Banyan boys look on in admiration.

'We are from Bhiwandi,' continues the boy.

'That's nice.'

'Only English-medium school in Bhiwandi,' he says with pride.

'Congratulations.'

Puro gets the ball. He steams ahead. Rishabh is well acquainted with that searching look on his face. He tears down the flank, hollering for Puro to notice him.

'Oye, where are you going?' yells his marker.

Rishabh receives the ball and tries to angle a shot in, but it goes wide. The crowd lets out an 'Ooooh!'

Ajinkya finally pants to a stop. 'You are too fast, yaar. Next time, go little slower.' Rishabh lets out a hollow, mirthless laugh and jogs to the halfway line.

The first half is frustrating for Sanghvi. They boast of almost all the possession but can't seem to convert in the final third of the pitch. Some kind of voodoo keeps deflecting their shots, smashing them against defenders and sending them inches wide from the goal. Rahul finds himself in space and lets rip a vicious strike only to see the ball ricochet off the left post.

'Post number one!' yells Rishabh.

Over the course of their training, Rahul has developed a rare disease. Once in every match, he unfailingly smashes the ball into the frame of the goalpost. The team has placed bets on how many times he will strike the posts during this tournament. Rishabh's guess is five, and he is fastidiously keeping track.

The half ends. The Banyan boys are chirping in delight. They've managed to hold on. The Sanghvites are shaking their heads as they walk off the pitch.

The coach was uncharacteristically calm. He told them to sit down and jiggle their calves. 'It's a strange problem, but it is happening: you boys are trying too hard. You are so desperate to score that it is not happening. And when it is not happening, you are getting shaken up. Just relax. Enjoy the game. It is on your ground. No tension. Just play like we always play here. Meaning, just become loose. Look at your opponents, just watch them—'

The boys turned to look at the Bodhi lads. They were squatting a little distance away, happily chatting and chomping on sandwiches and sipping from water bottles. They didn't have a coach or even the desire to get back to finish the match. But their free and easy attitude felt enviable to the agitated Sanghvi boys.

'Not a care in the world,' continued the coach. 'Just go out there and enjoy yourselves. Goals will come. There is no sense in winning if you don't feel good about winning. Understand?'

It starts with Dave, who announces before kick-off, 'If you don't score in the next five minutes, I'm leaving the goal and going in attack. I've forgotten what the ball looks like.' They laugh. But the minutes tick by and they still haven't shaken off their stiffness. Then, just as they feel the irritation creeping back in, Puro thunders a low, speculative shot from seventy-five feet out. It's a stunning strike—the kind that is born only when talent meets frustration. The net ripples, and the Sanghvi boys whoop with relief.

The minute they score, the Banyan boys appear deflated. All their pluck and cheer desert them. They start scampering around, trying to play harder, but end up opening up more space for Sanghvi to attack. The chances come thick and fast, just like the falling rain. Soon Rishabh launches the ball from the right, which finds Rahul, who strokes the ball in. 2–0.

'Nice kick, re,' says Ajinkya.

Rishabh nods in appreciation.

'How much you got your shoes for?'

'I don't know . . . some 3000 bucks.'

Ajinkya's eyes widen. He glances at his slippers. 'What does your father do?'

'What?'

'He must be in a good position, no?'

'Yeah, he's vice president of a company.'

'Okay, okay . . . Look, look, ball is coming!'

Rishabh turns to see that Bhupi has scudded the ball down the line. Rishabh canters forward to meet it. Ajinkya puts up a valiant chase, but suddenly Rishabh sees him drop away from the corner of his eye. He delivers a cross that Tejas sends wide. Turning, he finds that Ajinkya has stopped tracking him because his slipper has come off. He's hunting for it in the muck.

'It's over there,' calls Rishabh, pointing at a spot a short distance behind Ajinkya.

'Thanks very much!'

In the second half, they eviscerate the Banyan boys. Floyd grabs a goal and Puro gets a second. Towards the end, Rishabh tries hard to get on the scorecard but can't seem to put the finishing touches to a strike. The match ends at 4–0.

Sanghvi leaves to applause from the other teams watching from the stands. Some of the boys on the sidelines are pointing and laughing at the Bodhi players. Ajinkya waddles up to Rishabh and taps him on the shoulder.

'Good game. All the best for remaining tournament,' he says with a wide smile on his face.

'Thank you, man. You guys also played well.'

Ajinkya snorts. 'No, no! We know we don't play well. We don't have ground in school. We like to play so we practise on the side. But there is no support only. Today also we all just bunked school and came.'

'That's crazy.'

'Yeah. Because we listened to lot of good things about Sanghvi School. So we wanted to see. And we are all loving to play. So we played. We are happy we came. Thanks, haan, and all the best once again.'

Rishabh watches him join the rest of his team. The Banyan boys stand shivering in the rain, picking up their half-eaten sandwiches and their animated conversations. They are laughing and joking, enjoying their day out with their buddies. Looking at them, Rishabh feels no joy of victory. The Banyan boys have lost but they aren't beaten.

Off the field, the Sanghvi team felt the exertion in their legs. A throb of pain escaped their toes when they yanked off their muddy studs. On the field, Dingreja Educational Society narrowly defeated Hemu Vilasbhai Patel School. DES, who were among the favourites, made heavy work of their first round. They missed chance after chance and played a box-to-box game that was thoroughly entertaining for the spectators, but must have been tiresome for the players.

The most decisive outcome was provided by Kamani Krida Public School. The team in orange met MES High School in their first round. The MES boys didn't know what hit them. Within the first five minutes, they were three goals down. KKPS showed them no mercy. They went at them with the same rabid energy from the first to the final whistle. It was as if they were making a statement. With an 8–0 victory, everyone got it.

The buzz right after the match was about two boys in particular: Eklavya Bhamtekara, the KKPS centre midfielder, who had scored one and set up three goals, and Nagesh Kataria, their striker, who'd scored the three goals that Eka had set up. When the duo's notoriety reached Sanghvi's 5 A dressing room, Rishabh and Puro had to get a better look for themselves.

They found them lounging near the cash counters, their wet clothes draped on the backs of their chairs. Eklavya was a big lad. Easily topping six feet, his long limbs spilled over the tiny seats. He had a broad, chubby face. His large front teeth prised his lips open into a perpetual half-smile. He flapped his right foot from side to side, his eyes glazed in a relaxed stupor.

Then he rose and looked around lazily. In a moist voice, he slowly called, 'Prateek.' No one replied to his croak. So he repeated it a little louder. When he still didn't get a response, he leaned over, picked up one of his studs and, with wicked force, flung it towards a boy sitting cross-legged on the floor, a few feet from him. The stud slammed into the boy with an ugly thwack. Rishabh and Puro winced. Prateek howled in pain.

'Pass the water, you deaf piece of shit,' spat Eklavya.

Prateek scowled but didn't retort. He quietly passed a bottle to Eklavya.

'They're on the same team, right?' whispered Rishabh. Puro nodded.

'Can't pass the ball. Can't pass the water bottle also. Why did we bring you here, Prateek?' said a tall, dark, skinny boy with a venomous sweetness in his voice. 'Be more . . .' the boy wound up his wet jersey and slapped it across Prateek's back, 'attentive.' The lash seemed to echo for a full minute.

Suddenly Puro gasped. 'What's he doing here?'

'You know him?' asked Rishabh.

'Nagesh Kataria. He was with me in one of the athletics meets. I was with the under-12 lot, and he was in the under-15 category,' said Puro.

'So?'

'That was four years ago.'

'Oh! He's overage?'

'One hundred per cent. Just *look* at him!'

Rishabh now began noticing Nagesh's overaged-ness, and the more he looked, the more signs he spotted. There was the chiselled musculature, the tight abs stacked over his stomach. He had the bristly goatee of a man, which, combined with his lean, bony face and beady eyes, made him look like a billy goat.

'How old do you think he is?'

'Old enough to go for *The Da Vinci Code* on a real ID.'

'And he's still in school?'

'Does he look smart to you?'

They watched as Nagesh struggled to open a Tupperware box. It seemed like the concept of a lid had him baffled.

'What about Eka?'

'I'm pretty sure he's ancient too,' said Puro.

'Should we complain?'

'Yeah, we should tell Ghadge Sir,' resolved Puro. 'Can't let these grandfathers get away with it.'

Twenty minutes later, Ghadge Sir was vehemently shaking his head. 'They haeo submitted proper documents. You don't think about other player. Jusht you worry about your own game,' he said in a tone that prompted no further discussion.

Their next game was an hour later, against Abhinav Vidya High School. The Sanghvites began warming up under a light rain. The tiredness that they had eased out of their muscles seemed to have returned with interest. On the pitch, St Mary's ICSE was playing Stanislaus. Rishabh's gaze shifted from them to the Abhinav players, who were limbering up at the other end of the ground. He stumbled mid-stretch.

They were terrifying to look at. In Rishabh's estimation, they were each the dimensions of a standard gulmohar tree. Their maroon jerseys seemed to have to strain to contain their bulging proportions. One boy among them was bigger than all the rest and no less than Frankenstein's monster himself. Each of his thighs was like a king-sized mattress, and he lumbered about on them, jiggling them to scary effect.

'What's so interesting?' asked Dave, who was stretching next to him.

'Man, they look scary,' croaked Rishabh. 'Just look at the size of that big one in the middle! He'll squish Puro.'

'If he catches him.'

'They look tougher than us,' said Rishabh.

'That's what they're saying about us right now,' said Dave. 'Look.'

'Don't point, bey,' hissed Rishabh, following Dave's finger. Two Abhinav players were staring at them and talking in low tones. They didn't look confident at all.

'We're the home team!' said Dave. 'We've just scored four goals.'

'Yeah, but against a team from Bhiwandi.'

'Doesn't matter. I've seen them play. The only way they'll win is if they join our school,' said Dave. 'And last I checked, admissions aren't open.'

Rishabh laughed. The next stretch really loosened his hamstrings. He felt a surge of affinity for Dave. He was a good personality to have in the trenches because he was never fazed. In fact, the worse things became, the funnier he found them.

Like that time when the football team had been dragged to the vice principal for breaking a sixth-standard classroom window. Rishabh had made the mistake of standing next to Dave, who'd delivered a whispered reply to each of Janaki Srinivasan's rhetorical remarks.

'How could you do this?' thundered Janaki Ma'am.

'You just have to kick a ball. It's not that difficult,' whispered Dave.

'How reckless are you boys?'

'Sometimes I open my eyes during prayers,' muttered Dave.

'Should I put a stop to your playing?'

'Okay, everyone, time to retire,' purred Dave.

It had been all he could do to not burst into howls of laughter right in a hissing Janaki Ma'am's face. All that dread that he had felt while walking up to Janaki Ma'am's room seemed to disappear. Suddenly, it wasn't the vice principal deriding them for wrecking property; it was just a batty old lady losing her sanity over a silly situation. The more she spoke, the funnier Dave's asides got until Rishabh turned red in the face with stifled laughter and had to pretend to have a coughing fit just to get some of it out. He had left the room feeling glad that they had broken that window.

He felt that same joy now. He looked around him and saw the determined faces of his teammates, and his fear was diffused. He wasn't alone, he realized. If he felt overwhelmed, he could voice his apprehensions—from the corner of his mouth—to people who were going through it too, and they could take heart from each other's limited strengths. Or, at the very least, take laughter from Dave's bluffed bravado.

As it turned out, it was their mammoth size that proved to be Abhinav's undoing. They were lumbering and slow and couldn't keep up with Sanghvi's quick passing. Though they ran out comfortable 2–0 winners, Rishabh hadn't really felt at ease during the game. Every time he got the ball, he could see their towering maroon outlines bounding towards him. It made him empathize with every human character in Jurassic Park.

After a tentative first half, during which he'd teetered on the brink of bad form, he had made amends by providing the assist for Hriday Lokhande's crucial second goal. Lokhande had been the revelation of the match. He was a quiet, hard-tackling, harder-working defensive midfielder, whom the Mongoose had unearthed to shore up the defence when Khodu left. He was a mysterious boy; so soft-spoken that Rishabh often wondered if he got overlooked only because people genuinely forgot he was around. He had been subbed in for Floyd as the Mongoose had been looking to consolidate their lead but he had ended up extending it.

They had no more matches that day. It took the team a while to lift their bodies off the desks in their dressing room. Everyone ached and sputtered, groaning as they scooped up their things. The coach entered the room and clapped his hands. They slowly surrounded him.

'Well done, men. We're in the quarter-finals. Three matches,' he held up three fingers, 'we are three matches from being champions. Now, I want you boys to go straight home and sleep. No TV, no reading, no music, nothing. Your muscles need complete relaxing. Understood?'

The coach really didn't have to remind them to sleep. Some were carrying out his orders while he spoke.

'I want everyone to report at 9 a.m. sharp tomorrow. Got it? Purohit, you are in charge of this. Okay, good job and get moving,' finished the coach, clapping his hands and motioning them to pick up the pace.

Puro and Rishabh shared a rickshaw ride home. Puro was quiet for most of the journey.

'What did you think of the last game?' asked Rishabh.

'Your second half was better. The assist was good.'

'I know, the first half . . . I don't know what happened . . .'

'You need to be more consistent, buddy,' said Puro. 'We all do,' he added, a little too late.

Fifteen minutes later, Mrs Bala gave Rishabh a withering look as he made his muddy way through the hall and to his room. 'Don't touch anything,' she instructed.

Rishabh stripped off his wet, dirty kit and washed it. He hosed the muck off, scrubbed the jersey—careful not to scrub out the school logo—and then rinsed it. Then he took a long, luxurious hot-water bath. Under the shower, he noticed a purple mark below his ribcage, to the left; a spot which the number 17 of AVH must have mistaken for an armrest because he'd kept nestling his elbow into it. The bath had made him drowsy. He just about managed to spread his wet kit under a fan before collapsing in a heap on the bed.

The pain began the moment he opened his eyes. He felt like someone had moved him from his bed while he'd been asleep and placed him in a car accident. Every inch of his body screamed in agony. He felt wincing pain in places he didn't even recollect getting hurt—like his eyeballs. When he stood up, his calves felt so stiff that he wondered if he had bathed in starch the night before. It took him half an hour of slowly shuffling around to retrieve some of his motor skills. *Thank God I don't have a football tournament to play in today*, he thought bitterly.

He stopped by Puro's house and waited patiently as the latter hobbled to the rickshaw and gingerly hopped in.

'Aches like hell, doesn't it?'

'Not really. I'm feeling fit and fresh,' said Puro. His dogged denial was amusing to Rishabh.

'Great! You mind holding on to this for a second?' asked Rishabh, dropping his kitbag on Puro's thigh.

'FUCK!' yelled Puro, making the auto–wallah swerve in fright.

'Sorry, man, I thought you were fully fit and all,' said Rishabh, laughing.

'Fuck you.'

The school was shrouded in Sunday silence. Their footsteps echoed down the long, empty corridors. In the distance, they could make out the forms of two–three contingents along the ground. Dattatreya was, as usual, in the middle of the pitch, having waited till the last possible minute to redraw the lines. Rishabh was talking to Puro about how benched substitutes always seemed to enjoy more victories than the key players, when he caught sight of an apparition that made him freeze. Puro noticed his stricken face.

'Your eyeballs hurting again?'

'I think . . . I saw Tamanna . . .' whispered Rishabh in a tizzy.

'Where? Where?' asked Puro, spinning in all directions.

'I think she was in the corridor next to the ground. Uff, there's a pillar coming in the way now,' said Rishabh. 'NO! There she is!'

Puro looked towards the passage Rishabh was pointing at and saw Tamanna and Preetha walking down it. Puro was relieved. He had been worried about Rishabh's form in the last game and didn't want hallucinations to compound his friend's issues.

'So today you'll be in full form,' teased Puro, winking at Rishabh, who said nothing and ducked with surprising speed into the corridor that led to the dressing room.

When Rishabh opened the door to 5 A, he was almost thrown out by the sonic force of twelve voices simultaneously telling him, 'Tamanna is here!' He quickly shut the door behind him but was confident the announcement had reached her already. They were loud enough to be heard in Burundi.

'I know!' he hissed.

'You called her or what?' asked Tejas.

'No.'

'Then why is she here?' wondered Tejas, genuinely puzzled.

'Because she's in love with our champ. Personally, I think it's time . . .' began Rahul.

'Time for?' prompted Rishabh.

'Time to tell her, dumb-ass,' said Dave.

Rishabh blushed. He knew they were ragging him, but a part of him wanted to believe they were right: that she had come to see him, that she wanted to support him—and see him win—that the time had come for him to man up and come clean. In his head, he quietly mulled over the idea of asking her out. The team, quite done with his indecision by now, resolved to egg him on.

'Tell her! Tell her! Tell her!' they chanted in unison.

'Guys . . . I can't,' muttered Rishabh. He had lived with himself long enough to know that his cowardly soul couldn't go through with the task. He was feeling parched just *thinking* of it.

'You have to tell her sometime,' urged Sumit.

'Dude, I'm telling you—you aren't going to get a better chance than this. There's hardly anyone in school today. No one will know. It's a three-second job—"I love you." See how easy it is?' reasoned Rahul.

Rishabh looked at Puro, who hadn't weighed in yet. Rishabh hoped he would side with him and against the rabid bunch of Romeos. But to his horror, a sly grin crept across Puro's lips.

'Tell you what, let's leave it to destiny. You don't want to tell her now, that's fine. But . . .' trailed off Puro, holding off for the flourish, 'if you score in the next match, you will tell her. Deal?'

'Arre, if you don't want him to tell her, then say that, no,' yelled Dave.

'Now he'll purposely not score. Well done, Puro,' groaned Floyd.

'Deal,' said Rishabh.

He'd said it too softly; the bickering continued unabated. So he said it again, considerably louder.

'I SAID I'LL DO IT!'

Now he had the attention of the room.

'If I score in the next match, I will ask Tamanna out,' stated Rishabh Bala with a coolness and calmness that surprised even himself. His heart was battering against his chest. He felt it was beating hard enough for the others to see its imprint on his T-shirt. He didn't know what had prompted him to blurt the words out, but he felt relieved at having voiced a thought that had grown stale in his mind. Suddenly it was fresh again. Yet there was a reptilian part of him that stuck out its forked tongue and hissed, 'You've made a big mistake.'

Rishabh has never played under so much pressure before. They're playing Kala Mahavidyalaya. KM aren't that great a side, having won their last two matches on penalties. Only the Mongoose is taking them seriously. 'Remember, there are no bad teams in the good rounds,' he says. KM doesn't bother Rishabh in the least. What worries him is seeing Tamanna and Preetha sitting in the stands overlooking the ground.

'Play a good game, my boy,' Puro says with a wink.

Rishabh gives him a nervous thumbs up. He has no other option. It's the first time she's seeing him play. He's determined to impress her, to show her what he's capable of, to display his skill, talent and passion for the game, to put the last match behind him and move Sanghvi ahead in the tournament.

And he does exactly that for two whole minutes before slipping in the mud. He lands on his belly and skids by a foot before dragging to a halt. The ball bobbles ahead of him but his head snaps to the stands. Tamanna is looking in his direction, mouth agape. His face turns into a giant beetroot. *She's seen it*, he thinks. *I'm forever going to be the guy who swan-dived into muck. There's mud all over me. It's over!*

He's spiralling into crisis mode, when the coach's savage cries pierce his thoughts.

'COME BACK AND DEFEND, IDIOT!' comes the coach's voice at a volume that must surely have split the eardrums of the players closer to the touchline.

He wants to desperately tell the coach not to call him an idiot when his one true love is in earshot. It makes for a terrible impression. He puts up a hand to pacify the coach.

'STOP WAVING AND START DEFENDING, BASTARD!' comes back the roar.

Rishabh runs back to defend before the Mongoose escalates past 'bastard'.

Kala Mahavidyalaya prove to be a tough opponent to break. They're a staunch defensive unit. At any given point in time, there are at least eight KM bodies behind the ball, forming a fortress. They don't attack very often, though. Even their counter-attacks are polite inquiries instead of brutal assaults. They timidly stray forward, almost like they are asking, 'You mind if we get a goal?' In short, they are inert but unyielding, a combination that tests Sanghvi's resolve.

During the break, the coach railed about the untalented scumbags playing for a draw.

'They want shoot-out. Bloody bastards. No skill, no hard work, no ambition,' he thundered. Then he asked them to double their efforts towards scoring a goal. He correctly predicted that they should not fear a counter-attack. Their opponents were too timid to actually try and win a match.

'But you men should not play that way. You should have the balls to say, "We want to win. We have come to play a game, not to defend a game." Be brave. Attack them with full power. Make sure these cowards lose.'

Freed from the constriction of defending and galvanized by the constant abuse of the coach, they play with more thrust. On the right, Rishabh cleans his mud-stained spectacles. He's seeing precious little action on the wing. So he decides to drift to the middle. As time ticks by, his mind becomes wholly absorbed in extracting a win. He's forgotten about the girl who's cheering from the sidelines.

Just then, Rana bumps the ball forward in his rubbery, lethargic manner. His body language masks the quality of the move, which is pointed and deliberate. The ball finds Tejas on the left wing. Tejas trots forward, his stubby legs becoming a speedy blur. He lashes the ball towards the crowded KM box. Eight defenders fling themselves on it simultaneously. The ball pops out to Rahul Rawat. He sees it plop on to the mud, perfectly teed up. His eyes flash at the opportunity. He rushes to the ball, his body clicking into position, and thwacks it with his instep.

The crack is almighty. The flailing in the box stops as all eyes follow the sailing ball. The KM players wince. All Sanghvi jaws drop. Bhupi blows out air urgently, hoping to help the ball along in every little way he can. The KM keeper leaps forward. The ball gracefully loops beyond his reach.

Rishabh is standing at the far post. He sees the ball spinning towards him, as if it had been couriered by fate to his exact position. A thought is forming in his head but, before he can wait to find out what it is, he instinctually stabs at the ball with the business end of his boot. The volley sends the ball rocketing into the net.

I'VE DONE IT! the thought screams in his head.

He careens towards his teammates to celebrate. He feels hands grab him in delirious joy, yanking at his hair, tugging at his jersey. Then his eyes travel to the stands and spot Tamanna and Preetha clapping. Preetha is saying something to Tamanna, who nods vigorously.

'I did it!' he hollers. 'I scored!'

He's feeling pretty chuffed about giving his team the advantage, but the realization that he's done it in front of the girl he's cosmically connected to makes for a feeling that gushes through him like a Brahmaputra of happiness. He tears away from the clawing mob and does a victory dance in the middle of the ground. It's clunky and disturbing, like a washed-up eel gasping for water. Preetha stops clapping and claps a palm to her forehead. Tamanna's smile disappears as she stares at the spasms that Rishabh is having.

Thankfully, Puro, ever the keen friend, notices the effect Rishabh's dancing is having on the object of his adoration. He jogs over and hugs him, squeezing tight to stop the seizures. They prove difficult to contain. Rishabh's hands seem to have a life of their own. The emotion of joy is so strong that it floods his body with a need to groove, and he wriggles in Puro's embrace.

'Stop moving, you fucking idiot. You're scaring her,' mutters Puro.

'Who cares!' says Rishabh. 'I just scored!'

'I know. Now you have to ask her out. So stop doing this rubbish.'

The memory of the deal slithers back into Rishabh's mind. Suddenly the goal sours. Surely he isn't going to go through with it. Surely he can still back out. The doubts spread across Rishabh's face like a crack in a glacier. On the positive side, he stops dancing.

When the match ended, Rishabh didn't walk off the pitch as much as he floated off it. It turned out that it was his goal that settled the match. Even though all he had done was scavenge it by being in the right place at the right time, he felt a profound sense of accomplishment. *This was one for the books*, he thought. *When historians of the future will write about Sanghvi's progress to the semi-finals, they will see that it was Rishabh Bala's effort that led them there.*

In 5 A, there was great cheering. Rishabh's back grew sore with the congratulatory slaps that it received. Finally, Rahul said in a ringing voice, 'Now you *have* to ask her out!' All in the room collectively remembered the promise and, with sadistic pleasure, sang, 'Ask her out! Ask her out! Ask her out!' Rishabh's smile vanished. He realized the mob was on to him. He tried backing away. But they advanced on him with their teeth bared, singing in one voice and with a malevolent gleam in their eyes.

Puro stepped forward and raised his hands. 'Wait! Everybody, shut up. Let's not scare him.'

'Thanks,' whimpered Rishabh.

'No, you still have to tell Tamanna,' said Puro. 'A deal is a deal.'

'But I'm not ready.'

'And you never will be,' retorted Puro.

'Fucker, you just scored!' goaded Tejas.

'Tejas is right. You're in the magic hour,' said Puro.

'What's that?'

'Arre, the magic hour! When you play well in front of girls, then for one hour after the game, you are the star. Right now, she will fully fall flat for you.'

'Really?'

'Yeah, yeah,' said Puro.

'When you score on the pitch—' began Rahul.

'You score off the pitch!' finished Puro. The two exchanged a blustery high five.

'There's no better time than now. You are the star, bey. What're you worried about? Plus she's come all the way for you. You won't disappoint her, will you?' said Puro.

The case they made was compelling. Rishabh's temperature rose. He took short, shallow breaths that scrambled his brain. He felt the oscillation of his heart. He imagined the sweet release he would feel when his trapped emotions finally escaped his lips. All of it had brought him to the edge, but what pushed him over were Sumit's words: 'If you don't tell her, we will!' And when thirteen boys started chanting about making his proposal for him, Rishabh decided it was time to act.

'Fine!' he said. 'I'll do it.'

The cheering was deafening.

'I need your help.' Rishabh turned to Puro.

'Anything you want,' said Puro.

'I need you to make sure she's alone.'

'Done. Let's go?'

'Let's go!'

They moved towards the door, and the whole team tiptoed behind them. Rishabh whirled around and sternly said, 'Just Puro. Please don't follow us. If I see any of you assholes around, I will not say anything. Okay?'

Their faces fell but they nodded solemnly. Rishabh opened the door.

They found Tamanna and Preetha idly walking around the cash counters near the bus stop. As soon as Rishabh spotted them, he dived behind the nearest pillar and shook like a plucked guitar string. It took a few minutes before Puro could coax him to stop hyperventilating and they could go ahead with the operation.

The plan was simple. Puro would lead Preetha away from Tamanna, leaving Rishabh to swoop in and say the three magic words.

'Listen,' whispered Rishabh, a waterfall of sweat gushing from his forehead, 'should I go down on one knee?'

'*What?* Why?'

'People propose on one knee, no?'

'Abbey, that's for marriage.'

'Are you sure?'

'Look, go down on one knee, go down on both knees, do a handstand if you want—it doesn't matter. All that matters is that you tell her. Okay?'

Rishabh nodded.

'You ready?'

There was no honest way to answer this, so Rishabh lied and said, 'Yes.'

'Good. All the best, my boy! Don't forget me when you get a girlfriend.'

Rishabh smiled. He shook his head and, before it could come to a stop, Puro leapt out from behind the pillar and gallantly strode towards the two girls.

'Hey, Preetha! How are you?'

'Puro? Hi . . .' said Preetha, a tad startled.

'Hi, Puro,' said Tamanna.

Rishabh cooed. Even amid his rising panic, he could still appreciate her sunny disposition and velvety voice.

'Uh, hi . . . Accha, Preetha, Ghadge Sir has been looking all over for you,' said Puro.

'Why is he looking for me?'

'For the volleyball team. He's calling you to the gymnasium right this minute.'

'I don't play volleyball,' replied Preetha, narrowing her eyes.

'Well, he wants to recruit you,' said Puro without skipping a beat.

'Now? That's strange,' said Preetha thoughtfully.

'I know. Just come fast and sort it out with him, no,' said Puro.

He began escorting Preetha away according to plan, but Tamanna followed them.

'Where are you going?' demanded Puro.

'To the gym . . . with you guys . . .' said Tamanna.

'No, no. You stay here only. You are not required. Ghadge Sir will not like it. You wait. We'll come back here. Five minutes, promise.'

Tamanna protested and Puro explained how highly strung Ghadge Sir was.

'He's really angry for some reason. He told me to bring one girl, and if he sees I brought two, he'll kill me.'

'Shut up, yaar, Puro. I know Ghadge Sir. He won't do that.'

'Look, it's important that you stay here,' growled Puro. 'Please,' he mouthed so Rishabh wouldn't hear it.

Tamanna interpreted the imploring eyes. 'Okaaaaay,' she conceded warily. Her jaw was set firm, and her eyes were dark squints of suspicion.

'We'll be right back,' said Puro. Then, in hushed tones, 'Thank you!'

Puro led Preetha away. 'What's going on?' Rishabh heard her ask as they walked past him.

'Arre, just come, na,' insisted Puro. He turned his head to see Rishabh still clinging to the pillar and winked.

Rishabh took a deep breath. He exhaled slowly, looked up in the general direction of heaven and stepped into the long corridor that led to the counters.

Though in reality Rishabh walked a total distance of ten feet, it felt like he had completed the Dandi March twice over. For a brief moment after he started on his way, he simply forgot how to walk. He had to direct his attention to each muscle in his legs to stop from keeling right over. He staggered on. The corridor stretched on endlessly. He heard each sharp cry from the players on the pitch. The thump of the ball sounded like a bass drum. The plants that lined the corridor filled the air with a sweet, wet smell. The light was dull and diffused. Every pore on his skin felt clogged with the humidity of the rain-laden sky. And on he walked. Tamanna was staring at the ground. Her body was angled away from him. She had no idea her greatest admirer was shuffling towards her.

Finally, Rishabh reached the foyer. She still hadn't noticed him. So, with the unsung courage that all schoolboys mustered in these situations, he said, 'Hello . . .'

Tamanna jumped. Any girl in her position would do the same. If your best friend was whisked away under mysterious circumstances and you were asked to hang around lonely foyers, it was only natural that you would jump when accosted with a gurgling 'Hello!' She took a second to compose herself, then said, 'Hi . . .'

Rishabh had lived this moment a million times in his head. In his mind's eye, he had stood before her and told her what lay in his heart with confidence and lucidity. He had spoken with charm and wit and mystery and lust and in every other way that a boy could express his love for a girl. Yet now when the moment had arrived, his throat had dried up and the words had disappeared. He stared at Tamanna's slender face, into her questioning eyes, for what seemed like days. Sensing his awkwardness, Tamanna decided to help him out.

'You played really well.'

'Yes . . . yeah,' said Rishabh. 'Sometimes you play well, sometimes you play badly.' Once again, he was unable to stop himself.

'Hmmm.'

'In that match I played well, though,' he said and then slammed his jaws shut.

'I know. I saw,' said Tamanna. Her eyes travelled around the foyer. 'Congrats.'

They fell silent. This was the moment. Rishabh felt it. It was a moment of anticipation. Twice he opened his mouth and shut it. Tamanna pursed her lips and wiggled them from side to side. And just like that, the moment was gone.

'Okay, then, see you later,' said Tamanna, trying to make her escape.

That did the trick. Rishabh was jolted into action the moment he saw her leave. Three precious years of yearning couldn't be dashed by one moment of awkwardness. Fuelled as much by desperation as desire, he spoke up.

'Tamanna,' he said. His brain held up a placard with his next line on it. 'Wait . . . there's something I want to tell you.'

She stopped and slowly turned around. Rishabh walked up to her and looked into her eyes. A gust of wind swirled around the bus stop and a lock of her wavy hair wriggled across her face. She gasped. She knew it was coming. He knew it was coming. Still, she went through with the formality of asking, 'What?'

Mustering all the heroism and huskiness he could, Rishabh said the three words he had been longing to say for three years. He steadied himself. 'You know what.'

Wait, those weren't the words. Someone had switched his words when he hadn't been looking. His brain frantically scurried inside his skull, searching for the right ones. In the meantime, his face looked perplexed. Tamanna's looked yet more perplexed.

'What?' she repeated.

His brain still hadn't found the missing words, so it could only supply the horrific 'You know *what*.'

Rishabh felt disgust wrap him in a warm embrace. It was a proposal that even the worst of his pessimism hadn't predicted. The trauma was such that he started having a surreal out-of-body experience. He floated above the foyer, looking down at his hapless self. He had always imagined this moment to be filled with poetry, during which he would rhapsodize the rapture she made him feel. Instead he found himself hosting a quiz show: 'Guess the meaning of "what" in the phrase "You know what!" and you become the winner of Kaun Banegi Rishabh's Girlfriend!' His floating self wanted to shake him out of his stupor, but all it could do was look on helplessly.

'I don't know what you're talking about . . .' said Tamanna with feminine coyness.

She had thrown him one last lifeline. The moment sneaked its snout back. It reappeared like a wary dog, snuffling about for scraps in a back alley trash can.

Rishabh took it; without further thought or preparation, without rationale or logic, with all his adolescent recklessness, he took it. His pulse throbbed on like a racing car engine, his pupils dilated, his fingers and toes curled. And he gambled it all on that slight, wavering moment.

'Tamanna, I love you. I've loved you from the first second I saw you. I think you're *gorgeous*. And—uh . . . yeah. That's it. Will you go out with me?'

There was a pause. And, as any seasoned proposer would testify, this was the pause that lasted a lifetime. It being Rishabh's first proposal, he didn't know any of this. All he knew was that the pause went on and on, and just when he thought it was coming to an end, it went on some more.

Many thoughts raced through Rishabh's head during that pause, the majority of which involved fantasies of the earth splitting and swallowing him whole. Unfortunately, the tiled flooring of the foyer remained rather intact.

At long last, Tamanna did speak. She took a step back. Her tongue hit the roof of her mouth and Rishabh glanced at the rows of her glossy white teeth. *Her teeth have gaps*, he observed casually. *Shut up*, he told this observational part of himself, *she's about to say something*.

'No . . .' she said. Her voice trailed off.

It was not a loud or emphatic sound by any measure, yet it went off like a bomb in Rishabh's ears. They rang with the shock. 'No, no, no, no!' it reverberated.

'What?' said Rishabh, hoping she'd change her answer.

'No,' she repeated. It was even softer this time.

'But . . . But I thought you . . . You don't like me?'

'I'm sorry, Rishabh . . . I like you . . . just not in that way.'

This wouldn't be the last time Rishabh would hear that phrase but it was definitely the first.

'I don't understand . . .' he said truthfully. 'Didn't you come to watch the matches for me?'

Tamanna shook her head.

'Then why did you come?' Rishabh wondered aloud. Then his eyes widened in realization. '. . . for someone else?'

Tamanna nodded, but it felt like she had shot him at close range with a .22 calibre handgun.

'So . . .' He found it hard to move his jaw. 'That's it?'

'Yeah . . . I guess . . .'

Rishabh remained silent. He feared that if he opened his mouth, he would let out the howl that was developing in his gut. In his stomach sat a concentrated ball of acid that churned and churned.

'I'm sorry . . . Rishabh, I hope you understand.'

Rishabh smiled. His lips trembled.

'I have to go now . . .' she said.

She walked past him, moving briskly. After a distance, she dropped her head. He didn't know why she did that—whether she was embarrassed or shocked or if she just wanted to check if her laces were tied. She turned a corner, and then he could see her no longer. He puffed his cheeks out and groaned. It was the hollow sound of three years falling apart.

'What did she say?'

'How'd it go?'

'Did she slap you?'

The squawky questions flew at him from every corner of the dressing room. Rishabh stared at the concerned faces and began laughing. It started as a giggle but quickly escalated to a monstrous cackling. He pushed past them and climbed on to a desk.

'Do you want to know what she said?'

He waved his arms about like the conductor of his own tragic opera.

'I'll tell you what she said.' He leapt to a second desk. 'She said no!'

A gasp rose from his audience. Not on hearing the news but because Rishabh had leapt to a third desk, which had wobbled perilously before settling under his weight.

'Rishabh, come down, man . . . It's all right . . .' said Rahul. Puro looked away.

'NO! I won't. N-O. No! Do you understand what no means, Rahul?'

'Yeah—'

'WRONG! It means no. Not happening, negative, nah, naw, nope!'

'Dude, seriously . . .' said Sumit, 'that was a terrible joke.'

'NO!' he screamed. 'It's not a joke. It's the truth.'

'AYE!' came a voice from behind him. 'WHAT ARE YOU DOING? GET DOWN FROM THERE!'

Rishabh whirled around only to lock eyes with a glaring coach. All at once he felt drained and sheepish. No one made a sound as he, slowly and noisily, lowered himself to sea level.

'Where is your discipline?' growled the coach.

Every shoulder in the room sagged at the mention of the D-word. The shouting sessions that followed the word 'discipline' were always the longest and harshest. They braced themselves as the coach ripped into Rishabh for insubordination, disorderly conduct, disrespect to public property, damaging the reputation of the football team, flaws of character, questionable upbringing and lack of remorse. In fact, he listed every reprehensible charge that could be thrown at a person this side of arson, robbery and first-degree murder. Rishabh was verbally assassinated for simply standing atop a desk and lamenting the loss of his first love. What made it worse was that every time he tried to defend himself, or even apologize, he was shut down with fiercer criticism.

When the tirade ended, the coach straightened himself, cleared his throat and said, 'I just came to tell you that the match starts in one hour.' He glanced at his watch. 'Okay, now half an hour. Take rest and don't stand on tables and chairs.' He turned on his heel and stalked out of the room. They saw that other teams had gathered outside 5 A after hearing the commotion. Rishabh shut his eyes and let out a low groan.

But his embarrassment didn't last much longer. Soon the team was engrossed in warming up for the upcoming match.

Their next opponents were called St Mary's. They were a convent school from Mumbra and wore a green-and-gold jersey. An unspectacular outfit, they had quietly made it to the semi-finals by being stolid in their defence and clinical in their attack. They had ground out three consecutive 1–0 victories. The Sanghvi boys felt the odds were in their favour.

The birds were making their way back to their nests. As twilight wore on, the anticipation and exhilaration grew and the team jogged up the muddy patch of land between the ground and the basketball court. But Rishabh didn't hear any of the chatter. The thought of playing a game of football—a semi-final, no less—did not enter his mind. He was focused, instead, on the match being played on the ground as they waited. Kamani Krida were deep into the second half of their tie with Bryan International. They had quickly secured a two-goal lead in the first half and had shifted to a lower gear for the rest of the game.

In the stands, Tamanna was chewing her nails. Her dark eyes followed the game with rapture. She threw her hands up whenever Kamani Krida attacked. The acidic ball wound tighter in Rishabh's stomach. *Her heart is set on someone wearing the orange jersey of Kamani fucking Krida.* He was sure of it.

Towards the end of the game, Eklavya clipped the ball over to the fossilized Nagesh, who promptly walloped it into the net. The boys and the two men of KKPS erupted in jubilation. Then, as he watched, Eklavya turned to the stands with a cheeky grin and saluted. Tamanna turned red and buried her face in her hands. The ball in Rishabh's stomach spewed out its bile. He froze.

Eklavya! She loved that pumpkin-headed idiot, who was still a student despite being old enough to be a teacher!

What terrible taste she had. *That too from Kamani Krida, of all places.* His interior monologue threw up a little. What a traitor she had turned out to be.

If there is any mercy in the world, Rishabh doesn't find evidence of it that day.

He doesn't hear the whistle blow. He starts moving as a mechanical obligation when he sees everyone around him running. He has a glazed look on his face that makes his teammates reluctant to pass to him. Rahul takes a shot at a goal that is firmly grasped by the keeper. Rishabh continues staring at the keeper with a thousand-yard stare long after he has kicked the ball afield. He stares till the keeper begs a defender to stand between him and the ghostly gaze.

They get a corner. Rishabh listlessly jogs over to take it. He submits a ball that drags itself along the ground and comes to a pathetic stop acres from where his players are poised. Puro grabs him by the collar of his shirt and shakes him. 'You've gone mad or what? Don't fuck up this match over some stupid girl!'

It enrages Rishabh. How does Puro not understand him? Why is he so selfish? It's just a game. A stupid game, that's all it is. How is he overlooking the well-being of his best friend over a goddamn match? Rishabh spits on the ground. From the touchline he can see the coach gesturing violently at him. He can make out the expletives framed by his lips. His eyes are popping so far out of his head that someone on the pitch could have tripped over them. St Mary's are attacking, and the coach is frantically trying to get Rishabh to track back.

'Fuck you!' he yells but jogs to pitch in. Luckily, between Dave and Dutta, they put out the attack. A few more strained minutes pass before the half comes to a close.

'Rishabh, what has happened to you? Bastard, look at me!' spat the coach the minute Rishabh was within earshot.

Rishabh turned a glum face towards him.

'Standing on tables, playing like a bloody fool. My six-year-old daughter could have taken a better corner. You don't want to play, you tell me. I'll take you off right now,' said the coach. He was screaming so loudly that a murder of crows flew out of a nearby tree.

Rishabh mumbled an apology. He darted his eyes upward, to the stands. Blood rushed to his ears. Reclining on the steps was a laughing Eklavya. Tamanna sat beside him. Rishabh was certain they had heard the coach. They were laughing at him. At his ineptitude. He felt embarrassed and angry.

If Rishabh is lackadaisical in the first half, he's positively catatonic in the second. If the statistics of the match are recorded accurately, then they will show that the goalposts are covering more distance than Rishabh. He ambles around aimlessly and ends up being more a spectator than a participant.

The coach goes blue in the face just yelling at him. Rishabh's behaviour is baffling and blasphemous. The Mongoose doesn't understand why he's shirking responsibility so openly. Eventually he's left with no choice. He tells Pinal Oza to get ready, and the next time the ball rolls out for a throw, he signals the referee for a substitution.

Rishabh is awoken by three sharp blasts of the whistle. He's surprised when he sees Oza bouncing on his toes by the touchline. *Who's being subbed?* wonders Rishabh.

'Get off the pitch, fast,' says the referee.

'Who?'

'You!'

It takes a moment for his protests to begin. He raises his hand, telling the coach he's fine where he is. The coach has an apoplectic fit. He goggles his eyes, and a stream of invective flows out of his mouth. The outburst is so venomous that it makes the referee blush.

'Just go,' says Puro quietly.

'But I don't need to be subbed,' whines Rishabh.

'It doesn't matter. Just go,' says Puro. The steeliness in his voice cuts through Rishabh.

He bows his head and trots to the touchline. Oza has a hand up for a high five, but Rishabh jogs right past him. Oza shrugs and runs in the opposite direction.

Rishabh glances up at the stands. The good news is that Tamanna isn't present to see his disgraceful exit. The bad news is that she is probably off canoodling with that filthy Eklavya. Rishabh drops down on a step, defeated.

'What's wrong with you, man?' inquires Sumit.

'SHUT UP!' screams Rishabh.

He startles the entire bench. Sumit tells him where he can shove his anger, and the coach gives him a cold look. It's meant to intimidate him, but Rishabh holds his dead gaze till commotion on the pitch makes the coach turn away.

Rahul eventually broke the deadlock with a clean header from Purohit's corner kick. Even the substitutes jumped up in jubilation. Rishabh, however, reacted as if he were watching a particularly tedious poetry recital. He blinked in rapid succession to show he had comprehended the situation but was unwilling to display any more emotion.

When they won the match and everyone charged the field to celebrate their first qualification for a football final, Rishabh hung back. He kicked about on the fringes, unable to generate the pride or happiness that the occasion demanded. He felt a lump in his throat as he realized that he was completely forgotten by all his mates. Nobody cared for the grumpy boy who refused to join the scrum. No one stopped to wonder, *Hey, where's Rishabh?* They were content and self-sufficient.

They don't need me around, thought Rishabh.

The coach congratulated the team privately after their vocal cords had been sapped from screaming and sloganeering. Chillingly, he didn't even look at Rishabh or acknowledge his behaviour. The ghostly insignificance of his presence wounded Rishabh more than a thousand words ever could.

'You have lots of time before your final match this evening,' said the coach. 'I will call you. Till then, save energy, have food, have water. Be mentally relaxed. It's one more game, men, just one more.'

In 5 A, Rishabh took off his studs, wrenched off his soggy jersey, slipped into a cool, dry pair of clothes, put his head down on a desk and slept. He felt like his teammates had abandoned him. He didn't want the coach glowering at him. Most of all, he didn't want to see Tamanna and her slimy old boyfriend. He was very much done with reality and so decided to slip into a self-induced coma for a couple of hours.

It was a dreamless slumber. When he awoke, he realized he had dribbled all over the bench. The dim classroom was empty. He didn't know how long he had been knocked out for, but he knew the day had progressed because the light outside had gone from dull grey to charcoal grey. The sleep had thankfully erased the sourness of the last match.

But bad luck wasn't done with Rishabh Bala just yet. It hung around the fifth standard corridor and took the form of the lumbering Dutta. Rishabh saw him immediately as he exited 5 A. One look at Dutta's mournful face made his peace ebb away.

'KKPS are in the final,' said Dutta. The words floated on a heavy sigh. 'They crushed DES in the semis. 5–0.' Dejected exclamations rose from Dave, Rahul, Floyd and Lokhande, who hung about the corridor too.

Rishabh balked. Dancing before his eyes was a vision of Tamanna clapping her hands in glee.

Dutta inhaled deeply and then delivered the sucker punch on a breathy, defeated sigh that was deeper than the first one: 'And I think Puro's dying.'

'What do you mean?' Rishabh was alarmed.

'He's in the infirmary,' explained Dutta.

Rishabh didn't hear the rest of what Dutta had to say because he'd shot off towards the infirmary, which was at the end of the fifth standard corridor. Rishabh raced down the passage, came to a skidding stop at the infirmary and entered it, panting.

He met the nurse in the examination room. She shrieked on seeing him. 'Get all that mud out of my room!' She shooed him away by violently fluttering her wrists.

'Ma'am, is Puro here?'

'Who is this Puro? Look how dirty you are, completely dripping with mud and dirt. Chee! I just get the room clean and you arrive with all this dirtiness. So filthy, so filthy!'

Just then, Dave, Floyd, Rahul and Lokhande burst on to the scene. The sight of one muddy footballer had been enough to cause the nurse's sensitive blood pressure to spike. The appearance of an entire gang of them was giving her heart palpitations. Again she shrieked in horror and this time retreated into her cabin, invoking the holy spirit of the Lord.

The boys marched to the sickbeds. The infirmary only had three, in one of which lay Puro wrapped up like a newborn baby. At the far end of the bed, like a tense father, sat Ghadge Sir. His hands were under the blanket, and were moving vigorously. At another moment, Rishabh would have burst out laughing at the suggestiveness of the spectacle, but then he grew grave.

'What the hell is going on?' demanded Rishabh.

'AIDS?' said Dave.

Ghadge Sir glowered at them. 'He's pheeling weak.'

'In only two games his stamina is over?' said Floyd.

'Fuck off!' growled Puro. Ghadge Sir's glower transferred to him. He must have done something unpleasant beneath the blanket too because Puro winced. 'Sorry, sir. I meant to say, "Get lost!" I'm just feeling really cold.' He shut his eyes and shook like a leaf.

In a long, rambling retelling, Ghadge Sir explained the situation. Purohit was suffering from hypothermia. Being drenched in sweat and a steady drizzle for the last five hours and playing two intense matches had left Puro a shivering wreck. That's when they noticed that Puro's skin had turned the colour of a cow's tongue. Rishabh asked the dreaded question.

'Will he be able to play?'

'What s-s-sort of q-q-question is that, b-b-bey?' said Puro between shivers.

Rishabh ignored his machismo and looked, instead, at Ghadge Sir.

'What you think I'm sitting here, rabbing his legs phor? I want him to but—'

'But can he?'

'I wheel not rishk this boy's health,' declared Ghadge Sir. 'He wheel play iph he gets better. That's all.'

Ghadge Sir rarely showed such firmness. Yet, when the moment demanded action, he transformed from a floundering dancing bear to a growling grizzly. His word, they realized, was final.

Rishabh could only wonder how cut up Puro was feeling. For him to succumb to illness before a final was perhaps the cruellest twist that fate could rustle up. He deserved to play in the final more than any of the others. Since the moment his father had first rolled a football towards him and he had bumped it across the room, Puro had developed a devotion to the game that the others couldn't even come close to. For most of the boys, the sport was a hobby. It was something they enjoyed doing even as they saw themselves eventually picking a branch of study, settling into a job and containing their love for football to weekend games on the television. Meanwhile, all Puro wanted to do was to keep himself on a pitch for as long as luck, livelihood and longevity would allow. When he closed his eyes and dreamed dreams of the future, he saw a vision of himself wearing a blue jersey, an armband encircling his bicep, and singing the national anthem in a full voice, joined by a stadium packed with passionate people. The thought drove him to wake up early, train with ferocity and cast aside any doubts about his talent or destiny. He had worked so hard to be a champion, it hurt Rishabh to think that he wasn't playing for the championship.

There was nothing they could do except stand around and dirty the nurse's infirmary even further. As they were leaving, Puro called out to Rishabh.

'Get my bag and kit, no,' he said. 'If I get better, I don't want to waste any time.'

Rishabh looked at Ghadge Sir, who mulled over it plaintively and then finally nodded his head.

'Getting it right away.'

By the time he dropped off Puro's belongings, news had spread about his hypothermia. Fearful conversations erupted in every corner of the dressing room.

'I knew it in the last match only,' said Vade. 'I played him a ball and he couldn't run to get it.'

'That pass was fuck all,' groaned Rana.

'No, no. He was struggling. I could see it on his face,' insisted Vade.

'Wish he was playing,' mumbled Bhupi.

'Arre, we'll be fine,' reassured Rahul.

'I know,' said Bhupi, but his face suggested he didn't.

An hour remained till kick-off—time enough for Puro to make a miraculous recovery, the team hoped. The minutes ticked by painfully slowly. Their bodies began recognizing the beating they had taken over the last two days. There was a dull ache in Rishabh's shins and a sharp one near his knee. They had burned through their energy and couldn't move without wincing and whining.

Then came the nervousness, which began permeating the room as the countdown came to a close. The boys started kitting up. The sense of occasion mounted as they slipped into their muddy jerseys. Tejas wiped the school emblem clean. Studs clattered against the marble floor. The smiles were replaced by pursed lips. Brows came together. Bhupi let out a series of quick breaths in an effort to calm down. But he continued to buzz like a wind-up toy entangled in a rug. Sumit sat upright in his seat. His eyes were shut, his fingers were entwined, his lips moved rapidly. The final had put the fear of God in Sumit, and he wasn't even going to play.

Finally, Rahul said, 'Last one.' He thumped his chest and held up a fist. 'Champions!'

Rishabh curled his fists in front of his face and growled the anxiety out. The trophy. Tamanna. Eklavya. There was a lot he was fighting for, but there was more he was fighting against.

Going into the warm-up, Rishabh had felt that it was impossible for his heart to break any further. But that was before he heard the coach announce the team: 'Rakshit, Bhupinder, Dutta, Saurabh Rana, Arnav Vade, Tejas, Abel, Lokhande, Pinal Oza, Paras, Rahul.'

'Sir, me?' asked Oza.

'Yes.'

The coach had dropped Rishabh for many reasons. The chief among them was his feeling that Rishabh's mind wasn't on football. In fact, Rishabh was paying such little attention that he'd wandered on to the pitch despite the coach not calling out his name. He only realized this when Rahul sheepishly told him to leave.

'Sir . . . am I not playing?' he blurted.

'No. Now, sit down,' said the coach.

The news was jarring to say the least. From getting ready to play the biggest match of your career (thus far) to being told you were to watch the said match from the bench was a steep drop, and Rishabh was flung down it without preparation. Yes, he had angered the coach in the last match, but he had been sure the coach would play his best players in the final. Pinal Oza was a good friend, but as a player, Rishabh knew he was slow, unimaginative and borderline non-competitive. He had never told anyone this, but he felt that the only reason Oza had even made the team was because he'd stuck around diligently, obeyed the coach's orders and didn't complain about sitting on the bench. *And that's why*, thought Rishabh bitterly, *he's now on the pitch.*

Rishabh opened and shut his mouth rapidly as many thoughts and many words flitted through his mind. But in the end, he chose not to aggravate the situation and angrily sat down next to Sumit at the foot of the giant steps. He tried to angle himself away from Tamanna and the girls, but there was no escaping their view. They knew he had been benched.

Dark thoughts occupied Rishabh as he sat on the concrete. The sight of the coach rooted to the spot with his arms crossed burnt him up. He wanted to push him. He wanted to lunge at him. Force him to put him on the field. Rishabh's mouth had gone dry. He couldn't swallow. And he didn't move.

The players took their positions. Sanghvi lost the toss. Eklavya elected to shoot towards the basketball court end. As he jogged back to his position, he waved at Tamanna. Preetha and Krupa burst into giggles. Then he looked straight at Rishabh and winked. It was a loaded, knowing wink, which, coupled with that cheeky, confident smile, humiliated Rishabh. He felt weak and powerless. His legs shook with impotent anger.

Floyd and Rahul stood in the centre circle, with the latter's foot on the ball. The whistle was blown.

'Go, Abby!' hollered Krupa. She clapped her hands.

Rahul rolled the ball out. Floyd passed to Tejas, who was immediately closed down. Tejas panicked and fumbled the ball back to Lokhande. The pass was poor; the ball moved slower than a case pending in the Indian judiciary and then it got stuck in the mud. A KKPS player promptly swooped in and retrieved it. Then they launched an assault on the Sanghvi defence that ended in Nagesh's shot going wide. From a Sanghvi perspective, the scariest aspect of that attack was the way Nagesh shrugged off Dutta. At six feet, Dutta was by no means a pushover, but Nagesh had pushed him aside like an empty grocery cart.

They were overrun. They missed the creative force and endless energy of Purohit. Lokhande was putting in an honest, noble effort, but his head spun in all directions as the KKPS players passed at dizzying speed. The Sanghvi boys appeared directionless. All their energy was concentrated on not conceding.

Before the match, Mehfouz Noorani had given them one of those inspiring talks that coaches give before big games. He had mentioned the usual give-it-your-all stuff. He had bolstered their confidence with a rousing speech that seemed contrived and unoriginal to Rishabh. He had said many things, but, as Rishabh acidly noted, none of them seemed to be working.

Bad tackles mushroomed all over the pitch. When Eklavya ploughed into Lokhande, it became apparent to everyone except the referee that this was not coincidence. Sanghvi's greatest weakness was their physicality. They were like a romp of otters: fast and dexterous but rather small. The KKPS boys were all much bigger, even discounting the fact that two of them were fully grown men. They bossed around and bullied their opponents. They routinely barged into the Sanghvi players, sending them caroming into the dirt. At one point, Nagesh rammed his elbow into Bhupi's jaw and then shrugged his shoulders and beat his fake angel wings. And Eka unleashed a sordid tackle on Floyd. The sound of the contact was so thunderous that it confused the clouds. It even drizzled for a short stint before they cleared up the mistake.

'Tell him not to attack my poor baby,' squealed Krupa in the stands.

'So mean of him, na,' said Tamanna.

'If anything happens to my Abby, you see what I do to your fellow!' threatened Krupa.

'You aren't even dating him,' reminded Preetha.

'So what? I don't want anything to happen to that handsome face,' said Krupa.

Rishabh wished he could temporarily lose hearing. It sickened him to hear these conversations from two rows behind him. He was disgusted by how callous Tamanna was being. It hadn't even crossed her mind that the boy she had just turned down was sitting immediately in front of her. Couldn't she have the sensitivity to take her traitorous support and her delusional friends a little further away from him? By the time the half came to a close, he wondered if she was doing it on purpose, to rub her rejection in his face—or rather, to be accurate, the back of his head. He wondered whether she was being cruel or ignorant.

Rishabh could read the story of the first half from the way the two teams were walking off the pitch. The KKPS boys walked huddled together, cracking jokes and guffawing amid mutual backslapping. The Sanghvi boys limped off the pitch. They cursed with every step. Their eyes never left the ground. When they spoke among themselves, it was with accusations and finger-pointing. Their only consolation was that the scores were still level: 0–0.

The coach didn't wait for them to catch their breath before spouting a torrent of criticism. For the first time, Rishabh heard a note of fear in the coach's gruff voice. Mehfouz Noorani had seen his team cut down to size, his plans fizzle out and loss nearly averted. It had been a good while since he had competed for anything more than possession of the remote control, but his instincts hadn't disappeared. That rabid obsession that had driven him as a player, that had kept him running even in the ninetieth minute of the most forlorn matches, that stubborn something that journalists had called the 'killer instinct' still glowed bright in him. And it roared now, fuelled by the prospect of another trophy slipping away from him.

'Fucking worst half I have seen you men play,' he bellowed. 'Not one shot on the goal. Haan, Rahul? You want me to remind you how to kick the ball?'

'No, sir,' said Rahul. He avoided eye contact.

'Bloody hell kind of game you all are playing. You want to give them the trophy, then do it now only. Don't waste everyone's time like this. Simple, basic things you are not getting right. Aye, where is that Oza?'

Oza raised his hand. He had been hidden behind Rana and Dutta. They parted, and he peeked through. His post-puberty moustache was caked in brown. He looked like a sneaky ferret to Rishabh.

'Not one bloody cross. What I told you before the game? You are playing like you are scared. Arre, don't be scared, yaar. Just play your natural game,' instructed the coach.

Rishabh wanted to tell him that Oza *was* playing his natural game. It was just that his natural game was rubbish. Nothing poor Oza could do about it. Seeing the coach rip into his replacement gave Rishabh the cold satisfaction of revenge. He felt vindicated. He knew this was the closest the coach would come to admitting a mistake. Of course Rishabh wanted his team to triumph . . . eventually. He just didn't want them winning it with ease without him. He wanted them to miss him like they missed Puro. He wanted them to sigh and say, 'If only Rishabh had played.'

The second half, too, was brutal on Sanghvi. They struggled to keep possession of the ball. They scrambled in defence and were impotent in attack. Rahul was stranded in the opponent's half like Robinson Crusoe, without communication or supply. He paced the turf more and more sullenly. He threaded intricate runs through defenders, only to be let down by a wayward pass. He began giving an earful to the culprits—particularly Tejas.

Fatigue and a few aggressive challenges had caused Tejas to lose his fizz.

The KKPS boys could sense it. Every time Tejas got the ball, they would charge at him in a pack. They tackled him on a whim. It was sad to watch. The referee never once thought it was unfair. Mehfouz Noorani began complaining about the partiality of the official. Rahul bemoaned the lack of fouls. They were both dismissed by a wave.

Then came a tackle that the referee could not ignore. Tejas received the ball and cut inside the midfield to avoid getting smashed into by his nemesis, the KKPS right back. Little did he know that worse challenges awaited him in the middle of the pitch. Tejas was driving in, looking for an option, when he overhit the ball. It trundled ahead, landing between him and Eklavya. Both of them charged at it, and Eklavya flew into a challenge. As a football tackle, it left a lot to be desired; but as a kung fu kick, it was a resounding success. It caught Tejas square in the chest. He let out a howl so hellish that even the coach turned away.

The referee ambled to the spot and fumbled around for a card. He brandished a yellow. He held it above Eklavya's head. Eklavya complained about the decision even as Tejas roiled in pain on the ground. The referee then inquired about Tejas's well-being. He was answered by a series of screeches that led him to believe that the boy could carry on no longer. He looked at Mehfouz and signalled for a substitute.

'Sumit, go help that boy,' said Mehfouz. Then he chewed on his moustache thoughtfully. Finally, he heaved a heavy sigh and said, 'Rishabh, get ready. I'm sending you in.'

Rishabh knew it. He had known it the minute Tejas had fallen. He didn't acknowledge the coach. He didn't nod, he didn't smile, he didn't say a word. He leapt up and began stretching. He felt powerful. His muscles strained and reared to go. He knew he was being watched, and he was ready to put on a show. He touched his toes, and when he straightened himself, electricity coursed through his body. Tejas had made it to the touchline, propped up by Sumit.

'Go to the right. Tell Pinal to go to the left wing. I want you to help in the defence. That Bhupinder needs help. Give crosses to Rahul. Their left centre back is weak. Attack from there. Understood?' said the coach.

Rishabh nodded. He knew all of this. He didn't want to listen to things any more. He had goals to score, scores to settle.

'And listen,' added Mehfouz Noorani, 'focus.'

Rishabh blinked. The referee called him on to the pitch. It was in the thirteenth minute that Rishabh Bala entered the final between Kamani Krida Public School and Shri Sunderlal Sanghvi School.

Usually when a player enters a match midway, it takes a few minutes for him to acclimatize to the pace of the match. It takes a while before his legs warm up to the running and he can read the patterns of the game. But within the first thirty seconds of his introduction, Rishabh's entry has a positive effect on Sanghvi's game. His first run brings the subs to their feet. Rishabh is running like an escaped convict. Like he's playing the last seven minutes of his life. Football may be a team sport, but in this moment, he will personally beat KKPS if he has to. His radiance on the wing causes major problems to

Kamani Krida. He makes two more threatening runs and pings the ball into the centre. They get headed out before Rahul can get to them. But Rahul applauds his attempts.

The momentum swings in Sanghvi's favour. They are emboldened upon seeing the KKPS players scramble to protect their goal. They can sense it: the fear, the opportunity. Eklavya realizes what's happening. He remonstrates with his left-winger and left back.

'Hold on to him!' he says within earshot of Rishabh. 'How can you let this slow *chut* get away?'

'Why don't *you* mark me, asshole?' Rishabh goads.

'You're saying something or what?' says Eklavya, walking towards Rishabh. He comes to a stop inches from Rishabh's face. He's taller and broader. Rishabh can see his big white teeth by way of his snarl. The KKPS goalkeeper is waiting to take the goal kick. Rishabh doesn't flinch.

'Mark me if you have the balls.'

Eklavya gestures for the keeper to wait. He tells the left-winger to switch positions. He gives the referee a thumbs up. The goalkeeper takes the kick. Eklavya jogs alongside Rishabh.

'You're going to get such a beating. I feel bad for you already. That too in front of Tanna,' he whispers.

Tanna. The word pains Rishabh. It angers him. It's too intimate for him to hear. He tries concentrating on the passage of play, but his senses are shutting down. Eklavya slams into him while running. It throws Rishabh off balance. He swerves back into position with a growl. He glances towards the stands. She's watching.

'Rish!' screams Floyd just then, before launching the ball down the wing. It lands ten metres ahead of them. Rishabh is off. Eklavya starts a fraction of a second later. Rishabh's legs are pumping furiously. He's leaping and stretching, trying to swallow as much ground as he can with each stride. He senses Eklavya gaining on him. He's fast. Rishabh's eyesight narrows on the ball. He can hear ragged breathing behind him. Closer and closer. He *needs* to get there first. An arm thrashes against his side. It slams into him, setting off a sharp pain. He sidesteps into Eka's lane and cuts him off. The ball's within reach if he skids in. Just a few yards more. Rishabh wants oxygen. Just a little more. Through sheer force of will, he strains through the last few strides and gets to the ball. First. He nudges it ahead, looks up. Paras is to his left. He cuts the ball back to him. His body loses all intensity in that instant. He's floating for a second, and then Eklavya slams into him. He stumbles miserably, flapping his arms to maintain his balance. He eventually comes to a stop.

The move has broken down. The ball is dispatched back towards the Sanghvi end. Rishabh shakes his head and starts pelting down the ground to help out the defence. Eklavya is level with him again.

'*Madarchod*, substitute,' spits Eklavya, 'you're not good enough for a full game.'

Rishabh's shoulders tense up. His mouth goes dry. He turns red in the face. Eklavya can sense the effect he is having. He's relishing it.

'So cute you are, yaar. You thought you had a chance? I'm a captain. You're not even on the team.'

Rishabh shuts his eyes tight. *Calm, stay calm. Focus. He's messing with you.*

'You heard me, no?' says Eklavya. He taps Rishabh on the shoulder. Rishabh slaps his hand away with the back of his palm.

'Watch it, watch it,' says Eklavya with a clinical malevolence that startles Rishabh.

'Don't fucking touch me,' he says.

The ball is pinging in the Sanghvi half. This time, Eklavya makes a sudden burst. Without warning, he takes off towards the centre of the pitch. He's screaming for the ball. *He's going to get it and shoot*, thinks Rishabh. He races in pursuit. He can see the orange jersey fluttering ahead of him. He can see every ripple. Eklavya's black studs are spitting mud. The rest of the ground is a blur. There is no sound. He's gaining on him. He can see the second KKPS striker laying off the ball. It's bobbling towards Eklavya. He's a yard away.

Without a second thought, Rishabh goes for a tackle. He propels himself through the air, cutting through the dense humidity. He braces for impact. His right knee strikes the ground first and then skids forward. His left boot flicks out, and he connects cleanly with the ball. Eklavya swings his foot and slices viciously through thin air. Rishabh slides ahead. The follow-through scrapes him till his buttocks, but he doesn't feel the burn. He's bested Eklavya again! He looks in Tamanna's direction and fist-pumps the air. She looks away.

'Come on!' he screams.

'You're fucked now. And don't you dare look at my girl again,' says Eklavya.

'Or what?'

'Face me like a man, na. Haan!'

'Rishabh, attack! Attack!' comes a voice from the touchline. It's an unexpected voice. It's Purohit's voice!

He's standing at the touchline, wrapped in the sickroom's blanket, which he's struggling to keep from scraping the floor. He looks like a little white ghost. Despite his hypothermia, he manages to find his voice and yell at Rishabh to return to the match. The subs are on their feet, swaying nervously. The sight of Puro has literally lifted the team.

Rishabh begins the long jog back to Kamani Krida's half. After so many lung-bursting runs, he can feel the stitch in his side. He gulps in air. He wonders how much time is left. *It can't be much.* He's got to keep running. He makes it past the halfway line. Eklavya is tailing him like his shadow, constantly yapping insults. It's like being tuned in to a radio station, whose RJ is not only annoying but also abusive. Then, after a raft of incoherent slander, Eklavya finally strings together a sentence that manages to hurt Rishabh.

'I'll kiss her again after I kiss the trophy,' says Eklavya in a treacly sweet voice.

It's the detonator that causes something to explode within Rishabh. He sees them locked in an embrace. He sees the adoration in her eyes, the twining of his arm around her waist. She shuts her eyes as she leans forward. The bliss written on her face is killing him. He wants them to part. But they lean closer, and their lips meet. His flesh is being torn off him. He's crumbling. It's cold and dark, and he has no energy left. No will to motion. The contents of his head are swirling and swilling. The blackness is complete. He's swallowed whole. And then, in a zap, his eyes fly open.

He's on the pitch. The lofted ball is misplaced. It's falling to Lokhande. Floyd screams, 'On you!' Lokhande panics and doesn't wait to control the ball. He side-foots a volley in Rishabh's direction. The ball doesn't slow down. It's bounding towards him. Rishabh instinctively runs to meet it halfway. He's just trapped the ball, when Eklavya, unwilling to lose another battle, charges into him with cruel intent.

He leaps with his knee raised and smashes into the small of Rishabh's back. The force curves Rishabh into the shape of the letter C before he is ground into the mud with Eklavya landing on top of him. Dirt enters his mouth. His spectacles dig into the bridge of his nose. His back burns from the impact. But he doesn't register any of these sensations, because his mind is filled with spikes. His mouth is full of barbed wire. He pulls back his lips and, before he can stop himself, lashes out with his right foot, spinning it backward like a scorpion's sting. His heel misses Eklavya but, on its return, the stud grazes his face.

Now, Eklavya, the beacon of toughness and manliness, feels the prick of the boot and falls to the ground dramatically. He clutches at his face and rolls around like he's been shot. He's screaming like a woman giving birth. Rishabh is seething. He struggles to his feet. The KKPS players have swarmed around the referee, buzzing for him to show a card. Rahul rushes forward and elbows Nagesh away from the referee. The referee glares at Rahul. Floyd is cordoning the referee off from the malicious hounding of the KKPS players.

Rishabh stands over the thrashing Eklavya. He's disgusted by his cowardice. 'Get up, motherfucker.' He grabs his arm and tries to yank him up.

'Back off!' yells the referee. He tumbles to the spot, flicking his index finger in Rishabh's face. 'Don't touch the boy.'

Rishabh takes a few steps back. He rests his hands on his hips. The darkness is subsiding. He's feeling light-headed now. He watches serenely as the referee checks on Eklavya. Tamanna has her cheeks cupped in her hands.

'You, boy, number 7,' calls the referee, snapping his fingers, 'come forward.'

Rishabh ambles towards the referee. He sees the floodlight bouncing off his sweaty bald head. The wispy remnants of his hair perfectly outline his scalp. The swarthy referee plods two steps forward. He takes out the cards from his back pocket. He consults them. Then he picks a card and brandishes it in the air. Rishabh follows his pudgy arm, carpeted with matted curly hair, all the way to his Jenga-block fingers. Clutched in them is a card that's burning red.

Rishabh immediately spins away. His heart drops from his chest to his ball sack with a piercing pain. His mouth twists in despondency. 'No, ref!' he turns and says. 'I didn't do anything!'

'Move,' commands the referee.

'You're making a mistake. HE fouled ME!'

'Get out!' screams the referee.

'You're fucking blind!'

The referee takes two menacing steps forward. His eyes are straining in his sockets. He's biting his lower lip fiercely.

Floyd wraps a hand around Rishabh and shoves him back. 'Go, just go. We'll take care of this,' he says.

Rishabh begins walking off in a daze. He can hear Rahul's loud protests. They come to an abrupt stop when the referee pushes a yellow card in his face. Rishabh staggers across the pitch. It's the longest, quietest walk of his life.

'Sit down,' said the coach before he could speak. He jerked a thumb towards the bench. Rishabh stumbled to it. All eyes were on him. They averted, embarrassed, when he looked at them. Further up the hushed stand, three places were empty. The girls were gone. He swallowed, shook his head and sat down some distance away from the subs.

A hand fell on his shoulder.

'Why did you do it? What was the need?' interrogated Puro. He had cast aside the blanket and now sat down beside him.

'I don't know . . . It just happened . . . I'm sorry.'

'Don't say that. Forget it. I don't think it'll make a difference. There's only two minutes left, bey. They'll hold on.'

Rishabh dropped his head into his hands. He couldn't watch the match. The shame was overwhelming. He stared at a blade of grass that swayed gently as the wind whipped across the ground. He didn't see Rahul dropping out of an attack and into the midfield as Sanghvi reconciled with getting to the penalty shoot-outs. He didn't see the ferocity of KKPS's assault as they gunned for a winner against a depleted side. He didn't hear Mehfouz frantically trying to orchestrate the shape of the squad from the sideline. He didn't hear the referee's whistle ending the game. All he saw and felt and knew was the fatal flourish of that flaming card.

The team, panting and drained, ringed around the coach. He picked the players who'd take the penalty kicks. Rahul and Floyd were the only ones who stepped forward to select their spots. The rest hung back and nervously accepted their position when the coach declared it. Rishabh stayed far away, just in case his bad luck was contagious.

'Shoot-out's starting,' said Puro eventually.

The kicks were to be taken at the bus stop end, the side that was further from where the substitutes sat. So the coach and the subs had coagulated together on the touchline, craning to catch the action and praying for victory.

KKPS won the toss and elected to kick first. Eklavya walked up with the ball. It was agonizing to watch his tormentor coolly place the ball on the spot and then perfectly dispatch it into the top-left corner. Dave didn't stand a chance. But Rahul quickly made the scores level with a finish that sneaked past the keeper's left glove.

Nagesh confidently fired the ball into the goal, and then Floyd made the long walk to the penalty spot. He took a deep breath. His shoulders settled when he exhaled. But he blasted the shot over the bar. It was hit so powerfully and went so high that it's a miracle it didn't damage a satellite before making its way back down.

The Kamani Krida keeper roared. Their players hollered. Mehfouz's jaw worked angrily.

'It's okay, Floyd, no problem,' screamed Sumit.

The next two kicks were successes for both sides. The keeper dived in the wrong direction for Paras's attempt and Bhupinder's effort trickled in despite him almost tumbling over in the run-up. Puro jumped and screamed with vicarious triumph after every kick.

For their last kick, KKPS sent their keeper. He had a vile smirk on his face, his chest was puffed out and his chin all but pointed at the Pole Star. He stood with his hands on his hips and took a few seconds to start after the referee's whistle. He took a caricaturally long run-up, almost the length of a fast bowler, as he charged down the ground and poked the ball with his toe. It was hit hard, fast and directly at Dave's face. In part to fulfil his duty as keeper, though mostly to prevent his face from becoming a chapatti, Dave jerked his hands up, and the ball bounced off them and out of harm's way.

The Sanghvi team launched themselves from the ground like fountains. They were back in the game! Puro clasped Rishabh in a side hug. Rishabh fist-pumped the air. The excitement had overpowered his shame. He selfishly wanted them to win so that his sins would be forgiven, or at least forgotten, in the celebration. It was all in Dutta's hands. Or, to be more accurate, in his right foot. If he scored, it would go to sudden death. If he missed, it would be sudden death.

It was a lot of pressure for the bovine ninth-grader. His face was frozen in an odd expression. His left eyebrow stooped so low that it was almost a moustache, and his right eyebrow arched so high that it joined his hairline. It was what happened when both fear and determination contested for the soul.

'Come on, Dutta!' screamed Tejas.

Puro whacked him on the arm. 'Don't distract him.'

The moment finally arrived. Dutta strode forward in his loping run and side-footed the ball. It went to the left but not too much, it rose above the ground but not too much and it troubled the keeper but not too much. He parried it away with a conquering cry. Sanghvi had been defeated. The KKPS players burst out of their line in the middle of the ground and mobbed the keeper. They danced and whooped and took off their shirts and celebrated bare-chested.

On the pitch, the Sanghvi players collapsed where they stood. Bhupinder was flat on his back in the mud. Dave sat near the edge of the D with his knees wrapped in his arms. Dutta was clutching a post and sobbing. Rahul stared at the ground. Floyd was openly weeping. Puro made his way to his teammates and started helping them to their feet.

'Stop crying like widows. Stop it! Dutta, you're chipping the paint off the post,' he said.

Mehfouz didn't say a word. He was more angry than sad. He went over to the Kamani Krida coach and shook his hand. He applauded their players, who were now writhing around like dance bar patrons after their fourth drink. It was a celebration so ostentatious that the Sanghvi boys felt it was clearly being done for them to look at and feel bad.

But the ordeal wasn't over yet. As further punishment, they were made to wait for the prize distribution ceremony. Ghadge Sir handed KKPS the trophy to an even more animated, cringe-inducing round of revelry. Rahul had been shaping a ball of mud in his palms; Dave urged him to hurl it. At the conclusion of the ceremony, Rahul smashed it on the ground with vehemence.

'I want to see you all in the dressing room before you leave,' said the coach when the indignities were over.

They trudged across the brightly lit ground, recalling the glint of the trophy and the happy faces reflected in it. More painful than defeat were the mundane details of your life that persisted even after you'd lost. There were studs to clean, bags to pack and rickshaws to be hailed. To do these tasks normally was a chore, to do them as a loser was even more excruciating. They were reminders of your loss and the fact that the day was not done. They seemed endless because of how much you wanted to disappear and forget.

The coach arrived when they had nearly finished their laboured packing. He briskly reached the centre of the room and paced around while they stopped fidgeting. When he had their attention, he began softly, 'Team, good game. I mean it. I don't care about outcome. I care about effort. You gave a hundred per cent on that pitch. Don't let this result hurt you. Sometimes things don't work out. It is a part of life. Handle defeat like men because you played like men. Yes, there were moments of immaturity, but mistakes happen. Rest of you showed character—'

Rishabh blurted out, 'Sir, what mistake? You know I didn't deserve it!' He'd intended it to sound like a statement but it came out as an accusation.

'Did I say anything to you?' said the coach.

'Then why did you look at me while saying it? You don't even know what happened because you won't fucking talk to me for one fucking second. You can shove all these grand words up—' Rishabh didn't realize how loudly he had been screaming until the silence rushed back in when he stopped.

A chilly silence filled the room. It was biting enough to make Puro wish for his discarded blanket again. The coach looked straight at Rishabh with dead eyes. There was not a single emotion in them; just cold, cold indifference. Everyone knew that a line had been crossed. In all his years as a professional, Mehfouz Noorani had never been spoken to with such disrespect. The tone, the content, the face of the person saying it—all of it stung Mehfouz. He hadn't become a coach to be cursed at by a boy, especially not one who had let his team down when they'd needed him the most.

The coach's face twitched. It was the angriest anyone had ever seen him. His eyes looked past Rishabh's right ear. His moustache quivered with indignation. Seeing him so furious, Rishabh's shame and guilt resurfaced like a foul-tasting burp.

'I'm sorry, sir. It won't happen again,' he said curtly.

Almost at once the coach cut in, 'I know it won't. You'll need to play another match to get another card, no?'

What a terrible thing for a boy to hear.

SECOND HALF

October 2006

THE MONSOONS HAD moved southward, just as Pinto Miss had taught the class they would. Yet there hung a dense mustiness in the air. It was as if the clouds had departed but left the humidity behind. The change was welcome, though. On the first morning of clear sunshine, Mrs Bala wrung her hands heavenward and shrieked, 'FINALLY! The clothes will dry!'

Rishabh didn't share her enthusiasm as he sat in class one October morning, observing the bustle before the day began. Ratiksh Palkar's massive head was blocking the light from streaming in through the large windows. It cast a cool shadow across Rishabh's desk, who marvelled at the largeness of Ratiksh's head. It was at least the size of a melon. Ratiksh was smiling—he was always smiling in a dull, amused way. He wiped snot from his nose with the back of a meaty palm. Interestingly, Ratiksh's nose was always leaking. *That's what must make his head so big*, thought Rishabh. *It's filled to bursting point with snot.*

Elsewhere in the class, Swara Gokhale and Viti Goel chatted animatedly. They were talking about the results. The tenth standard was due to receive their first-term papers later that day. While the scholars were excited and the backbenchers were bracing for impact, the majority of the students would agree with Swara when she said to Viti, 'I just want it to get over as fast as possible.' She let out a tired sigh. As the years would pass by, Swara would use that trademark line and that patent sigh for her wedding ceremony, the birth of her children as well as the approach of her retirement as bank teller at the Naupada branch of Dhanlaxmi Bank. What she didn't realize was that every time she made that wish, things never got over as fast as possible. In fact, they always went even slower. The third day of October 2006 was no exception. It was going to be a long, long day for all of them.

It began when Puro bounced into class. His hair was wet, and dirt caked his forehead. He looked flushed but was inwardly glowing. As had been the ritual the whole week, Puro entered the class with a wide, lingering smile that vanished abruptly when he saw Rishabh's gloomy face. Then Puro would mournfully set his bag down to the right of his desk and his football kit on the left. This morning, he did just that but also proceeded to dolefully shake his head.

'Training sucks, yaar,' he said without conviction.

'Puro . . .' said Rishabh.

'No, really. Mehfouz doesn't know what he's doing. Anything he makes us do,' continued Puro. He added another rueful bob of the head to the act.

'Really, you don't have to.'

'Plus it's not the same without you. That Oza is fine, but the fun is missing,' said Puro, this time with more sincerity.

'Puro, stop!' snapped Rishabh, 'It's all right. This is between me and Mehfouz. You don't have to hate football for it.'

Puro remained silent. Relief was rippling across his face. Then he looked at Rishabh sharply. 'But we do miss you, man. At least I do. You should come back.'

Rishabh laughed a hollow one. The reason he scoffed was because they both knew where things stood between Rishabh and the coach. To put it into perspective, India had a greater chance of winning the World Cup than Rishabh had of getting back into the Sanghvi football team.

Training had resumed the previous week, after a break of what felt like the longest fortnight in the boys' lives. For two agonizing weeks the team had lived with the bitter aftertaste of the final. For fourteen straight days they had haunted the school with their heads bowed, failure flickering in their eyes. It had seemed odd when Puro went a whole week without getting hauled to the coordinator's office. By the second week, it had become worrying. Kaul Miss had taken him aside and asked him if everything was all right.

'Purohit,' she had said, 'why aren't you interrupting any classes?'

'We lost, miss. It's over . . . and I couldn't do anything . . .' a glassy-eyed Puro had responded.

His reply had set alarm bells ringing in the staffroom. The teachers resolved to send all the boys on the team to the school counsellor. The day they'd decided this, the boys miraculously recovered. This had coincided with Ghadge Sir's simple declaration: 'Boys, coaching is phrom Monday morning, 6 a.m.' Later that day, as Kaul Miss signed a remark in Puro's calendar again, she realized how much she had missed doing it.

There had been no closure for Rishabh Bala. He hadn't met the coach since the final with KKPS. He hadn't spoken to Tamanna either. They had briefly ghosted past each other during a lunch break, and he had once spotted her online on Yahoo Messenger. He had even opened her chat window and typed a number of messages, each one more swiftly backspaced than the previous. The confusion had swirled from his head to his stomach.

He couldn't really remember the days immediately following the final. It was as if the tumult of that day had forced his brain to take a vacation, as if it were saying, 'I can't do this any more. Hey, Stomach, why don't you take over for a while?' And so Rishabh had vacuously drifted through the days, preoccupying himself with stuffing his face. He had constantly been shovelling food into his mouth—the oilier the better, and the sugary the best. Coupled with seven–eight hours of TV-watching, Rishabh's consumption patterns had managed to block the ebb and flow of all his feelings. He had been numb. The food had been giving him a semblance of emotion (it was mostly just energy and quite possibly gas), while the television subbed in for thought.

But despite his best efforts, the sadness had crept in. When he would shut his eyes, in that oppressive darkness before sleep, the card would flare into vision without warning: bright, red, searing. It would burn into his brain. He would flail helplessly.

Mrs Bala wondered why the sheets were in such a tangle each morning, then remembered her son's hormone-riddled age and regretted wondering about the sheets.

Rishabh's crust of daytime indifference had finally cracked when he'd heard that coaching was resuming. For the first time in days he'd felt excited. He'd realized again that the world had colour. He'd hummed songs in class, much to the annoyance of Barkha. But as he'd been packing his kitbag the night before training, the dread had returned. He'd recalled the coach's glowering face, his stony eyes, his shrivelled mouth. *I'll have to say sorry*, Rishabh had thought. His own disappointment had been so great that he had forgotten about the disappointments of others. They had swum to the fore now as he'd zipped up his bag and perched on the windowsill.

His teammates had forgiven him, he knew. They had looked him in the eyes, clapped his back, squeezed his shoulder, ruffled his hair and had variously said, 'Forget it', 'We understand' and 'Next time you get a card, make sure you do more damage'. The coach's mind, however, had remained beyond prediction. None of the boys the coach had let go of had ever returned to the fold. He wasn't the benevolent sort; less forgive and forget and more retaliate and remember.

Rishabh hopped off the windowsill. *Well, I'll find out tomorrow*, he had said to himself as he'd headed to bed.

The coach had been reading a newspaper in the shed next to the ground. Rishabh and Puro were the first to arrive. The coach had looked at them over his reading glasses. If he had been happy to see them, he did not show it. Rishabh's stomach did a somersault. Beside him, Puro cried out, 'Sir!'

The coach nodded.

'How are you, sir?' asked Puro, shaking the coach's hand.

'First class,' said Mehfouz.

'Good morning, sir,' said Rishabh tentatively.

'Morning,' croaked the coach. The morning chill clung to his voice. In fact, it was so icy that Rishabh felt he needed to wear a sweater just to hear it.

They had waited for the others to trickle in. Puro had been happily chatting with the coach, his innocence making for easy conversation. Soon more boys wandered in. Rishabh had been surprised to see the junior team had also been called. They bobbed in, chattering, energetic and excitable. Every boy had been greeted with a warmth and cheer that the coach was withholding from him. Rishabh suddenly felt distant from the merry group. He couldn't join the boisterous banter. He dragged his bag a little away from the assembly and laced up his boots in silence.

The coach told them to gather around him once they were on the ground. His jaw worked like a piston, his floppy hair wafted on the wind and his eyes bore into his team.

'I know you didn't want it, but players need to take breaks. It was a difficult tournament, but you know what I'm happy about? You all gave full effort. Maximum. Whatever happened in the final, happened . . .' The coach's icy stare glided over Rishabh, who dropped his eyes to his studs. 'But from our side, we did our best and that is what matters. Trophies matter a little more, but it's okay. You did well.

'Now, remember, you have to practise so we are the champions next time. Understand? We cannot come second again and again. Otherwise life will just go past you.

Understand? You will think, "Arre, there is a lot of time!" and then one day your time will be up. Whistle is blown. Game is over. Understand?'

The boys hadn't really understood, but the coach took their perplexed faces to mean yeses and continued. 'Good. From now on, the junior team will also train in the morning.' He looked at Joy Chakraborty, the speedy junior captain, and said, 'I want you players to observe your seniors. Watch what they are doing. Learn. And senior team, you have to help the juniors. Now, start warming up. Purohit, lead the senior team on that side.' He pointed towards the bus stop end.

Rishabh had been peeling away with the rest of the seniors, when the coach had called out, 'Aye, Rishabh! You are not there. You will be with the junior team.'

Everyone had stopped. A flurry of emotions had flitted across Rishabh's face: confusion, surprise, incredulity, shock, worry, grovelling and, finally, humiliation.

'But . . .'

'Don't waste time. Go with the juniors.'

Veer Chanchalani, a sixth standard pipsqueak, sniggered at the suggestion.

'Why, sir?'

'You don't know why? You want me to say in front of everyone?'

'If you don't want me on the team . . . I'll leave . . .'

The coach didn't answer immediately. His eyes smouldered under their hoods. He uncrossed his arms across his chest and placed them on his hips. Rishabh thought, *How much drama this old man does!*

'I want you to train with the juniors. If you don't want to, then you can leave.'

The coach had come straight to the point. Rishabh's bluff had been called. The power had never vested in him, and the coach had uncloaked this fundamental flaw in Rishabh's assessment. It was time for plan B: outright begging.

'Sir, I'm sorry! I just really want to play, and I promise I will make up for my mistakes if you take me back in the team.'

'I don't trust you in my team. When I trust you, you will play in my team.'

There was a collective sharp intake of breath from the players. If this were a soap opera, the camera would have cut to their faces: a shocked Rahul, a disagreeing Puro, a smirking Chanchalani. The coach's statement had hurt Rishabh. He had never prided himself on being the best player on the pitch, but he sure did count himself among the most reliable players. He had never skimped on effort, had always followed orders, he had never even been late to a single training session. His dedication to the game had never been in question, until this moment. It was like Gandhiji being told, 'You'll be back in the movement once you prove your love for the nation.'

'Sir, please, I'm really sorry . . .' Rishabh had sputtered with downcast eyes.

'*Sorry?* For what? You don't know only what you did wrong. That is the main problem. When you realize it, then I will accept your sorry. Okay, everybody, debate is over. Chalo, start moving. Come on, come on.'

The senior team had started moving and buzzing like a beehive as the junior team had bobbed away in the opposite direction. The coach had headed to the shed to get rid of his windcheater. Rishabh had stood alone in the middle of the ground. He'd seen the sympathetic glances from his teammates, and it had enraged him. He'd wanted to punch Rana for thinking he needed pity. He'd felt alone, helpless and embarrassed. He'd cursed under his breath and jogged over to train with the juniors.

Rishabh felt ridiculous towering over them as they stretched. They twittered around him. He knew what they were talking about but it seemed different. It was like listening to a language he understood but in a dialect he didn't. He was only four years older than the youngest kid on the team, but in school years they had a gap of a couple of generations. He was most conscious of his age when they spoke about football. The rug rats only spoke about three teams: Arsenal, Chelsea and Manchester United. They never spoke of technique or skill but only about wins and losses. Rishabh was listening to Shubham Chettiyar—a short boy with terrible posture and an annoying habit of stopping his sentences exactly at moments of the highest suspense—talk about the last Chelsea game.

'You should have seen how Drogba scored. Lampard got the ball and . . .' Shubham blinked and swallowed while everyone waited expectantly. 'Gave a long pass to him and he . . .' Rishabh clenched his fist. 'Took it on his chest like this . . .' Here Shubham broke the line to demonstrate. He leaned back awkwardly, almost falling over in his recreation. Then he scrunched up his face, received an imaginary ball on his chest and kicked some air into an imaginary goal. Then he wheeled away to celebrate the goal he had scored in his head, doing his best Drogba impression. Rishabh shook his head. What an insult it was to Drogba to have Shubham imitate him.

'But Chelsea are so boring,' offered Rishabh.

All heads turned to him. He hadn't said a word for the longest time, and they had all concluded that he was an uppity senior who thought it beneath him to mingle with them. They ogled at him now, not knowing what to make of his comment. Finally, a tubby boy spoke up. 'No, they are not.'

'They only win matches 1–0,' said Rishabh sagely.

'So what? At least they win matches,' retorted Chanchalani.

Rishabh hadn't known he was capable of hating someone as quickly as he'd begun hating Chanchalani. Everything about him—from his cheeky little face, with his hair combed in a Hitler-style side-parting, to his whiny, high-pitched voice that fluted annoying half-formed opinions—made Rishabh want to lay him down with a swift uppercut. But that day he'd managed to keep control of his right arm, instead choosing to expose the imp's ignorance.

'What about winning with style? Playing with flair? Look at Arsenal. They were unbeaten for a whole season, and they played beautiful football.' Rishabh thought he had eviscerated Chanchalani, but he'd thought wrong.

'You're an ASS-nal fan! Ha ha! And they lost to Chelsea! Stupid, loser ASS-nal!'

The whole bunch of them exploded with laughter. Anger rose from Rishabh's stomach like an acidic belch. He wanted to smash Chanchalani's teeth into his oval face. Their mean-spirited cackling made up his mind for him. How dare these kids bully him? How dare they not respect him for the senior player that he was? He could outrun, outscore and outwit each of these runts without breaking a sweat. And yet they disregarded him to the point of laughing in his face. How low had he fallen?

I'm done with this stupidity. I don't deserve to train with these monkeys, he thought. Then he strode over to Chanchalani, lifted him by the front of his shirt and tossed him in a heap on the ground. The laughter stopped abruptly.

'Okay, okay, don't fight,' said Joy Chakraborty nervously.

'I'm a Madrid fan, just so you know,' spat Rishabh in Chanchalani's ears, who was now on the verge of tears.

The coach had been putting the senior team through a drill and hadn't seen the unfair altercation. All he had seen was Chanchalani being hoisted up by his teammates and Rishabh stalking across the ground towards the shed. He hadn't seen Rishabh at training after that day.

All of this had happened a week before they were to get their papers. Rishabh's exit had made things mighty awkward for Puro. He liked his friend well enough and wanted to show solidarity, but he liked football a little better. He was so glad that they had finally cleared the air. He didn't need another thing to worry about on the day they were getting their exam papers.

Soon they found out that they were due to get all the papers at once in the lecture right after the lunch break. The news caused anxiety even in the most confident of nerds. For Puro, it was terrifying. He felt like a goat being told when Eid would be celebrated.

'How many of your ships are sinking?' whispered Puro.

'What?' asked Rishabh.

'Arre, how many of your eggs are cracked?'

'I have no idea what you are saying.'

'How many *baingan*s in your bharta, dude?'

Rishabh whirled around. 'What the fuck do you want?'

Rishabh had picked the worst possible moment to vent his frustration. It was the exact moment when Ramnarayanan Sir had stopped droning on about integers and had turned to the board to demonstrate something remarkably dull, causing a vacuous hush to fall upon the classroom. It was that fragile silence that Rishabh's irritable voice had pierced.

All eyes turned to him. 'Fuck,' hissed Rishabh. It was a whisper but was heard even clearer than the previous interjection.

Mr Ramnarayanan gaped at Rishabh. The three lines of sandalwood paste on his forehead turned into exclamation marks.

'Rishabh, what is this behaviour?' demanded the portly maths teacher at long last.

'Sorry, sir,' mumbled Rishabh.

'I did not hear that. Please say it louder than your abuses,' said Ramnarayanan Sir.

'Sorry, sir!' yelled Rishabh.

'May we all know what made you use such beautiful, dare I say, poetic language?' interrogated Ramnarayanan Sir with smug sarcasm.

Rishabh heard some of the boys sniggering at the back of the class. 'Nothing, sir. I was talking to Purohit—I mean Abhay.'

'Talking to Abhay Purohit,' repeated Ramnarayanan Sir, drawing himself up to his full height. 'Once you see your paper, no, you will stop talking only.'

Rishabh's heart rate picked up. His palms turned sweaty. He had been most worried about his maths result, and the relish in Ramnarayanan's voice sounded ominous.

'And, Abhay, I feel bad for you, haan. I wish I could give you marks for talking in class. At least then you would get something.'

With that, Ramnarayanan Sir turned to face the board with a chuckle and continued his calculations.

'Arre, I was asking how many papers you're failing,' whispered Puro.

Rishabh turned around and glowered at Puro, who bit his tongue in regret.

'Never mind,' said Puro. He shook his head and returned to finishing his masterpiece: a doodle of Pamela Anderson.

The lunch break in the tenth standard corridor was a sombre affair. The anxious chattering of teeth replaced the usual scampering of feet. When the bell rang, the standard collectively gasped. The hour of reckoning had arrived. They dived into their classrooms and cowered at their desks. Time slowed to a crawl as they waited.

Then they heard the footsteps. The teachers made their way through the corridor like a death squad. Their slippers slapped against the floor ominously as they stalked towards them with bundles of papers in their arms. They entered their classrooms. *Thud-thud-thud-thud-thud* went the papers in synchrony as the teachers dropped them on the desk.

Kaul Miss leaned over with a mischievous smile spread across her face. 'Come roll–number–wise and take your papers. If you want to cry, go to the toilet. I want no noise in this classroom.'

Aabhas Acharekar was the first to the slaughter. All eyes were trained on his oblong face. He picked up his eight papers, his expression changing from hopeful to astonished to dismayed to horrified before finally settling on resignation. As he made his way back to his seat, the rows on either side whispered, 'How much did you get?' He swatted the inquiries aside with irritation.

'ABHAY! Come fast!' yelled Kaul Miss.

'All the best!' called Rishabh as Purohit shot past him.

Purohit's shoulders drooped as he reached the teacher's desk. He scooped up his papers in a hurry. When he turned around, he widened his eyes and pulled back his lips in mock horror. The class laughed on cue. Rishabh knew he was doing his best to make light of the situation, but the results sure had rattled him too.

'All my buffaloes are in the water,' admitted Puro.

Rishabh glanced at the open chemistry paper on Puro's desk. It was a bloodbath. The entire script was marked in red. Pillai Miss had written more in the answer sheet than Puro had.

'This is not good,' muttered Puro, shuffling through the papers and assessing his marks. He hadn't passed a single subject. His father's face swam in front of his eyes, and he let out a low moan.

Rishabh now waited for his turn, tapping his foot violently. At this point, simply passing all his papers would be an achievement. His stomach flip-flopped like a fish pulled out of water. Finally, Kaul Miss called out his name.

He took a deep breath and stood up as Purohit patted him on the back. He strode forward, right foot first. It was silly of him to be superstitious, but he sincerely believed that his actions could still influence the results. That the marks were in a state of flux until his eyes fell on them.

'You must work harder, Rishabh,' said Kaul Miss in a low voice. He looked at her sharply. She pursed her lips and shook her head. 'I expected more from you.' With shaky hands, he snatched his eight papers and bolted.

It was a disaster. He hadn't failed, but he had done the next best thing: he had passed maths, physics and chemistry on grace marks. His English marks were the biggest surprise. His confidence in the subject was not reflected in the 61 marks he scored in it. But it was the snide remark at the end that enraged him:

Keep answers brief. Use fewer big words.

'Bloody Bobde!' spat Rishabh. He couldn't believe an English teacher was asking a student to use less English. Then he noticed the second remark:

-5 for poor handwriting

Ironically, this was written in handwriting so atrocious that it could only be justified if Bobde had written it with her left hand in the middle of an earthquake while suffering a stroke.

'She hates me,' whispered Rishabh. 'Bitch.'

'Rishabh!' Barkha exclaimed and immediately slapped him on the arm.

'Ow! Sorry,' said Rishabh, massaging the stinging spot. 'How many subjects did you top?' He sounded bitter.

'I don't want to talk about it,' said Barkha.

Rishabh leaned over and snatched the papers from her desk.

'RISHABH! Give them back!' shouted Barkha, clawing at him. Her reaching fingers pattered against his arm.

'Holy moly! 89, 92, 90—you got a bloody 90 in bio?' exclaimed Rishabh.

'It's soooo bad!' moaned Barkha.

'I don't know what your definition of bad is, Barkha.' He handed the papers back to her.

'How are yours?' she asked, mostly out of courtesy, and she regretted asking almost immediately. To her relief, Rishabh brushed it aside with a smile.

'Superb!' said Rishabh. 'My father always wanted me to get 37 in maths. And this 42 in physics was my mother's dream.'

Barkha laughed. It wasn't one of those giggly, girly laughs. It was the full-throated barking of unselfconscious glee. It was probably the way the light fell on her, but for the first time Rishabh noticed how pearly white and perfectly enamelled Barkha's teeth were. *Look at those two in the front,* he mused, *they're like pearls in an oyster.* Not that he thought her face was an oyster. On the contrary, he found it rather appealing. Her clear, pimple-free skin (a rarity in their classroom) and neat bob caused his pupils to dilate. He was surprised he hadn't noticed these things ever before.

Suddenly the below-average marks didn't seem so bad any more, and he felt the need to sit up straight for the remainder of the periods. Occasionally he sneaked a sidelong glance in the direction of his neighbour and saw her radiant face trained on the teacher. He was impressed by her focus. He would never be able to pay attention in class for that long. His personal best was nine minutes, that too because it was Avantika Miss teaching the reproductive system.

Rishabh wondered what it would be like to have Barkha pay attention to him. Then he wondered why he wondered that. But, he had to admit, the thought did seem wonderful.

The school day ended when the bell rang, but not Rishabh Bala's bad day.

He sat in the bus, heading home and looking out of the window with unseeing eyes. Thoughts gathered in his head like angry storm clouds. He was thinking furiously about how best to break the bad news to his parents. When one got 46 per cent in their exams, the utmost tact was necessary in dealing with the mom and pop. He toggled through all the simulations: telling them outright, lying about his results, running away for good and starting a new life in a new city. But no matter which option he chose, the outcome always seemed bleak.

He got off the bus and had almost decided on suicide, when he remembered something. His aunt and grandmother were dropping by in two days' time. Rishabh realized he could just withhold the results till the day his relatives arrived. His parents surely wouldn't unload on him in front of an audience. Besides, if things did get ugly, he could count on his aunt and granny to be in his corner; it would be better than facing the music alone. It seemed like an appealing option and, at any rate, kept him from chugging a bottle of phenyl.

The next two days were tough nonetheless. Firstly, at home he had to pretend as if everything were normal. He put in his usual shift on the sofa, wasted the adequate amount of time watching TV and refused to eat the vegetables his mother plonked on the dinner table. He felt guilty, but it was the only way to not arouse any suspicions.

Secondly, on the day after they got their results, a rumour began snaking through the corridor: Tamanna had scored 100 in biology. She was the only person to get a hundred in any subject in the entire batch. During the short break, kids Rishabh didn't even speak to were walking up to him to congratulate him. Grins and thumbs ups were flashed at him as if *he* had managed to get full marks. While Rishabh was relieved that nobody knew about his failed proposal, he was also pained by their teasing.

Then in the longer lunch break, just as he was heading to the toilet, Tamanna skipped out of 10 A. She was walking in the opposite direction, and it was too late for either of them to change destinations. At the moment they passed each other, Rishabh suddenly found a chart about waste recycling tremendously fascinating and swung his head towards it and away from Tamanna.

His heart had skipped a beat upon seeing her, and there was a part of him that still wanted to sneak a glance. But his pride stopped him. If a man kept hankering after the girl who broke his heart, then was he really a man? No. Her rejecting him was her loss. He would stoop no further in his pursuit of her. So what if most of his biological functions failed on seeing her? That didn't mean anything. *Pfft*. There was a long line of girls behind him, just waiting for him to turn around.

He whipped around and saw Adil Bambawala digging his nose with a dreamy look on his face.

Well, not literally, of course, he thought.

There's nothing more daunting than telling your parents you've done badly in your exams. It was therefore understandable that Rishabh Bala waited outside his door, finger on the doorbell, rehearsing how he'd break the news. After ten minutes of deep breathing, he finally pressed the bell, stood back and braced himself.

His mother opened the door. She was smiling. Rishabh took that as a good omen.

'Rishu, guess who's here?'

Rishabh now had to pretend as if his grandmother and aunt's visit hadn't been the only thing on his mind for the last forty-eight hours. He faked the appropriate amount of surprise and bounded into the living room. As advertised, sitting on the sofa were his relatives by blood. Vidya Bala sat on one corner of the three-seater, a frail old lady who was born when India was still part of the British Empire. Most of her saris were about as old, but you couldn't tell because she wore them ironed to a crisp. Like all grandmothers, she was a jukebox of stories, which, though overly moralistic, were always enjoyable. Really, the only disagreeable aspect of his granny was her love for cooking brinjal and her insistence that everyone eat it.

Rishabh dived at her feet and she clasped him to her as he rose. 'So thin this one has become!' Dadi exclaimed, holding him at arm's length and shaking him to prove her point. Rishabh couldn't believe that a septuagenarian had such strength.

'Tch!' uttered his aunt. 'He's almost bursting out of the uniform. What, fatso! How are you?'

That's the thing about family: no matter how much you weigh, you will always be too thin for half your relatives and too large for the other half.

But he liked his aunt best of all. Vinaya Bala was like Santa Claus—jovial, kind and usually seen during festivals. She was a professor of biology at Shekhawat College, Vikhroli, and insisted that of all the animals she had studied, the weirdest ones were those related to her by blood. She had a keen sense of humour and a hearty laugh. Rishabh loved spending his summers in the more relaxed home of his aunt. He liked the company of his cousins—an older brother, Vignesh, and a younger sister, Shreeja. His aunt usually cooked him fish, and he was allowed to watch as much TV as he wanted for he didn't have to study during those carefree months. Just having Buaji around gave him fortitude.

But his spirits sank once more when he saw his father. Mr Bala sat dourly on the sofa, twiddling his thumbs and acting formal even with his mother and sister. It was as if the many years of corporate rigour had squeezed the cheerfulness out of him. Now the only interactions he understood were those he had with colleagues, and every meeting—even one with family members—was a board meeting.

'Rishabh, you are looking very scruffy. We have guests at home. Go freshen up and come,' instructed Mr Bala.

'But they're not GUESTS!' Rishabh wanted to scream, but then he remembered his marks and ate his words. He spent two soapy minutes wondering what his exact words would be when he made the shameful reveal. Finally, he settled on a plain-spoken denouement.

'I got the first-term papers today,' he said.

Dadi had been in the middle of a rather ripping account of her rheumatism, which she paused as Rishabh fished out his papers and handed them to his father.

Mr Bala took a deep breath in preparation and plunged into the papers. With each successive script, his breath quickened. The blood drained from his fingers even as they held the answer sheets. His face contorted. He looked like a spoonful of Dadi's brinjal sabzi had been shoved down his throat.

'You . . . 37 . . . you got 37 in maths,' stated his father. Dadi pulled her starched *pallu* to her mouth.

'It doesn't mean anything. It's just a term exam,' reasoned Rishabh. His eyes sought out Buaji for support, but he couldn't manage to tear them away from the bloodshot ones of his father.

'What do you mean it doesn't mean anything? You are in the bloody tenth standard. This means everything!'

Dadi hissed at the curse word. 'Don't use that kind of language,' she said.

'I'm holding back only because you're here,' said Mr Bala. 'His work deserves much worse.'

'Show me the papers,' demanded Mrs Bala, who'd been playing observer next to her husband. Now she couldn't contain her anger any longer. She took the scripts and her jaw moved restlessly as she shuffled through them.

'What is this?' she said at last. 'You are hardly getting 50 per cent overall.'

His mother was genuinely shocked. From senior KG onwards, her son had done well. Agreed, he had never topped or even come close to topping the class, but he had always been gloriously above average. These marks were alien to her. She double-checked the name on the sheets. No, there was no wishing it away. It was her own son who had produced these atrocious numbers.

'Is there a problem? Is there something bothering you? Do you want to talk to us about it privately? Should I tell Dadi and Buaji to go? SHOULD I TELL THEM TO GO?' Mrs Bala had become quite hysterical, and she only calmed down when Mr Bala put a firm arm around her shoulder.

'Nothing is wrong with him. He's just lazy and distracted. All the time I see him lying on the couch like a maharaja and watching TV. He doesn't understand the importance of—'

With the paternal unit yelling at you, the best course of action was to remain silent, take the abuse and hope they forgot about it in a couple of days. One of the worst courses of action was to answer back. Worse still was to answer back with something sarcastic.

'Papa, *you're* not understanding. These are term papers. The final exams are in March. What month is it right now? October. Therefore, this doesn't count. Hence proved.'

It was a bad idea and Rishabh had known it, but there was something black and bilious inside him that he couldn't hold back that afternoon. It gave him twisted satisfaction to see his father's face turn to stone, stunned as he was by his son's insolence. However, that victory was a small one. Soon his father's features squeezed together, his mouth opened and a deafening stream of invective spewed out.

'Shut up! Just shut up!' screamed Mr Bala. 'I don't care when the goddamn exams are. I can tell you now only that you won't do any better. This is not about your marks. It is about your attitude. You just wait and see how hard life will be when you screw up your tenth!'

'Ram, ram, ram, ram, ram,' chanted Dadi, her eyes rolling heavenward.

Mr Bala turned to his sister. 'Vinaya, look at this. He's done the worst in the sciences. How will he get admission into any good college?' His aunt remained silent. Mr Bala faced his son again. 'Do you know how high the science cut-offs get?'

'Have you asked me if I want to study science?'

'Accha, so now you want to quit?'

'I have to do something to quit it, no? I'm not going to do science. I don't want to do engineering. I don't want to do an MBA. I don't want to run a stupid business. That's what you want me to do, no?'

'Rishabh!' hissed his mother.

'Okay,' said Mr Bala, 'take the easy way out. You don't want to do science? Fine. What do you want to do? Play your goddamn football? You get out of my house and try to feed yourself playing football. Let's see how long you last. We give

186

you a roof, give you hot meals, get you 3000-rupee football shoes—' He turned to Rishabh's aunt. 'Vinaya, 3000-rupee shoes! Can you imagine? It's gone to his head.' He locked eyes with his son again. 'You take all of this for granted, no? You go and earn and see. Then you'll know how hard it is. You quit science, quit studying, quit everything—just play your FUCKING FOOTBALL!'

'OM NAMAH SHIVAYA!' screamed Dadi. Showing surprising agility for a rheumatic person, she bounded in between Mr Bala and Rishabh. 'When did your language become so unclean? I thought I raised you right,' she said to her son. She turned to Buaji and gave her a small nod.

Buaji floated over to Rishabh. 'Let's go to your room. Come, come.' She grabbed him by his shoulders and gently steered him to his room.

Meanwhile, Dadi took Mr Bala to his room and, in an impromptu tag-team effort, the two women tried to diffuse the situation.

'Be honest with me—is something bothering you?' asked Buaji. Like most teachers, she wore bifocals and was gazing at him concernedly over the frames.

'No . . . I just didn't study enough,' said Rishabh, leaving out the part where he had lost two football tournaments, got rejected by his long-time crush, hated his teachers and was barred from playing the sport he loved with his own team. 'I'm sorry. I know it's my fault . . . but I don't understand why *he's* so angry with me. All. The. Time. I said I'll do better in the final exams, no? What more does he want?'

Rishabh had worked himself up again and was pacing about his room. His aunt considered his condition. She liked her nephew. He was a soft-spoken, well-behaved boy on most days. He did have a streak of mischief and a hint of wickedness, but then so did Lord Krishna and he'd turned out just fine. It hurt her to see him so cagey and confused, and she decided that there was only one way to arrest his turmoil. She would have to tell him the truth. And adults, as a rule, didn't like telling the truth because children exposed to reality too soon tended to malfunction. But she decided to chance it.

'Your father isn't angry. He's just very afraid,' she said.

Rishabh stopped pacing and looked at his aunt sceptically. The reaction had felt pretty angry to him.

'He's afraid, Rishu. He's been where you are. In fact, I was there too. I've seen it before. This same thing.' She chuckled to her herself. 'Do things ever really change?' she asked of no one in particular.

'What do you mean?' said Rishabh, who wished she would have epiphanies on her own time.

'Yeah, yeah. So impatient, just like your papa. So much in common and you still can't get along. He's afraid, babu. When he was your age, he was *worse* than you. He got 58 per cent in his tenth and 42 per cent in his matriculation. Sorry, the twelfth, as you now call it. Everyone made so much fun of him. All our relatives. They would come and tell our father, "What is your son doing? He will never amount to anything." Only difference was our father never let that pressure touch us.'

She drifted off into thought. Rishabh hadn't heard much about his father's early years, and now he understood why.

'So, your father,' said Buaji, snapping back. 'He had to really struggle for years afterwards. He worked so hard, you know, to get into IIT. For four years after his twelfth, I didn't see his face only because there was always a book in front of it. He used to sit in a banyan and shorts and read, read, read. "Vinaya, I'm trapped by my marks," he used to tell me.

And when he finally got into IIT, he cried so much, you know. I remember it so well because he never used to cry. But that day, oho, our whole house was flooded. He cried because he had escaped certain failure. He went to IIT, then IIM, and then there was no looking back.

'But before he got in . . . his fear was huge. You're still better off. Our father had even less, and Hari wondered if he didn't do well in life then how would he survive? See, we don't tell children this, but you should know: money is important. Thinking long-term is a must. And the key is education. Tomorrow, you will have a family of your own, and you will want them to live well, no?'

Rishabh didn't respond.

'Of course you will. For that, you will have to earn money. And if you do well in these exams, you will get into a good college; and if you do that, then you will get a better job and you will be settled for life. That's what your father wants. He isn't worried about the marks; he's worried about your future. Trust me, babu, he's seen too much—we all have—to not be worried. The world is a pretty harsh place. The least you can do is not add to your own problems.'

'But he has no faith in me or what?'

'He does. He's just afraid to show it. He's doing what he thinks will be best for you.'

'*Why* is he so scared? Why doesn't he know how to handle things?'

This was the reaction Vinaya Bala had been worried about, but she had decided to tell the truth and she would tell all of it. 'Because none of us do.' It was an odd admission of weakness from his fifty-year-old aunt. Her eyes shone, but her face looked tired and older than before. Her vulnerability flooded her voice. 'I hope you see where he is coming from.

And I want you to promise me you will work harder on your studies, yes?'

There were many questions Rishabh wanted to ask and many injustices he wanted justified, but he suppressed them all. He was surprised to find his eyes were moist. He couldn't explain it. He felt angry and helpless but also guilty for not being a better son. He blinked back the tears and nodded.

The tears would flow eventually and unexpectedly.

The next day, Rishabh was catatonic in class and equally vegetative in his Hindi tutorial. Prasad Sir asked him two questions just to check if he was alive. Puro, too, was concerned about his best friend's lack of liveliness, and as they hiked back from the coaching class he tentatively probed, 'You seem a little . . . down?'

No response.

They kept walking.

'You want to talk about it?'

Rishabh's gaze didn't shift from the road and his lips remained firmly shut.

'Is this about Tamanna? You deserve better than her. I'm telling you, bey. She's stupid and her hair looks like a crow's nest and everybody hates her.'

Suddenly a tear trickled down Rishabh's face. His eyes crinkled, his lips parted and a low wail escaped him. Water now gushed out of his sockets, enough to irrigate the entire football field. Puro was alarmed.

'I'm sorry, I'm sorry . . . I didn't mean any of that about Tamanna. She's not all that bad . . .'

But it didn't stop the bawling. Rishabh was embarrassed. It had been years since he had cried in front of any of his friends. He'd had his best crying spell as an eight-year-old, when he had wept for a whole week for a G.I. Joe figurine (and had got it too). Since then, his stats had fallen and his crying average had come down drastically. His friendship with Puro rested exclusively on football, jokes and boyish high jinks. Emotions, feelings and especially tears were never part of the deal. He didn't want Puro to rip up their contract because of this flagrant violation. Besides, Rishabh had always felt that crying was for the weak and the powerless—and now he cried because that was just how he felt.

'I'm sorry, I'm sorry, I'm sorry,' he chanted to Puro.

Puro didn't know how to react. His crying average was even lower than Rishabh's and, what was more, he hadn't encountered many weepy people. He remembered that when someone erupted in sadness in the movies, the characters around them put an arm around their shoulder or patted them on the back. So he attempted this. The execution was awkward. His arm rested on Rishabh's shoulder like a wooden log and his attempts at back-patting came across as violence against an already crying person. He stopped doing whatever he was doing when Rishabh picked up the wailing a notch. He was now in full widow mode.

Rishabh tried stopping himself, but the more he tried the harder he cried. He felt an acute pain in his chest, as if it were his heart that was pumping out the bodily brine. He cried for all the horrible things that had happened to him: the results, the rejection, the red card. And then, to his horror, he found himself crying about things long past: having to leave his friends behind when his dad got transferred, seeing both his goldfish floating belly-up in their bowl one afternoon, the ending of *Rang De Basanti*. It was like his tear ducts had been building up a reserve over the last seven years, waiting to let it all out at once one day.

Finally, at long last, Rishabh was able to compose himself enough to give Puro an explanation. He told his friend about the showdown he had had with his father. It was a miracle Puro managed to understand him through the juddering sobs that rocked him every few seconds, but that's what best friends were for.

After hearing the tale, Puro laughed. It was insensitive and, frankly, a bit insulting, but before Rishabh could feel bad, Puro patted him on the head. 'You fucking idiot. You let out that waterfall for this?'

Rishabh glowered.

'Don't be angry, re. I'm only asking why you are taking your dad so seriously. Dads are supposed to say rubbish. That's their job. You know how grannies tell stories and mothers tell you to wear sweaters? Just like that, fathers say mean things. You are supposed to hear it from here . . .' He pointed to his left ear. 'And take it out from here.' He pointed to his right ear.

Rishabh remained sceptical.

'Arre, compared to my father, your father wrote you a love letter. My dad once told me, "You will amount to nothing."'

'You didn't feel bad?'

'No, he's probably right.'

Puro flashed a grin and, before he could stop himself, Rishabh laughed.

'Jokes aside, my dad is doubly frustrated. He can't criticize me because I am his fault.'

'You mean he should have worn a condom?'

'You want to cry again or what?'

'I'm joking.'

'I know. So truth is, my father was a footballer. In his time, he was a forward for a local team, Tembhi Naka Tigers. He had long hair, sunglasses, earring, rode a Bullet.' Puro saw the incredulity on Rishabh's face. 'I only believed it because I saw photos.'

Puro went on. 'He played for a long time, but he didn't get very far. I think they won the Thane District league, but that was it. Then he had to take up a job. He keeps saying that he wasted all that time. Says he could have put those five–six years in his job and earned a better salary.

'Then he says his second mistake was teaching me football. He says that he got carried away because he had a son. He used to take me to the ground when I was four years old and make me run. Trust me, he doesn't put as much pressure on my studies as he used to put on my running. Full evening he used to make me run. Then we would play pass–pass with the ball. Back then I hated it, but I have stamina and skill now only thanks to that.'

'That makes sense,' said Rishabh.

'Yeah . . . Problem is that at first he only encouraged me and now he's only saying that I spend all my time playing football. That I should study. What is his line? Haan . . . "You are not playing football, you are playing with your future."'

'Wah, wah!' Rishabh clapped.

'I let him say what he wants. As long as he isn't whacking me, it's okay.'

'He hits you?'

'Yeah, sometimes. Just the belt. Nothing crazy.'

Mr Bala had never hit him, though he had come close. Put in perspective, Rishabh's problems did seem trifling.

'I do agree with one point your dad made,' said Puro.

'Which point?'

'That you shouldn't quit.'

'But I haven't even chosen science. How can I quit something I am not even doing yet? I just want—'

'No, you have quit something you were doing.'

Rishabh understood the implication. But in his opinion, he hadn't quit football; he had been forced out.

As if reading his mind, Puro said, 'I know you shouldn't be playing with the juniors, but that is no reason to give up. The coach doesn't hate you. If he didn't want you to play, he would have told you to leave right away. He just wanted you to learn a lesson. I'm sure that in just a few days he would have brought you back to the team.' He paused. 'Where you belong.'

'Yeah, but would *you* stay if this was done to you?'

'Yes. I love playing. He could have made me train alone and I still would have come. I just want to be on the pitch with a ball. Everything else is a bonus.'

The words swam around in Rishabh's head.

'You don't want to study because you don't like it, so don't do it. I support you. In fact, if you want, we can drop out of school tomorrow. To be honest, I'm just waiting for one person to leave so I can join them. We waste at least eight hours every day on this rubbish. When will I ever use algorithms?'

Puro looked off into the distance, playing out his school-leaving fantasy. After a few seconds, he snapped out of it.

'Listen, thing is, when you leave something you love, you are doing yourself the most harm. We will hate passing to Pinal Oza, but we'll do it. The team will suffer. That is true. But we won't suffer as much as you are suffering. I see you in class, yaar. Without football, you are like a plant without water.

194

You sit around like this, see.' He mimed a drooping, wilting flower. 'Do it for yourself. Don't be a quitter. Because, think about it, by not trying, you're just proving your old man right,' Puro finished dramatically.

Rishabh darted his eyes up and down the stretch of the road. He had been reluctant to admit it, but he had run away from the Mongoose's challenge. At the first sign of difficulty, he had bolted and, in doing so, had proved the coach right. He hadn't shown any spine, any character, any real repentance. And if he kept walking away, he would be a quitter. No matter what his ego told him.

'Hey,' he heard Puro say, 'screw all this serious stuff. Take these. They'll cheer you up.'

Rishabh looked up to see Puro brandishing two blue film CDs. The girls on the covers had breasts that were bigger than the CDs they were on.

'Got them from the guy at Thane station. They're new, and very, very good. Last one is the best. Watch it till the end.'

'Of course I will,' said Rishabh. 'You think I'm a quitter or what?'

After that clearly inspiring tête-à-tête, Puro expected Rishabh to bounce into training the following morning. However, the next day, too, saw the school ground free of Rishabh Bala. In fact, even 10 F didn't have the pleasure of Rishabh's company. It would be two whole days before Purohit would see his best friend again. On the first evening, more curious than concerned, he rang up the Bala landline and was met with the voice of Mrs Bala. When asked if he could speak with

Rishabh, she said, 'Sorry, Abhay. He's fallen ill. He's actually resting at the moment. I'll tell him to call you when he feels better.' The call was not returned, and by the second day, Puro was more concerned than ever.

The truth was that Rishabh wasn't ill. He'd just wanted some quiet time to think things through. He knew that voluntarily bunking school was not an option. He would have to manufacture a reason. So he had sneaked into the bathroom and, shoving two fingers so far down his throat that they almost reached his lungs, had probed around in his oesophagus until he'd hurled up the previous night's dinner. He had then shown the mess to his mother, who'd immediately told him to get into bed and not get up the whole day.

Another bout of self-induced morning sickness meant that he had secured another day's reprieve, as well as his father's head-shaking disapproval. 'The last thing he needs is to miss school,' said Mr Bala.

'Leave him alone. He's sick, poor thing,' protested Mrs Bala.

'How long will he just lie there? At least make him read a textbook.'

'He needs rest.'

'Am I asking him to run a half-marathon? Reading doesn't take effort.'

'He'll do it once he's better.'

'Bullshit. You wait and see, the first thing he'll do is go play football again.'

'Shhhh, don't make a commotion! You go do your work. Let him rest.'

And so Rishabh lay on one side of his double bed, a heap of rumpled blankets beside him, and stared at the ceiling fan.

Since his breakdown in front of Puro, he'd been feeling numb. All emotion seemed to have escaped his body with the tears. He felt lonely and broken. *I've hit rock bottom*, he thought. *I've messed up everything I loved and pissed off everyone who loved me. Now what?* He contemplated the question as the planet turned away from the sun. His attention was fixed upon the fan and his mind spun faster than its blades.

At night, he tossed and turned like he was being roasted on a spit. He sweated through his sheets. He woke up with anxiety hanging around his neck like a millstone. His only comfort was the hypnotic spinning of the fan. He thought and thought, and when he got tired of thinking, he remembered. Every forlorn moment from the past four months was replayed on the white expanse of his damp ceiling. He forced himself to look at them till he cringed with disgust. When he had run through all the thoughts and memories his mind could conjure up, finally there was silence. His eyes were open, but all he saw was a black ocean of infinite nothingness and then a flash of light and then, once again, the spinning of the fan.

On the morning of the third day, Mrs Bala woke up at 6 a.m. as she always did. She received the milk, brought it to a boil and made herself tea. She had scarcely settled into her chair and unfolded the paper, when out came her son, freshly bathed, wearing his football clothes, school bag on his back and kitbag in his hand. And just like that, Mrs Bala's face lost all colour. She wondered if she was looking at an apparition. As she may well have been. If you'd tucked in someone at night who'd looked like they were in need of a saline drip and the very next morning, they sprang out of their room, ready to play football, you'd be well within your rights to question their corporeal existence.

'Where are you going?' asked Mrs Bala in a daze.

'For training and then school.'

'But . . . your health?'

'I'm feeling much better now.'

'No! Don't go for football.'

'I have to. I know I haven't had breakfast, but there's no time. Here,' he picked up an apple from the table, 'I'll have this on the way.'

The morning drowsiness all but left Mrs Bala, and she grasped that this was reality and that her recently bedridden son was going off to exert himself by playing an exhausting contact sport. 'WE HAVE A CODE RED SITUATION!' went her maternal instincts. Without further thought, she leapt from the dining table and latched a vice-like talon on to Rishabh's arm.

'You are not going anywhere. HARI! HARIIIIII!' screamed his mother.

Rishabh knew this was bad, because his mother only called his father by his first name in the direst of emergencies. The last time he had heard her do so was when the city had been hit by an earthquake. Mr Bala now came rushing out of the bedroom, eyes half-open, hair standing up and an expression that said, 'This better be worth it.'

'He says he wants to go play football.'

Mr Bala blinked. Questions—many questions—were forming inside his sleepy head. Firstly, who wanted to play football? And secondly, and more importantly, why was that his problem? And then he spotted his squirming son and his confusion gave way to rage that petered into exasperation. He couldn't deal with his son's shenanigans in the middle of the day; there was no way he was going to be able to handle them this early in the morning.

'Just let him go,' he said.

'WHAT!' squawked Mrs Bala.

Mr Bala turned to his son. 'Will you take responsibility if you faint or collapse?'

'Yes, Papa.'

'Okay. Chitra, let him go. There's no use stopping him.'

Mrs Bala let go of her son while Mr Bala shook his head and groggily blinked at the floor. Rishabh stood rooted to the spot. It hurt him to see his parents this distraught, but he was getting late. He hurried towards them.

'Papa, Mumma, I know what I'm doing. Trust me.'

Then he scuttled to the door and let himself out. Before shutting the door behind him, he shoved his face in and said the words he had really been meaning to say. He said them fast to reduce his embarrassment.

'I love you both, and I'm sorry.'

And then he shut the door behind him just as quickly, before the words could escape the house and follow him. Apologizing first thing in the morning could set the tone for the rest of the day.

The players were already kitting up by the time Rishabh arrived. He heard the gasps, he heard the hoots and cheers, and he felt every eyeball ping-ponging between the coach and him. He didn't acknowledge any of it, homing in on the coach instead. The ground grew still. Each ear strained to hear what was going to be said next. The coach's moustache moved furiously, his eyes were narrowed in scepticism.

'Sir, I'm sorry. I was a stupid boy, and I'm sorry.'

The coach opened his mouth to say something but Rishabh continued.

'I know what you're thinking. This is just the beginning of my apology. The main part is where I come to training every day, work really hard and hope that, one day, I win my place back on the team. May I please train with you?'

The coach scanned Rishabh's face. He detected remorse but, more satisfyingly, he detected determination. Finally, the lad was repenting. The coach nodded, let out a gruff sound that could be interpreted as a yes and pointed to where the junior team was kitting up.

Rishabh made his way to them.

'Rishabh!' he heard Puro scream.

He looked towards the senior team, who jumped to attention in synchrony and saluted him, and just when the emotion was going to overpower him, they brought their hands down, crossed their arms over their crotches and shouted in unison, 'Suck it!'

'Aye!' roared the coach, but Rishabh didn't hear it over his own laughter. It was the perfect welcome.

It was heavy weather, returning to practice after a gap of two weeks. His sides began burning while warming up, and he heaved and wheezed through the session. The smiling mid-October sun had replaced the cool shade of the clouds. It made Rishabh's throat dry and his skin itched as it was gently toasted. At the end of the hour, he almost regretted his decision to return.

Somehow he dragged himself to class, and his legs throbbed out of mercy when he finally sat down. Next to him, Barkha smiled.

'Are you okay? Where were you?'

'Wasn't feeling well for a while, but I'm finally better.'

Looking at his grimy, haggard face, Barkha couldn't believe he was feeling better, but she said she was glad.

Rishabh turned to Puro, who had been staring at him with a pen between his teeth.

'Puro, I just wanted to say—'

Puro took the pen out of his mouth and said, 'Shut up. Just shut up.'

'Fuck you, man.'

'That's much better.'

Though he had reconciled to training with the junior team, it still took some effort for Rishabh to treat the pipsqueaks around him with respect. As a senior, he was used to ordering them around and making them work like valets. Within the first few days of his return, he asked Ranganathan, the tiny centre back, to clean his studs and put them in his bag. It was only when a chorus of protests went up that he realized he had made a mistake. He apologized immediately and made a mental note to keep his sense of superiority under control.

On the pitch, however, his superiority was unquestioned. He routinely scored three–four goals in five-a-side games. His strength and speed were no match for the striplings. He swatted them aside like they were gnats. The junior team keeper, Aalap Tople, couldn't handle his fierce senior-team-level shots and got into the habit of curling up into a ball of cowardice every time Rishabh even entered his half.

He didn't think it would happen, but gradually Rishabh got used to the little fellas. They weren't too bad once he got to know them. They fretted about their marks, liked girls, hated teachers, watched football and dreamed of playing with their idols—just like the seniors. The only difference was that the seniors did these things in longer pants. Sometimes, though, they would rail about a particularly sixth-standard problem, like when Sudhanshu, the forward, was worried sick because his name had appeared on the board for talking in class for three consecutive days.

'What will happen now?' he bleated.

'Nothing. Purohit and I are on the board all the time. They don't rub out our names only!' Rishabh laughed.

'But miss said she'll take strict action.'

'Arre, what's the worst that will happen? She'll give you a remark. So what?'

The juniors gasped. It amused Rishabh to see that remarks still had this kind of hold over them.

'I'll tell you a secret? Girls love guys with remarks.'

Soon more and more of them started coming to Rishabh with their problems, which he solved with his wisdom, experience and bullshitting prowess. He enjoyed helping them on and off the pitch, and before he knew it, he was simply enjoying himself. Of course, if you had asked him if he liked training with the kids, he would have huffed and puffed in denial.

The only blip that remained was the coach's lack of forgiveness. Mehfouz Noorani wasn't warm with any player. However, if the rest of the players were in the fridge of his affection, then Rishabh had been shoved into the freezer. For the entire first week, the coach had refused to even call Rishabh by his name. Instead he used various epithets, like 'Boy!' and 'Aye! You there'.

That changed one Tuesday morning because of a series of extraordinary events that began with Mehfouz Noorani forgetting to buy a pair of double A batteries. The batteries had been needed for the alarm clock that sat beside the coach's bed and had stopped in the middle of the previous night— at 3.16 a.m. to be precise. Stopped clocks may be right at least twice, but they don't sound alarms even once. As a result, Mehfouz Noorani groggily opened his eyes and realized that he was running behind by half an hour.

He whirled through his routine and rushed downstairs, where he patted his pocket and realized he had forgotten the keys to his bike. He cursed his forgetfulness as he glanced at his watch. There was no time to run up the four floors to retrieve his keys. He simply couldn't afford to be late. Thanks to his self-righteousness, he now had a reputation to maintain.

So he hailed a rickshaw. He made good time, and at the end of the bumpy, back-breaking ride, he had managed to arrive at the school gate five minutes earlier than he usually did. The rickshaw-wallah stopped the meter, which displayed Rs 35. The coach reached for his wallet and, for the second time that morning, patted a pocket and found its contents to be missing. In a panic, he massaged every inch of his clothing, right down to his socks, but the wallet remained elusive. This was bound to happen because wallets forgotten in the cupboard in haste do not appear on your person merely by patting.

Mehfouz Noorani got out of the rickshaw. He explained the situation to the rickshaw-wallah, a man of broad Maharashtrian build, who impassively stared back at him with puffy eyes and a slack lower lip. After hearing Mehfouz's story, the rickshaw-wallah said, 'I don't care. Thirty-five rupees.'

The coach now pondered his next course of action. It was clear he would have to borrow the money, but from whom? And just then, he saw a figure bouncing down the road. It was Rishabh Bala. The coach cringed. *Why him?* he thought. *Why couldn't it have been anybody else?*

Rishabh Bala was indeed sauntering to school with a sunny disposition. A chocolate sandwich for breakfast was fuelling his upbeat outlook. Upon seeing the Mongoose, though, he immediately switched off the spring in his step. He wondered why the coach was standing beside a rickshaw, glowering at him.

He approached the coach cautiously. 'Good morning, sir,' he said. The coach uttered a churlish grunt of acknowledgement. The rickshaw-wallah looked at Rishabh, then looked at the coach and then wagged his head in Rishabh's direction. The coach violently shook his.

'Look here, I have things to do, places to be,' said the rickshaw-wallah.

'Yes, yes,' mumbled the coach. Then Mehfouz Noorani took a deep breath and said, 'Rishabh.'

Rishabh, who had walked ahead, heard the voice and froze. He wondered if he had imagined it. Then he heard it again.

'Don't just stand there wasting time, come here FAST!' said the voice. Rishabh had definitely not imagined that.

'Yes, sir,' he said, whipping around.

'I need some . . . help,' said the coach, the word hardly getting past his moustache. 'You see, I forgot my wallet . . . The rickshaw . . . Would you have any . . .'

'How much do you need, sir?'

'Thirty-five rupees.'

Rishabh fished out a hundred-rupee note from his school bag and handed it to the rickshaw-wallah, who flicked his head in annoyance, grumpily returned the change and sped off—but not before throwing the coach an ugly look.

The coach was studying Rishabh with hangdog eyes. 'Sorry about that. I'll pay you back tomorrow without fail.'

'It's all right, sir.'

'And . . . thank you.'

Rishabh nodded. They entered the school together. Rishabh continued to train with the junior squad, but the coach started calling him by his name again.

It was 9.47 a.m. The short break was about to end, so Rishabh hurried to the loo. He was busy at the urinal, when Bhargav Chigulur and Gagan Gowda walked in and took up the stalls on either side of him.

'She's cute, man. I'm telling you,' said Chigulur.

'What! No!' retorted Gowda.

'Have you seen how pretty her face is?'

'No, I haven't. I only see her hand because it's always raised.'

'Oh, come on.'

'Of all the girls in our standard, I can't believe you find Barkha hot,' said Gowda with a sorrowful shake of his big blocky head.

Rishabh's pee abruptly stopped flowing. His eyes widened.

'Who has a crush on Barkha, yaar?' continued Gowda.

Rishabh cleared his throat.

Chigu and Gowda looked at him.

'Rishabh, what do *you* think? Is Barkha cute?' asked Gowda.

'She's all right,' said Rishabh. 'Why?'

'Chigu loves her.'

'Is that right?' The words came out in a low gurgle.

'NO . . . I just find her cute, that's all. She has a very pretty face.'

'Hmmm,' sighed Rishabh. He had a vision of grabbing Chigu by the neck and hurling him to the floor in a thunderous chokeslam.

Chigu and Gowda finished emptying their bladders and washed their hands at the sink. Rishabh remained rooted to the spot.

'You know what I'm going to do?' said Chigu.

'Get your eyes checked?' said Gowda.

'No, fat-ass.'

'Watch it,' said Gowda, waving a fist the size of a bowling ball in Chigu's face.

'Arre, you know I was joking.'

'Make better jokes next time.'

Rishabh sighed again. He wanted to find out what Chigu was going to do.

'Right. So, anywayyy . . . I'm going to ask her for her notes,' said Chigu, unveiling his master plan as he washed the soap from his hands.

'Smart,' said Gowda.

'I know, right. It's the perfect excuse.'

'No, *she's* smart. Her notes will be really helpful,' said Gowda.

Chigu sucked his teeth.

Gowda flashed a shark-toothed smile in the mirror. 'I'm just joking,' he said.

'What do you think?' asked Chigu.

'Yeah, do whatever. She's too nerdy to fall for you, though. Raman should date her. Mr and Mrs Genius. Their kids will come out solving equations,' said Gowda, running his hand through his already thinning hair.

Rishabh now had a vivid vision of grabbing Gowda by his considerable girth and giving him a body slam. Chigu, who was patting his hair into place, interrupted his fantasy.

'It's worth a shot,' he insisted.

'Just admit it, you have a crush on her.'

'Okay, fine. Maybe I do.'

Rishabh felt a tremor of jealousy run up his spine. He rocked in his place, in front of the porcelain urinal. By now he wanted to deliver a running clothes line on both these chumps. He caught himself enjoying this imaginary violence and was surprised by his emotions. His relationship with Chigu, up to that point, had been pleasant. He couldn't explain why he suddenly felt like administering WWE finishing moves to his classmate. *All for what?* thought Rishabh. No, the real question was, all for whom?

'Rishabh?' said Gowda.

'Hmm?'

'You okay?'

'Yeah, why?' asked Rishabh defensively. He wondered if they could sense his resentment.

'You've been peeing for a very long time.'

'Oh,' said Rishabh, relieved. 'Yeah, had a lot of water.'

'Okay,' said Gowda with an unconvinced shrug and ambled out with Chigu.

In the long break, Rishabh spotted Bhargav Chigulur awkwardly trying to make his move. He sidled up to Barkha's desk and asked her for her maths notes. Barkha politely refused, saying she didn't share her study material with anyone. Chigu nodded in false understanding and slunk away to the sound of Gowda's booming laughter that bounced off the walls of the classroom.

And witnessing the squashing of Chigu's hopes and dreams made giddy with joy the boy who sat next to Barkha.

Ghadge Sir's face was scrunched up and his tongue lolled over his lower lip like a Labrador's. This was the face of a man concentrating. He had a sheet of paper in one hand, which he carefully positioned on the board, and with the pin in the other, he honed in towards the top-centre of the sheet. As the pin got closer, so did the huddle of boys crowding around Ghadge Sir. It so happened that, in his excitement, Bhupinder leaned too close and jogged Ghadge Sir's arm. The pin jerked over its mark, and Ghadge Sir let out a roar.

'ERRYBODY, SHTAND BACK! Iph you want me to put phixtures on board, THEN SHTAND BACK!'

The elastic throng pulled back. Ghadge Sir took aim once more and managed to pin the sheet without incident. He then turned around with an accomplished, avuncular smile and said, 'Now you can see.' He stepped aside, and the crowd flocked back to the board.

The sheet was titled 'Inter-House Sports'. The football team had been looking forward to these fixtures for a long while. The race for the house cup was tight this year. Though Yamuna was on top, a galloping Vindhya had cut down their lead. The remaining two houses, Himachal and Ganga, though at the rear, were still within striking distance. Now that they were approaching the business end of the competition, the race had begun to heat up. The footballers were particularly excited, because the football trophy contributed the maximum points among all the sports, and they were dying to help their respective houses win it.

Sumit, who had muscled his way to the front of the mob, screamed out the football fixtures, 'Football matches to be held on 20th October—Himachal vs Vindhya and Ganga vs Yamuna!'

A groan went up from the assembly. It belonged to Yamuna voices. Calling the fixture a contest between David and Goliath would be an insult to David. The Ganga team was the strongest side that had ever played in a blue T-shirt. It boasted the likes of Purohit, Rishabh, Rahul, Pinal Oza, Khodu, Sumit and the speedy Joy Chakraborty. Meanwhile, Yamuna had Bhupinder. Any side in which Bhupi was the best player was a poor side indeed. Yamuna weren't the underdogs, they were the dogs under the underdogs.

'You people wheel be more happy with news coming tomorrow,' said Ghadge Sir benignly.

'Why, sir?' asked Rahul.

'You wheel see. It is surprise.'

'What is it, sir?' insisted Bhupi.

'ARRE, BHUPINDER, IPH I TELL YOU SURPRISE THEN HOW IT WHEEL BE SURPRISE? USE BRAINS, NO, SOMETIME!'

Bhupinder was having one of those days that couldn't end soon enough. He shut up and thought dark thoughts while the rest of the teams discussed what surprise lay in store for them.

It wasn't hard to guess what the news could be. The options were narrow when a physical education teacher told a football team that hadn't played in a while that there was good news around the corner. The football team wouldn't go around guessing glad tidings, like 'Good news? Oh! Is the coach pregnant?'

Nevertheless, at the end of the next day's training, when the coach announced that they were going to play in a tournament to be held in MES High School, the cheering was substantial. There were a bunch of 'What did I tell you?'s, which were met by a bunch of 'It was obvious!'es. The coach waited until the din had died down before continuing.

'Collect your forms from Ghadge Sir and submit them by Friday latesht. The tournament will be held on the 28th and 29th of October.'

The boys gasped. The collective positivity took a nosedive. The coach sensed something was amiss.

'What is the matter?' he probed.

'Sir, that weekend we have tests at our coaching classes,' said Floyd.

Floyd was referring to the series of tests that was going to be held at Oswal's. It was the first major round of assessments to be conducted in their tutorial groups, and the tutors had been emphasizing their importance for the last two weeks.

'How many of you go for these classes?' the coach asked.

Nearly every hand went up. The coach was surprised. He chomped on his moustache meditatively.

'This is bad timing. I understand it is an important year. Studies are important. *I* would put them before football. So I am asking you: how many players don't want to play in this tournament? If you raise your hand, don't worry; I understand. I will not hold it against you. How many don't want to play?'

Only three hands went up: one belonging to Rakshit Dave, Abel Floyd and Dhrupad Dalal each.

'Don't do this, re,' urged Puro.

The coach held up a hand and Puro fell silent.

'You boys are sure?' he asked softly.

Dave gave a small, sad nod. Floyd followed, uneasily dragging his foot in the mud. Their shoulders had drooped. Their eyes didn't meet those of their teammates'. Even Dhrupad, the substitute stopper, stood with his arms folded and his chin buried in his chest.

'All right. We will respect the decision. If you like, you can train with us till then, you are more than welcome,' said the coach before returning to the shed.

It was a body blow. The team was losing two of its most vital players and Dhrupad. What Rishabh couldn't fathom was how quickly Dave and Floyd had made up their minds. It was ominous. The boys surrounded them and demanded answers.

'What the hell is wrong with you two?' interrogated Puro.

'It's not even school exams. Who cares about tutorial tests?' huffed Rahul.

'My father does,' said Dave.

'And my mom. You guys know my mom,' said Floyd.

They shuddered. They were well acquainted with the academic despot that was Floyd's mother. She was a wild-eyed woman with messy hair that looked like a raven's nest. While most mothers were polite if not reasonable, Floyd's mother was loud and unwavering with her marks-mongering. Rishabh recalled the Christmas they had visited Floyd's house. His mother had taken the opportunity to warn them about not taking their studies seriously. 'If you don't study hard, Jesus's sacrifice will have been in vain!' she had said, forcing them to put down their glasses of Pepsi and their plates of cake. Rishabh was sure that the last thing Jesus would have liked on his birthday was for his sacrifice to be brought up, but he'd kept quiet about his opinions lest he provoke Mrs Thottapalli into another sermon.

Though they knew that Floyd and Dave were in a hopeless situation, they felt it was their duty to convince them to stay. And so they did. But the boys would not relent. Rishabh could see the pressure their parents exerted. There was no talking them out of it. That epiphany couldn't be induced by football teammates, especially when they'd surrounded you and were squawking at you like seagulls. Rishabh knew that two months ago, he might not have had the courage to defy his parents either. Had he not spiralled to the bottom, he might never have charted an independent course up. Floyd and Dave would have their own journeys to make, but they would not begin now.

'Stop it,' said Rishabh. 'ENOUGH!'

The rabble quietened down.

'Look, it's already hard for them. We're making it worse. Everyone's situation is not the same. You know these two would never let the team down if they could help it . . .'

'Hey, me also,' piped up Dhrupad.

'Shut up, Dhrupad,' said Puro.

'But if they have made up their minds, let's respect it.'

'Thanks, man,' said Floyd.

'I'm not saying it's a good thing. Or the right thing. But you know what's best for you. And at least come for practice as long as you can. Yes?'

Rakshit Dave and Abel Floyd said they would.

'I may not be able to come from next week,' added Dhrupad.

'Okay, Dhrupad,' said Puro.

'But I'll try and convince my parents—'

'You don't have to,' said everybody.

The same time a week later, Rishabh Bala knotted his shoelaces, stood up and took three mighty gulps of air. He felt like his stomach had bloated with nervousness and risen to his chest. He hadn't felt this way in a long time. Surrounding him was his pride of blue-clad Ganga teammates. As his eyes roved from face to face, he took heart. Ganga was solid. In the distance, Bhupinder Chatwal, the Yamuna captain, waddled around, trying to get his team to kit up. Most of the Yamuna team didn't even have studs. They were lacing up their white Bata school shoes. Ganga was going to win. The question was by how much.

'Good to go?' asked Purohit, the Ganga team captain.

'Yeah,' said Rishabh.

'Show him a game so good that he has to have you back,' added Puro with a wink.

Puro was giving Rishabh this pep talk because the coach was in attendance. The position of senior team keeper had remained vacant ever since Dave had opted out. The coach had promoted Aalap Tople, the junior team goalkeeper, to reserve keeper and regretted it instantly. Tople had a habit of cowering pitifully whenever powerful shots came his way—a tendency that had become far worse once he was put between the senior sticks. Rahul, Puro and Sumit had even made a sport out of not shooting for the goal but aiming at Aalap Tople. He got thwacked so consistently that on the second day he'd clung to the post, with a slightly more crooked nose than before, and cried until he was relieved of his duties.

'Who can bloody keep for you people?' the coach had hollered, exasperated by Aalap Tople's breakdown.

That's when Tej Jaykar's name had come up. Tej, or TJ, as he was affectionately known, was Yamuna's goalkeeper. He was an excellent keeper, with reflexes so quick that strikers who came up against him routinely complained that he shouldn't be allowed to break the sound barrier in a bid to block shots. But there were no rules regarding that sort of thing, so referees never took any action. The only reason why Tej wasn't on the school football team was because he was already gainfully employing his reflexes in table tennis. He was number three in the country's junior table tennis rankings, leaving Dave to be number one in the school football team.

As it turned out, Jaykar had readily agreed to help the team out for the tournament, but the coach decided he would wait till he had seen him play in the inter-house matches. That's how the coach had landed up in the shed next to the ground and caused Rishabh to have a mini myocardial infarction. Suddenly, the game had changed from a routine drubbing of Yamuna to a make-or-break audition for his spot on the team.

'Also, don't look behind the goal,' said Puro.

Such instructions were almost always futile. The minute you were told not to do something, instinct dictated that you attempt to do just that just then. Alongside imagination and empathy, it was something that made one human. So Rishabh's head instantly snapped towards the goal near the basketball court. There he saw, camping on the grass, a group of Ganga house girls; and among them were the wavy tresses of the one girl who had crumpled up his heart and tossed it aside.

'Oh, God,' groaned Rishabh.

'Why did you look, bey? I told you not to look,' said Puro.

'Why did she have to come?'

'What difference does it make? Look here, listen to me,' said Puro, grabbing Rishabh by the shoulders, who was vibrating like the hindquarters of a cow atop which was perched a fly. 'She shouldn't matter any more. All that matters is this match. Play hard. Show her what Rishabh Bala is capable of. Show her that Rishabh Bala doesn't care if she's here or not. Because Rishabh Bala deserves better than her.'

'I do?' asked Rishabh. He caught Puro's eye and quickly asserted, 'I do.'

Soon the players were called to the centre of the pitch. Rishabh walked on, jelly-legged. He could physically feel the pressure crushing him. This was the first competitive match he was playing since his stupid sending off, and it seemed like the list of people he had to prove himself to just kept growing. There was the coach who didn't believe in him, the girl who had dumped him and the Ganga house spectators who had heard of his card and had come to see if he would receive another. The only ones missing from this set of doubters were his parents.

His spirits rose when they lined up against the green-shirted Yamuna team. This was because the Yamuna football team was also almost the Yamuna cricket team. After totalling all the footballers in the house, Bhupinder had found that they were eight players short. So he had drafted the cricketers. *At least they're sportsmen*, Bhupinder had thought, displaying the glass-half-full optimism that was classic Yamuna.

Fate might have dealt him a poor hand, but Bhupinder was afforded some luck before the match. He won the toss and decided that Yamuna would shoot towards the bus stop end. Which meant that Ganga would be shooting towards the basketball court end and Rishabh would spend the first half facing both the coach and Tamanna. Rishabh was determined to do his best, but the butterflies in his stomach suggested that he should go easy on his estimates.

As it turned out, Rishabh needn't have worried. Ganga decimated Yamuna 9–1. Rishabh scored two goals and set up two others. It was a mauling so brutal that it would remain the most comprehensive victory in the school's history for many years to come.

At the end of the match, the Yamuna players had to be rolled off the pitch from where they had fallen in exhaustion and grief, to the tune of boos from the handful of their supporters. Jaykar was the worst affected. He knew he had blown his chance of making it to the school team. His shoulders sagged so low that his fingertips almost grazed the grass.

The Ganga boys, on the other hand, glugged water and landed heavily on the grass. They shook their calves and waited for their hearts to settle. On the field, the white T-shirts of Himachal were lining up against the orange jerseys of Vindhya. Rishabh cast his eyes towards the basketball court end. The girls had disappeared. He wondered what she'd made of the game. Surely she had seen him dominate the second half. She had definitely witnessed him score the goals. Did she regret turning him down?

What the hell is wrong with me? he thought to himself. *I scored against Yamuna. Which girl would be impressed by that?* Then he dwelt on it further. *Why the hell should it matter what she thinks anyway? Though I'm sure the scoring-from-the-corner thing must have impressed her. Not that it matters. Just objectively, it was impressive even if it was against Yamuna. But she can also go to hell. I hope that's where she went. Not that it matters where she went. I wonder if she saw the ball I played to Rahul—*

'Good game,' said a bashful voice.

He looked up at Barkha's bright face. She had a smile on her lips and shyness in her eyes.

'Hargh?' uttered Rishabh, mid-gulp.

'I'm sorry. You must be tired.' She turned away.

'No, no, I meant thank you,' said Rishabh.

Barkha faced him, now beaming more radiantly than before.

'I don't watch much football, but it was such a thrilling match. Actually, I came because of Riya. She didn't enjoy as much. Poor thing, Tej.' She pointed towards the stands.

Tej was curled up like a dejected prawn. Riya Bose, his girlfriend, rubbed his back soothingly and whispered encouragement in his ear. Rishabh felt a pang of envy. It was true that Tej had been beaten nine times, not to mention once from a corner kick, but at least he had someone who still believed in him. He had someone he could share his grief with. Here Rishabh had played an inspiring turn in a magnificent comeback, and still he had not a soul to share his spoils with. Suddenly, he felt desperately alone. The match seemed distant. The victory lost its sweetness.

'I think you really are tired,' said Barkha. Concern coloured her features. She didn't know what to make of Rishabh's forlorn gaze. 'I just came to say congratulations,' she added hesitatingly. She stuck out her hand.

Rishabh looked confused, as if it were the first time he had encountered a handshake. Then he shook himself like a dog ridding itself of water and reached out and grasped her hand. He felt the warmth and softness of her palm, and giddiness overtook him.

'Thank you,' he said hoarsely. He didn't know what he was thanking her for. He held her hand for a fraction too long, and she withdrew it coyly. The two of them looked in every direction but at each other. Rishabh caught Rahul's eye, who, along with Sumit, stood behind Barkha; the two were grinning mischievously. All of a sudden, both attacker and defender were overcome by a coughing fit that seemed too loud and pointed to be allergic.

Barkha straightened herself and nervously tucked her hair behind her ear. Turning around, she announced in a quick, high-pitched squeak, 'Well played, all of you!'

'Glad you saw the rest of us playing too,' said Sumit with a snigger.

Barkha hit him hard on the arm and hurried to the stands. Rishabh was about to ask her to return but stopped himself when he saw the coach. Mehfouz Noorani was standing at the entrance of the shed, diagonally behind him. Rishabh didn't know how long he had been standing there. *She was* just *congratulating me*, he told himself, suppressing his guilt.

'Aye, call that Romeo goalie,' said the coach.

Rishabh breathed a sigh of relief. If the coach had seen anything suspicious, he hadn't brought it up. Sumit fetched Jaykar, who stood before the coach with his face scrunched up and ready for the rejection. The team gathered around to hear the verdict.

The coach knew they were waiting and dragged out the suspense. Rishabh couldn't believe he was relishing this announcement. Jaykar was growing increasingly jittery as the coach sized him up with a steady, studious gaze.

Finally he spoke. 'Firstly, all this coochie coo you do somewhere else. Not on the ground. Okay?'

'Sorry, sir—'

'Shhh!' hissed the coach sharply.

Jaykar winced.

'Secondly, your positioning was wrong for the second goal. You have to stay closer to the line.'

Jaykar gave a sorrowful nod.

'Thirdly, you are a keeper, but you don't have gloves?'

Jaykar shook his head.

'Now you can speak.'

'Sorry, sir. I'm not selected, no, sir?'

'No,' said the coach. 'When you get gloves, you will be on the team.'

Tej Jaykar's spine had managed to wilt further, but suddenly it straightened up. He didn't know if he had heard right, and, from the looks of it, neither had the rest of the boys.

'Sir, I didn't understand?'

'You will come to practice from day after.'

'I'm in?' verified Tej.

'Is he stupid or what?' asked the coach. Then to Tej, 'You . . . will be . . . our keeper. Come to practice . . . from day after.' He said it slowly and with gestures to ensure Tej got the point.

'Yes, sir, okay, sir, definitely, sir!'

'And remember, gloves. Now you will be professional. Understand?'

Tej was dazed. If one had asked him what he was experiencing at that moment, he would have replied, 'A miracle.'

The coach dismissed him. Jaykar tottered to the stands, but kept a cautious distance from Riya Bose. He didn't want to jeopardize his newly acquired position.

Puro asked in a low voice, 'Sir, how come you picked him?'

The coach was annoyed. 'What is this stupid question, Purohit?'

'No, sir . . . I mean . . . we thought . . . after that kind of a match, you wouldn't choose him.'

'What do you mean? He had a superb game.'

'No, sir . . . I mean . . . we scored nine goals against him.'

'Arre, you could *only* score nine goals against him. It doesn't matter how many you scored, what is important is how many he saved.'

Now there were fewer doubts as to why Tej Jaykar became the keeper and none as to why Mehfouz Noorani was the coach.

Rishabh flung the stone with savage violence. It struck the water at a hard angle and sank with an angry plop. Puro and Rishabh were at Upvan Lake. Leaning against the iron railing, Purohit was enjoying the breeze that cut across the water even as Rishabh could do nothing but be aggravated. For the last three minutes, he had been chucking stones into the water. Puro was afraid that if he didn't stop his friend soon, he would end up throwing all of Thane into the lake.

'He's messing with you, bey,' said Puro.

'I don't get it. You saw me in the house matches, no? What did you think?' demanded Rishabh.

'Are you joking?'

Ganga had faced Vindhya in the finals and had eviscerated them too. The only time Vindhya managed to keep the ball for longer than a minute was when Tejas fell on it and refused to get up until a Ganga player was booked for tackling him. This summed up Vindhya's match, and so it had come as no surprise when Ganga won 5–0. Out of the five goals, Rishabh had assisted in three and scored one. He was unanimously named player of the tournament. It was a mighty triumph for Rishabh. The trouble was that it was a triumph for him alone. Apart from being a partial redemption of his ability, the award changed nothing.

When he'd shared the happy news with his parents, they had been quick to remind him, 'It's nice but it's no distinction.'

Winning player of the tournament wouldn't get him more marks in the tests at Oswal's, nor would it reduce any of the remarks that continued to fill his calendar (Kaul Miss had to staple an extra sheet to continue jotting down disparaging comments about him). But those he could deal with. The reaction that had perplexed him the most was that of the coach, who couldn't have ignored him more if he had been the 'Beware of crocodile' sign at the entry to Upvan Lake. Rishabh had continued to train with the juniors, feeling like anything but the player of the tournament.

'What more do I have to do?' protested Rishabh, hurling another stone. Puro noted that, worryingly, the stones were getting bigger and bigger.

'I don't know,' said Puro truthfully.

'We're less than two weeks from the tournament. I don't think he'll select me.'

'Be positive, bey. It'll work out. As captain, I'm 100 per cent going to recommend your name. He's still not made the team sheet, you know.'

'So there's a chance?'

'A big one.'

'He was there for both matches. He saw me play.'

'Yeah. He said you played well also.'

'What!'

'Oh, I didn't tell you?'

'NO, you idiot!'

'Yeah, he said you played well.'

'Tell me *exactly* what he said!' said Rishabh, resisting the urge to grab Puro by the shoulders and shake him.

'Let me think. He said something like, "You boys played well. Even that Rishabh."'

'Even that Rishabh or especially that Rishabh?'

'Even that.'

'Oh, shit. But there is a chance. I'm going to be back on the team, Puro.'

'And the team is going to back you.'

Rishabh whooped and threw a large rock into the lake.

'Enough now,' interjected Puro, 'you'll disturb the crocodile.'

'Yeah, right,' scoffed Rishabh. 'It should be honoured that the player of the tournament is throwing rocks at it.'

They continued chatting, oblivious to the faint plop from the middle of the lake.

As a rule, Rishabh was a player who gave it his all in training. It was the only way to make up for his talent. In the following days, he went a step further: he gave it his all-est. He trained with a determination that bordered on damaging. He ran ceaselessly, so much so that his legs would scream with agony towards the end of the session but he would keep going, swaying drunkenly. Sharp pain would shoot down his sides, but it spurred him on, like the heels of a jockey jabbing into the flanks of a horse. He howled at himself in fury if he misplaced a pass or shot wide of the goal. He berated himself louder than the coach would ever have done. His teammates remembered their loved ones if they ever made a mistake, in case the psycho Rishabh Bala strangled them in his frustration.

His manic intensity yielded twice as many goals. The teams he was part of never failed to win a practice match. He even raised the skill level of the youngsters who played alongside him. Yet the coach left him stranded in the junior squad. He nodded appreciatively every time Rishabh shone but never invited him to train with the team that was to play in the tournament at MES High School.

As they entered the final week, Rishabh doubled his already doubled efforts. He arrived half an hour earlier than anybody else and practised his free kicks with monklike devotion. One in every ten attempts would go precisely where it was intended. The others would sail over the bar or meander to the sides. Rishabh would stoically collect them, line them up and boot them all over again. Ball after ball, day after day.

What Rishabh achieved through all this was a more consistent free kick manoeuvre, which was generally a good thing but rather pointless if he was not going to be playing any matches. So he decided to amp up his efforts another notch. Not only would he come in earlier and hoof balls into the goal, he also began staying back after training to practise penalties.

On the first day of his penalty improvement drive, the coach walked up to him, bemused. 'What's happening here?' he asked.

'Sir, I'm taking penalty shots. I had missed that one time . . . I don't want to make another mistake.'

The coach considered the situation. He couldn't make out if the boy was dedicated or if he was trying to con his way back into the fold.

'How long will you be here?'

Rishabh wanted to answer, 'As long as it takes to go for the tournament.' Instead he went with 'Ten minutes.'

'Hmm,' went the coach. 'You will put the ball back after this is over?'

'Yes, sir,' said Rishabh.

The coach took a long pause before speaking again. 'Look, I have seen you in the morning, I am seeing you now. Dedication is good. I just want to tell you—'

Rishabh's pupils dilated. This was the moment. The coach was going to take him back. He wondered what his reaction should be. Gratitude? No, he had earned it. Glee? No, he wasn't three years old. A curt thank you would do.

The coach continued. 'You should work on your technique. Make sure you aim for the sides of the goal. They are the hardest for a keeper to reach. Keep practising. It will happen soon.'

Rishabh wilted. Reality burst his bubble. His chin crashed into his chest.

'Yes, sir. Thank you, sir,' he said.

In addition to not helping him get back on the school team, his penalty-practising sessions had one more result—they rankled Poulomi K. Bobde. He wasn't hitting his shots with as much precision as he was hitting a particularly raw nerve with the teacher. The additional ten minutes that he spent on the pitch meant that he walked into class ten minutes later than everybody else. And Bobde took the first period on three days of the week: English on Mondays and Thursdays and history on Wednesdays.

The first day he sauntered in after everyone else, she wagged a menacing finger at him.

'Rishabh, why are you late?' she demanded.

'Miss, I had football practice.'

'You also have English class. How come Abhay is on time?'

'Miss, he is good at penalties. I am not. I have to practise them.'

'I don't care,' snapped Bobde. She resented the boy's calm insouciance. 'Come late on any other day, I don't care. But be on time for my lectures.'

'Sorry, miss,' said Rishabh. 'Can I sit?'

'May I sit.'

'Yes, if you want,' said Rishabh. The class erupted in laughter. Poulomi K. Bobde almost burst a capillary. She had not gone to teaching school to be made fun of by teenagers.

'NO! STUPID BOY! The right usage is "May I sit?"' she roared.

'Okay, may I?' Rishabh was too tired to get fazed by semantics. All he wanted to do was place his buttocks on a bench and give his creaky knees a rest.

'Sit. But don't come late—'

She didn't get to complete her thought because Rishabh had already shot past her. He set his bags down and let out an 'Aaaah!' The class sniggered. They were thoroughly enjoying the show.

Bobde had never encountered such a situation before. She tried to frame a remark in her head but couldn't find the words. It was the boy's first offence and he had been apologetic. 'This is to inform you that Rishabh has not been taking my rebukes seriously' sounded more like a failing on her part. Growling under her breath, she let the matter slide and returned to providing a terrible interpretation of the poem 'An October Morning'.

When she entered the classroom the next morning, the first thing Bobde noticed was that Rishabh Bala's seat was empty. Purohit saw her eyes jump to the vacant spot in front of him and gulped. The classroom buzzed with low-decibel chatter.

Bobde cracked her knuckles and sat behind the teacher's desk. She tapped the table with her fingertips. She didn't tell them to take out their textbooks. She didn't say a word. She didn't have to. The class shared her anticipation. Every soul in 10 F was waiting for one boy.

Precisely on time, ten minutes late, the dusty, wet-haired figure of Rishabh Bala staggered into the door frame. His steady eyes betrayed his preparation. He knew a showdown was imminent. Upon seeing him, the class collectively took a sharp intake of breath. Barkha shook her head solemnly. Everyone waited to see who would flinch first.

Bobde fired the opening salvo.

'What is the time?' she asked.

'Sorry, miss, I don't have a watch.'

The class tittered. Rishabh 1–Bobde 0.

Bobde knew he had bested her, so she set aside the banter and got down to brass tacks. Rising from her chair, she screamed, 'QUIET!'

A hush fell upon the class.

'The time is 8.11 a.m. This class starts at 8 a.m. Rishabh Bala, you are late again.'

Rishabh pursed his lips.

'I am taking you to the principal. Right now,' said Bobde. She briskly strode over to the door and grabbed him by his arm.

'Miss, please!'

'I am not listening to any more of your please-wease, sorry-worry,' spluttered Bobde.

'Please can I at least put my bag down?'

The request caught Bobde off guard. She was expecting a protestation, but the entreaty had thrown her. Seeing her silent, Rishabh ventured, 'Sorry, may I at least put my bag down?'

The class burst into peals of laughter. Puro guffawed the loudest. Even Aaditya Raman, the boy genius, chuckled softly. Bobde's eyes almost torpedoed out of her skull. She had comprehensively lost the duel and the class's reverence. She hadn't been this insulted since that suitor her parents had arranged for her to marry had rejected her, saying, 'Her tea tasted like rat poison.' For an English teacher, she suddenly fell mighty short of words. She gaped and goggled and, finally, she said, 'Just you wait. I will see that you get the strictest punishment.'

Rishabh's exhaustion prevented him from showing it, but he was a tad concerned. They had seen Bobde livid before, but this time she had come positively unhinged. Her nails dug into his arm and she tugged at him with enormous force. He tottered behind her with all his bags crashing against him.

The corridor of the tenth standard had seen many strange sights but never before had a teacher dragged a student down it, berating him so wildly.

'No manners. No respect. No concern. This is the tenth standard! You will regret this attitude for life. Mark my words!' shouted Bobde.

She decried his future prospects, cursed him and threatened him. 'You think you are too smart, no? I will take all the smartness out of you!' she bellowed. They left behind a corridor of peeping heads in their wake as teachers popped out of classrooms like weasels to see what the commotion was all about. The embarrassment fuelled her rage further.

'See what you have done! Look, everyone is watching now!' she snarled, but her fury eclipsed her dignity.

As they reached the stairs, her grip tightened. Rishabh winced.

'What is it?' spat Bobde.

'Miss, please don't hold my arm like that. It's hurting.'

'Good! Take this also,' Bobde said and struck him hard on the shoulder.

'Aye! Don't hit him,' said a voice from the bottom of the stairs.

Rishabh saw the Mongoose looking up at them. His hands were on his hips, his moustache quivered with indignation. This was the first time in months that Rishabh had been genuinely happy to see the coach. He breathed a deep, happy sigh. Bobde, on the other hand, had an adverse reaction. She had struck Rishabh in what she had considered to be the perfect place—near the stairs, out of sight of the prying eyes of other teachers. Now confronted with this stern, blue-tracksuit-wearing, moustachioed man, she loosened her grip around Rishabh's arm.

'And who are you to tell me what to do?' she stuttered.

'I am this boy's coach. Football coach,' said Mehfouz Noorani.

'Brilliant,' said Bobde, her anger returning with the mere mention of football. 'Then may I ask you why this boy has been coming late for MY classes?' The words ground out from between gritted teeth.

'Because I told him to stay back,' answered the coach.

Bobde was taken aback by this response. In the school, there was a general code among the adults: always agree with each other, especially if it meant getting a student in trouble. This football teacher had flagrantly violated this agreement.

'If he has disrupted your classes, it is my fault. I apologize. I will talk to him. It will not happen again,' assured the coach.

'No,' said Bobde. 'I have given this boy enough warnings. He's coming with me to the principal.'

The coach's eyes hardened. He looked at Bobde's clenched lips and then at Rishabh's helpless face. Without saying a word, he began climbing the steps until he was on the same landing as Bobde and Rishabh.

'Ma'am, I am asking nicely. Let him go. Or I can also take you to the principal for beating a student. You know the rules, no?' It was the stillness in his voice that made the threat more potent.

Bobde withdrew her talons from Rishabh's arm. She knew the coach was right. She had violated a major code of conduct in the schoolteacher's rule book. In Shri Sunderlal Sanghvi School, teachers were allowed verbal abuse of any kind—they could indulge in sarcasm and insult—as long as it didn't involve assault. Just three years ago, a Sanskrit teacher had been sacked for using a ruler on the palms of students who hadn't submitted their homework. The principal had condemned the 'barbaric deed' and had promised the parents at the annual PTA meet that she would stamp out all corporal punishment. 'I'll beat it out of the system,' she had quipped, but the parents hadn't laughed.

Bobde was well aware of the school's anti-student-pummelling policies. A smarmy smile spread across her face. Rishabh was repulsed on seeing it.

'Yes, of course. I was simply concerned for the boy. I am sure he had a good reason for being late. And I would appreciate it if you spoke to him about it. I hope we can all resolve this matter amicably. Yes?' Rishabh was truly impressed by how she could speak entire sentences while holding that smile.

'Fine. I will talk to him,' said the coach gruffly. 'You can leave him with me.'

'Right now?' asked Bobde.

'Yes.'

'Great! Send him back to class whenever you are done. Rishabh, please listen to your sir, haan?'

Rishabh almost puked at the sweetness in her voice. If he'd had any doubts about her being bipolar before, they had all but vanished now. He wagged his head.

Bobde withdrew. She made her way down the corridor with her arms by her side and her head bowed.

'Sir, thank you!' breathed Rishabh.

'Come with me,' said the coach. He descended the stairs and Rishabh followed.

The sprinklers chugged away on the field, leaving the grass to glisten in the morning light. The coach and Rishabh sat on the giant steps overlooking the ground. Mehfouz Noorani had brought him to the stands and asked him to sit down but had said nothing else for the last couple of minutes. Rishabh was growing awkward and fidgety. He began to question the coach's benevolence. Why had the coach saved him from Bobde? Was it so he could yell at him now? Was he going to tell him to stop coming to training? Were the sprinklers a metaphor for how the coach sprinkled wisdom to help them, the players, grow?

At last, the coach spoke.

'Why did you get that card?' he asked.

'Sir . . .' began Rishabh. Of all the possibilities his mind had made up, this train of thought had not occurred to him. He composed himself and recollected his sending off. 'Sir, I didn't deserve the red card. It was a yellow challenge. I just touched him, and he went flying. It was a dive, sir. Very clear. And that guy is a *haraami*. Sorry for swearing, sir, but he is. You don't know him. He's very cunning. And you saw how many fouls he had done before that, no? It wasn't my fault—'

The coach put his index finger to his lips and then held up his palm, indicating for Rishabh to stop talking.

'I did not ask you *how* you got the card. That I saw with my eyes. I asked you *why* you got the card.'

Rishabh started to make more noises, but the coach shut him down.

'That card,' said the coach, 'was coming. Whether you fouled or not. Because after the quarter-final, your whole attitude was different. It was not the attitude of a professional. You were aggravated. Undisciplined. Frustrated. So now tell me, why did you get that card?'

Visions of that rainy day flitted across his mind. He thought of Tamanna. Once again he clearly heard her soft 'No.' The potato-shaped face of Eklavya grinned in front of his eyes. And more painful than all the rest, he saw the neon red card. He saw the raindrops trickling down it as it was brandished high in the stormy sky, like a lightning conductor of bad luck.

'It's okay. You can tell me everything. I will not mind it,' said the coach.

'Sir, from the beginning?'

'From the beginning.'

'But it will take time.'

'Don't worry.'

'Sir, you promise not to judge?'

The coach barked an affirmative.

'Sir, promise?'

'Aye! Say fast.'

'Okay. So it starts with a girl,' said Rishabh.

He told the coach everything. How puberty had hit him like a truck and he had fallen for a girl called Tamanna in the seventh standard. He told him about the years he had spent in silent longing. How he had taken up football because he thought it would impress her.

'That's why you are playing the sport?' asked the coach, not masking his incredulity.

'Yes and no, sir. I started because of her, but I continued playing for myself.'

'Hmm. Go on.'

Then he told him about the fateful day he had asked Tamanna out and the hopelessness he'd felt when she had rejected him. For the first time, he put in words how lost and hollow he had felt. A large chunk of his life had been made meaningless by a one-syllable word that had taken a second to utter. Before that it had never occurred to him that others lived a life independent of him. He had been so consumed by his own selfish infatuation that he'd never stopped to wonder if she felt the same way. He told the coach that he had been confused by her love for Eklavya and then, slowly, that confusion had transformed into rage.

He apologized for his bad behaviour. He admitted that he had jeopardized the team to exact a personal revenge. Eklavya was no saint, but Rishabh was no vigilante either. A part of him had been aware that the tackle he'd made wasn't for the ball.

'I deserved that card,' said Rishabh finally. He was startled by his own admission. His heart rate dropped, and his eyes were caught by the beads of water cascading on to the ground. At long last, he had clarity on what had happened that rainy September evening.

Rishabh had answered the coach's question, but he couldn't stop. He was in such good form when it came to confessions that he decided to go on. He told the coach about his results and how his parents were breathing down his neck to study. He spoke with feeling about the pressure of being in a board year, with the end-of-the-year exams looming on the horizon, casting their long shadow on all the days before them. He told the coach how much football aggravated his parents. And when he had run out of his own grievances, he even told the coach about Puro's problems with his father. Finally when Rishabh was silent, the coach turned to him.

'Is that everything?' he asked softly. Rishabh was surprised that the coach could speak without his voice sounding like it came out of a cheese grater.

'That's everything,' confirmed Rishabh, staring ahead.

A slight chuckle escaped from beside him. He saw that a smile had opened up underneath the Mongoose's bushy moustache and that his eyes had crinkled with laughter. It occurred to him that he had never really heard the coach laugh before. He had an odd fluty squeak for a laugh. And then it struck Rishabh that maybe the coach was laughing at him. He felt gypped that his heartfelt outpouring was met with ridicule.

The coach was oblivious to Rishabh's dark sentiments. He continued tittering to himself and then struck his forehead with his palm. 'You know,' he said, 'I forgot that you all are only boys. I am coaching a team of boys. And I forgot! How old are you, Rishabh?'

'Sir, fifteen.'

'Fifteen! Boys for sure. Mehfouz! How could you forget, yaar?' The coach slapped his forehead once more.

'Sir, what happened?'

'I made one mistake, Rishabh. And it is not a small one. All this time I have been thinking that I was coaching bloody

Mohun Bagan! But you are only kids, yaar. You are boys! You have hormones and foolishness. And that's a good thing,' added the coach, seeing Rishabh frown.

'You see, Rishabh, a man forgets where he comes from. I also used to show off when my wife was in the stadium. My coach would know. He used to say, 'Mehfouz, today too many step-overs. Nazneen has come or what?' And you know what? She used to get impressed also!' The coach upturned his collar.

'Those were the days, yaar. I had a team like yours only. All the boys were there: Swapnil, D'Mello, Roger, Baldeep. We won so many trophies. Santosh Trophy, Durand Cup—all of them. Sunday afternoon was beer day. So many times I've carried Baldeep home. Bloody bastard was so heavy! Now we are all bloody old. We get hangovers just drinking water.' The coach grew quiet. In the mist of the sprinklers he saw the sunny days of his prime, when his knee was sturdy and his body was unbreakable.

'Main thing was that we had fun. My father was like yours. I told him I want to play football. But he didn't like it. He said, "Passion and all is fine, but can passion fill your stomach?" He was very much against it. But I did it anyway. And you know what? I don't regret it. My career ended because of this, see.' He hiked up the right leg of his trackpants and revealed his knee. It was gnarled and twisted like an old tree trunk.

'I played at the top level for only ten years. But I played it all, haan. Indian league, Indian national team, Maharashtra team. Everything. Only ten years . . . then it was over. But they were the best ten years of my life. Till the day he died my father said I wasted my life, but I will tell you—ten years of happiness is enough. Most people—even my father—don't even get one year.

'And football is so beautiful at your age. When you are playing only because you like playing. You boys are so lucky. You don't have to think about the rent, children's fees, *biwi ka kharcha*. You can just bloody play!' He chuckled again. 'And then I come along and keep bugging you people. Aye, do this, do that! You know, I was treating you like men, yaar. But you are only bloody boys. You will fall in love. Enjoy it. You will fall in love many times, but never like the first time. And yes, pay attention to your studies. I have said it before and I will say it again: it is important. And enjoy this time on the pitch, yaar. You will never get it back. My mistake was that I made you play from here,' he tapped Rishabh's foot, 'when you should always play from here.' He patted Rishabh's chest.

'Now, getting that card was a very selfish mistake. Because you were hurt, you hurt the whole team. But I guess boys make such mistakes. What I like is that you have finally understood how to say sorry. I have been watching. You are on time . . . sorry, *before* time. Free kick practice. Penalty practice. Very good. My coach used to say, "You are a man when you change your capability and not your challenge." I can see the maturity in you. And I will also be a man and say that I am also sorry, Rishabh. I will be happy if you train with the senior team. You deserve it.' The coach extended his arm and almost hugged Rishabh but, at the last moment, settled for three pats on the back.

Rishabh turned his face away and flicked the tears out of his eyes. He had spent the last two months in the pursuit of these very words. He was overwhelmed, but the coach had called him a man. He took a few seconds to compose himself and then said in a moist voice, 'Sir . . . does this mean I am on the team for the MES tournament?'

'Aye! Did I say that?'

'No, sir . . .'

'See, you have not trained with the senior team. I cannot take a chance. But you start coming for practice and the next tournament pakka you will play. Okay?'

'Yes, sir.'

Rishabh took the coach's leave. He hoisted his bags and made his way to class. When he found himself alone, his eyes filled up with tears again. If one had placed him on the ground just then, he would have done a better job than all the sprinklers.

November 2006

'NOT EVEN THE quarter-final, *behenchod*!' spat Purohit, making the group of girls walking in front of them jump and scurry.

'Shit, man . . .' mumbled Rishabh.

'Those DES *chutiya*s didn't deserve to win, bey,' continued Puro.

'I wish I were there.'

'We needed you, man. That Oza didn't make one right pass. The goalpost moved more than he did!'

Sanghvi hadn't had a happy campaign at MES High School. In fact, few campaigns had been worse. The Sanghvites' reputation of being a formidable footballing force had been built over years of terrific tournaments. They weren't a team that crashed out in the round of 16. That was the forte of schools like Bluebell Academy, which is why it had come as a surprise to all when Satvik Mukherjee of Dingreja Educational Society scored in the final minute of extra time to eliminate S4.

So huge was the shock that Ghadge Sir still hadn't spoken to them.

Two days later, Purohit was still shaking and thrashing about with anger as he related the events to Rishabh. Their tutorials had just got over, and they were standing near the bus stop in the narrow lane outside Oswal's.

'Who won the tournament?' asked Rishabh.

'We did,' said a voice to their left.

Often people found themselves being at the right place at the right time. Eklavya Bhamtekara had a knack for being at the wrong place at the wrong time. Or so Rishabh thought as he stared at Eklavya's bulbous head and buck teeth. He had his arms crossed over his chest and was leaning against a Pulsar motorcycle.

'Kamani Krida are the champions again,' he said in a mock announcer voice.

'Oh, God, not again,' groaned Puro.

'Is that what you said when DES beat you? We saw you losers. It was too funny.'

'Buddy, not now,' said Puro quietly.

'I would have said 'Well played' but I don't want to lie.'

'Okay. I don't know what you're doing here, but get the hell out,' snarled Rishabh.

'Good question. I'm waiting for my girlfriend. I don't know if you know her . . .? Her name is Tamanna.'

Puro put a hand on Rishabh's shoulder. He expected Rishabh to blow a fuse, to rush at Eklavya, to at least lash out with some degree of violence. Rishabh brushed off his hand. Puro stepped forward. *Here it comes*, he thought. But Rishabh burst into . . . a smile. Puro did a double take.

'I'm so glad she's not my girlfriend because she's clearly into losers.'

It was now Eklavya's turn to get flustered. He sprang forward. 'I heard you play with the juniors now.'

'I've heard you've always been doing that. How old are you, dadaji?'

Eklavya's breathing had quickened. Still, he persisted. 'Be honest, did I end your career? Is that why you didn't come? I was looking forward to whacking you at MES too.'

'Puro, do you think it would fix his face if I punched it?' asked Rishabh dramatically.

Purohit gave him a sidelong stare. He was as proud of his friend as he was concerned. The Rishabh he had first met in the seventh standard had been a diffident runt with an atrocious middle parting, who read books and wore his trousers an inch below his spectacles. For most of their friendship, Rishabh had left the trash-talking to Puro, preferring to mumble in fear in the background instead. Puro hadn't noticed when the boy growing up beside him had brushed back his hair, lowered his pants to his waist and begun quipping like a thug. As glad as the change made him, though, Puro worried if Rishabh had the will to back up the words.

Rishabh's jibe had penetrated Eklavya's ugly mug. It took him a few seconds to process it but when he did, he bellowed and rushed Rishabh. He grabbed Rishabh by his shirt front, who gripped his combatant's neck in a vice.

'Say that again, you bastard!'

'I knew you wouldn't get it the first time.'

Purohit tried his best to prise the two apart, but their ferocity repelled him. He could see that Eklavya was gearing up to slam his fist into Rishabh's gut. He was about to grapple the older boy from behind, when Tamanna exited Oswal's building. She immediately saw her boyfriend and her admirer locked in combat and shrieked.

'STOP IT!'

But the two boys neither stopped it nor let go. Their teeth were bared. Tamanna grabbed Eklavya by the shoulders and pulled as hard as she could.

'Look, your girlfriend's here, do you really want to do this?' panted Rishabh.

'Are you jealous?' sneered Eklavya.

To call the question intelligent would be going too far, but as far as Rishabh was concerned, it definitely was thought-provoking. An instant after Eklavya spoke, Rishabh looked at Tamanna. Her face was contorted with the effort of hauling Eklavya away. Then he looked at the leering melon that Eklavya called a head. A thought crossed his mind: *If this is what she wants, I am happy for her.*

'Not at all,' Rishabh said and released his hold on Eklavya, who rubbed his palm along his throat.

'Good. Because if I see you near her, I'll kill you!'

'You won't. Because I like someone else.'

Rishabh's gaze didn't flinch from Eklavya, but he could see the effect his words had had around him. Tamanna cocked her head; Purohit put his hands on his hips; Eklavya spat at his feet.

'Stay. Away,' he warned in conclusion and then mounted his bike.

Tamanna joined him angrily. She threw a glance at Rishabh and bobbed her head. It was an ambiguous nod. Rishabh couldn't tell if she was being apologetic, annoyed or envious. The bike vroomed to life.

'A fifteen-year-old with a license? Very believable!' Rishabh screamed after them.

Eklavya held up his middle finger, which was promptly swatted by Tamanna.

Good riddance, thought Rishabh.

'Are you sure about this?' asked Puro.

It annoyed Rishabh that he had been asked this question for the twentieth time. The first ten times he had put down to caution and the next nine to friendly concern, but this last instance was just insulting his intelligence.

'Just say it, Puro. You don't like her?' said Rishabh.

Puro's shoulders bounced, his mouth opened and shut and opened again. 'It's . . . Barkha. And it's you! All I am saying is . . . *are you sure about this?*'

'I am *very* sure about this. She's a lovely girl. She's smart, she's cute, she's got great taste in pencil boxes. Have you seen hers? I like that shade of green. Elegant design too.'

'Pencil boxes? You know nothing about her, bey!'

'We've talked.'

'Three times. For three minutes each.'

'You just don't like her because she writes your name on the board,' said Rishabh.

This was true. Ninety per cent of the trouble Purohit had got into that year had begun because Barkha had done her job as class monitor too diligently. She had told on him for every possible offence, ranging from the mundane (talking in class, not submitting homework) to the memorable (throwing the duster out of the window, pelting Pinto Miss with a paper plane).

'Yeah,' admitted Puro, 'but I'm also worried that you're jumping into this too soon. Just two months ago you were about to cut your wrists over Tamanna and now you're thinking of dancing in the fields with this Barkha girl! It's a little too fast, no?'

'Firstly, I was never going to cut my wrists over Tamanna. She doesn't deserve that kind of sacrifice. And secondly, it takes only one second to fall in love.'

'Love! You're seriously in L-O-V-E with Barkha? It's not like? Or lust? Or having-a-crush-on-her-because-she's-literally-the-only-girl-who-has-smiled-at-you-since-Tamanna-said-no?'

Whether he'd intended it or not, Purohit had raised a reservation that Rishabh had indeed been wrestling with. There had been a definite uptick in the fondness he felt for Barkha but, worryingly, it had coincided with Tamanna giving him the thumbs down. However, he'd reminded himself of the epiphany he had experienced. Towards the end of his scuffle with Eklavya, he'd had a searing vision of Barkha. Her bright, pleasant face had popped up in front of his eyes. He had felt a warm, tingly shudder. She was everything that Tamanna wasn't. While Tamanna was callous, she was caring. While Tamanna was impulsive, she was measured. While Tamanna liked Eklavya, Barkha liked him. She was the one.

'I do love her.'

'But you said Tamanna was your one true love.'

'Yeah, I know I did,' snapped Rishabh. 'But do you know what it means when your true love doesn't work out?'

Puro shook his head.

'It isn't true love after all.'

The bell rang and the short break ended. The kids began racing back to their classrooms. Rishabh left his friend looking out over the bridge. He turned around when he'd reached the other end. 'I'm going to ask her out. In the lunch break. I hope you'll wish me luck.'

'All the best!' yelled Puro.

'Not now, bey. In the lunch break.'

'Oh, sorry,' said Puro. He raced to join his friend. 'Tell me something,' he began. 'How do you know she likes you?'

Rishabh smiled. 'She gave me her notes,' he said warmly.

Puro rubbed the back of his head. *For all his new badassery*, he thought, *deep down the fucker is still a nerd.*

Just as the bell was sounded for the long break, Puro wished him luck (rather reluctantly) and Rishabh Bala sallied forth. He had asked Barkha to meet him near the staircase at the rear of the corridor. There had been a minor hiccup in his plan when she had benignly asked him, 'Why?' It was not a contingency he had prepared for but, being quick on his feet, he'd improvised, 'I have a civics doubt.' Thankfully, she had seen the pleading look in his eyes and did not ask aloud why someone would need civics doubts answered specifically near the staircase.

With a pounding heart, Rishabh strode out of class, mentally running through his prepared lines. He rounded the corner and, as the Beatles eloquently put it, 'saw her standing there.' Even with arms folded across her chest, she looked as close to an angel as a person could without having the wings or the halo.

He walked up to her, putting in some effort to make sure his back didn't give in to gravity. Standing in front of her, he cleared his throat.

'Well,' he began.

'Yes?' she said. 'What's your doubt?'

He was surprised by his own composure, which he put down to this being his second proposal of the year. *At this rate*, he thought to himself, *pretty soon I'll be a veteran proposer.*

'My doubt is,' he said, 'Barkha Kotwal, I really, really, *really* like you. Will you go out with me?'

He had rehearsed the line in front of the mirror. Each 'really' was accompanied by its own inflection. The first was delivered low and smooth, the second was affirmative and bold and the third was explosive with a hint of seductive thrown in.

The effect of the words on Barkha was instantaneous. However, her reaction wasn't exactly what Rishabh had imagined. In his forecast of the situation, she'd swoon and say, 'Yes, yes! For a handsome, dashing boy like you, always and forever YES!'

But back in the corridor on that November afternoon, Barkha's eyes first leapt to the side of Rishabh's head, then to the floor, and then she let out a low whimper and burst into tears. Without saying a word, she shot into the girls' bathroom.

Rishabh couldn't believe his luck. When girls weren't outright rejecting his proposals, they were bursting into tears and running off into loos. Surely he had to have a long, hard think about his MO, because, in current form, it was utterly failing him. He kicked the air in frustration and made his lonely way back to class.

In class, Purohit debriefed him and grew visibly joyous as the narration went on. At last he spoke. 'I'm so glad you have this effect on women, my boy!'

But Purohit had spoken prematurely because Barkha's sobbing had had nothing to do with Rishabh asking her out. At least not in the way the two boys thought it had. The truth was that Barkha had been dating Dhruv Kelkar, the school captain, on the sly for the past two years. Rumours had abounded, of course, but the couple had laughed it off expertly. For all practical purposes, they were just another platonic pair that was teased in the corridors.

However, around the time Rishabh had applied for the position of boyfriend, Dhruv and Barkha's relationship had soured. Their liaison was what the tabloids would have termed as being 'on the rocks'. It was the usual culprits that drove a school couple apart: they had shifted to different classes, taken different optional subjects, slowly grown apart, she'd complained he didn't spend as much time talking on the phone, he'd said she didn't understand how much homework he had been getting.

All of it had taken a toll on the couple, leading up to the moment when Barkha stormed out of the girls' bathroom, face flushed with tears, cornered Dhruv in the corridor and, in no uncertain terms, declared, 'I can't take it any more! It's over! OVER! You understand?' It being over came as a surprise to everyone in the corridor because no one had known it was actually going on to begin with.

Dhruv looked about sheepishly, as a boy who's had a wailing girl tell him it was over was wont to look. Barkha then stormed right back down the corridor, turned into 10 F and came to a stop at Rishabh's desk. 'Yes, I like you too,' she said.

It was under those angry, tearful and, if truth were told, wee bit scary circumstances that Rishabh Bala finally found himself single no more.

Rishabh hadn't read those Mills & Boon romance novels that the girls in his class were glued to, but he imagined that the plots couldn't have been better than his first week with Barkha. It was nothing short of enchanting. When he sat beside her in the mornings and caught her eye, the ache and strain of football training would disappear. He couldn't take his eyes off her. Constantly staring to his right caused a crick to develop in his neck. He wanted to tell the world that the studious beauty who sat an aisle away from him was his girlfriend, but he couldn't because she didn't want anyone from school to find out.

After all, secrecy was the norm in school romances, and for good reason. Merciless teasing inevitably followed if the class caught a whiff that a couple was in their midst. Plus a girl of Barkha's academic stature had a reputation to maintain. One couldn't be taken seriously as monitor of the class if they were also seen gallivanting around with disreputable elements from the football team. Not to mention the teachers. They always frowned upon the couples of the class. Rishabh didn't care much about what Kaul Miss thought of his private life, but Barkha insisted that the less she knew the better it was, and he deferred to her judgement. She hadn't been the teacher's pet for so many years without knowing a thing or two about the teacher's psyche.

Besides, the clandestine nature of their togetherness only added to its thrill. Each day of that first week, he felt like they were two spies on a mission, sharing codes that only they understood—like when they smiled ever so slightly while passing each other in the corridors or when his hand brushed lightly against hers while forming a line for the computer labs or when he put a poem in her bag.

Putting a poem in a girl's bag was like wearing three-fourths. It would seem awfully cool at the time, but in a few years' time one was wont to wonder what they'd been thinking. Years later, Rishabh Bala would be doing something mundane, like reading the newspaper, when he would suddenly remember the time he had slipped a poem into Barkha's bag and it would leave him cringing with embarrassment for the rest of the day.

Even when it came to the matter of dropping sonnets into one's beloved's bag, there was a right way to do it and a wrong way. For instance, it was universally accepted that one must not deposit the composition in the front pocket, where the tiffin box was kept, as the chances of discovery by the partner's mother became exponentially higher. And Rishabh had done just that. If one did stow the note in the front pocket, which contained the tiffin box, one had to at least ensure that their significant other was made aware of its presence. This Rishabh did not do.

As a result, that evening when Barkha's mother opened her bag to extract her tiffin box for its daily cleaning, out tumbled the note. Barkha denied knowing anything about it. She said it had to be a secret admirer from class. 'Your secret admirer calls himself David Beckham?' her mother said with arched eyebrows. The next day, Rishabh got a dressing-down that dissuaded him from planting furtive poems in anyone's bag ever again.

Then, as if to equal the score, Barkha called on Rishabh's landline a few days later. He had told her not to ring his home under any circumstances, yet here was his mother screaming, 'For you. Barkhaaaaa!'

LIC agents had called the Bala landline more than girls had. Besides, girls didn't ring for Rishabh Bala. He didn't have any female friends because all his friends were on the football team. Hence he had explained to his girlfriend that if she were to call out of the blue, suspicions would arise. And he had been right.

The minute he kept the receiver down, he was held for detailed questioning. He was badgered about the identity of this mystery girl and what business she had calling him. He cooked up a flimsy, loophole-ridden story about how she was helping him with project work.

'Rishabh, you'll have enough time to do your "project work" once you're done with your boards,' said Mr Bala.

Rishabh knew he had dodged a bullet, and the next day he told Barkha, in no uncertain terms, that she should burn the sheet that bore his number and erase it from her memory too, if possible.

The beginnings of their amorous engagement led to a happy time in Rishabh's life. For the first time in months, he found himself springing out of bed, eager to face the day, and not cowering under the blankets, bemoaning his alarm, his mother, school, life, the universe—in that order. He found pleasure in the small, mundane activities that made up most of daily living. The smell of El Paso tickled his olfactory senses once more and he sang in the shower. Music returned to his life. He would find himself jigging alone in his room to the latest MP3s that Sumit had pirated and provided on a pen drive.

One lunch break, Kaul Miss called him to her table and inquired, 'Is everything all right, Rishabh?'

'Yes, miss. Why?' asked a worried Rishabh. Had she found out?

'Nothing. It's just that you've been paying attention in class. I wanted to know if something was wrong with you.'

She beamed at him, amused by her own cleverness. It was refreshing to see such childlike glee in a woman so old. Besides, Rishabh was simply relieved that she hadn't caught wind of his super secret love affair.

'No, miss, everything is okay.'

'Good. She's having a positive effect on you.'

She beamed harder. Rishabh stared at her, mouth agape. Their cover had been blown! He didn't know where Kaul Miss stood on class romances, so he stood silent, shuffling his feet.

'Don't worry. If I cared so much, I would have changed your seats a long time ago.'

Rishabh stepped closer to the desk. 'Miss . . . how did you find out? Did someone tell you? Was it Purohit?'

Kaul Miss laughed. She had a hearty, boisterous laugh that drew the attention of the entire classroom. She glared at the rest of them and said, 'You people eat your food. Do your work.' Then she rested her chin on her downturned palm and looked up at Rishabh with ancient, twinkling eyes.

'I have been teaching for two decades. I've seen countless children pass through this classroom. Each batch as filled to the brim with hormones as the last one. I see them fall in love. I see them stare at each other from across the classroom. The boys are more obvious, the girls are more cunning. And they all have one thing in common—they think that us teachers are either blind or stupid. They think we will never find out. The two of you are always red like tomatoes. It's hard to miss that colour.'

'Oh.'

'You are not as smart as you think. Kaul Miss is an old fox, remember that. She was here before you came and she will be here long after you are gone. You remember that.'

'I will, miss.'

'And I like that girl. Good monitors are rare to find. You treat her well, otherwise . . .' She wagged a mock-threatening finger at him.

Rishabh blushed and nodded.

'And cut down on this football business. It's too late in the year for silly games.'

'Now you're asking for too much, miss,' said Rishabh, grinning,

'Uffo . . .' Kaul Miss sighed tiredly. 'Every batch listens to Kaul Miss less and less.'

The most surprising reaction came from his teammates. He broke the news to them as they were warming up for training one chilly morning. As soon as they heard that he was dating Barkha, they burst into a chirping that out-chirped the seventeen mynahs that were pecking at the earth a short distance away. Rishabh probably imagined this, but he thought the mynahs looked annoyed at the racket they were making. Up until then, he had assumed that a bunch of footballers that prided themselves for being tough young men wouldn't revel in gossiping. But seeing their eager eyes and hearing their prying questions made him revise his opinion.

'When did this happen?' quizzed Tejas.

'More importantly, *why* did this happen?' asked Bhupinder, who instantly disliked anyone whose GPA was higher than 3 (Barkha's was a 4 point something). Bhupinder felt that scholars were part of the establishment. They were bland 'sell-out's who had bought into the academic system and were not to be trusted. Few knew it then, but he was showing all the makings of the first-class hipster that he would eventually become.

'She's really nice once you get to know her,' said Rishabh defensively.

Purohit snorted. He continued to stretch with a distant look of deep dissatisfaction stamped on his face. Puro's reaction was typical of the person whose best friend had suddenly acquired a girlfriend. Rishabh seemed totally absorbed in her. He'd stopped loitering down the corridors with Puro in the lunch break, choosing instead to sit and chat with that girl. After school, too, he'd go off with Barkha, and Puro rode the bus back alone. When they spoke, they talked off superficialities—studies, training, match scores. Rishabh would keep the marrow of his thoughts and feelings for Barkha. He now found it easier—and more exciting—to talk to her. Her sympathetic cooing and thoughtful inputs towards even his most inane revelations enthralled him. This was usually the case when young boys first had a deep conversation with a girl. They suddenly realized the callousness of boyish conversation.

For the first time in his life, Rishabh was made aware of aspects of life like emotion, affection, empathy and understanding. For once, he could be vulnerable about his hopes and fears, his insecurities and afflictions. Discovering this was new and thrilling, and he found himself spending more and more time glued to Barkha at school. But he hadn't stopped to think about the toll this was taking on his best friend. He'd assumed Puro would understand that things had changed, but Puro didn't. He simply missed his friend and wished he could say as much.

'Arre! It's unbelievable!' Rahul whistled.

'What? That I would ask her out?'

'No! That she would say yes.'

Rishabh flung a pebble at Rahul, who dodged it.

'How long before they break up?' Sumit asked of the boys.

'Why would we break up?'

Sumit laughed a grim one. 'Come on. You both are too different.'

'But opposites attract,' argued Rishabh. 'Don't they?'

'Yes. But similar sticks together.' It was the coach.

The team quit bantering and snapped into warm-up positions in record time. The coach shook his head.

'So who's the lucky man?' he asked.

Everyone unanimously pointed at Rishabh. The coach clapped his hands. 'Of course it's Rishabh Bala. Persistence paid off?'

'Er, not exactly, sir. It's not the same gir—'

But the coach carried on. 'Good timing also, haan. Team, come closer. Juniors, keep stretching.'

The senior team swarmed around the Mongoose. Rishabh still felt an electric buzz of happiness over being part of this hive again. He liked his juniors well enough now, but he would never want to be banished ever again.

The coach spread his arms out. 'Are you boys ready to play?'

The team declared that they were indeed ready.

'Good. Because the next tournament is in December. It's a big one. You know where it is being held?' He took a dramatic pause, leaned in, curled his lips and growled, 'Kamani Krida Public School!'

Spontaneous whoops and jeers of varying degrees of aggression erupted from the boys, drawing the judgement of the mynahs once more. On their first day of training after the MES debacle, the coach had told them to train with sincerity because another tournament was around the corner. He had promised to supply more details soon.

'This is the one I was talking about. We have one full month to prepare. It's time for revenge. What say, Rishabh?'

Rishabh shook his head. 'Sir, I'm not dating that girl,' he said diffidently.

'Oh,' said the coach, 'you found another girl?' His features hardened. 'How many girls will you fall in love with? You're falling in love or buying onions?'

The players laughed. The coach flashed an impish grin. 'You'll date all the girls or you'll leave some for them also?'

'Sir, please, yaar . . .'

The coach put an arm around him and, in an instant, gripped his head in a lock. 'Aye, you date any girl you want. Date the teachers also, but—'

Savage oohs and aahs escaped the boys at the mention of dating teachers. If a collective thought bubble were placed over the heads in that congregation, then only the face of Avantika Miss would occupy it.

'. . . you owe the team a victory. You will pay your debt?'

'Yes, sir,' squealed Rishabh. He was in such close proximity to the coach's armpit that he finally figured out how the coach managed to wear the same blue tracksuit every day. The trick was that he didn't wash it.

'What is this *choo-choo* you are doing like a mouse? Say clearly. You will score the winning goal?'

'YES, SIR!' he squawked.

'Rest of you?'

'YES, SIR,' came the chorus.

The mynahs took flight but not before shaking their tiny heads at the barbarians they shared the ground with.

Kamani Krida Public School was like chewing gum that had got stuck to the sole of Rishabh's life. There was no ridding himself of their sticky presence. No matter how much time passed, Sanghvi was fated to duel Kamani Krida as if they were two arch-enemies: Real Madrid and Barcelona, Batman and the Joker, Clinic All Clear and Dandruff, Eklavya and Rishabh.

The more Rishabh thought about this, the less sense it made. How had the universe presented him with this opportunity? He was going to be up against the team that had ruined his year, up against the boy who had made his world bleaker.

He remembered the fiery eyes of Eklavya Bhamtekara from when they had scuffled outside Oswal's. His pride had burned in his sockets. Rishabh wanted to extinguish the blaze. He wanted to see Eklavya suffer. There would be nothing more satisfying than watching Eklavya's insufferable cockiness be confronted with defeat. He wouldn't know how to react. Like a star dying out, he would implode. Rishabh became consumed by the tournament. A month seemed too long a time to wait.

He was so motivated that he mused, *It's a pity Kamani Krida isn't up against us in studies. I would top the board if it meant beating that overage bastard.* Trembling with excitement, he paced his room to walk the energy off, but it only fed off his emotions and kept building. He wanted to talk to Barkha. He needed her calm voice to soothe his rattling spirit.

Calling Barkha was quite a task because of their strict no-calls-at-home policy. He first called Tej, who in turn called Riya, who rang up Barkha and told her to stay near the phone. Riya then relayed the message to Tej, who passed it on to Rishabh, who finally dialled Barkha's number. It was a ten-minute ordeal but well worth the wait, because when she answered the phone, he felt like a Labrador whose master had come home.

'Hullo! Barkha! Thank God you answered.'

'Rishabh? What happened?'

'It's going to happen. I can't wait for it to happen!'

'Is this about that football match?'

'It's not a football *match*. It's a tournament.'

'Yes.' One of the consolations of being on the phone was that Barkha could freely roll her eyes at his boyish touchiness.

'Can you believe that it's happening at Kamani Krida? How is that possible?'

'There are only four major schools in Thane. KKPS is one of them, Rishabh. I can see it being very possible.'

This was the trouble with dating toppers. They could never see the miracles of the world without ruining them with logic and common sense.

'Noooo,' moaned Rishabh, 'it's karma. That's what it is. They cheated against us. Now they're going to pay.'

Barkha laughed. She found it adorable that Rishabh could make even the most random events about himself.

'Is it?' she humoured him.

'Yup. I'm going to show that fucker Eklavya his place. Thinks he's better than me because he's dating my girl. I'm going to destroy him. Just you wait!'

It was only when he'd finished that the words that had come out of Rishabh's mouth reached his brain. He winced. There was silence from the other end. He could hear her breathing.

'Barkha? Hello?' he said. His voice trickled out of him.

The lack of response cut into his chest.

'Hello?' he tried again. 'Barkha, are you there?'

'Yes.'

'I'm sorry. It's not what you think. I said that out of habit.'

'Hmm.'

'Barkha, believe me. You know what happened. I got that card because of that guy.'

'Is this really about the card, Rishabh?' The hurt in her voice was palpable. The receiver was clammy in his hands.

'Fully, totally, 100 per cent about the card. I don't care about her. I don't even care about her!'

'Okay.'

'Barkha, believe me. It's not about her. I called you because I'm afraid. I know I seem brave and all, but I'm just scared about letting the team down again. What if I mess up? Then what?'

Barkha closed her eyes. She held the receiver away. It was a good thing he wasn't in front of her.

'Then you won't have to go through it alone,' she said.

Rishabh gawked at the wall in front of him. Her compassion made him feel even stupider. He thumped his chest in anger. How could he have made such a foolish mistake? He was still debating whether to tell her how special she was or to apologize profusely, when she spoke.

'Rishabh, I have to go now. I'll talk to you later.'

The jarring static kept buzzing in his ear long after he'd kept the receiver down.

The ties that bound lovers together were woven with the threads of trust and delusion. After that fateful phone call, Rishabh had stretched the tie to its limit. It had begun to fray. Subsequently, Barkha was not herself in class. She grew quiet and became withdrawn. It hurt Rishabh to see her suffer, but the more he tried to make amends, the more demure she became. She treated Rishabh as if he were speaking in a foreign language—she would listen attentively but with a blank, confused look on her face, and if she answered, she did so in monosyllables. One day Rishabh penned a heartfelt ode titled 'My Aching Heart' and this time sneaked it under her desk after the last period. The next morning, he found it lying on his desk, tightly crumpled into a ball. If anything, it only made his heart ache more.

Thankfully, for Rishabh, things were looking up on the football pitch. He enjoyed training in the crisp winter mornings. The boys were playing well together. Even Jaykar had seamlessly integrated into the team. But the major revelation of these practices was the blistering form of Amar Verma. The slender, soft-spoken Vindhya house left back had long been warming the benches. He had pace and intelligence, but he'd just never seemed to assert himself in matches before. However, in these November sessions, he had finally come into his own. He played like a dogged defender and his devilish speed made it impossible to get around him.

'*Where* were you all these days?' said the coach, smacking him on the head.

'Here only,' said Amar in his lilting Uttar Pradesh accent.

'Arre, where was this form?'

'Sir, it came from Siddhivinayak.' He joined his palms and uttered a soft prayer.

It turned out that Amar's parents had taken him to Siddhivinayak Temple in Prabhadevi, so that Ganesh could knock some sense into the boy about his studies. Little did they realize that in his private chat with God, he had asked instead for a chance to play on the school team. With God literally on his side, Amar's confidence had soared to the point where he was on the brink of replacing Vade. Meanwhile, his parents continued to wonder what else they would have to do to get one good hour of studying out of him.

Rishabh should have known that the going was too good to last. Soon the football team would face a major setback. All thanks to Pinal Oza and his fragile right hand.

Being made of churan, Pinal Oza's bones were genetically predisposed to getting pulverized. The Ozas were a brittle bunch. His grandmother, Saritaben Oza, had undergone two hip replacements. His father suffered from chronic slipped discs. Pinal Oza himself couldn't remember a single year of his life during which he hadn't had a cast on some part of his body. This had reached a point where those close to Oza were bored of writing lewd messages on his pristine plaster casts.

Therefore, when Tejas flicked a ball upward, which struck him on his wrist, Oza immediately knew it had cracked. He howled in pain and hopped up and down, clutching his limp wrist.

'It's broken!' he screamed.

'What rubbish! The ball barely touched you.'

'It's gone!' wailed Oza.

The coach cleared the mob around the writhing Oza.

'Show me the hand,' he commanded.

The coach had seen the ball that had hit Oza. It was going slower than a bill through Parliament. He was convinced that there was no way the impact could have done more damage than a slight sprain. So when Oza presented his arm, the coach immediately grabbed the wrist and manoeuvred it to the left and the right and then up and down. If the wrist wasn't broken before that, it sure was then. In sheer agony, Oza kicked the coach on the shin, freed his paw and, bellowing, ran down the pitch to the infirmary.

The next day, his mother stormed into the principal's office screaming so loudly that if the football team had heard her they would have thought she had broken a bone too. Mrs Asha Oza was livid. She accused the school of negligence. 'HOW,' she thundered, 'WAS FOOTBALL PRACTICE STILL ALLOWED TO TAKE PLACE SO CLOSE TO THE BOARD EXAMS?'

Her son had fractured his right hand, his writing hand. He had almost jeopardized his entire career by kicking a ball around. Thankfully, the doctors had assured her that his wrist would be in fine condition well before the exams. But who would have taken responsibility if the Oza bones hadn't been so used to fusing up quickly, thanks to the repeated damage. 'Tell me, madam principal, would it have been you or that *lafanga* football coach?'

It was powerful rhetoric powerfully delivered. The principal was moved to action. She promptly called Ghadge Sir to her office and, venting her own ire, demanded that the school cease football practice for the tenth standard with immediate effect. He in turn rained the news on to the boys.

'There wheel be no more phootball phor tenth shtandard boys phor resht oph year.' He had predicted the outcry that followed, so he swiftly added, 'This is order phrom principal. Iph you are not liking it, please talk to her itselph.'

'Sir, please,' they begged.

'No.'

'Sir, last tournament.'

'NO! I SED NO!'

The team wrote a letter to the principal but received an unequivocal response in the negative. She wrote back saying that if any tenth standard student was found practising on the school premises, the culprit's parents would be called and they would be suspended—the culprits, not the parents, of course. Furthermore, letters had been dispatched to their homes, informing their parents that football practice stood cancelled for the final year students. The quashing of the team was complete.

As hope evaporated, some turned their wrath towards the source of their problem. The boys had to do all they could to restrain Sumit from breaking the remaining bones in Oza's body. Puro called for peace. 'It's not Oza's fault,' he reasoned.

Rishabh begged to differ. He had always seen Oza as a usurper of his place, and now the weasel had graduated to stealing their tournament from them! *One just had to marvel,* thought Rishabh, *at how good Oza was at ruining things for the football team even when he wasn't on the pitch.*

They fought the ban for two more days, taking turns going to the principal's office. The only outcome of the pleading was that the principal's secretary was now on first-name terms with the entire football team. He would greet them with a cheery smile and tell them that the principal was not in. Once Rana had even seen the principal standing outside the door, but Yadav, her secretary, vehemently insisted that she was at a conference in Ulhasnagar.

On the third day, the finality of the decision finally sunk in and turned Rishabh and Puro into sulking, slouching messes.

They lay draped on their desks, gaping at the teachers with unseeing eyes. When the bell sounded for the short break, Rishabh felt a tap on his shoulder.

'What's happened to you?' asked Barkha.

It was the first conversation she had initiated in a whole week. One of the odd things about couples was that at any given point in time, only one of them could be upset. Barkha had been exacting her vengeance for all these days but now, seeing Rishabh so mopey, she melted.

'Never mind. It's football stuff, you won't like it,' grumbled Rishabh.

He was right. There was a part of Barkha that had hoped Rishabh was feeling bad because of what he had said to her. She sighed. *Of course it's about football. Why would it ever be about you?* she thought. She wondered if she should leave him alone, but her better instincts dictated that she probe further.

'It's all right. You can tell me.'

Rishabh shifted in his seat, scanning her face. On it he saw warmth and genuine concern; so, slowly and cautiously, he unspooled the chain of events. He was careful to not let slip anything about KKPS, Eklavya or Tamanna. He stuck to the facts. Then, involuntarily, he began telling her about how terrible he would feel if they didn't end up playing in this tournament.

'I didn't go for the MES tournament and we probably won't go for this one. You know what kills me?'

Barkha made an attentive sound.

'I've possibly played my last game for the school, and I didn't even know it.'

Barkha was touched by the feeling he had for the game. She could sense his grief. It made her jealous that he had never once spoken about them with the conviction with which he spoke of football. Maybe one day, she hoped.

'Don't worry. It'll be fine soon,' she said.

'How? The coach will never take us to play without training.'

Barkha considered the dilemma. She wanted to help him but knew nothing about football. So she resorted to applying a broad soothing philosophical balm.

'Everything happens for the best,' she offered. She meant it sincerely. She even smiled to make him feel better. However, her kindness produced the opposite effect. Instead of improving his mood, Rishabh's features darkened.

'How is this for the best?'

'Maybe . . . maybe if you don't go for this tournament, you will get more time for your studies. See, every cloud has a silver lining.'

Rishabh had just told her how his school football career had been tragically cut short, and here she was talking studies and silver linings! For the first time, he saw what Purohit meant when he had said that she was not his type. She sympathized with him, but she didn't *understand* him. If she didn't get that football was his sole preoccupation, did she even get anything about him?

'Who the fuck cares about all that?' His voice was high-pitched with helplessness.

'Rishabh! Don't curse!' reprimanded Barkha.

'I'll curse all I fucking want. *What's wrong with you?* Look, you may like studying—Ms Goody Two Shoes, four-pointer, topper. And you get to do that and win awards and all. Good for you. I like playing my sport. But I'm not getting to do that. It hurts. How hard is that for you to understand?'

'*Who are you?*' she said. Then she rushed out of the classroom. The people who saw her leave immediately turned an accusatory eye towards Rishabh.

Rishabh dropped his head into his hands. *What have I become?*

'Ma'am, I have a doubt,' said Rishabh.

Biology period had just got over and Rishabh had followed Avantika Miss out of the classroom, calling out to her as soon as he was out of sight of his classmates. Avantika Chandra was the teacher who had caused an early onset of puberty in many a Sanghvi schoolboy. For the hormonal teenagers, her appeal lay in the fact that she was one of the few teachers who hadn't been alive when India was still a part of the British Empire. She was in her late twenties and wore jeans to class. This, coupled with a figure that Shakespeare would have described as 'bodacious', meant that she widened the eyes of the XY chromosome–having population of the school.

Rishabh didn't know whether he had the doubt before wanting to meet her or if wanting to meet her had made him have a doubt. That point was immaterial. He had a peachy question that guaranteed him audience with Avantika Miss; and so he took his chance.

'Miss, what exactly is the epidermis?' he asked in his most earnest voice.

'Oh,' said Avantika Miss. The sheer number of people who had doubts after her classes always surprised her. It made her question the effectiveness of her teaching.

'It's quite simple,' she began. 'You see, the epidermis is the layer of tissue between the bone and the skin.'

But Rishabh didn't hear the end of her explanation because at that very moment he saw Rahul looming up from behind Avantika Miss. Rahul noticed whom he was talking to and gave him a thumbs up. Rishabh shook his head as inconspicuously as he could. Rahul then mimed that Rishabh should follow him.

Now, Avantika Miss, on seeing Rishabh's vacant expression, assumed that he wasn't following her explanation. 'Let me explain in simpler terms,' she tried again. 'Show me your finger.' She reached out and raised his index finger.

Rishabh couldn't believe this was happening. But Rahul kept jerking his head violently in the direction of the corridor. *Come, come*, he implied, *we have to go*.

Rishabh nodded his head ever so slightly towards Avantika Miss. *Are you mad?* was his implication. *Not now.*

'See, the epidermis is the layer between your skin,' she touched the surface of his finger, 'and the bone.' She knocked on the bone under his nail.

'Er . . . Rishabh,' interrupted Rahul, realizing that it was going to be impossible to extricate Rishabh without intervening, 'sir has called us.'

'Sir? Which sir?' quizzed Rishabh with monumental annoyance.

'Mehfouz sir. Football coach.'

In a flash, Rishabh's finger was out of Avantika Ma'am's grasp, epidermis and all.

'Right now?'

'Now. Call Puro.'

Rishabh nodded. He dashed back to class and hollered for Puro to follow him.

'Got it, miss. Bone, skin, between!' shouted Rishabh as he sprinted down the corridor.

Avantika Miss could only look on, bewildered, as the boys raced towards the gymnasium.

The coach stood in the middle of the gymnasium. Ghadge Sir stood beside him with an expression that betrayed no emotion. The players surrounded them. Their eyes were wide with anticipation. Questions trembled on their lips. The coach held up a hand. All motion ceased.

'Meeting is about the tournament,' he began.

The players held their breath and leaned in closer.

'I've thought a lot before coming here. And having spoken to some of you, I'm sure this is the correct thing to do.' He addressed this to Rishabh. There was a gleam in the Mongoose's eye that they had never seen before.

'I know you want to play. After a lot of thinking, I also want you to play. If I can, then I will keep this team together as much as I can.' He paused. 'Problem is practice. Without practice, there is no sense in going for a tournament. Correct?'

There was grumbling among the team. They had seen eye to eye with the coach on many matters, but on this last point, they seemed to have a difference of opinion. They really wanted to play this tournament; practice was just a means to that end.

The coach dismissed their chatter. 'I will not send any team of mine without practice, so forget about it. But,' he continued, 'if you find a way to practise for the next twenty days, there is no way I won't send you.'

Dutta and Rana high-fived. Rahul looked heavenward. Tejas cocked his head. Only Sumit held reservations.

'Sir, but the principal doesn't want us to go.'

'No. She doesn't want you to practise. She said nothing about playing,' corrected the coach.

Ghadge Sir unfolded his arms and piped up, 'That all you don't worry about. I wheel get you leave. You concentrate on practice.'

'But, sir, where will we train? We can't use the grounds.'

'You can't use the school grounds,' retorted the Mongoose. 'There is a ground outside school. Just outside the gate. That we can use. If you are okay, then I am happy to train you there.'

'Sir, we were always okay. If you want to start now, we are ready to go. Right, team?' asked Puro.

'Hold on,' persisted Sumit. 'They've sent letters home, remember? My mother is happy that football training has stopped. She won't let me come.'

He had finally succeeded in dampening their enthusiasm. They all recalled the circulars that had reached home and how their parents had reacted. The average of their remarks had been: 'Finally, good sense has prevailed on the school authorities.'

The coach rubbed his chin. 'So you boys cannot train?'

'Not unless we can convince our parents,' said Sumit.

'Okay, I am giving you three days to decide. After that it will be too late. In three days if you are not at the ground, then tournament is over,' declared the coach. 'Go now, I'll see you soon.'

The pitch opposite the school was the zilla parishad ground, but everyone called it ZP for short. It had an ill-maintained stony surface and was half the size of the Sanghvi ground. When players ran down it, the ground coughed up plumes of dust. It was a ground that either made you a player or an asthmatic. But given the special circumstances they were in, the Sanghvites were more than happy to train there.

The problem of permissions persisted, though. The coach had asked them to report at the ground the coming Tuesday. On Saturday, after Oswal's, all the boys spent the afternoon at Café Coffee Day, coming up with strategies that would convince their parents to let them play. By the end of it, they had amassed a pageful of ideas, the catch being that none of them were viable. For example, Tejas had suggested holding their parents hostage: 'Tell them, "If you don't let me play, I'll not study on purpose."'

Puro said it wouldn't work. 'I'm not going to study even if they let me play.'

Bhupinder spurred them to revolt. 'Let's burn our uniforms and drop out!'

'It's a school tournament. If we drop out of school, then we won't be eligible,' reasoned Rishabh.

'Dammit,' mumbled Bhupi. 'Didn't think of that.'

Dave suggested they threaten suicide. 'And it wouldn't be just one of us, right? It will be mass suicide. Just imagine. Who will say no to that?'

It was at that moment, they admitted, they were out of ideas.

The next morning, Sunday, Mrs Bala opened the door to Rishabh's room and found him asleep even as the alarm clock sang and danced on his study table. She shook her head. More than half the school year was over, but the boy still showed no signs of seriousness. On days he had to go for football practice, he jumped out of bed without any external stimuli, but when it came to going for tutorials, even trumpeting elephants couldn't wake him.

With the tired sigh of a mother chained to her duty, she began the familiar cycle of waking up her son. It was a step-by-step process that had been perfected over a decade. She began by shaking him awake and, as expected, he grunted and rolled over. Then she shouted out his name three times, each intonation rising in decibel. This made him flap his sleepy wrists in her general direction. Then she informed him he was running late for tutorials. At this point, he usually begged to sleep for a proverbial five more minutes. But on that day, Rishabh veered dramatically off script.

'Wake up, Rishu! You'll be late for coaching!' crowed Mrs Bala.

'Coaching . . .' he mumbled.

'Yes, you have to get ready. Come on! Up, up!'

'Coaching . . .?'

'Yes, coaching. Oswal's. The tutorials we've paid a lot of money for and so you can't afford to miss.'

It was understood that when humans slept, most of their body shut down, except the brain. Such was the case with Rishabh too. Circuits fired in his grey matter, sparks flew through his synapses and an idea bloomed in his sleepy head. Then Rishabh's eyes flew open.

'Coaching!' he said joyously, springing out of bed. He hugged his mother and sped out of the room.

That day he got ready in record time. Mrs Bala was amazed. Never before had he shown such passion for tutorials.

Maybe she had been wrong about her son. Maybe he had started taking things seriously after all. Little did she know that she had unwittingly gifted Rishabh an idea that was going to make his teammates very happy.

That Tuesday afternoon, the minutes ticked by slowly for Mehfouz Noorani. He was standing under the shade of a solitary banyan tree, watching a tornado of dust swirling in the middle of ZP ground. It was five minutes past the scheduled time and the team hadn't shown up. Five more minutes by the stopwatch, and he was going to leave.

Then he heard the pattering of feet and saw the bobbing heads of the boys from Shri Sunderlal Sanghvi School burst through the entrance. He smiled. The boys apologized for being late.

'Won't happen again, sir,' said Bhupinder, who huffed the hardest.

'I am surprised this has even happened,' said the coach, beaming at his flock. 'I thought you boys wouldn't come.'

'No chance,' said Dave.

The coach cocked his head. He looked at Dave suspiciously. 'Aye, your father wanted you to study, no?'

'He still does, sir,' confirmed Dave with a devilish grin.

The coach now paid closer attention to the faces present and soon caught the eye of Floyd, who waved back merrily.

'What have you told your parents?' interrogated the coach. He supposed the lie had to have been pretty bold if Dave and Floyd, too, had managed to return to the fold. He just wanted to know what it was so he could tell how much trouble there would be if they were to be found out.

'Sir, we didn't say anything,' confessed Purohit. 'The school did.'

Saying so, he stepped forward and handed the coach a rectangular piece of paper. With great trepidation, Mehfouz Noorani read it. And as his eyes reached the bottom, his lips curled into a smile. The paper looked like an authentic school circular. The boys had even got the school's letterhead printed at the top. The text read:

Dear Sir/Madam,
As the exams are drawing closer, we are holding extra lectures and test series for your wards. Please make sure they attend the same. The lectures will be held from 4 p.m. to 6 p.m. from 15 November to 15 December.

Thanks,
Principal

'Ah! *Very* smart. Parents cannot say no to extra classes.'

'Sir, my mother forced me to come! I'll toh get whacked if I go home before 6 this evening,' said Floyd, chuckling.

'Superb,' said the coach. 'Whose idea was it?'

Rishabh raised his hand as his teammates pushed him forward. The coach nodded. He stuck out a hand. Reluctantly, Rishabh shook it.

'Good job,' said the Mongoose. 'Only one mistake you've made.'

Concern flashed across every face that stood around him. The coach remained silent for a few extra agonizing seconds before he spoke.

'The principal does not say "Thanks". She says "Regards".'

ZP ground was filled with cheers and every whoop was louder than the last.

December 2006

RISHABH PEERED INTENTLY at the mirror. He had worn the cleanest uniform in his cupboard. It was crisply ironed and perfectly tucked in the right places. His shoes, for once, were polished. Even though he knew that they wouldn't be seen, he didn't want to take a chance. It was for the tenth standard photograph after all. Shri Sunderlal Sanghvi School had a tradition of taking a photograph of every passing batch—all 320 students—and cramming it as a fold-out in the school magazine, *The Sanghvite*. Photographs were taken in the lower classes too, but those were always shot class-wise. Only in the tenth standard was the entire batch made to stand together on the steps next to the ground and told to look into the camera and smile.

The picture had always fascinated Rishabh. The odd thing about that photograph was that even though the faces were different every year—not to mention funnier looking—the photograph appeared the same. Even the date above it did not seem to matter, because each batch gave off that identical heavy stench of hope. Each thoroughly scrubbed face with their neatly combed hair and puffed-out chest looked ready to never look back. They could see the finishing line to their school lives and seemed buoyed up by that vision. They looked like a pack of academic wolves that was ready to pounce on the world, grab the jugular of hard work and devour the meat of success and . . . you get the point. The spirit of anticipation in the image was so strong that sometimes the magazine glowed in the dark.

But here he was now, getting ready for his own tenth standard photograph. He remembered having a fleeting thought about it at the start of the year. *It's far, far away*, he had mused and promptly started thinking of something else. Now the year had raced past, and the day of the photograph was indication that all of it really was coming to an end.

Mist clung to the ground. His shoes became moist with dew as he made his way towards the giant steps. He was one of the last to reach. Excited chatter rippled out in all directions. His entire batch was milling about before him, looking as good as they could possibly look in a uniform that had one item in the colour brown. Rishabh was searching for friendly faces, when he spotted Barkha. She was talking and laughing with Riya Bose and Mukta Gawde. Her bob was neatly swept into place and held there with a white hairband. Her skin glowed in the diffuse morning light.

He was too far to hear what she was saying, but he could imagine her floating sing-song voice and her simple jokes, and before he knew it, he was ducking to avoid her. They had started speaking again, but he felt they had nothing left to say. It was an awful, hollow feeling that flipped his stomach and turned his heart black. So many times he had come close to telling her how he felt, but his courage always failed him. He didn't know how much longer he could keep up the facade. It had become genuinely painful for him to go on deceiving her, but he was just as afraid of coming out with the truth. So he came up with a new solution: of avoiding her as much as possible.

He skulked behind people, keeping a careful eye on her all the while. In conversation, she absently turned her head, this way and that, as if searching for someone. Rishabh knew he was the searchee. He could sense that urgency in her behaviour. He knew she wanted to talk to her boyfriend before the tenth standard photograph, to ask him whether she looked all right. And the question would break his heart.

At that moment, Ghadge Sir appeared and barked at them to get into position. The clumps of students dispersed and re-clumped at the base of the steps. It was an obvious, hypocritical school formation: the girls, secretive and giggling, were bunched together at one end and the guys, macho and feigning nonchalance, parked themselves at the other. Very quickly, the lower steps were filled. Rishabh spun about in confusion, until an arm grabbed him. Puro yanked him up the steps.

'You didn't hear me or what?'

Rishabh shrugged.

'Was calling your name for ten full minutes.'

They were at the rightmost edge, away from the mass that seemed to coagulate in the centre because that's where people thought they would get photographed best. To his left were Sumit and Tej.

Moments before the picture was taken, he happened to look down at the herd of classmates and found a face staring

273

back at him. Barkha, seated on the far left of a lower step, had been waiting to catch his eye. When their eyes met, her face broke into a smile.

'All right, everybody, look straight ahead . . .'

Her eyes were on him. She waited.

'Smile . . . 3 . . . 2 . . . 1.'

Click.

There he was, in the second-last row, on the far right, stuck for posterity: a puffy-haired boy, standing next to his buddies, mouth open and with nothing to say.

The flash of the camera had made up his mind. He paced the corridor next to the ground, a metallic ball of fear in the pit of his stomach. People talked and laughed all around him, making his dread and sadness more pronounced. Soon she came down the stairs, looking apprehensive. She regarded him as if she couldn't recognize him. *She knows*, thought Rishabh.

He wondered how he should broach the topic. He was a veteran of proposals (two), but this was his first break-up. Thankfully, she spoke.

'I know what you want to say.'

'You do?'

'Yes. I've known for a while.'

'For how long?'

'Since the beginning.'

This was news to Rishabh. In the beginning, he'd been certain he wasn't going to break up with her. In the beginning was when he had liked her. And why would he break up with a person he liked? That would make no sense!

She saw these thoughts wrinkling his face, and it made her laugh. It was a bitter laugh, which made Rishabh shudder.

'Don't pretend, Rishabh. You know this was a rebound.'

He genuinely didn't. Unless she meant a ball getting knocked against a surface and returning to the kicker. But he doubted that was her implication.

'What do you mean?' he asked.

Barkha sighed. 'It means you were never in love with me. You weren't even remotely interested in me until that other girl rejected you.'

'That's not true.'

'Before this, did you even speak to me?'

'There was that one time, when I asked you to rub my name off the board—'

'A *conversation*, Rishabh,' said Barkha, losing patience.

Rishabh cast his mind back to the years they'd shared and came up empty. She was right. He had only started noticing her after Tamanna had exited the scene.

'But . . . what I felt for you was real.'

'It might have been for you. For me, it felt like I got the leftovers of the feelings you had for that girl.'

'Did you really feel that way?'

'Yes. And it hurt, Rishabh. I wanted to be someone's choice, not someone's backup.'

The words stung. She had said them in her soft, even tone, and yet Rishabh flinched. In that moment, he woke up to the recklessness and ignorance with which he had barged into her life and the damage he had wreaked.

'And what did you want to say now?' she continued.

Rishabh remained silent. He couldn't even get himself to look at her. He stared at the floor.

'You wanted to break up?'

The resignation in her voice unsettled Rishabh. He felt callow and undeserving. She had believed in his magic, but all he had to offer were a bunch of lies and a bag of tricks.

'I'm sorry,' he said.

'For whom? I hope it's for yourself. Because you're stuck, Rishabh. And I'll tell you why: because you don't have the strength to move past it. In fact, I'm surprised—and a little bit happy—that you even took the decision to break up. I didn't think you would have the courage. I was going to do it myself. I have had enough. You were so careless and selfish sometimes, Rishabh. It hurt. I want you to know that. And I took it all with a smile. Only because I cared. I genuinely liked you, Rishabh. It takes more strength to let someone into your heart than it does to hold them away. I let you in. But you never could. I *still* like you, Rishabh. I like you a lot. But I know this is over, because I know who you are.'

Rishabh looked up.

She held his stare without anger or loathing. 'You're just a silly boy who doesn't know what he wants.'

Life took a turn for the worse for the newly single Rishabh Bala. Almost immediately, Barkha asked for her seat to be changed and Kaul Miss shot a deadly stare in Rishabh's direction. She puffed up her cheeks and shook her head in disappointment. Rishabh shrank in his place.

He thought football would offer respite, but his mind wasn't in the game. He made mistakes in the training sessions, and his form fell faster than stocks during a depression. The change was dramatic and worrying. The coach noticed his drooping shoulders and his distracted gaze. *Something must be wrong*, he surmised after watching Rishabh hit a free kick so wide that he almost scored in another dimension. After another listless performance, he took Rishabh aside and asked him what the matter was.

Rishabh was reluctant to divulge details, but the coach persisted. He finally gave up when the coach threatened to drop him from the team. Slowly, and with great embarrassment, he offered the gory narration of his break-up with Barkha. For the second time that year, Rishabh confessed to the coach that a girl was the source of his troubles.

Mehfouz Noorani promptly whacked him on the back of his head. 'Aye! This is why I don't like all this girlfriend–boyfriend circus.'

'I know, sir. It won't happen again.'

'It better not.' The coach glowered. Then he tapped Rishabh on the shoulder. 'But she's right about you. You don't know what you want.'

Ever since Barkha had uttered those words, Rishabh had been haunted by that one question: what *did* he want? He'd pondered it for days. He had plumbed the depths of his desires and, worryingly, found them to be rather vacuous and surprisingly shallow. But even in the otherwise pristine blankness of his mind, there was an answer.

'Sir, I don't know about the big-big things in life, but right now, I really want to win this tournament.'

The coach threw his head back and laughed. The boy was stupid, but at least he was honest. 'Good. That is a start,' he said. 'And if you want to win that trophy, then forget everything else and play the damn sport.' He patted Rishabh's back. 'Because you know what's better than knowing what you want?'

Rishabh shook his head.

'Getting what you want.'

Years later, when Rishabh would be asked about the best advice he ever got, he would rummage in the attic of his head and say, 'If you know you want the trophy, forget everything else and play the damn sport.' It was the simplest, clearest instruction he had ever received, he would add. He would smile, and his eyes would be illuminated by a light from long ago as he would say, 'And it worked wonders for me.'

Setting the trophy in his sights blurred all the distractions. His focus returned and brought his form with it. As the days passed and the tournament drew closer, he became more and more obsessed. On the final day of training, two days before the tournament, the coach named his first eleven: Dave, Amar, Dutta, Rana, Bhupinder, Tejas, Floyd, Purohit, Rishabh, Paras and Rahul. Before he could stop himself, Rishabh let out a loud, primal roar. The sound erupted from him spontaneously, but it had been rumbling inside him since the cold days of his exile. He had suppressed his anger, fear and resentment, and now that his comeback was complete, it burst out of him without restraint. The other players heard their names announced in a squad; Rishabh heard his pride being restored.

As he brought the final session to a close, the coach said, 'I can't believe you crazy people did it.' He chuckled. In his twenty-five-odd years of playing professionally, he had seen every situation and every circumstance that a footballer could encounter, and yet these boys had pulled off something unique, the likes of which he'd never seen. He marvelled at the way they had got through the month.

They couldn't tell their parents that they were sneaking out to play football after school, so they had stowed away their studs and one pair of training clothes in the gymnasium lockers. And they had worn these same clothes without complaint for the whole month. By the end of it, they smelled like a heap of rotting carcasses. It was a level of commitment that even the coach couldn't fathom.

'I glad you did it, but I'm happy it's over,' he said. 'I can't take this smell for another day.'

On the eve of the tournament, Rishabh packed his football kit for the last time that year. He neatly arranged the crêpe bandage, the can of Relispray, extra stockings, shin pads and his studs. He was about to zip it shut, when his father entered his room.

'There's a call for you,' said Mr Bala. 'Some girl called Tamanna. Or Tameeksha. Or something.'

Rishabh froze. 'What?'

'Phone. Tamanna,' repeated Mr Bala.

Rishabh had heard him fine the first time. He just hadn't believed him. Was his father joking? He peered at the man's face. He had his standard-issue dour expression and haggard eyes. There was not a hint of humour on his map. Besides, Rishabh had not heard his father crack a joke in his living memory. (This was true; the last time Mr Bala had cracked a joke, the Berlin Wall had still been standing.)

'Are you sure?'

Mr Bala worried for his son. How was Rishabh going to pass his board exams when he couldn't comprehend simple sentences plainly spoken?

'I'll tell her to call later . . .' he said in weariness.

'No!' yelled Rishabh. 'I'll take it.'

He sprang out of his chair and sprinted to the phone.

'Hello?' he said tentatively.

'Hi,' came the voice from the other end. He recognized the uncertain, husky timbre. It was certainly Tamanna.

'Uh . . .' He fumbled for words.

'I hope it's okay that I called.'

'It's okay.'

'I just needed to tell you something,' said Tamanna. Rishabh gulped. 'Be careful tomorrow.'

'What?' Many possibilities had raced through Rishabh's mind—everything from her proposing to her asking him to explain what the poet meant when she said, 'life is a prism of my light and death the shadow of my face'—but a warning had not been one of them.

'They've planned to target you. They think they can get you sent off again.'

'Kamani Krida?'

'Yeah.'

'Who told you?' He instantly regretted asking this question. 'Of course. Your boyfriend?'

'He told me, but he's not my boyfriend any more.'

It was a startling bit of news. Rishabh didn't know how to react. It was one of those situations wherein anything he said would seem inappropriate, so he chose to stay mum.

'It's all right. I should have done it a long time ago.'

'That's right!' he wanted to scream on the line, but better sense prevailed and he vocalized like a creaking door instead.

Tamanna giggled. 'You don't have to be awkward. I'm sorry for all the trouble he gave you.'

'What trouble? No trouble.'

'The card and fighting with you on the street. That stuff.'

'Oh. Ah. It happens.'

'I'm sorry anyway.' She paused. 'I've heard you're dating Barkha.'

'No,' said Rishabh. 'Not any more.'

'Oh. I'm sorry to hear that.'

'It's all right. She's better off without me.'

'Don't say that.'

'She told me that herself.'

Tamanna laughed, but then she realized that was inappropriate, so she coughed to cover it up.

'Why did you break up with him?' asked Rishabh when she had stopped.

She took a few seconds to compose her thoughts and answered, 'He wanted me to come for the tournament tomorrow.'

'That's a good thing, no?' said Rishabh. He was genuinely surprised that inviting people to watch football matches was grounds for break-ups.

'So that it would affect you,' she added.

'Oh!'

'Yeah. It's such a shitty thing to do.'

'I agree. But it wouldn't have affected me, to be honest.'

Tamanna balked. 'Come on. It would affect you a little bit,' she said.

Rishabh couldn't believe he had managed to offend her. 'No. And . . . I have to tell you something too. It was good that you . . . uh . . . said no when I asked you out. It hurt a lot for a while. But in the end, it was the right thing to do.'

'Why do you say that?' asked Tamanna. She sounded subdued.

'Because I don't think I knew what I wanted. I'm just happy at least you did.'

They fell silent. In Naupada, with the phone pressed against her ear, Tamanna Vedi thought about the dorky, spectacle-wearing boy who would stare at her like she was an animal in a safari. She wondered what she would say if he asked her out again, right now. There was a distance between them that she knew she couldn't cross. And yet she had called him.

'Tamanna,' said Rishabh, 'thank you.'

'Oh, this was nothing. I thought I should let you know—'

'No, for everything. I liked you since the seventh, you know. I fell for you when you were patrolling the bridge. Do you remember?'

She made a noise that indicated she hadn't the slightest clue.

'You were. And I spent four years trying to impress you. I sometimes used to wonder whether you felt it.'

'Felt what?'

'Felt your life changing, because you changed a lot of mine. I have so many memories of you that you probably don't even remember. For all of that, thank you.'

'Where was all of this when you asked me out, you idiot?' said Tamanna. She felt rueful about letting him down.

'No,' said Rishabh, 'I said exactly what I wanted to say. I spent a lot of time thinking about it. Trust me.'

'So dumb it was.'

'It wasn't so bad also.'

'Oh, please.'

'Too late now. And I don't think I'd change it even if I had the chance. You were the first person I really wanted. But it was not meant to be. And you—'

Just then, a third voice joined them. That of a lady. 'Tamanna? You're still on the phone?' It was her mother. 'Leave the phone and sit down to study!'

'*Haaaaaan*, Mumma!' screamed Tamanna. 'You keep the phone first.'

A receiver clicked into place, and it was the two of them again.

'Sorry. My mom. She has no understanding of privacy. She always picks up the other line and tells me to study.'

'It's all right.'

'Anyway, I better go now. You take care tomorrow. All the best, and I hope we win!'

Rishabh thanked her and said goodbye.

He zipped up his bag and headed to bed. His chest felt lighter. His heart beat freely for the first time in years.

All for the best, he thought, *all for the best*.

They had been instructed to report to class, give attendance and submit their 'On Duty' leave notes. Knowing how touchy the principal was about football, Ghadge Sir had taken the trouble of forging fake 'On Duty' notes. The entire football team was supposed to be going for some athletics meet that day.

'But be carephul,' Ghadge Sir had warned. 'Iph teachers phind out, then *poora* plan *phail hoyega*.'

They had never seen worry lines on Ghadge Sir's brow before. He was clearly concerned, and so they'd vowed to be cautious.

But as luck would have it, their first period of the day was English. Bobde sashayed into class and dumped her textbooks on the desk.

'Take out your copies of *Julius Caesar*. Act four, scene three,' she said.

Rishabh nodded at Puro and raised his hand. 'Miss,' he said, 'Puro—I mean Abhay . . . and I have an inter-school tournament. Can we—I mean may we leave?'

Bobde squinted at Rishabh. 'Which tournament?'

'Miss, it's athletics. Running and all,' piped up Puro. 'We have a letter also.'

Bobde crooked her index finger. 'Bring it to me.'

Rishabh's face was rapidly turning red. Things were not going according to plan. He felt apprehensive about giving the letter to Bobde. He knew she was on to them and wondered if the doctored letters would hold up under scrutiny. It was too late to worry about that, though. Puro and Rishabh got up from their seats, walked up to the teacher's desk and handed their letters to Bobde.

She smirked at them and began inspecting the notes. Time slowed down. In the morning light, Rishabh could see the soft hairs on her earlobes as she bent over the sheets of paper, scanning them for dishonesty. Nervously shifting his weight from foot to foot, he wondered what would happen if she caught the deception. Then he looked up. No longer under observation, the class had gone back to its default state of confusing chatter. Suddenly, his troubled eyes met a pair of burning black ones. They belonged to Barkha.

She waggled her eyebrows. 'All okay?' they asked.

Rishabh gave a micro shake of his head.

Barkha grew concerned. 'What happened?' asked a single raised eyebrow.

Rishabh's eyes directed hers to the note.

Barkha's mouth fell open. *Oh!* Then her hand shot up. 'Miss!'

Bobde looked up from the note.

'I have a doubt,' said Barkha. 'Why did Cassius condemn Lucius Pella?'

Bobde reacted as if it were the first time she was hearing the names. And it could well have been the case too. It was her first year teaching the play, and she was having a hard time keeping up with all these Roman blokes who had banded together to do Caesar in.

'One minute, Barkha. Let me finish reading this,' answered Bobde, continuing her forensic analysis of the leave notes.

'Miss,' persisted Barkha, 'why is it that Caesar talks in Old English for the whole play but when he is stabbed, he suddenly says, "Et tu, Brute?" in Latin?'

'Barkha, I said give me a minute! Do you understand that or should I say it in Latin?' shrieked Bobde with venom on her tongue.

Rishabh and Puro could see that her patience was wearing thin. Behind her back, Puro began silently inciting the class to ask more questions by wringing his palms. Gowda was the first to get it.

'Miss, I have a doubt,' piped up Gagan.

'What?' spat Bobde.

'How come you can't kill politicians so easily nowadays?' he asked with genuine curiosity.

Eventually the whole class caught on to the game, hands mushrooming all over the room.

'Miss,' asked Parth Popat, 'my cousin has a German shepherd called Brutus. Should he be worried?'

'Miss,' asked Barkha, 'which came first: the name Brutus or the adjective "brutal"?'

'Miss,' asked Amay Khatri, 'is it true that Caesar was the first caesarean baby?'

Poulomi Bobde looked around at the eager faces and raised hands. Usually the kids sat in class like stuffed animals, but today, all of a sudden, the light of learning shone from their eyes. Bobde had never been drowned in such a deluge of doubts before. She smiled benignly. Deep down, she had known that it would take time, but that one day, she would get through to them. She was glad that day had finally come. She handed the notes back to Rishabh and Purohit. They could go to hell; she had the attention of thirty-eight other kids to bask in.

'Leave my class quickly. Don't make a noise,' she growled at the two.

'Yes, miss. Thank you, miss,' said Rishabh.

They scooped up their bags and rushed out of the room. As they left, they heard Bobde say, 'Who had the question about the dog?' Rishabh stood outside the door at an angle that hid him from Bobde but put him in sight of Barkha. He waved his arms to get her attention. She looked.

'Thank you,' he mouthed.

'Gooooo!' she mimed, moving her hands rapidly.

As they ran down the corridor, Puro asked, 'Why did Barkha help us?'

'I don't know,' said Rishabh, unable to fathom the largeness of her heart that enabled her to do so much for someone who had only let her down. 'I don't know.'

On the bus, they retold the story of how Bobde had almost sniffed them out and how Barkha had started an avalanche of questions that had buried Bobde's curiosity in their notes. The bus was filled with laughter as they bounced along.

'Legends,' said Bhupinder, clapping Rishabh and Puro on the back.

'But just imagine if Bobde had caught you all,' said Sumit.

'The first thing she would have said is, "Et tu, Barkha?"' quipped Dave.

Mirth rippled through the bus afresh. They jabbered ceaselessly for most of the journey, but as the vehicle approached Kamani Krida Public School, they fell silent. Their energetic conversations were replaced by a quiet contemplation. Looking around the seats, Rishabh could feel the emotion coursing through all his teammates. Ever since the sixth standard, he had been playing with these boys. They knew him better than almost anybody else on the planet. He trusted them. He loved them. They had been the Golden Generation of the school, the ones who were destined to win trophies and glory. And now they were down to their last tournament. As he gazed out of the window, at the blurry world outside, he felt the weight of expectation on each of their shoulders. This was their final chance to fulfil their potential. And he knew they were going to make good on it.

When the Sanghvi boys got out of the bus, some sections of the white-and-blue Kamani Krida crowd in the stands jeered them. It gave the boys their first taste of the hostility that was going to come their way. A shudder ran down the length of Rishabh's body. He could imagine them sending shards of sound when he'd battle Eklavya in the middle of the pitch.

Kamani Krida Public School was a sprawling, modern, modular building block that was painted a dull grey colour. It felt forlorn and bleak as the Sanghvites gazed at the imposing monolith. What was more, the KKPS ground looked like the surface of Mars. It was a red, grassless rectangle that lay adjacent to the building. On one end of the ground was a large banyan tree. On the other end was a flagpole, on which fluttered a bright orange flag, bearing the Kamani Krida insignia.

The boys first made their way to the board on which the fixtures were put up. It being December and so close to the final exams, fewer schools had sent their teams. There were sixteen sides in total, divided into two groups. Their first match was against a team called B.L. Bhosale School. If the S4 had a case of nerves going into the first match, they were settled right then. They knew B.L. Bhosale was a small school situated near Thane station, whose team had been on a hot streak to see how many tournaments they could go without winning a single match.

It was a run that had extended to at least a decade. The Sanghvi boys had grown up watching B.L. Bhosale always getting bundled out of tournaments in the first round. If anything, they were consistent. And they were cheerful. It was as if they knew they had a reputation to maintain, and feeling bad about their losses would only make their work harder. It had reached a point, Rishabh thought, where they would be inconsolable if they were to win a match.

Their fixture was the second match of the tournament, and the coach told them to kit up and then start warming up. Adrenaline flooded Rishabh as he put on his shin pads, stockings and studs. Then he took off his shirt and slipped into his jersey. He inhaled its musty scent from the cupboard corner in which it had lain for three months. He looked down the front, at the logo they had designed, and felt the memory of every match he had played that year trapped inside it. Puro was sitting in front of him, his face a study in concentration.

'What are you thinking about?' he asked Rishabh.

'What happens after this?'

'We reach the quarter-finals.'

'No, after all of it.'

When Rishabh was younger, say, in the fourth or fifth standard, he never thought he'd reach the tenth. It had seemed so far away. The boys and girls in the final year seemed so big and intimidating. He just couldn't picture himself being one of them. By the time he had reached the eighth or even seventh standard, he'd been in school for so long that he had resigned himself to it. *This is my life. And there's nothing I can do about it*, he would think. He never felt that a day would come when he would wake up in the morning without hearing, *'Jaldi utho, brush karo!'*

But here he was now, in the December of his final year. He had been in such a hurry to grow up that he hadn't realized when it had happened. Soon he would be a man. An adult. What would it be like then? Would he be any good at it? Would it be any fun? He had rarely seen men smile. Did the joy go away or did responsibility overtake it? He realized he had more questions than answers. One day, he would answer them, but now they had a match to play.

'It'll be fine,' Rishabh said to his friend, 'and it'll be better if we win this tournament.' He clapped Puro's hand and hoisted him to his feet. 'Come on, captain. It's showtime.'

They warmed up in silence. It was as if everyone had had the same existential crisis at once. The sense of an ending clung to them. This would be their last tournament regardless of the outcome. No trophy could adequately compensate for their disbanding. It would just be an excellent way of honouring their time together.

Mehfouz Noorani had terse instructions before they took the field. Most of them were strategic in nature. But he concluded with 'We all know how this team plays. They are not good.

Doesn't mean we don't have to be. Same intensity. Same focus. Every game is final. Every game is last. Respect your opponent. Don't be arrogant. If you feel you will not enjoy this victory or that you will not accept defeat, then realize you're being arrogant. Stop it, at once. Go have a good game.'

He clapped his hands. The boys patted each other on their backs and got ready to face their first challenge.

Before kick-off, Rishabh found himself opposite B.L. Bhosale's striker, who wore the number 8 and kept shouting and clapping at no one in particular. 'Come on, come on!' he would scream, and not a soul would look in his direction. It was like the mad barking of a rabid dog. The only one who paid him any attention was Rishabh. He finally caught the striker's eye.

'Nervous?' asked Rishabh.

'Not at all,' said the boy, his eyes shifting in his sockets like ping-pong balls.

'How many games have you not won?'

The striker thought about it. He counted on his fingertips and offered a number. 'Twenty-two tournaments.'

It was now Rishabh's turn to applaud. 'Well done,' he said.

'Thank you. In some time, we will talk to the guys behind *Limca Book of Records*.'

'Very nice. Who gets the credit, though? The players? The coach? Who?'

The question made the number 8 run the upstairs machine again. 'I think the school. They showed a lot of faith in our failing.'

'Are you ready to lose today?'

'If luck is on our side, hopefully.'

'But you don't plan to lose?'

'No. It's not fun then. There has to be some suspense.'

In the meantime, Purohit had won the toss and elected to kick off. B.L. Bhosale chose to defend the half they were standing in, so Sanghvi had their shots targeted towards the banyan tree end.

Within seconds of the match commencing, Rishabh can feel the difference in the side. Two things stick out in particular. Firstly, every player in the black Sanghvi jersey has the focus of a grandmother with acute far-sightedness trying to thread a needle. Secondly, they are quieter than eagles soaring the skies while scanning for mice. They complete their passes and don't fumble with the ball. They spot each other without hollering. They run rings around the hapless B.L. Bhosale defence. Scarcely have two minutes passed, when Floyd splices the ball through two centre backs. Rahul burns some fuel, catches up to the through ball and calmly slots it home. 1–0.

Even their celebrations are muted. The Kamani Krida spectators grumble in disapproval, which becomes louder three minutes later, when Rahul strikes the ball from the edge of the D and into the top-right corner to bag his second goal of the match. 2–0. Then Purohit, in a dazzling bit of individual brilliance, makes a run to remember. He collects the ball from the centre circle, beats an onrushing Bhosale player, cuts to the left, nudges the ball forward, snakes past a second player, runs around a third, deceives the goalkeeper, drops a shoulder to the left and pokes the ball to the right. 3–0. It's a goal so magical that even the staunchest KKPS supporter is stunned into silence. A patter of applause emanates softly from the stands.

'It's a walk in the park,' says Puro with carefree pride.

As the half is about to draw to a close, Rishabh receives the ball. He looks up for options and sees Floyd darting forward. He passes to Floyd and shoots ahead.

'Give!' he says. Floyd can see a defender closing in on Rishabh. He's reluctant to pass. Rahul is open to the left.

Rishabh follows Floyd's gaze; spots the defender. *I'll get past him*, he thinks. 'Floyd! Pass!' he calls.

It's the conviction in Rishabh's voice that makes up Floyd's mind for him. He knocks the ball forward. Rishabh spreads his arms and plants himself in the ground. The defender slams into him. Rishabh shifts all his weight backward, shielding the ball from his opponent. He twists this way, then that. He spots a gap. He rushes into the space and rifles a shot. It smoothly rolls past the keeper, hits the post with a *thunk* and ricochets into the net. 4–0.

It's a clinical, satisfying strike that propels Rishabh skyward. He lands on his feet and punches the air. A wave of aggression rolls through him. Ever since the tournament was announced, he has dreamed of the day he would score within the walls of Kamani Krida. The distant rumbling from the stands sounds like a symphony.

When the whistle was blown for half-time, Sanghvi left the pitch elated but the B.L. Bhosale boys looked happier. They were on course for another well-deserved defeat and a step closer to record-book glory.

Usually in the interval, the boys would rasp for air and fall to the ground, exhausted. That day, they didn't feel like they had played a game at all. For most of them this was metaphorical, but for Dave it was literal. With neither a shot to defend nor a kick to make, he had spent the half staring at the back of the heads of his busy teammates. He came off the pitch yanking at his gloves and grumbling to himself.

'Anybody has a book or something?' he yelled. 'Super bored out there.'

They settled down as the coach cleared his throat. 'Good half,' he said. 'The match, as I see, is over. In the second half, play a relaxed game. Don't waste energy. The tournament is long, and you will need it soon.'

'Sir, I spend more energy playing chess,' quipped Rahul.

'Aye!' barked the coach.

Rahul winced. He knew he should have kept his smart alec comments to himself, but an innate Rahulness made him blurt it out.

Surprisingly, the coach broke into a wide smile. 'Funny,' he said, before continuing. 'Okay, team, drink water. Sumit, Lokhande, Chakraborty, warm up. Rahul, Purohit and Rishabh, you will be on the bench.'

Rahul's eyes widened. Fear crawled all over his face. 'I'm sorry, sir. I was just joking!' he pleaded.

'I know,' said the coach.

'Sir, then why are you taking me off?' Rahul had scored two goals, and in B.L. Bhosale's rickety defence he could see the inevitability of a hat-trick. In the tradition of every full-blooded striker, he was greedy for goals and gutted when he was hauled off the pitch.

'I want you to rest for other matches,' reasoned the coach.

'But, sir, I have the stamina. Don't worry.'

'Aye, you know better or I do?'

Rahul had some opinions on the matter, but he saw the moustache flare out and managed to bottle up his views. Rishabh shared Rahul's sense of regret, but he was also flattered that the coach had identified him as a key player for future matches. He rolled down his stockings, unclasped his shin guards and stretched his legs out. For once, he would enjoy being on the bench.

The second half belonged to the substitutes. Rishabh was happiest about Sumit's inclusion. The mynahs that pecked at the Sanghvi soil had spent more time on the pitch in a single morning than Sumit had in a year. Yet he had never let his lack of playing time curb his enthusiasm. It didn't help that Sumit lived forty-five minutes away from the school. For a long, punishing year, he had awoken at a time when even roosters snuggled under their blankets and taken a rickshaw to the bus stand and then a bus to school. He'd put in all that effort for the hard task of being left on the bench. Rishabh had often wondered what drove Sumit despite the disappointments. Watching him gambolling about on the pitch now, he realized what it was: a pure and simple love for the game. It hurt Sumit not to play, but it would have hurt him more not to try.

Given his opportunity (but more likely because of the opponent), Sumit was majestic. He towered over the B.L. Bhosale strikers. He flicked them off the ball like they were ticks. He bullied and heckled every player who wandered within earshot. He slammed into the enemies like an angry rhinoceros. Within minutes, the B.L. Bhosale players were reluctant to go anywhere near him. So he started advancing towards them. He rushed to clear balls as far ahead as the halfway line. Once, he booted the ball so hard, it possibly struck a space station before landing well outside the school walls.

'Abbey, how small is this ground?' Sumit bellowed at the Kamani Krida stands.

And how the Sanghvi players clapped. They applauded him till the skin of their palms threatened to chafe.

'SUMO! SUMO!' they cheered.

Higher up the pitch, the attackers kept busy too. Tejas bagged Sanghvi's fifth goal early in the half. He celebrated by sticking his tongue out and thumping his chest. Then the young striker Joy Chakraborty, freshly promoted from the junior team, added a sixth. He would go on to score many more goals for the senior team, but the one he scored on the red earth of Kamani Krida would remain his most vivid strike.

Towards the end of the match, Floyd dinked the ball over the B.L. defence, and Paras bobbed up like a seal and managed to get his head in contact with the ball. It looped dramatically over the keeper and bounced into the goal. It was a rare goal for Paras, and the only one he would ever score with his head. On the touchline, Rahul struck the ground with a fist.

'Paras scored!' he said in disbelief. Then, wistfully, he added, 'I should have been playing.'

If Paras had bagged a goal—was Rahul's implication—then he could have easily got a double hat-trick.

The Sanghvi boys were favourites even going into the tournament. They became the favouritest after winning 7–0. It wasn't just the score that made people take notice. It was the vitality of their playing that had caught their eye. Their game was more an artful display than a mechanical slicing and dicing. They were even talked about in hushed tones. 'Seven–nil, seven–nil,' went the whispers.

The boys were aware of the effects of their result even as they walked to the touchline. There could have been no clearer announcement of their intent. They had put B.L. Bhosale's head on a pike and said, 'This is the fate that awaits those who cross our path'—metaphorically, of course.

Their next match was in an hour's time, against Bluebell Academy. They were a competent team but rarely made it past the quarter-finals. After seeing the way Sanghvi had eaten alive, digested and belched out B.L. Bhosale, they had started the bus engine and decided to keep it running. From the looks of it, they would be out of the tournament pretty soon.

'Eat something. Drink water. Rest. You have half an hour,' said the coach once his team was off the pitch.

They parked themselves in one corner of the stands and got as comfortable as they could while still being in their soggy clothes. A match was already under way on the ground. Father Ignatius's High School were playing Lord's High School. It was a hotly contested match, but Father Ignatius's had most of the possession. They were a tough side from Vashi and crammed full of skilled players. Rishabh watched them dodge and swerve and dart about like dragonflies skimming over a pond. It made him nervous. Regardless of how well they played, other teams always seemed stronger, faster and better prepared.

He turned his attention to his teammates. Most of them had opened up tiffin boxes and were chomping on food with feverish hunger. His mother had packed some grub too. He opened his box and saw two limp sandwiches. Sauce had seeped through the surface of the bread, making the poor sandwiches look like they had been shot. For years his mother had smeared sauce on two slices of bread, slapped them together and passed it off as a snack. The sauce wouldn't even be evenly spread. It was usually daubed in the centre, which meant that for 90 per cent of his sandwich-eating exercise, Rishabh was chewing through plain fluffy white bread.

Looking at it now made him nauseous. After a decade of quietly eating the same stuff, that day, Rishabh decided that he had had enough. He replaced the lid, got to his feet and dusted himself down.

'Wwww oooo goooog?' asked Puro through a mouthful of poha.

'What?'

Puro gulped his food down. 'Where are you going?'

'Oh. To the canteen. Getting something to eat.'

'Here, have this,' said Puro, thrusting forward the serving of poha. No matter what the dish, someone was always tired of having it.

Rishabh politely declined and made his way out of the stands. The Kamani Krida canteen was situated at the rear of the school, inside a garage. There were three tables, complete with benches, and the floor had white tiles. The place smelled of disinfectant and had more flies than people. Rishabh hoped the food was better than the ambience. He was scanning the menu, when he heard footsteps behind him.

'Arre, hi, yaar!' said Eklavya Bhamtekara, thumping Rishabh hard on the back. 'Long time. How's it going?'

Rishabh winced. His back stung from the contact, but he bit his tongue and didn't let out a sound. Whipping around, he found Eklavya and Nagesh grinning at him like thugs from an '80s Bollywood movie. With a grimace, he said, 'Don't touch me again.'

Eklavya looked at Nagesh. 'What, I can't say hi to an old friend?'

Nagesh flashed his protuberant teeth. The smile stretched his skin, making his face look even more hircine.

'Not your friend,' said Rishabh, turning away. His fingers had bent the laminated menu card.

'I heard you people scored a lot of goals,' continued Eka.

Rishabh didn't answer. He was staring at the menu, but his eyes were glazed over. His muscles were taut as he waited for the trap to spring.

'I also heard you got subbed,' hissed Nagesh. The trap had snapped. Nagesh let out a dry chuckle and tapped Rishabh's elbow.

Instinctively, he swatted Nagesh's paw away.

'Can't believe you're still a substitute,' goaded Eklavya.

Rishabh faced him. 'And I can't believe you got dumped.'

Eklavya's mouth opened and shut like a guppy's. His eyebrows waggled.

Meanwhile, his crony looked on, concerned. He glanced at Rishabh and they had a silent exchange. 'You shouldn't have said that,' Nagesh indicated with slow shakes of his head.

'Why?' signalled Rishabh with a toss of his.

'Apologize, now!' commanded Nagesh, pulling back his cheeks in a snarl.

'Pfft,' blew Rishabh.

'That bitch didn't dump me,' roared Eklavya.

'Oh, sorry. Then I guess she lied to me when she called me,' said Rishabh.

Nagesh threw his hands up and turned his head to the heavens. He was disappointed in Rishabh's disregard for personal safety. He knew Eklavya and how upset he was over Tamanna. And few things outside the realm of hell were as destructive as an upset Eklavya. Dutifully, he scanned the surroundings to make sure there weren't any knives or sharp objects around. He spotted a stray fork and quickly snatched it off the counter.

'She called you?' repeated Eklavya in a low whisper.

'Yeah. On the phone. Told me everything.'

'What did she say?'

'I can't tell you that. I wouldn't want to hurt an old friend,' retorted Rishabh with relish. He knew that information would enrage Eklavya but half the information would drive him positively insane.

Eklavya advanced towards Rishabh. 'Tell me,' he growled, 'NOW!'

Rishabh looked at his twisted, angry face and he saw Eklavya for what he truly was: a scared, overgrown child whose self-respect rested on being admired by those younger than him. At once, Rishabh's fear turned to pity. But pity wasn't going to stop Eka from clobbering him.

Eklavya had already encroached to within inches of him. Rishabh could see an aggrieved vein on his forehead. Without waiting another second, he shoved Eklavya in the chest. Eka stumbled backward on to Nagesh, and Rishabh darted out of the canteen.

'Eklavya, she's gone. Leave her alone. Sort yourself out,' he called out after him.

Shortly before noon, Sanghvi took the field against Bluebell Academy. The harsh sunlight made Rishabh squint. At the far side of the pitch he saw Amar standing listlessly, one hand on his hip and the other screening his eyes as he waited for kick-off. He looked more like a clueless spectator who had wandered on to the pitch by mistake than a player about to play in a quarter-final. One could fault him for his posture but not for his performance. Ever since he had replaced Vade, the left flank had thrived. His piston-like legs regularly propelled him past Tejas, who was left trailing like dust behind a comet.

And then when attacks broke down, he charged back to defend without complaint or fatigue. Simply watching him motor up and down the flanks could induce motion sickness.

The Bluebell Academy attacking pair made their way to the centre. One of the boys clamped the ball under his stud. Amar let down his handmade visor. He cast his eyes over the ground and saw Rishabh flashing a thumbs up. He held up his thumb in reciprocation. He felt delighted to be on the ground under that bright sun on that wintry day. All was right in the world for Amar Verma. He couldn't understand why his teammates were hanging their heads and waggling their limbs in nervousness. It amused him to see them behave like his father, who had a hefty home loan on his head. The fear of bankruptcy and losing the roof over their heads was concretely worrisome. This was just a game. But for all his perspective, his heart skipped a beat when the whistle was blown, and he leapt to attention as the ball was set in motion.

Bluebell Academy are respectful towards Sanghvi. Rishabh sees it in the stricken face of his marker, in the crablike retreat his defender makes every time Rishabh rushes at him with the ball. But Sanghvi don't reciprocate the feeling. Rather than displaying the panting intensity they had shown in their first contest, they resort to a confident, mellow passing game. They roll the ball around the ground lazily. And Bluebell Academy are happy to chase it in the middle of pitch. It's better than having to fish it out from the back of their net.

When Sanghvi do decide to attack, they are met with a compact, organized Bluebell Academy defence. They keep tight, well-manned lines and mark their players with an obsession that borders on stalking. They leave little space for Rahul to wiggle through. A burly boy, roughly the size of Kanchenjunga, marks Paras. Once, Paras manages to get a lead on the mountain. He drives forward with the ball at his feet but, within seconds, the defender covers ground and lands a powerful shoulder charge—one that sends Paras skidding a good twelve feet. After that, Paras goes missing from the game. He's reluctant to receive passes and doesn't call out for the ball.

Rishabh is one of the few Sanghvi players who are having a good game. He's been flying up and down the flank, like a honeybee going from flower to hive, making tackles, threading passes and supplying crosses. He pings ball after ball into the middle of the D, but they get repelled before Sanghvi heads can get to them. When Bluebell Academy attack, Rishabh doubles back to help Bhupinder and makes one critical tackle.

Bluebell Academy's number 9 turns Rajput and bursts into the open space. Rishabh at once chases after him. The boy pulls his right foot back, rearing to shoot. 'No!' screams Rishabh and slides in between the boy and the ball. He knocks the ball out for a corner; but his foot takes the place of the ball. The number 9 is already in the middle of a sweet strike. He follows through and wallops Rishabh in the ankle. There's a sickening sound as leather crunches into bone. Rishabh yowls like a cat in heat and rolls around, clutching his ankle. Pain is shooting firecrackers into the darkness of his closed eyes.

When he opens them, he finds himself in shade, under the canopy of the concerned faces of his teammates.

'Don't get up,' says Dave. He kneels down, grabs hold of Rishabh's ankle and gives it a fine twist.

'Ahhhhh!' he screams.

'Do you feel like kicking me in the face?'

'Yes!' Rishabh winces.

'Good. Then it's not broken. You can walk it off,' advises Dave with the confidence of an orthopaedic doctor with twenty-five years of experience.

Rishabh is hoisted to his feet, and he gingerly places his weight on his left foot. It still hurts, but he can continue. He looks to the bench. The coach has been pacing the dugout with his hands behind his back. When he sees Rishabh on his feet, his eyes sparkle. He rolls his hands, checking if Rishabh needs to be substituted. Rishabh holds up his palm in negation. The coach signals back, as if to say, 'Perfect!'

Rishabh plays with a slight hop for the remainder of the half. He feels a twinge each time he rests his weight on his left foot. Thankfully, the half comes to a close soon, and Rishabh hobbles off the pitch.

Rishabh was desperate to play the remainder of the match, broken foot be damned. When the coach asked him how he felt, he did a jig to demonstrate he was fine.

'Your foot is fine but your dancing is broken,' said Rahul wryly.

The coach was not happy with the half. His brows had come together and his moustache was moving in agitation. He waited for them to catch their breath and sip some water. He had a long address to make and he wanted their full attention when he spoke to them. At last, he said, 'Not good. What I saw was not Sanghvi School. How many shots on target this half?'

He glared around the team. No one answered.

'Zero,' answered the coach. 'You boys have to realize this is a different team. This is not like the first match, where you could play easy and win. You have to work hard against this team. You have to show that you want to win. You have to show initiative. Where was the desire?'

He turned his gaze to Paras. For the coach, Paras's performance personified the half—weak and anonymous.

'Aye, Paras, you are hiding on the pitch. I know the defender is tough. He's not giving you much chance. But when you don't have the ball, at least make a run. At least defend from the front. Try to get the ball. Help your teammates. You have bloody disappeared! Not one pass has come to you in the last fifteen minutes. You know why? Because you are afraid of taking responsibility. Otherwise, how can it be that on such a small pitch, with only twenty-two players, nobody can see you?'

He ran his angry stare over all of them. Purohit tugged at a tuft of grass; Rishabh noticed the force with which he was yanking at the vegetation. *He's angry*, thought Rishabh. *That's a good thing.*

'Only this Rishabh is calling for the ball. Full match, I can hear him. Even when it is with Tejas on this side of the pitch, that bastard is shouting for the ball. That is the initiative you have to show. Be in the game. Take charge. Make things happen.'

Rishabh's back straightened. He felt proud that his contribution hadn't gone unnoticed. He had worked his socks off for the whole half and now, after the coach's critical acclaim, he was ready to throw himself into action all over again.

'We can do this,' he said and clapped his hands. 'Put those goals in. Come on!'

'Yeah!' yelled Rahul.

Purohit threw a fistful of grass to the ground. 'Enough being nice and all. Let's get them!'

They jumped to their feet and shook themselves out.

303

'That's the spirit, boys. Move your lazy asses. Ask for the ball. Push for the win. Go for what you want or you will have to settle for what you get.'

The pungent smell of Relispray is driving his marker crazy. Rishabh has applied about half the bottle to his left ankle. It's serving as a repellent while providing some relief. The boy keeps a foot away from him; his ankle feels cool and numb. The pace of the game has picked up in the second half. Sanghvi's play has more attacking intent. But their waves of attack keep crashing against the same solid defence.

Puro has grown more vocal. He compliments Tejas when the left-winger delivers a peachy cross that sails inches over Paras's head. He roars in admiration for Rahul's stinging shot that slams straight into the Bluebell Academy goalkeeper. He bellows for the defence to keep their shape as Bluebell Academy advance with the ball. And they aren't empty words. He leads from the front. He takes players on, dribbling past defenders and chipping away at Bluebell Academy's resolve.

But for all his effort, the score remains unchanged. The minutes tick by. Bluebell Academy make a few attacks, and Rishabh starts noticing a pattern in their play. The Bluebell Academy raids peter out instantly because they are carried out by a maximum of two players. It's as if the rest of the team is forbidden from entering Sanghvi's half.

'They're playing for the draw,' he says to his captain.

'Yeah,' says Puro. He, too, has sensed their ultra-defensive mindset.

'Let's blitz them,' proposes Rishabh.

'No, they can counter.'

'We don't have much time. They want to drag us to shoot-outs, Puro. If we have to do something, we have to do it now.'

Puro looks around the ground. An ominous feeling surges through him. He has seen these circumstances before. He knows how much it hurts to lose a game to the cruel lucky draw of a penalty shoot-out. And Sanghvi are cursed. No team of theirs has won a penalty shoot-out in twenty-six years.

'All out, bey. It's time,' decides Puro.

He relays the message to the coach, who immediately catches their drift and yells out command after command to direct all resources towards getting a goal. Amar moves up the pitch permanently. Tejas tucks in more centrally. Floyd drops deeper, functioning as a holding midfielder, freeing Puro to roam further up the pitch. The coach tells Chakraborty to warm up.

They get closer. They secure two corners in quick succession. Rishabh floats two balls in, but the boy-giant niftily clears them. As the match enters the final few minutes, the game becomes ever more frantic. Scruffy shots blast from the Sanghvi players. Even the Bluebell Academy defending is desperate and last-ditch. The pressure is on Sanghvi, and they transfer it to Bluebell Academy. Chakraborty is ready to come on.

The ball rolls out for an innocuous throw-in. But before the coach can signal the substitution, Amar has scooped up the ball and hurled it. It drops into a little cavity between two Bluebell Academy players and lands at the feet of Paras. In a flash, his XXXL-sized dance partner joins him. They match each other step for step. When Paras goes right, the big lad lurches right. When Paras goes left, the defender lugs his weight to the left. They're spinning in circles. Then Paras drops a shoulder to the left. The wall cabinet marking him takes the bait. He spills to his right. Paras strokes the ball forward, through the behemoth's legs. It threads to the other side and Paras retrieves it. The titanic boy takes a few seconds to realign. That's all the time Paras needs. He skitters into the box and hurries to the byline. He looks up and sees the sprinting form of Rahul. Paras squares the ball into Rahul's path. Without hesitation, Rahul pulls the trigger and breaks the deadlock.

The Sanghvi boys scream in relief and rush over to Paras. They pat him so violently that he will develop bruises the next day. It turns out to be his last contribution to the match—the coach is replacing him with Chakraborty. Paras takes his own sweet time getting off the pitch. He makes it to the touchline with the speed of an octogenarian needing a hip replacement. By the time Chakraborty enters the fray and the match resumes, time is up. The referee blows the whistle and Sanghvi hands shoot up in triumph. They're through to the semis!

A mighty roar erupted from the stands when the quarter-final between Dingreja Educational Society and Kamani Krida ended. It was in part to celebrate KKPS's victory but mostly because it meant that the home team was to play Sanghvi in the semis.

The din made the Sanghvi players sit up. They had been studying the KKPS match and had watched how clinically DES had been carved open and cast aside. KKPS had won 4–0. Eklavya had scored twice; Nagesh and Sandeep Sinha had supplied the remaining goals. The match had had none of the uncertainty and hesitation that had marred Sanghvi's quarter-final. It made a few of them nervous. Rana and Dutta had both stopped watching after the third goal.

When the final whistle sounded, Rishabh cheered with the rest of the spectators. It made Dave and Puro, who were sitting next to him, raise their eyebrows. He smiled back at them sheepishly. This was the match he had come to play. It was the contest that had consumed him for thirty straight days. In his visions, the match always took place in the final, the perfect farewell to his school career. He was a tad disappointed to meet them earlier. *It's a pity*, he thought. *Would have been more fun beating them in a final.* But it was a minor change in plan. He would now get revenge before the trophy instead of the two of them together.

As he waited for the semi-final encounter, time flopped down and stretched out to take a nap, and refused to budge. Rishabh ate his lifeless sandwiches and got himself a glass of lemon juice from the canteen. It was sour and viscous. *It takes special talent*, thought Rishabh, *to make nimbu pani badly*. Then he sat back in the stands and watched the clouds drift by in the sky. He looked at the Kamani Krida students in the stands as they ate potato chips and watched Father Ignatius's play St James's High School. After some minutes, he found Puro, and they rehearsed elaborate celebrations for when they would score against KKPS.

Forty-five minutes before the match, the team huddled around the coach and looked at him with expectant eyes.

'You have made it to the semis. It is no small achievement. Well done,' began the coach.

The team cheered half-heartedly. The coach nodded his approval, and they added the rest of their heart.

'Now, you know whom you are playing—'

The boys let him know they were well aware of their opponents.

'It is going to be a tough match. Maybe even tougher than a final. Firstly, we are on their home ground. Look there.' He pointed to the stands.

Crowds had begun filling up the seats. No one wanted to miss Sanghvi vs KKPS. There were a few girls in the cluster, but the stands were predominantly, aggressively male. Rishabh could spot the mischief on their faces. They were waiting to scream and shout, to boo and bay for the blood of every Sanghvi player. He could smell the expectation wafting from the stands. It was going to be no ordinary match. It was going to be a blood sport.

It was as if the coach had read his mind. 'Don't worry about them. The best way to shut them up is to play well. I am telling you about them because they will make noise. I want your communication to be loud. Shout. Talk more. And whatever happens, do not react to the crowd. No matter what they say. Understood?'

Although the coach had dispensed this as a general warning, Rishabh couldn't help but think it was exclusively intended for him. He nodded vigorously.

'Secondly, I know they are cheats.'

Now this statement had a pronounced effect on the team. The coach had struck a groundswell of emotion. The boys chimed in with their opinions on exactly what kind of cheating scum Kamani Krida were. The coach heard them out patiently. Finally, he held up a hand and they fell silent.

'I said I know,' he said. 'What I want to tell you is this: In school, age group and all matters. But in some time, school will be over. You will be men. The world outside is tough. Not everyone follows the rules. They bend them. They break them. But just because others do it does not mean you should bend or break. In my time, I have come up against many such crooked people. I can say this with full confidence—they might think they are getting an advantage, but there is only one way to win. You know what that is?'

Rishabh was about to say, 'Discipline', when the coach added, 'To play by your own rules. Because in the end, we have to live with ourselves. We have to be who we are. Do what you love. Love your family. Enjoy life. Live with yourselves. In the end, that is all that matters. They can cheat and lie and win trophies, but when they shut their eyes, does winning like this mean anything?' He paused for breath. 'I have won many things in my life, boys. And the ones that matter, I didn't have to play for.'

Mehfouz Noorani stood with his arms folded across his chest, staring at the ground. They could see pictures flicker in his eyes, though they couldn't see what he was seeing. His moustache moved. A smile spread across his face.

'Thirdly, don't hold back for the final. Don't go easy now. Don't conserve energy. Run like this is the last one. Play like this is the last one. The final generates its own energy. In the semi-final, you have to bring your own. GIVE IT EVERYTHING AND YOU WILL TAKE EVERYTHING!'

The boys cheered as the coach reached a crescendo. At that moment, Rishabh was willing to give his life up, if only the coach asked. He had never felt this way before. That he himself was insignificant; that there were things bigger than him and that he was ready to surrender to them.

'Now, warm up. Do it properly. Purohit, lead the team. It is match time.'

Rishabh carefully wrapped the crêpe bandage around his ankle. He had carried that bandage in his bag for four years; he was glad to have used it at least once in his time on the school team. It seemed like he hadn't wasted the bandage's time.

The stands were packed. The clamour washed over the ground in waves. He couldn't tell what was being shouted, his heart was beating so fast in his chest. His laces kept slipping because of the patina of sweat that coated his fingers. Time had slowed to a crawl. He knew he got this way when he was afraid. Except this time it was different. He could feel his pulse humming in his wrists. He couldn't wait to walk on to the field.

He jumped up and bounced on the spot. 'Come on!' he yelled.

He caught Purohit's eye, and his friend's face broke into a wide grin. It was the same smile that he had seen when he had first met the captain all those years ago on a rainy day in the seventh standard.

'Come on!' Puro yelled back.

'This is our game!' said Rahul.

The crowd roared around them, but Rishabh heard each Sanghvi voice the loudest. Sunlight slanted over the ground, the red earth glowing in the dying light. He thought of the trophy. He felt his fingers curling around the golden metal. His heart stopped for a single second before resuming its function again.

Beside them, the KKPS players were tucking in their jerseys. *Not this time*, he thought. *Not while I'm on the pitch.*

Purohit patted him on his number. 'This one is for you.'

Rishabh beamed. 'And the next one will be for all of us.'

Nothing has prepared them for the jeers they are greeted with when they take the pitch. It is the sound of 200 virulent voices. Rishabh soaks it in. He basks in the hatred. It fuels the adrenaline already coursing through him. In the first half,

Sanghvi are shooting at the flagpole end. Rishabh takes his position on the right, away from the baying crowd. He jumps and tucks his feet in. His muscles are loose and raring to go. His ankle is stiff, but the pain has vanished.

A louder racket erupts as the Kamani Krida players walk on to the field. They wave back at the crowd. Their smug faces revolt Rishabh. *They think they are going to win*, he realizes. He shakes the anger out of his body. The familiar stocky frame of Eklavya floats out of the clump of orange jerseys. He pads his way to the left flank. *Welcome*, says Rishabh to himself.

'I'm going to kill you, boy,' says Eklavya by way of greeting.

'How long did it take you to come up with that?' taunts Rishabh.

Eklavya glares at him. 'I can smell the fear on you.'

'It's Relispray, genius.'

Eklavya's eyes drift to his feet and he spots the bandage. Rishabh winces. He knows he's made a mistake by revealing his injury.

Eklavya is smirking. 'I'm going to finish that job,' he promises. 'Upgrade you to a plaster. Maybe even crutches.'

Rishabh doesn't reply. Coolly, Eklavya touches his toes and flexes his back. His T-shirt strains against his muscles. Rishabh looks down the line. Puro is watching him. He holds up his palms. 'Easy, easy,' he indicates. Rishabh nods.

'Rishabh!' Rahul yells. 'Kick-off!'

Rahul is waiting at the centre circle. Rishabh shakes his head and runs over.

'Sorry, I forgot,' he says.

'As long as you remember to not get a card, it's fine,' says Rahul.

The referee, a lean, bald man with hooded eyes and a hooked nose, jogs over to the circle.

'Ready?' he asks.

The boys nod. He puts the whistle to his lips and blows. The crowd roars. Rishabh rolls the ball out. Rahul traps it and side-foots a pass to Puro. Once the game begins, Rishabh loses all his pre-game nerves. The crowds transform into a blur. The only sound he hears is the quick intake of his breath. He drifts to the right flank. He is shoved forward. He stumbles but maintains his balance.

'Watch where you're going,' calls Eklavya with a grin.

Floyd is holding off a KKPS midfielder, looking for passes. Rishabh glances around the ground. Puro, Rahul and Tejas are all too far ahead. He breaks away from the touchline and drifts towards the middle. He's in an ocean of space.

'Floyd! Look!' he yells. Floyd acknowledges him and cuts the ball to Rishabh. It's a trap. As soon as he traps the ball, three KKPS players pounce on him like wolves bursting from the bushes. A foot hacks into his vulnerable ankle. He goes down in a heap of agony and screaming. Another well-aimed stud drives into his back. He twists in anguish. A player bounds over him, and he sees the orange jerseys streaming past him. His eyes are shutting as pain shoots through his back and ankle.

Then he hears the crowd boom. A tsunami of noise washes over the ground. He stops squirming and sees Eklavya billowing away from the Sanghvi goal with his arms outstretched. He comes to a stop in front of the stands. Nagesh jumps on to his back. Rishabh staggers to his feet just as Dave is stooping to pick up the ball from the Sanghvi goal. That's when it sinks in. Kamani Krida has scored. Eklavya has scored. And Rishabh let it happen.

'BEHENCHOD!' he screams. He buries his face in his palms. His fingers rend his hair. His heart sinks into his sock. His stomach turns to ice.

If there is a worse way to start this match, then Rishabh can't imagine it. All around him, Sanghvi heads drop. Kamani Krida jog back to their half. As Eklavya passes him, he shouts, 'Thanks, sissy!'

Rahul is standing in the centre circle. His arms are on his hips as he's rolling the ball on the spot in anger.

'I'm sorry. I'm sorry. I'm sorry,' says Rishabh to every teammate within earshot. He looks to the bench. The coach is squeezing his lower lip between his thumb and his index finger. He has no sage advice to offer now.

The whistle rings in their ears again. This time, it sounds ominous. Rishabh is still shaking. Rahul puts his hands on his shoulders.

'We'll do this. Don't worry. Not this time. Not again.'

'PLAY!' yells the referee.

Rishabh jumps to attention. Jerkily, he nudges the ball forward. KKPS has always had the skill and now they have the momentum too. They begin dominating possession. The crowd flares up in appreciation with every pass completed by their team. The Sanghvi players sense the desperation with which KKPS seek their second goal. Puro is pushed back. Floyd is back-pedalling. Dutta and Rana are overrun. Almost every Kamani Krida player is camped inside the Sanghvi half.

Bhupinder is struggling to keep up with Eklavya. In a perilous moment, Eklavya skips past Bhupinder, reaches the goal line and sends a cross sailing in. Dutta jumps, but it's a Kamani Krida head that gets to the ball. Nagesh powers a header into the ground. The ball ricochets upward. Dave launches into the air and his fingertips prove to be the difference between the status quo and Kamani Krida going two goals up.

KKPS take the corner quickly and the pressure doesn't relent. They shuttle the ball around from the right to the left.

313

Eklavya gets the ball. Bhupinder advances towards him. Rishabh holds up a hand. 'He's mine!' he yells and rushes up to contend with Eklavya.

'Want some more?' asks Eklavya.

Rishabh doesn't respond. His eyes are riveted on the ball. Eklavya's feet dance over it in a series of step-overs. Rishabh dives in with a challenge. His right foot knocks the ball out of Eklavya's foot. His trailing foot takes out Eklavya's standing leg. Puro is about to mount an attack, when the referee blows the whistle.

'Foul!' shouts the referee.

Rishabh jumps to his feet. 'I got the ball!' he protests. On the touchline, the coach is punching the air in frustration.

'Foul,' says the vulture-faced referee, quietly and definitely.

Rishabh is about to let loose a torrent of abuse, when Paras wraps an arm around him and pushes him back. 'Let it go,' he whispers.

Rishabh shakes his head and steps back.

Eklavya is rubbing his knee. He grimaces at Rishabh. 'You thought you'd be a hero? Now watch.'

The free kick is twenty-five yards out. Eklavya places the ball on the spot and takes three measured steps back.

'Wall! Wall!' screams Puro.

Paras, Rahul, Puro and Rishabh link their arms and stand as tall as they can. They cover their genitals with a palm and wait. Rishabh can feel Paras jittering. Sweat is dripping into his eyes. He blinks it away. The Nike logo flashes as Eklavya plants his foot more firmly into the ground. *Please don't let him score. Please. Please*, he begs God, his guardian angel, anyone who has any cosmic say in the outcome of this situation.

Eklavya takes a short run-up and strikes the ball cleanly. He hits it with tremendous power and pinpoint accuracy. The ball rockets into its intended target: Rishabh Bala's face.

Rishabh feels the bridge of his spectacles dig into his mug and the sharp cut of their metallic frame before he feels the blunt trauma of the ball. He rocks back and falls to his knees, clutching his face. The skin has peeled off his nose, and it burns in the cool wintry evening. Soon a small stream of blood trickles down his cheeks. Eklavya runs up to him in mock concern. He bends over the fallen Rishabh.

'Are you okay?' he asks.

Rishabh groans.

'Good,' Eklavya says as he yanks at the back of Rishabh's head before straightening himself.

Puro shoves Eklavya in the chest. 'Get away from him!'

Eklavya smirks but retreats. Paras hands Rishabh his glasses, which had fallen from the impact. The frame is bent out of shape. They sit askew on his face but are still usable.

'Get off the pitch. Clean the blood off your face and then return,' commands the referee. He's looking down at Rishabh with a cold, apathetic stare. He seems less concerned about Rishabh's well-being and more worried about protocol.

Rahul and Puro hoist Rishabh to his feet, and he stumbles his way to the touchline.

The coach is concerned. He is the first to get to Rishabh. Ghadge Sir shuffles after him, carrying the first-aid kit.

'Can you carry on?' asks the coach.

'Yes, sir.'

'That cut looks bad.'

'Sir, I can play,' says Rishabh, his voice rising.

His eyes are still fixed on the match. His mind is still racing. Ghadge Sir pulls out a tuft of cotton, wets it in water and dabs it on Rishabh's face. It singes his wound. Rishabh yowls in pain and swats away Ghadge Sir's hand.

'Shtay shtill!' shouts Ghadge Sir. 'Otherwise it wheel take longer to put you back on.'

Rishabh apologizes and holds still, though the cut burns like an ember flaming on his face. When the blood has been wiped off, Ghadge Sir administers a Band–Aid in haste. As a result, the Band-Aid is lopsided and doesn't cover more than half the gash.

'You wheel wear shpecs like that?' asks Ghadge Sir.

'Yes, sir.'

'It is little crooked.'

Rishabh grabs the glasses off his face and bends them into some semblance of their pre-impact form. Then he shoves them back on.

'Okay, now you can go.'

Rishabh waits impatiently for the ball to go out of play so he can return to the pitch, but the game goes on uninterrupted for what seems like decades to him. From the touchline, it looks like the two teams are playing different sports. Sanghvi are playing football while Kamani Krida are playing rugby. Rishabh watches as the KKPS players commit a series of fouls that go unpunished. A player yanks Puro's jersey. Another elbows Paras off the ball. Two KKPS players ram into Dutta from both sides, compressing him into a chapatti. And the Vulture overlooks it. It's only when Amar makes a clearance, sending the ball over the touchline, that Rishabh gets to return to the field. And when the KKPS player takes the throw, he finds himself back off it as the referee blasts his whistle for half-time.

In the heat of the match, Rishabh had forgotten his mistake. As he left the pitch, he saw that the scoreboard read Kamani Krida 1–Sanghvi School 0, and guilt took hold of him once more. His breath grew ragged and he pursed his lips. He saw the leering faces in the crowd and remembered crumbling to the ground. He recalled the vibrant KKPS jersey as Eklavya had torn towards the goal. He could have fended them off. He had let them overpower him. He had lost the ball. He had cost them the match.

He found the coach overseeing the bandaging of a cut Bhupinder had sustained over his right eyebrow. It had happened when Bhupinder had leapt for the ball along with Eklavya. Eklavya had jumped with his elbows spinning like the blades of a chopper. His elbow had crashed into Bhupi's face and bust it open like a watermelon. So many Sanghvi players were bruised, battered and bandaged that they looked less like a football team and more like the casualty ward of an army hospital.

Rishabh made his way to the coach and hung his head. 'I'm sorry, sir,' he said. 'I should have done better.'

'Sorry for what?'

'The goal, sir. They fouled me . . . But I could have still done something, sir . . .'

'Look at me,' said the coach. 'It's not your fault.'

'Sir . . . I will make up for it.'

'It is NOT your fault. I saw what happened. They didn't tackle you. They mugged you. There were at least three fouls committed on you and one criminal assault. *It was not your fault.*'

Rishabh remained silent.

'Don't think about it, Rishabh. First, have water, rest your legs and sit with the team. I'm coming in one minute.'

Mehfouz Noorani took a minute to gather his thoughts. It was a rare situation for a coach to be in. At one–nil, the team had far from lost the match, yet they seemed beaten. They had lost their vitality. Their faces were glum. Their bodies were broken. He could see the throbbing pain in their calves pulsing all the way through their drawn-back lips and narrowed eyes. The most foreboding realization for the coach was that he could ask nothing more from them, because they had nothing more left to give.

He squeezed his lower lip and brushed his moustache with his fingers. His eyes fell on Rishabh, who was busy drenching his ankle in whatever remained of the Relispray. He recalled the look in the boy's eyes as he apologized for a mistake he hadn't committed. It was a stark emotion, reflected deeply in the clear pools of the boy's eyes. It was fear.

As he peered at the rest of his team, he saw that fear had cloaked them all. They were afraid to lose. They were afraid of being fouled. They were afraid of disappointing him, the coach. They were boys pretending to be men, failing in the face of fear. And an idea formed under Mehfouz Noorani's orange mane. He clapped his hands and said in a loud, uneven tone, 'Team! Make a circle around me.'

The boys hurried to attention and surrounded the coach. Mehfouz Noorani beamed at them. He took a deep breath. 'Boys,' he began, 'that was a good half. You are still in the game. As a coach, there is nothing I can change. That is why I want you to change as players.

'Aye! Let me finish,' barked the coach when he saw the exchange of perplexed glances.

'I have seen thousands and thousands of teams, but I have seen few like you. You know what's so special about you? You boys are good individually but much better as a team. And what is even more rare? I have never seen anybody have more fun than when you people are together. You are all idiots.'

He laughed. The boys sniggered. They adjusted in their places. They sat up and leaned in closer.

'That's what makes you special. I have seen you play. I know what you are all capable of. When you people enjoy playing is when you play the best. That other team is playing ugly, ugly football.

'These other boys are kicking and fouling and cheating. That is ugly. You go on that pitch and show everyone how beautiful this game can be. Play your game. Enjoy yourself. The winners never made this sport beautiful. The results never made it worth watching. You know what makes it beautiful? The passing. Giving what you have to someone else. The teams that conceded but never gave up. The players that danced after they scored. Our spirit is more powerful than our situation. Isn't it amazing to see how much happiness we are capable of sparking off? That is why football is called the beautiful game. Because when it is played right, it can teach a man to live. It has taught this man,' said the Mongoose, jabbing his index finger into his chest.

'Sir . . . you have taught it to us,' said Rishabh. The rest of the team heartily agreed with this assessment.

'Good,' said the coach. 'So will you enjoy yourselves?'

'Yes, sir!'

'Will you have as much fun as you can?'

'Yes, sir!'

'Will you play the beautiful game?'

'YES, SIR!'

'And remember, whatever happens, I am proud of you boys and I have your back.' He clenched his fist and thrust it forward.

The team applauded and hooted and jumped to their feet. They felt re-energized and ready for the second half.

'I feel fresh!' exclaimed Puro.

'He's like glucose for the soul, man,' said Floyd.

And Rishabh felt he couldn't have put it any better than that.

If someone ignorant about the score watches the two teams returning to the pitch, they will find it hard to tell which one was in the lead. Sanghvi walk on with their heads held high. They look serene. They flash ironic smiles as the crowd boos. They talk to each other constantly as they take their places on the field. They look composed. Their confidence shakes the screaming, jeering students in the stands.

The Kamani Krida players make their way to the pitch with swagger. Their eyes stare darkly from under their hooded brows. They sneer at the Sanghvi players. They take up their stations in silence. Eklavya and Nagesh plant themselves in the centre circle. Rishabh wonders if they practise being smug, because they've got quite good at it.

In the second half, Rishabh is on the flank adjacent to the stands. He can feel the hateful eyes trained on him. He can feel the contempt these people feel for him. It's amazing how they've worked up so much emotion for a person they don't even know. He continues loosening his body even as insult after insult washes over him. They don't make him angry.

He looks in the direction of the onlookers and says, 'I understand. I would also be this frustrated if I were studying here.'

The hive buzzes with consternation and hurls back more abuse in retaliation. The coach looks sharply at Rishabh and flashes a small grin. Before Rishabh can acknowledge it, the referee blows the whistle and the game begins.

Kamani Krida pick up from where they left off. They knock the ball around as much as they knock people. Their centre midfielder, Prateek, puts a palm over Tejas's face to prevent him from getting the ball. Another time, Purohit and the Kamani Krida number 19 both vie for the ball as it soars in the air. They jump together, except that Puro leaps like a footballer and the number 19 springs up like a trained assassin. He has his boot out, and it slams straight into Puro's chest. It's a tackle so vicious that Puro goes down and rolls a couple of times, screaming and holding his chest. Puro is not one to fake injury, so his reaction is worrying.

More worrying yet is the reaction of the referee. He waves for the players to play on. 'Foul!' scream the Sanghvi players. 'FOUL!' screams the coach. But the referee only stops play when Dutta clobbers a clearance into the stands. Puro is still on the ground. The Sanghvi boys congregate around the spot. Bhupinder, Rahul and Paras cordon off Puro from the attention of the Kamani Krida players. The referee asks for Puro to be removed from the field.

'He's halting the game,' he says in a slick, pitiless voice.

'It's what you should have done!' Floyd says and receives an icy stare for his troubles.

Rishabh helps Puro to his feet. 'You okay, champ?' he asks.

'Yeah,' he says through gritted teeth. 'But we have to be careful. This ref isn't right.'

Rishabh agrees with the assessment. If anything, Purohit has put it lightly. The referee isn't just 'not right', he is plain wrong. He has displayed a glaring and blatant amount of partiality. He blows the whistle if a Sanghvi player even moves in the general direction of a Kamani Krida boy. Meanwhile, Purohit has suffered a challenge that was intended to break all his ribs, and still the whistle remained clutched in the referee's closed fist. This is the story of the entire match, where challenge after challenge from Kamani Krida has gone unpunished. In effect, Sanghvi realizes, they are playing against twelve people.

'It doesn't matter!' screams Puro when he's caught his breath. He directs his words to all the Sanghvi players. 'As long as we can run, this match is ours!'

'YEAH! YEAH!' returns the cry from Dave. 'Go, Sanghvi!'

If the injustice of the referee is meant to have a demoralizing effect on KKPS's opponents, then the plan has failed spectacularly. The foul on Puro galvanizes the team. Their anger makes them more focused. It starts with Rana, who snatches the ball from Nagesh and calmly boots it forward. Floyd makes a trademark powerful run that sends Kamani Krida scrambling, before laying the ball off to Rahul. Rahul takes a shot that thunders off the bar and goes out for a throw.

The crowd gasps. Their team has been picked apart in an instant. Kamani Krida are shaken by Rahul's efforts. They find it harder to pass the ball around. Rishabh nicks the ball from Eklavya and delivers a cross that Paras puts wide.

'He is less your striker and more our defender,' hisses Eklavya.

'Just like the referee is more your player than our referee?' says Rishabh.

'Oh, did we make it that obvious? We like you, Rishabh. We thought we'd get you a card.'

'So sweet. If you had done this much for Tamanna, maybe you wouldn't be single.'

Eklavya shoves him in the back. 'You're not going to walk off this pitch on your feet.'

'Yeah. I'll be carried off it by my friends when we win.'

'Only if you're friends with a stretcher.'

He runs past Rishabh but not before kicking him hard in the back of his thigh. The pain is sharp and the first of many attacks that Rishabh is to sustain over the next ten minutes. Eklavya smacks him on the back of his head. He tackles Rishabh with only the faintest interest in getting the ball. He pulls Rishabh's jersey till it rips near the collar. And all through the abuse, Rishabh doesn't react. He bites his tongue, grits his teeth and carries on playing.

It is the complacency that the Kamani Krida players have about the referee that will be their undoing. It begins with a move started by Tejas. He dispossesses Nagesh and, with his glorious left foot, floats a long ball to Paras. Paras knocks the ball down Purohit's path. Rishabh, sensing an opportunity, breaks into the D. Puro spots his run and perfectly passes the ball to his path. Rishabh traps it and drags it to the left, into space. The lithe Kamani Krida defender, who's been on Rishabh's tail since he got the ball, decides he's had enough of chasing and scissors in from the back. He doesn't get the ball but sends Rishabh skidding face down across the hard, abrasive ground. It's a shameless foul inside the box.

'PENALTY!' scream eleven voices in unison. The referee turns down their plea and the match is about to resume, when the linesman, who saw the incident at close quarters, runs on to the field, his flag streaming behind him.

Elton D'Souza, the linesman, is an honest official from the Referees' and Linesmen's Association of India. He's completed his B license and is working his way up to becoming a referee. He has a sense of justice and duty that hasn't been seen in the world since Yudhishthira exited the scene at the end of the Mahabharata. Elton is horrified with the way the match is being officiated. He has quickly caught on to the fact that the decisions the referee has been making are overwhelmingly in favour of the home side. It is everything that he stands against, for it maligns the game and brings disrepute to the refereeing community.

Alas, being a mere linesman, he doesn't have much to do beyond raising his flag for offside. He has been standing by the touchline and waiting for the moment when he can intervene. Finally, that moment has arrived in the form of a hideous tackle. Now Elton stands in front of Mahoob Riaz, the bald referee, and says, 'Give them a penalty. I saw it from up-close.'

'It is not.'

'Mr Riaz, it is as clear a penalty as there can be.'

'You will decide that or I will decide that? Who is the referee and who is the linesman?'

Elton has had enough of this beak-nosed, bribe-taking hairless man. 'If you don't give them a penalty, I am reporting you.'

Mahoob Riaz glares at the young linesman. Two righteous eyes stare back at him unflinchingly. Mahoob Riaz has got a fair sum from the Kamani Krida coach, but it won't cover his expenses should he be tossed out of the Referees' and Linesmen's Association of India. He snarls at Elton, but acquiesces to the demand. He blows a tired whistle and points to the spot.

The Kamani Krida players rub their eyes in disbelief. It seems to them that they are collectively hallucinating. Surely the referee didn't just give a decision against them? Who does he think he is—a regulator of fairness in the game? Then, as Purohit places the ball on the spot, reality sinks in. They rush the referee and bemoan the decision. Mahoob Riaz can't look them in the eye. He blows his whistle and asks them to leave.

'You double-crosser! How can you do this!' yells Eklavya.

'Careful. I don't want to card you,' says the referee quietly.

'Oh, now you'll give us cards also. Great! Good investment you were.'

The crowd boos as a yellow card is dished out to the Kamani Krida captain. The decision stands. Sanghvi are to take the penalty. Puro finishes teeing up the ball. When he rises, he sees Rishabh next to him.

'Let me take it,' says Rishabh.

Puro hesitates. 'I'm the designated kicker.'

'I want to take this.'

'Look, you don't have to prove anything . . . You're emotional right now. Just let me take it. I'm the designated taker anyway.'

'Puro, I won this penalty. I need to take it. This is for me. I promise I won't let you or the team down.'

Rishabh's voice is even. His features are set. His face, it seems to Puro, is covered in two things: sweat and determination. He looks at the ball, the keeper and then Rishabh, and makes his decision.

'Take it,' he says. 'From a captain, for a friend. But make sure you nail the motherfucker.'

Rishabh nods. He measures his run-up and stands still. The cacophony of the crowd swells. The sweat pours out of him in buckets. His grazed knee burns. But all Rishabh can see are the ball and the lanky form of the KKPS keeper.

Eklavya yells to distract him, 'MISS IT, YOU FUCKER!'
Pfffeeeet.

Rishabh takes a deep breath. Then he runs. He angles his body, leans back and side-foots the ball to the left-hand post.

The moment he strikes the ball, he knows he's scored. He doesn't wait to see it go in. He sprints away from the penalty spot and yanks his shirt front, displaying it with pride to the silenced Kamani Krida public. His teammates rush forward to hug him. He screams and screams till all the anguish since his card in September breaks free and escapes his body.

The coach runs up to the boys and sifts through them till he finds Rishabh. He clasps the boy by his shoulders and says, 'I'm happy you took it. But I'm happier you asked to take it.'

'Thank you, sir! This one was for that card.'

'You made up for that a long time ago.'

Rishabh hugs his coach.

'Aye! Get off me. Sweat is making my clothes dirty.'

The match is choppier on resumption as Kamani Krida grow frantic for a win. More tackles fly in all directions. Nagesh and Eklavya single-handedly try to bulldoze their way to the goal. Once, Eklavya takes a wild stab at the goal from twenty yards out. The ball flies over the bar and, fittingly, smacks a KKPS supporter full in the face. Eklavya returns to the touchline, swinging his arms and cursing in frustration. Rishabh is relishing his helplessness.

'Try to be more accurate,' says Rishabh. 'You know, like my penalty.'

'Shut your bloody mouth!' Eklavya screams and swings a fist clean into Rishabh's jaw. There's a deafening crack. Rishabh's head jerks to the right, and he stumbles and then falls to the ground. The crowd gawps at the violence. Rishabh can taste the metallic blood filling his mouth.

Don't react, he tells himself.

The incident takes places in front of the team dugouts. The coach runs down the touchline to see if Rishabh is all right, but the latter turns to Eklavya with a smile. 'So many years older, and you still punch like a little boy.'

Eklavya bares his teeth. He rushes up to Rishabh and spits. It's a giant gob of spittle that lands with unerring accuracy on Rishabh's cheek and slides down it. Rishabh wipes it off with disgust. His hands are shaking. He wants to break Eklavya's face. *Eight minutes*, he thinks to himself. *Hold on. Please.*

Then he looks up, and his eyes meet the coach's. 'WHAT ARE YOU WAITING FOR?' screams Mehfouz Noorani.

In the course of the year, Rishabh has followed hundreds of the coach's orders, but this one brings him the most joy. He springs to his feet and dusts himself down. Then he runs up to Eklavya and taps him on the shoulder. He waits for Eklavya to face him before he clocks him with a fist made of bone and anger. And before Eklavya can recover, he wallops him with an open-palmed slap from his left hand. Eklavya's eyes go comically wide, and he spins to the floor.

A KKPS player tries to grab Rishabh from behind. Puro drives his elbow into the boy's back and gets him off Rishabh. Another boy tries to jump Rishabh, but Sumit comes roaring from the bench and clotheslines the attacker.

'*CHAL, BHOSADIKE!*' he shouts. It's a cry that turns the football pitch into a wrestling ring.

Rahul and Bhupinder knock down Nagesh. Dave gets a short midfielder in a headlock. The Kamani Krida coach tries to intervene but is laid low by a beautifully executed uppercut by Mehfouz Noorani. 'Get 'em, boys! It's a knockout tournament!'

Mahoob Riaz, the referee, is horrified by the turn of events. He blows his whistle relentlessly, but gang wars are rarely played by the rules.

The Sanghvi boys batter Kamani Krida. They have never been beaten more soundly. Security guards run in from the gates to prevent the spectators from leaping down from the stands and joining the fray. Soon, order is restored and Mahoob Riaz frantically blows his whistle. He calls off the match and declares Kamani Krida as winners. In his final act of the match, he gives each and every member of Shri Sunderlal Sanghvi School a red card. Every time he shows one of the Sanghvi boys a card, they scream and clap as if they are receiving a medal.

Rishabh Bala asks the referee if he can take the card home. 'What! Why?'

'It's better than a trophy,' says Rishabh.

And he is right. Years later, he will think back to this match and remember what makes his school team so special. So many school teams won trophies. But to have the whole team sent off—now that was a rare distinction.

EXTRA TIME

March 2007

RISHABH WAS WRITING his last board exam: biology. His hand moved swiftly across his answer sheet. He had a good feeling about the paper, save for a few true-and-false questions. He glanced at his watch. He was half an hour away from the end. His fingers had gone numb because of the manic speed with which he had written his answers. His elbow felt frozen from overuse. At long last, he completed his paper and set his pen down on the desk.

As he nursed his aching fingers, he looked around and saw he was the first person to have finished. Everyone else was still slogging away in different poses of concentration. They were seated in the gymnasium, as it was the only room big enough to accommodate the whole batch. Diagonally ahead of him sat Puro, who was scribbling furiously. Here they finally were.

It seemed like a dream. It seemed like he had lived a lifetime in the span of a year. The boy who now sat with his biology paper in front of him was not the boy who had been bathed in the white light of the TV that night when Zinedine Zidane had brought his dome down on Materazzi's chest. He had ridiculed Zidane for that moment of madness, but it finally made sense. Everyone has their own personal Eklavya. Zidane's was called Materazzi. And no glory comes close to the satisfaction of walloping an Eklavya.

Rishabh grinned as he thought of that semi-final at Kamani Krida. They had returned to school on the bus, twirling their jerseys and singing all the way. The coach's had been the loudest voice. He'd even taught them all the old, filthy anthems that had rung across the terraces of Salt Lake Stadium. The boys had roared along. The coach's eyes were glistening as he'd watched a new generation join the chorus.

When the bus had come to a stop, he'd gathered the boys together.

'It is time I tell you this because I say this very rarely: I am very proud of what you boys have done. You boys are special. I hope you play on. Football deserves your talent. When the time comes, I hope you are brave enough,' he chuckled, 'or stupid enough to continue playing. Give it a try. And if you need anything, I am there. Don't worry.' He'd looked at each of their faces in the fading light and smiled. Even his moustache had seemed happy for once. 'I'll miss you, boys.'

'Sir, thank you for—' Rishabh had begun.

'Aye, all this senti stuff you say at my funeral.' And just like that, the coach had shut the tiny window of vulnerability once again.

They had hugged the coach and thanked him. As they'd waited at the school gate, they heard the steady puttering of a motorcycle. They'd watched till the coach had drifted away.

Towards the end of December, something strange had happened. Purohit called Rishabh early one morning. His voice was ragged with excitement. 'Read the newspaper right now!'

Sleepily, Rishabh had shuffled through the pages. There, in a small box on the right side of page seven, was a picture of a large crocodile thrashing inside a metal box. The succinct caption read:

Twelve-year-old crocodile caught in Upvan Lake. It was relocated by forest officials.

'Unbelievable,' said Rishabh.

'It was right there the whole time!' said Puro.

Rishabh had cut out the newspaper clipping and stuck it on his desk. It felt like a good omen that something hidden all this while had finally surfaced.

For the remainder of the school year, Rishabh had sat behind a fortress of books on the same desk. He'd take his food at his table. He'd take naps at his table. His mind settled into the dull routine of academics. And so the days had passed by swiftly, and the boards had commenced.

'Last five minutes!' screamed the invigilator, making the many brain cells and tendons around her jump into overdrive.

Now here he was at the very end—the last five minutes of his final paper. Now all he had to do was wait. It was such a long, leg-shaking, heart-aching wait. And then the bell rang. The teacher collected the papers. She counted them. Then she turned to the hall. 'Now you may leave.'

A bubble popped inside him, followed by a familiar rush of adrenaline. He scrambled out of his seat. He didn't ask people how their paper went. He couldn't be bothered. There was only one thought on his mind. He picked up his bags from outside the examination hall. Skidding into the first toilet he could find, he tore off his school uniform with wild urgency. He fumbled into his football kit. His heart was racing.

Rishabh runs on to the ground. Puro's already there. 'You're too slow,' he says.

Slowly, the rest of the team make their frantic entries. Floyd, Rahul, Dave, Tejas, Sumit and Bhupinder. He looks at them with pride. *What an honour it is to play with these legends*, he thinks. They split into teams and start playing. Soon, other boys from the tenth standard join them. They slip in and pick a side at random. No one seems to mind or care. The game goes on.

Eventually he scores, and wheels away in delight. Instinctively, he looks at the shed next to the ground. There is no tall, moustachioed figure to nod in acknowledgement. He's on his own from today. The coach will be there for those that come after him. And there will be many. He wishes them all the magic and heartbreak that was his. The game goes on.

It's two o'clock in the afternoon and the sun glares down on them. Then a shadow passes over the ground. Rishabh looks up and sees a big gloomy cloud cover the sun. It's one that looks familiar, like a straggly remainder of the clouds that had appeared at the start of the school year. The cloud passes, and the game goes on. They play until Ghadge Sir drives them away and brings to an end their last game on the school ground.

Acknowledgements

THERE IS A lot of pressure to write this section because for a lot of my friends, this is the only page they're going to read. The writer puts down words alone, submerged in the glow of a lonely laptop screen, but a book gets written by the dozens of people who bathe him in their attention and affection. This is to thank all those generous, wonderful people.

The first and foremost thanks is to my parents, without whom this would literally not have happened. The quote rings true—the older you get, the smarter your parents become. Their patience astonishes me and their wisdom elevates me.

A big hug to Siddhi. Not only did she inspire the writing of the final draft of this novel, but she also saw me through the torturous process of writing it. As if that was not enough, her talent and imagination are behind the beautiful cover. I am so glad I swiped up.

Next I have to thank the people who suffered me through the teenage years that formed a large part of this novel. A lot of my gratitude goes to my aunt Veena Srivastava, uncle Rajendra Nayak, cousins Shrinkhala and Vibhor Nayak and my grandmother Vidya Srivastava. The Neelkanth years will always be among my favourites. Thanks for all the fish!

Abhishek Ambekar—Ambe—thanks for the company, the laughs, the passes and the adventure. Can't wait to see you play for the Indian national football team.

I had the time of my life playing on the school football team. We never won anything other than each other's friendship, but it turned out to be enough. A special thanks to Pavan Powar, George Jose, Aman Choudhary and Suyash Sawant; our coach Manzur Arfin, who is one of the fairest, finest men I have met. It was an honour playing for you, sir. And Shedge Sir, whose gruff warmth I miss even after all these years.

I owe a debt of gratitude to Smt. Sulochanadevi Singhania School. It was a pleasure to walk the corridors and inhabit the classrooms for as long as it took to write this book. It is, was and will be where the magic is. A sincere thanks to all the teachers too, along with an even more sincere apology. I can't begin to understand how you tolerated the unruly, ungrateful kids that we were.

This book would have always remained just a document on my laptop if it wasn't for Vivek Tejuja. Thank you for tweeting and for steering the book to the right people. Thank you to the wonderful folks who've put in their hours and expertise into this book: Anupam Verma, Niyati Dhuldhoya, Kankana Basu and everyone else at Penguin Random House India who has helped transform this book from a Word doc to something that can be found in a bookstore.

Acknowledgements

Next are all my friends who've heard me talk about this book incessantly for the many, many years it's taken to write it. Thank you for not thinking I was insane, or at least for not letting me know you thought it. This starts with RGDC (Neehar Jathar, Prithika Vageeswaran, Tanvi Vaidya, Sankalp Kelshikar, Sailee Rane and Sayali Marawar), Zameer Vikamsey and Praveen Patil, Nikhil and Daisy Taneja, Ankit Joshi and Sandeep Narayanan, SnG Comedy (Aadar Malik, Neville Shah and Varun Thakur). And finally, thanks to the first girl I dated. You know who you are.

I'd also like to thank A to Z Printers for keeping their shutters open well past closing time just so I could get the first spiral-bound copy of my book. A thank you to Sunanda Pednekar; your effort and dedication make writing easier by the day. Rahul Bheke, thank you for your generosity. And James the cat for being adorable.

And lastly, a thank you to anyone else who's reading this and feeling offended that their name hasn't been mentioned. You know I love you.